FOND MEMORIES

A pale path of moonlight lit up the darkened room as Adam saw Holly sleeping quietly. Strong desire swelled up in him as he gently brushed away a strand of hair that fell across her face. Memories of that face had given strength in the prison camp.

When their eyes met, a million unspoken words passed between them. His hands slid under her back and pulled her against him. He kissed her throat and shoulders, pushing her nightgown slowly down as his lips followed.

He closed his eyes and let her love surround him. Never before had their lovemaking been like this.

"Holly, I missed you so much," he cried.

"Adam, Adam, Adam . . ." she sighed.

He did not want to leave the sanctuary of her body ever again. But he knew that with morning came a new reality—and that he somehow had to tell Holly that they might lose the farm . . .

FICTION FOR TODAY'S WOMAN

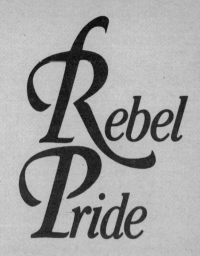

Rebel Pride

BY SYLVIE F. SOMMERFIELD

ZEBRA BOOKS

KENSINGTON PUBLISHING CORP.

ZEBRA BOOKS

are published by

KENSINGTON PUBLISHING CORP.
21 East 40th Street
New York, N.Y. 10016

Printed in the United States of America

Dedicated with affection
—to my brother-in-law
James R. Fusco

Rebel Pride

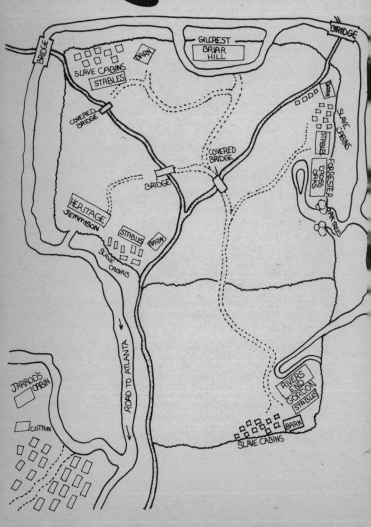

When two strong forces meet
    like water and rock,
It's a basic law of nature that
    one will hold and the other must yield.

The water will strike again and again
    and though the rock wins each individual time,
Over the years the water wears away the rock
    and wins a slow victory.

    Because
whenever two objects have a conflict
each is hurt by the experience.

Chapter 1

The hot Georgia sun did nothing to ease the severe headache that caused Graham Forrester to swear and pull sharply at the reins of the horse he was riding. The horse had shied at some imagined object, and the following jerk made Graham feel as though his head would definitely explode. If he could have seen the tightly controlled smile on the face of Bram, who followed behind on his mule, and the wicked glitter in his eyes, he would have cursed even more fiercely.

Bram, short for Abraham, was Graham's personal slave and had been so since his birth and Graham's on the same day twenty years before. Though he was very respectful of Graham at all times, for he knew his fierce temper, he did not have any affection for him. After having a good night's sleep himself in the stable, he was enjoying Graham's discomfort.

Tall and slender, yet muscular, his face was devoid of any Negro features. His eyes were widely spaced and intelligent. His nose, very slightly widened about the nostrils, was long and slender. His skin was a light, creamy brown, almost the same color as Graham's. The predominant feature about him was his eyes. Not quite brown, they had bright, golden flecks in them that attracted immediate attention. Graham realized at an early age that Bram's father must have been white. Being

9

a slave, his mother must have been some part black, but Graham was sure she was not fully so. After some curiosity, Graham finally gave up trying to find out and accepted Bram as black.

Graham could never quite accomplish saying Abraham when he was a child. All he could manage was Bram, so it remained.

Bram had spent his entire life in Graham's shadow but felt if Graham had been away from his father, he would have been a stronger man. While Graham was being educated, his mother had insisted Bram be there in the classroom. Consequently, Bram was well educated also. His quick intelligence told him this was dangerous, so he kept his ability well hidden. Occasionally, when it was possible, he slipped books out of the house to take to his bed and read by the light of the fire. Now he slipped back to the language that was expected from him.

"Yo Pa gwine be mighty mad wif you 'bout las' nite."

"Shut up, Bram," growled Graham.

"Yassah, but he still gonna raise thunder."

"Bram, you don't shut your goddamn mouth, I'm going to shut it for you." He winced as the pain struck. "Just as soon as I get rid of this headache."

"Yassah," Bram said softly, but the glitter in his eyes attested to his amusement at the situation.

Graham was also contemplating his father's anger. For the past two years, he was trying to arrange a wedding between Holly Jemmison and Graham. He knew Holly had just come home from school. He also knew why last night's dinner party had been planned. The parents would have gotten them together over a luxurious dinner, then after the men had retired to their cigars and whiskey, talk would have gone from houses, planting and slaves, then to the inevitable plan for marriage between their children. Last night, Graham had felt trapped, and instead of facing his father, he had saddled his horse and

10

rode into town for some gambling and drinking, meaning to come back in time for dinner. This morning, he had woken in a whore's bed with a rotten taste in his mouth and the pain in his head.

Now the thought of facing his father was really stretching his nerves.

Graham Forrester was an extremely handsome man. Standing well over six feet, he was large boned and had big, strong hands that had served him well in many a fight and yet could be as gentle as a woman's when handling a horse or a girl. His hair was a gleaming, blue black, and his skin was deeply tanned, contrasting sharply with the deep, sea green of his eyes.

They crossed the river over the old, covered bridge that was the boundary of Forrester land, and before long, they turned up the long, curved drive to the main house.

Cross Oaks received its name from two, huge oak trees that stood on either side of the main drive. Their branches entwined with each other causing a shady arch over the drive.

The Forrester plantation was one of the showplaces among homes that existed in the area. It had been built with loving care and detail by Graham's father, Richard, when he and his wife, Merilee, were first married, when she had turned seventeen. She had been raised gently, and being well bred, had brought to her husband's home the exquisite taste acquired from generations of wealth and breeding.

Graham stepped down very gingerly from his horse, but in spite of this precaution, he still winced when his feet met the drive. Bram took the reins of Graham's horse and walked around the side of the house toward the stable, his face cracking in a broad grin. Once at the stable, he rubbed the horse and mule down and put them in their stalls. With a tuneless whistle, he went about his duties for the day, ignoring the inquisitive stares of the rest of the slaves at his sudden show of lightheartedness.

Graham moved slowly up the four steps to the front door, and after hesitating for a few moments, opened it and stepped inside, closing it quietly behind him. He was hoping he would reach the safety of his room before he met his father or mother, and with one hand on the banister, he moved quietly and slowly up the spiral staircase. About halfway up, the click of a door latch stopped him in his tracks. He closed his eyes for just a moment, then opened them and turned around.

Richard Forrester stood in the doorway of the study and glared coldly at his only son. Although they were father and son, the two men facing each other were as different as night and day. Where Graham was dark, his father was light haired and blue eyed. But the dissimilarity did not end there for they were completely unalike in temperament.

Graham, when away from his father, was a man of pleasant disposition and delightful sense of humor. It was only in his father's presence that he closed himself off completely. As a child, Graham felt a strain between him and his father. In subtle ways, Richard had made him feel he was an unwelcome, unwanted burden. No amount of effort on Merilee's part had brought the two any closer together. It had made Graham feel inferior whenever he was around his father. When he was five, he had developed a stutter whenever his father was present, and it did not go away until he left for school at fourteen. After that, he had gained some control over himself and could at least survive in Richard's presence without letting him know how he really felt.

"A trifle late for dinner, aren't you, Graham?" he asked coldly.

"Pa—" he began hesitantly.

"Come into my study, I want to talk to you," said Richard, and turned away to reenter the room without

12

looking back to see if Graham would follow or not. He thoroughly expected obedience.

For one minute, Graham contemplated the reaction his father would have if he just went on to his room, but only for a moment. He had never had the ability to cross his father's anger. Now he wished he had returned for dinner the night before. He moved slowly to the study door, stepped inside, closed the door behind him and turned to face his father.

Richard Forrester seated himself behind the big desk and gazed coolly at Graham. Perspiration beaded on Graham's forehead, and he could feel his knees weaken. His father was always capable of causing this effect. Even as a small boy, Graham had never been able to lie or to cross his father.

"Pa—" he began again.

"I don't want to hear any of your excuses, Graham. You should have been here last night. You've embarrassed me like that for the last time. After you've tried to make yourself half decently presentable, you will ride over to the Jemmison's and apologize, especially to Holly. You know very well why this dinner was held. The Jemmison's land borders on ours. Together, we have the greatest producing piece of property in the state. Do you understand me Graham?"

"Goddamn it, Pa! . . ."

"Don't swear at me boy," his father answered angrily, his face growing red with the anger he was trying to control.

"I don't want to get married, Pa. Holly and I don't love each other. We're just good friends."

"After you've married Holly, you'll have plenty of time for your other affairs."

"Pa, I can't do that to Holly. She's not the kind of woman who'd put up with that. I know Holly better than you do. She's not a woman you can cheat on. Besides,

13

she's too nice. She doesn't deserve that kind of treatment."

Richard looked at his son in silence for several minutes, knowing the havoc he was causing by doing so.

"Graham, you're my only son. I would like to leave you an inheritance that you could live with in pride and dignity. I would like to, but I don't think it will be possible. I have made a great deal of debts by trying to expand my holdings. At this moment, we are mortgaged to the hilt, not only the house, but everything we own, including next year's cotton crops. I've sold off all the slaves it is possible to sell without leaving us too short for harvest. After Holly's father agreed that the two of you could marry, I thought we were saved, that you two could unite two of the biggest holdings in the state of Georgia. Now, I find that my only salvation, my son, refuses to help me when I need him the most. We'll lose everything."

Graham stared at his father, speechless at this confidence. If anything should have warned Graham, it should have been this sudden, quiet reasoning on his father's part. All his life, his father had given orders, and Graham had obeyed. Now to have him suddenly explaining their difficulties, threw Graham off guard, and this was exactly what his father wanted. Since it had never happened before, Graham was at a loss to handle the situation.

Deep inside himself, Graham had always wanted his father's respect and love. He hated the way his father continually looked at him as though he were an ignorant child.

Richard Forrester kept his secrets well, and because Graham didn't know many, he respected and halfway admired his father for what he had accomplished in his life. Richard Forrester, along with Tyler Jemmison and Matthew Gilcrest had built their three connecting

14

plantations to what they were by sheer strength of will. What was now three connecting plantations had been one large square with two rivers starting at the upper corners and meeting at the bottom, slicing it neatly into three triangular pieces. For several years, the three men had worked the land together, eventually dividing it into three separate pieces as each married and built his own home. It was impossible for Graham, who loved his home deeply, to even consider it ever being lost to them.

"You, you mean . . . everything, Pa?"

"I didn't want to tell it to you like this, Graham, but your marriage to Holly is the only way I can see right now to pick up the notes against Cross Oaks. Her dowry could get us back on our feet. You see how important the dinner was to me—to all of us?"

"I'm sorry, Pa. I didn't know. Maybe if you'd told me before, I could have helped some way."

"What way, Graham? Outside of a good marriage, there's nothing you could do."

Graham let his shoulders droop; he had never felt more defeated or trapped in his life. He knew, as always, that his father would have his way. Cross Oaks and his family meant the whole world to Graham.

"All right, Pa," he said resignedly. "I'll ride over to the Jemmison's today and talk to Holly."

"Good, good," his father said. "You won't be sorry, Graham. Holly is a lovely girl. She'll make you a beautiful wife."

Graham turned away and started for the door. He felt suddenly very sick and tired. He wanted only to reach the security of his room and lie down. Without another word, he left the room, closing the door behind him.

His father looked at the closed door for several seconds, then a slow smile of triumph formed on his lips, broadening into a delightful grin. What he had told Graham about Cross Oaks was a lie, but he wanted the

15

marriage between Holly Jemmison and Graham because it would form the most powerful alliance between the two largest plantations in Georgia. When he was gone, Graham would inherit great wealth. There was no nudge in his conscience about Graham's or Holly's happiness. Richard Forrester was used to getting what he wanted.

Graham walked slowly up the stairs and pushed open the door of his bedroom. Inside, he removed his jacket and lay down across the bed. He lay staring at the ceiling for quite some time, trying to form words he could say to Holly to convince her of an affection he did not feel.

Holly and Graham had been very close friends since the days of their early childhood. They played together and exchanged confidences and depended upon one another for trust. He remembered so many times he had run to Holly for sympathy and understanding when life with his father became unbearable. She had always understood and seemed to share an inner strength with him. Sometimes, he thought she was a little angry with him, instead of his father, but she never showed it. Instead, she offered him the comfort of a sister. He knew that was the way she felt about him, and it was the way he felt about her. "How in God's name will I ever be able to propose to Holly? She'll laugh me out of the house!" he thought in angry desperation.

He rose from the bed two hours later as devoid of words as he was when he had lain down. He washed, changed his clothes, left his room and started down the stairs. He met his mother coming up.

Merilee Forrester had never lost the beauty of her youth. Her figure was still slender. Her dark, black hair was coiled atop her head in a severe style that accentuated the beauty of her deep green eyes. She was a quiet woman and held her thoughts and feelings to herself. At times, she seemed aloof with everyone else except her son. Graham was her life. Sometimes, she felt

16

guilty about this, but Graham was the one who held her deepest affection. She often thought of the situation surrounding Graham's birth and each time promised herself to tell him the truth, because she knew of the feelings between father and son. She continually put it off until suddenly Graham was a man, and she realized one day he would marry and leave his father's house. Then she finally decided the secret was better kept with her.

"Graham," she smiled. "Where were you last night? We missed you at dinner, especially Holly. She asked about you."

"Not you, too, Mother," he groaned.

"I see you've already spoken with your father." She chuckled. "He was a little angry last night."

"A little! I think that's the understatement of the year," replied Graham sourly.

Merilee Forrester gazed intently at her only child. There was a special place in her heart that belonged specifically to Graham. "Someday," she thought, "there were things she must tell him about his past."

She had no way of knowing the pressure Richard had just put upon him. If she had, she would have taken steps to stop it, for she alone understood Richard Forrester as no one else ever would. She knew immediately after their marriage that Richard did not love her, but her background and family did not permit her to do anything about it.

"Where are you going, Graham?"

"Over to the Jemmison's . . . to apologize to them and—"

"And?"

"And propose to Holly."

"Oh, Graham, that's marvelous! Holly is such a beautiful girl."

She reached up on tiptoe to kiss his cheek, then

17

stopped suddenly alert to his expression.

"What is the matter, Graham?" she asked quietly.

His Southern male pride forbade him to cry on his mother's shoulder. If he had been able to bring himself to tell her, she could have remedied the situation by putting a stop to the story his father had told him. As it was, he straightened his shoulders and smiled at his mother.

"Nothing, just a little nervous, I guess. After all, a man doesn't propose every day, does he?"

He gave his mother a swift peck on the cheek and continued on down the stairs, calling back over his shoulder as nonchalantly as possible, "See you at dinner, Mother."

Merilee continued to watch the door after it had closed behind him. She would have given her life gladly to keep Graham from unhappiness. Now she had the deep feeling there was something wrong. She turned her eyes toward the door of the study, then she slowly moved in that direction. She gave a light knock on the door, then opened it and stepped inside before Richard could think of a way to stop her.

Richard looked up quietly at the rap on the door, but before he could say anything, Merilee was inside closing the door behind her. They looked at each other in silence from across the room. It was Richard's eyes which dropped from hers first.

"Richard, what's the matter with Graham?" she asked softly.

"Matter? Did he say something was the matter?"

"You know he wouldn't say anything. But I know him better than you ever will, and I'm asking you again. What's the matter with Graham?"

"Outside of his being a little upset at me being angry with his not showing up last night, I can't think of anything else that would bother him. Of course," he sneered, "Graham is such a weakling, that—"

18

"Richard!" she said, her face pale and her eyes flashed with anger. "You really know nothing about Graham at all after all these years, do you? Graham is far from a weakling, and someday you are going to push him a little too far."

"And what will he do?" Richard laughed. "Run to his mother for help?"

Merilee's face became frozen with deep anger, her voice was cold as ice as she said slowly.

"Graham has never come to me for help in his whole life, and I have admired his courage. But if he ever does come to me, Richard, if you ever push him until he does, I shall do everything in my power to help him no matter what! Do I make myself clear, Richard? There is nothing I wouldn't do, no one I wouldn't hurt to help Graham, and that includes you. I shall tell Graham all the truths he needs to make him strong!"

She turned and walked from the room closing the door softly behind her. Richard stared at the closed door long after she left, then in sudden frustrated anger, he slammed his fist against the desk and said softly, "Damn you, Merilee. . . . Damn you!"

Chapter 2

Holly Jemmison controlled her laughter with difficulty as she sat on the edge of her bed and listened to her younger sister Steffany's incessant chatter.

Steffany was sixteen, and her whole life revolved around fun and laughter. She was a bright-eyed, bubbling girl. Small and very slender, she was very pretty and gave all signs of turning into an extremely beautiful woman. Her skin was a clear ivory white. Her eyes were a crystal green, slanted up at the corners and filled with a look of secret amusement that took the interest of every male in her presence, making them wonder just what she saw so much fun in and anxious to share it with her. Her hair was a deep auburn that fell to her waist with a natural curl that gave it a vibrant life of its own. She had a wide, beautiful smile that exposed dimples on each cheek. The only thing that distressed her was the small bridge of freckles that ran across her pert, upturned nose.

"Holly!" she exclaimed with bubbling enthusiasm. "You're home from school at just the right time. There's a ball at the Gordon's tomorrow night, and it's going to be fabulous. I even hear Adam Gilcrest came home just for the party, and I think he's still sweet on Diane Gordon. He sure was when his pa sent him away. I heard they caught them together one night and him only eighteen and her sixteen and I heard—"

20

"Steff, you shouldn't repeat idle gossip. It's not very ladylike. You have no idea what's the truth and what isn't. Diane's a nice girl; she wouldn't do a thing like that."

"Oh, Holly, sometimes you're so trusting that I think I'm the older sister and you're the younger. A good-looking boy like Adam wouldn't have any trouble getting his hands on any girl he wanted, and he really wanted Diane."

"Steff, if you're going to keep up this kind of talk, I'm going to shoo you out right now, and you'll never see what I brought you."

"Oh, Holly! What, what did you bring me?" Steffany clapped her hands together in delight, her eyes sparkling and her cheeks flushed in excitement.

It took so little to make Steffany happy, thought Holly. A new party dress, a trinket of some sort, laughter and parties were her whole life. Holly wanted suddenly to shake the silliness out of her, but she knew it would be useless to try to explain to Steffany the seriousness of what was happening in their world. Holly had taken her education in a Northern school very seriously. She had been listening closely to what was happening, and a terrible fear had enveloped her.

She realized the true position the South was in if a war started, and from all the talk, she felt certain it would. She had tried to talk to her father once when she had just arrived home, but her father had reacted like all Southern gentlemen, brushing her fears aside with, "Now don't you worry your pretty, little head about these things, Holly. You just get married and give me some grandchildren."

She had flushed red at his words, and he, with a chuckle, thought it was shyness. It wasn't; it was anger.

"I'm not a child, Papa," she said stiffly.

He laughed again and patted her shoulder.

21

"You sure are a baby, my child. You're only eighteen, Holly. There are a lot of things you don't understand. Now just let us men worry about those things. You just marry Graham Forrester and give me a house full of babies."

She had controlled her anger with an effort. "I'm not going to marry Graham Forrester, Papa. Y'all might as well understand right now, I don't love him, and I won't marry a man I don't love."

"Now, baby," he said softly. "You've got to understand some things, too. Graham's the man for you. Why it will bring together the two biggest plantations in this part of the country."

"Is that what I am to you, Papa, a piece of property?"

Now it was her father's turn to redden. What she had said was so true that it made him angry.

"You will marry Graham Forrester, Holly, and I don't want to talk about it anymore. You're going to be obedient to me in this matter, my girl, or—"

He caught himself before he finished. "We're just not going to talk about it anymore. It's settled." He turned away from her and left the room. She had watched his retreating figure with a mixed feeling of anger and helpless despair. She knew he would be able to make her do as he wished.

She roused herself from the bitter memories and let her thoughts drift to last night's dinner party. She was grateful for Graham's absence, but she knew it was only a delay of the inevitable. There was no doubt in Holly's mind that she was fond of Graham, but it was the fondness of childhood friends. Holly knew of his dalliances with the slave girls on both his plantation and the surrounding ones and his tendency toward drinking to forget the fact that he was not a strong enough man to face his father and to prove his independence. Holly felt that the day would one day come when Graham would be

22

his own man, but until it did, she could not respect or feel toward him the way her father demanded. Along with these realizations was the fact that there was no way for her to fight her father's control, no place for her to run and no one to turn to.

"Holly! Are you listening to me? What did you bring me?" Steffany's insistent voice broke in on her thoughts.

"Oh, Steff, there's a package in my portmanteau for you."

Steffany squealed with delight and rummaged through Holly's things until she brought forth the gift. With rapid fingers, she unwrapped it and lifted a beautiful, white, lace shawl.

"Oh! Holly, it's bee-you-ti-ful!" she shouted with delight as she swirled the shawl about her shoulders. "Just perfect to wear with my green gown to the party tomorrow night."

Now she rushed to Holly and flung her arms about her, kissing her firmly on both cheeks, then rushed to the door.

"I must show Mama. Oh, won't Darcie Mitchell be just pea green with envy!" She giggled with laughter as she closed the door behind her.

Holly sat back on the edge of the bed and recalled her sister's words. Adam Gilcrest . . . She remembered the last time she had seen Adam. She had only been about fourteen and he seventeen. She and Graham had run across the group swimming in the river that bordered the Forrester and Jemmison property.

Dixon and Deline, Adam's twin brother and sister, his youngest brother Brian and Diane Gordon had been enjoying the coolness of the water on a blistering hot day, when Graham and Holly arrived. Shouts of laughter had drawn them to the river, and it did not take much persuading to draw them in. For a considerable time, they romped in the cool water, then gathered on the bank

23

to talk.

The conversation turned to courage, and an argument developed over who was the bravest. Dixon, Graham and Brian had finally taken turns jumping off the highest tree limbs they could climb to when a shout had called their attention to the covered bridge that crossed the river under which they were swimming. All eyes were riveted to the side to which Adam clung. Her heart had leaped to her throat and strangled the cry that would have come out. His long, lean sun-browned body had held for another moment against the side; then he jumped. He struck the water and disappeared. They all watched, holding their breath until they became alarmed. She had begun to cry when his head finally broke the surface, and he laughed and waved at them. She had never been so frightened or angry in her life, and as Adam pulled himself up, she had gone to the edge of the bank and shouted at him.

"You're crazy, Adam Gilcrest, and the next time you pull a dumb stunt like that you make sure I'm not here."

"Why, Holly? Were you afraid for me?" he asked, his slate-gray eyes looking deeply into hers. They were serious, and for a moment, she thought they were trying to say something to her. Then the look was gone, and he laughed.

Her anger, combined with her fear, exploded, and placing her hands against his chest, she had pushed him backwards into the river.

"I hate you, Adam Gilcrest," she had shouted at him, "I hate you!"

With these words, she had gathered her clothing and, with Graham following close behind, had almost run from the scene.

If she had seen the look on Adam's face as she left with Graham following, she might have been quite surprised. He glared at Graham's retreating back for a while, then

24

his face had softened and the gray of his eyes shadowed to a deep blue. "Holly," he had mumbled softly once to himself, then swam to shore and joined the group that waited for him.

Holly chuckled to herself with the memory. Combining that with what she had just heard from Steffany made her wonder again about Adam's recklessness. He had always seemed to be trying to prove something to someone.

With a sigh, she pushed every other thought to the back of her mind. Somehow, she must persuade her parents that she shouldn't marry Graham, and she was at a loss to think of how to accomplish that. Holly had never been the type of girl to simper and play coy. It was impossible also for her to plead since she was possessed of an abundance of pride. It was obvious in every move she made.

She went to the wash basin and poured out some water, splashing it onto her face. Then she removed her dress and slipped on a white dress of sprigged muslin. A wide, green band trimmed her slender waist and the neck and sleeves. She looked at herself in the long mirror as she recoiled her long, auburn hair into a bun at the nape of her neck. No matter how she tried, fringes of soft curls escaped to frame her face. Large, emerald-colored eyes enclosed in a fringe of deep brown lashes slanted over a slender, straight nose. Her face was oval shaped with high cheekbones and pouting, sensual lips that had stirred the hearts of most of the young men in the county.

She gave herself one last look in the mirror, then set her jaw determinedly and went down to join the rest of her family.

"Somehow, I'll persuade Papa," she thought grimly. "But if he won't listen to reason, I'll have to do something desperate. I will never marry a man I cannot love and respect."

With these thoughts, she shut the door firmly behind her.

Holly's parents sat together in the large drawing room, and both looked up as Holly entered.

"Darling." Her mother smiled fondly at her and rose to accept Holly's kiss. "I'm so glad you're home, child."

"Thank you, Mama. You have no idea how good it feels to be here. Our world is so much more beautiful," she answered, as she moved to her father's side and kissed him also. "Papa," she murmured.

Tyler Jemmison could tell that Holly was still upset with him, but he patted her hand and smiled at her.

Holly was just about to launch into a soliloquy on why she should not marry Graham Forrester, when he was announced by the butler. All three people were taken by surprise.

Holly's father requested he be sent in to them, and the butler left the room to return in a few minutes with a request that Graham be able to see Holly alone.

Holly's father smiled smugly to himself, which raised Holly's ire toward him. Her cheeks flushed slightly with anger as she rose quickly and, with chin lifted, moved rapidly toward the door taking the advantage of slamming it after her.

Graham was waiting for her nervously in the library. He could never think of himself and Holly as anything more than the close friends they had always been since they were children. Now he felt sure she would see straight through him as she always could.

"Holly," he smiled at her when she entered the room, and she smiled in return, for she truly cared for Graham.

"Graham, what are you doing here this early in the day? I thought you slept till noon, lazybones."

"I usually do, Holly, but I had to see you before the ball tonight. First, let me say, Holly, I'm really sorry about not being home last night."

"Oh, Graham, that's all right," she laughed. "We're too good of friends to worry about things like that. We'll be seeing a lot of each other anyway this summer."

"Holly, I . . . I've got to talk to you about something very important."

"Yes, Graham?"

"Well . . . Holly . . . ah . . . you know I'm very, very fond of you."

Holly knew instantly what Graham was going to say. She felt sympathetic toward him, yet angry that he was again allowing his father to maneuver him into an unwelcome position.

"Graham, is this going to be a proposal of marriage?" she asked bluntly, then knew she was right when he flushed with embarrassment.

Holly moved close to him and put both her hands on his arm.

"You and I have been almost family all of our lives, Graham. We're good friends. No matter what anyone else wants, I'd like to keep it that way. I feel you do, too, Graham. Let's not let anyone push us into something neither of us wants."

She almost laughed aloud at his look of relief. Then he smiled down into her eyes.

"You always were the smartest of all of us, Holly. You know I care for you. I just knew you were much too good for me. I'm happy to have you for a close friend. Maybe you won't want to be after I tell you what I have to say, but I think you have the right to know." He proceeded to tell her how their fathers were trying to join together their two plantations through them.

"I know, Graham," she smiled. "I realized that a long time ago, but we'll fool them all, Graham. We'll both marry who we please, and we'll both stay friends."

"I wouldn't want to lose your friendship for anything in the world, Holly. I hope you find someone you really

27

love. In the meantime, what are we going to tell our parents?"

"For now, let's tell them you proposed, and I'm thinking it over. Maybe something will happen to change things and to guide us both to what we really want."

With relief, she heard hoofbeats on the drive and saw her father leave for the fields with the overseer.

"Good," she thought. She would not have to face him, at least until tomorrow, to answer questions about Graham.

She sat down on the edge of the bed with a sigh, and for some unaccountable reason, her thoughts drifted to Adam Gilcrest. She hoped he would be at the ball tonight. Maybe seeing him and judging for herself, she would be able to satisfy herself about the truth in the stories that had passed around about him.

Chapter 3

Adam cursed softly to himself as he swung his long legs over the edge of the bed and stood up. Another light, impatient knock sounded on the door.

"I'm coming," he answered. He knew who was on the other side of the door, and at this particular moment, his mother was the last person he wanted to talk to. Her ability to read him like a book upset him, for she was the only person who had ever been able to do that.

He opened the door and let his mother enter, closing it quietly behind her. Jessica Gilcrest looked closely at her son. She hadn't seen him for almost two years.

"Adam, I'm so glad to have you home."

"I'm glad to be back, Mother."

She went to his side and took both his hands in hers and, reaching up, kissed him gently. "You will stay now, Adam, won't you?"

"Mother," he said gently. Then disengaging his hands from hers, he turned away lest she see the hurt in his eyes.

"It really wasn't my idea to leave in the first place, now was it?"

"Adam . . ."

"I know, Mother, but I shouldn't have let father force me to leave. I should have stayed and faced everyone. After all, I really was innocent of their nasty little thoughts."

"What really happened, Adam? Can't you tell me?"

"Why don't we just forget it, Mother. I've come home to stay, and no one will ever make me run again."

She sighed, but did not question him further. "Will you be coming to the Ball tonight with us?"

For a moment, Adam didn't reply, but his eyes seemed to be seeing something far away.

"Adam?"

"Yes, yes, Mother, I will. There's someone I have to see . . . to talk to . . . to explain if I can."

"Holly Jemmison?"

He gave a startled jerk and turned surprised eyes toward her.

"Oh, Adam," she laughed. "Adam, my darling, I've known you cared for Holly since you were children. I was wondering when you would know."

"Is there anything about my thoughts you don't know, Mother?" he laughed.

She looked at him affectionately, this tall son she loved so dearly. He had changed since he was away, and she was not as sure of him as she was before. He had grown taller, but it was not just his height which caught her. He exuded a feeling of strength although he seemed slender. It reminded her strangely of a young male lion she had once seen in a zoo. Pacing back and forth, he had seemed to mesmerize her with a feeling of barely controlled violence. Adam gave her the same feeling. His slate-gray eyes watched her closely now, darkening to a deep hue of gray blue.

"Why," she thought, "he's afraid, of what, I wonder?" But she did not voice this aloud, instead she smiled at him.

"Very little, Adam, for I love you, you see. Maybe sometime soon, you'll be able to tell me. For now, let me just welcome you home."

30

"Thank you, Mother."

She was just about to reach for the door handle when a loud slam of a door and shouting, angry voices came to their ears. Adam and his mother exchanged exasperated glances.

"Dixon and Deline," they said in unison, then laughed aloud together.

"Mother!" a young masculine voice shouted. "Mother, where are you?"

Jessica opened the door and stepped out into the hall with Adam behind her, just in time to run into a young girl laughingly flying down the hall with a young man hard at her heels. Adam laughing, grabbed his young sister in his arms, and Jessica stepped between them and her angry son.

Dixon and Deline were fraternal twins. Outside of the fact that Deline was female, it would have been almost impossible to tell them apart.

"Whatever is wrong now?" Jessica questioned.

"Mother," Dixon almost shouted, "will you do something about her before she ruins my reputation? I swear, I'm going to murder her."

"Well, if you tell us what happened," said Adam, dropping his sister's feet to the floor but still holding her about the waist, more for her protection than anything else, as her brother glared at her over his mother's head.

"She dressed up in my clothes again and went over to Selena Mitchell's house and actually had the nerve to serenade her from the garden at dark. Selena thought it was me, and it's been spread all over town." He panted as he stopped talking and continued to glare at his sister.

Adam almost choked holding back his mirth, and Jessica was hard put to contain herself.

"Deline," her mother said sharply, her voice as firm as she could keep it as she tried to camouflage the glitter of humor in her eyes, "You absolutely must stop this

31

consistent harassment of your brother like this. It is not ladylike, and it is unfair to Dixon."

"Well," giggled Deline, "he's sweet on Selena, and he's such a poke, I just thought I'd hurry him up a little."

Her brother groaned as if in agony and, throwing up his hands, began to mumble under his breath as he turned away from them and went to his own room, slamming the door behind him.

Jessica turned to Deline, who was leaning now against Adam, and they both were convulsed with laughter.

"Now you both stop this. Deline, it is really terrible the problems you cause your brother. I expect you to apologize," she smiled, containing her laughter with difficulty, "just as soon as Dixon will allow you near him."

"All right, Mama. I'll apologize. But really, Dix is such a poke. He'll never get any girl if he doesn't get out of those books."

"That's not your problem, Del," said Adam with the remnants of his laughter dying in his throat. "You leave Dix alone, little girl, or I'm going to paddle your bottom like I did when you were a baby."

Deline, whose love for Adam was close to adoration, looked up at him and her smile faded. She had deep blue eyes and they filled with gentleness as she looked at him.

"I'm too old for you to paddle, Adam," she said quietly. "But I won't cause Dix any more problems, I promise."

"Good girl." Adam smiled down on her and squeezed her tightly against him, kissing the top of her head lightly. "Now run along and get ready for the party tonight. I'd like you to save me one dance at least, okay?"

She nodded and moved toward her room without question.

"Oh, Adam, I really am glad you're home. You are the only person who's ever been able to handle those two."

32

"Don't worry about it, Mother. I'll go talk to Dix now. It will be all right."

"Adam," she said softly, looking into his eyes, "you have always been the strong one. Save some of your strength for yourself."

"I'm perfectly all right, Mother," he grinned at her. "No problems, honest."

"I just don't want anything to hurt you anymore. If you need any help, Adam, you will come to me?"

"Sure, Mother," he said, with a confidence he was far from feeling. "Now don't worry, I don't want the most beautiful lady at the Ball to have dark shadows under her eyes."

She smiled, but she felt deeply the unspoken words between them.

Adam watched her move away from him, and his smile faded. There was a darkening in the gray shadows of his eyes for just a moment before he got himself under control.

He went to his brother's door and knocked. A muffled "come in," sounded from inside, and he opened the door and walked into the room.

Dixon was still furiously fuming as he moved about the room. Three to four inches shorter than Adam's six-foot-two inches, he was slender, yet gave the same feeling of strength as his brother. His hair was sandy blond, worn a little long, and it was thick and wavy. His eyes, the identical color as his twin, looked at Adam with the same look of trust and love. Sometimes the sameness of the two would shake Adam. He knew, as everyone else did, that there was more between Dixon and Deline than just being twins. It was as though they were held together with an invisible tie. It amazed everyone the way each of them knew what the other was feeling, and they had a love for each other that was completely different than their feeling for others. It was as though they lived inside

33

each other's body, sharing and caring far beyond what anyone else could comprehend.

"Dix, take it easy."

"God, Adam, how am I going to go to the Ball tonight and face Selena? And how about all my friends?"

"I'll tell you, Dix. If you were really smart, you'd take advantage of what Del has done."

"Advantage, how?"

"Well, when your friends ask, just say you're sorry they didn't think of it first. And when you're dancing with Selena, she'll fall all over you for being so romantically inclined. Just take the credit for it and enjoy her gratitude."

"You really think that will work, Adam?" he asked, hopefully searching his brother's face.

"I've always found, Dix, that facing a problem head on is usually the best way to solve it. I'll bet you'll find Selena hanging on your every word all evening."

Dix straightened his shoulders and grinned at Adam. "Maybe Del's idea wasn't so bad after all," he chuckled.

Adam slapped him on the shoulder and laughed with him.

"Then maybe you'd better be nice to Del before you go to the party, or she might take it upon herself to tell Selena the truth. Then your goose would really be cooked."

"Maybe I'd better go make up with Del right now," he said rushing toward the door. He was gone in a few seconds.

Adam chuckled to himself; then, as quickly as it came, the chuckle died and his gray-blue eyes clouded again. His thoughts drifted to Holly Jemmison and his hopes of seeing her that evening.

Adam had loved Holly Jemmison since they were children. Never once could he bring himself out of his boyhood shyness to say anything to her. He remembered

34

the burning jealousy he felt for Graham Forrester when he realized Graham held a special place in Holly's affections. Because of this, and no matter how hard Graham tried, Adam could never bring himself around to being friends with Graham. He remembered how often he came close to telling Holly how he really felt, but when she would turn her emerald-green eyes to him, he would suddenly become flustered and tongue tied. Only one time was he really tempted, and there had been too many people around for him to speak. He still remembered the look of fear on her face when he had jumped off the bridge. He had seen her often after that, but remembering her anger at the bridge, he felt it would be useless. Then this awful incident with Diane had occurred, and he had taken the blame for a situation he was not responsible for. And then his father had sent him away to school, in anger. But now he was back to stay, and his running away days were over. Tonight, he was going to tell Holly how he felt.

No matter what the outcome was, no matter how it hurt, he had to tell her. He had to know how she felt or if she could begin to care for him. In his mind, a million times, he had fantasized a romantic courtship and marriage to Holly. He would push his dreams away no longer. Tonight was the time for truth.

Chapter 4

River's End, the Gordon's plantation, so named because it began where the two rivers met, was the most beautiful in the area. Charles Gordon had spared no expense in its building nor in its furnishings.

A large, two-story building, its front was framed by four white pillars which held a veranda that circled the complete house. Doors from each bedroom upstairs opened onto this veranda. Two huge, oak doors opened from the circular drive into a large foyer. Entering the house through these doors, one faced the most magnificent circular stairway, behind which large windows faced the morning sun. Black tiles graced the foyer floor, and the stairway itself was carpeted in thick, deep red carpeting. The balustrades were white, and the total effect of severe black, white and red, combined with the rustling colorful gowns of the ladies was inspiring.

Every room was brilliant with the glow of hundreds of candles. The soft sound of music floated lightly through the open doors and windows as one carriage after another arrived and the occupants were warmly greeted at the door.

Adam and his family had arrived some time before Holly's, and as soon as they entered, Adam had begun to watch the door. Occasionally, he would dance with one girl or another and stop to talk to small groups of his friends, but always, his eyes returned to the door.

It was surprising then that, when she entered with her family, he missed seeing her, for at that moment, Diane came to his side and put her hand on his arm.

"Adam, I have to talk to you. Please?" she said with a quiet urgency.

He gazed down into her face and his jaw tightened. She could see the muscle along the side of his face quiver with the clenching jaw. His gray eyes darkened as his brows came together in a scowl.

"What do we have to say to each other, Diane? You had your chance to talk two years ago, and you chose to keep quiet."

"Please, Adam, just for a moment," she replied softly, her eyes moisture filled.

"All right, Diane, but just for a moment. I've got something very important to take care of tonight."

She took his arm, and they were about to turn toward the veranda when Adam looked one last time toward the door. Holly stood there, splendidly beautiful in a turquoise and gold gown, allowing her creamy shoulders and the soft rise of her breasts to rise above the draped neckline. It accentuated her small waist; then yards of turquoise and gold lace cascaded in a wide circle.

"She looks like Venus in an emerald ocean," he thought as he stared at her.

She looked directly at him, and her eyes changed from a warm, happy glow to a cold, frigid stare. Suddenly it dawned on him. With Diane on his arm, all the stories she must have heard would appear to be true.

"Damn," he thought to himself, "of all times for this to happen." He and Diane moved slowly out of the large French doors and the last glimpse he had of Holly, Graham Forrester was offering her his arm, and she was smiling up at him.

His anger and sudden burning jealousy of Graham

almost overcame him for a moment. He hesitated, but at that moment, Diane turned toward him.

"Adam, I have never had the chance to tell you how grateful I am for what you did for me. If it hadn't been for you, I don't know what would have become of me."

"You picked a sorry way to show your gratitude, Diane, letting me take the blame in front of your parents."

"What could I do then, Adam? If I had told them the truth—well, I don't know what they would have done. Probably sent me away in disgrace."

"What is the truth, Diane? Who were you meeting?"

"I can't tell you, Adam. Not even you, no matter how grateful I am."

"It's over, Diane. Let's just let it die."

Tears came to her eyes, and she tried vainly to smile again.

"I just want you to know, Adam, I am grateful, and I'll never forget it. Maybe sometime I can tell you. If you ever need a friend, I'm here."

He gazed down into her eyes, and his face softened. It was all past now, and there was no sense keeping it alive any longer. Diane watched him closely.

"All right, Diane," he smiled. "Let's forget it. It's over. We'll be friends again."

She sighed with relief. "Thank you, Adam. I'll never forget you." She kissed him gently on the cheek and turned away to reenter the ballroom.

He watched her for a moment, then turned his back to the lighted doorway and looked out over the Gordon's garden. Inhaling the soft summer air, he watched the millions of bright stars light up the black-velvet sky.

"This is home," he thought, and his mind raced back over the past two years to the night Maribell, Diane's personal maid, had come to him secretly and told him tearfully that Miss Diane was running away to join a

38

married man. She had refused steadfastly to tell Adam who the man was but had begged him to stop Diane before it was too late.

Young and foolishly chivalrous as he was in those days, he had dashed off immediately to find her and bring her home before anyone knew what had happened.

He had found her in Atlanta, alone and in tears, for the man who had led her on had disappeared, leaving her to fend for herself. It was nearly dawn when they had arrived at the Gordon home, and her father had been up to meet them. Coldly, he had ordered Adam to leave his house and said he would come over later to speak with Adam's father. Adam had been stunned with Diane's silence. His amazement turned to pain, then to stubborn anger. He would not give her father the satisfaction of pleading his case.

Later, closeted with his father, he had refused quietly but firmly to marry Diane. His father had given him an ultimatum. Either he married the girl or he would be sent away to a school with firm discipline. Again he had refused, and his father's wishes had been carried out, at least as far as he knew. Because Adam, in his anger, had never stayed at the school. Instead, bribing a schoolmate to forward his letters, he had wandered about the country, doing odd work here and there and trying to escape the painful memories of home.

At one time, he joined the crew of a sailing ship and traveled for almost fifteen months from port to port, but his heart was always at Briar Hill. Then he grew weary of the self-imposed loneliness and gave in to his deep desire to see his home and especially Holly. She was never out of his dreams, no matter what girl he was with, and he was with many, for his charm and good looks had brought women to his side no matter where he was.

His reverie was interrupted by the soft swish of a gown against the stone patio. He turned and faced Holly, who stood in the light of the door. He was sure she could not tell who stood in the darker shadows outside the range of light.

"Oh, I'm sorry," she said. "I didn't realize there was anyone else here." She turned to go.

"Holly," he said softly. "Don't go." He moved to her side and looked down into her green eyes.

"Adam," she whispered softly, for when his eyes captured hers, she felt a flood of warmth tingle through her, making her suddenly aware of everything about him.

His warm, smoky, gray-blue eyes held her fast, and she appraised him, taking in the strong square jaw with the tiny cleft on his chin. He was very tanned, and although he appeared slender, still, he gave her the sensation of tightly reined strength. She had no realization of how tightly he held himself in check, for his urgent desire was to pull her into his arms, hold her and bury his face in the fiery glow of her hair.

"I've been wanting to talk to you all evening, Holly. Will you walk in the garden with me?"

She gave one hesitant look back toward the ballroom.

"Afraid?" he asked bitterly. It was not the word but the pain-filled way he said it that brought her eyes back to his. Then she lifted her stubborn chin and tucking her hand into his arm, she nodded, and they walked out through the garden in silence.

They walked for quite some time without speaking, but it was not an uncomfortable silence. She felt the warmth of him close to her and the feeling was good.

Beneath a tree on the far edge of the garden, he stopped and turned to her.

"You said you wanted to talk to me all evening. What is it, Adam?"

"You're as beautiful as you always were," he said softly.

"Adam," she laughed. "As a child one could never

40

have called me beautiful! I was so skinny and had all those horrible freckles and that terrible ugly-colored hair."

He looked at her seriously. "You were always beautiful to me, Holly."

They did not speak again for several seconds. They were caught in the emotion of the moment. He cursed himself silently. Why could he never find the words to tell Holly how he felt about her?

Adam had never been hesitant with a woman. With ease and charm, he had taken them as easily as lifting a glass of wine. Why now, after all his determination, was he suddenly tongue-tied and shaken? Was it because *he* was afraid . . . afraid?

"Holly, I'd like to see you again soon when we can spend some time alone. There are things I want to say to you, things I can't say when someone may interrupt us at any moment. If I came to your home tomorrow, would you consent to go riding with me?"

Perceptive as Holly was, despite his cool, quiet manner, she could read the hesitancy and . . . what in his eyes? It piqued her curiosity, and despite what others might think, she found herself accepting. His quick smile of pleasure took her by surprise, as it did everyone, for the rough, square contours of his face had brightened as though someone had lit a candle behind his eyes.

Quickly he bent and just brushed her lips with his, but the shocking current that passed between them startled them both. He pulled away, and his smile faded. They stood close together, both suddenly caught in the stream of something they did not understand. Then, very slowly, his arms went about her waist, and he pulled her gently and lowered his head to cover her mouth with his.

He was irretrievably lost, and he knew it. Somehow he had to make Holly his. Never before in his life had he felt such a desire for a woman. The warm softness of her

41

melted against him, and her lips were moist and yielding under his. Slowly, they parted, and his tongue touched with a tentative searching of hers. A soft sound of pleasure escaped her, and he felt her arms creep up about his neck.

Her mind swirled in a tempest as reality slipped slowly away from her and she felt nothing but the demanding insistence of his lips and the joyful giving of her own. She realized beyond a shadow of a doubt that after tonight, it would be completely impossible for her to even contemplate marrying Graham Forrester, for there was no thought in her mind except that one day she would belong body and soul to Adam Gilcrest.

"We'd best go inside now," he said huskily.

She realized the wisdom of his words, but they were both reluctant to comply. Slowly, they walked toward the large, open doors. Then, as they reached the light, she took his arm, and he guided her to the dance floor, where with a warm smile, he took her into his arms, and they whirled about, oblivious to the others.

Tyler Jemmison stood on the dark corner of the veranda and watched the two cross the garden and enter the house. He ground his teeth in anger, and his face became suffused with suppressed rage.

"Adam Gilcrest," he muttered. He leaned back against the wall. For some time he stood in deep thought, then he smiled to himself and went back into the ballroom.

Once inside the ballroom, Tyler stood by the open doors and let his eyes scan the crowd. It was several minutes before he found Richard Forrester on the opposite side of the room in deep conversation with several other gentlemen. He made his way slowly through the crowd to Richard's side.

"Richard I would like to speak to you in private for a few minutes." He smiled warmly at the others. "If you gentlemen would excuse us for a few minutes."

He and Richard made their way to a secluded corner.

"What's the matter, Tyler?"

"I thought we had the marriage between Holly and Graham arranged?"

"We do!"

"Well look around. Right now she's dancing with that rascal Adam Gilcrest."

"For Christ's sake, Tyler, she's at a party. She's just being polite and dancing with him. Don't jump to hasty conclusions."

"Well, what about the two of them out in the garden kissing. And I don't mean a brotherly welcome home kiss, either."

"You're sure of what you saw?"

"Hell, yes, I'm sure. He was kissing her, and she was enjoying every minute of it."

"Well," Richard said softly, his eyes watching the dancers on the floor. "We'll have to put a stop to that, Tyler, or all our plans are for nothing. If that boy comes around Holly, it's up to you to chase him away. You understand."

"Don't worry. I'll see he gets no courtin' time in my home."

Richard turned to him and said quietly, "You'd better, Tyler. You'd better."

Chapter 5

Deline Gilcrest felt the vague stirrings of unrest begin as soon as she opened her eyes. She stretched her slender body, lifting her arms over her head, then relaxed. After a few more minutes, she pushed aside the covers and rose from the bed. Going to the washstand, she poured some cool water from the pitcher into the basin and splashed her face. Patting it dry, she moved to the full-length mirror that stood in the corner. Her long hair was plaited into two braids. Slowly she worked the braids loose with her fingers until her hair fell about her in tawny waves to well below her waist. Then she removed the long cotton nightgown she wore and studied herself in the mirror. Her body was slender with small breasts that rose high and were pink tipped. Her hips had acquired the soft, ripe curves of womanhood, but her stomach was tight and flat. Her skin had a golden, creamy smoothness.

She closed her eyes for a moment and tried to imagine how it would feel to have a man hold her now. Then she shook her head negatively. No matter how many of the local swains were enamored with her, and there were many, she had never felt the desire to have one of them.

"I wonder if something's wrong with me?" she queried miserably. She had spent many hours with girlfriends who had chattered endlessly of this man's charms or that one's romantic prowess. Still, though she had flirted

44

shamelessly, she had no desire to carry it any further than that. She thought of her twin, Dixon, who was always in love with one girl or another, and after listening to him and Brian discussing the subject, had firmly believed that all women responded immediately to a romance. "Then why not me?" she thought miserably. "Why can't I find someone who really cares for me?"

Her thoughts were interrupted by a knock on the door, and she slipped the nightgown quickly over her head and got back into bed.

"Come in," she called.

Her brother, Dixon, came into the room fully dressed for riding. They smiled at one another across the room. Dixon and Deline were closer than just brother and sister, they were especially attuned to one another's thoughts.

"Good morning, lovely lady," he laughed happily as he bounced down heavily upon the edge of her bed.

"Well, I guess you're pleased with yourself about last night," she grinned.

"Li'l sister," he laughed, rolling his eyes, "you have no idea how grateful I am at this moment."

They laughed together, then the laughter slowly ebbed as Dixon narrowed his eyes at his mirror image.

"Del, why don't you tell me what's wrong with you lately? You haven't been the same girl for the last few months."

Deline was amazed to find that for the first time in their combined lives there was no way to explain what he could never understand. Instead, she tried to change the subject.

"Where are you riding to?" she asked and looked away from the questioning eyes of her brother.

"Over to Cross Oaks. Graham and I are going hunting this morning. Want to ride along?"

"You go on ahead. As soon as I get up and dressed, I'll

45

be there," she answered.

He gave her one last intense look, then shrugged his shoulders. "All right," he tossed back over his shoulder, "but remember, we aren't waiting all day for you, so get a move on."

She watched her brother's broad back as he moved to the door, and she continued to watch long after he had closed it behind him, her eyes clouded with thought. Now she lay back comfortably among the pillows and allowed a gentle lethargy to overtake her. Her mind drifted to her family. Mama and Papa so happy with each other had made their home a place of laughter and contentment. For as many years as she could remember, there had been the feeling of love and warmth among them. Then her thoughts turned to Adam, Adam whom she loved to distraction and had missed so desperately when he was sent away. She had never understood why he had suddenly left. She only knew she missed him terribly, but now he was back again, quieter and gentler than ever before.

"Maybe I'll talk to Adam. Maybe he'll understand," she mused.

She thought also of Brian, sweet-smiling, warm-hearted Brian. He teased her unmercifully, yet he also was a strong shoulder on which she knew she could lean if necessary. Brian resembled Adam in many ways; his hair had the same tawny color, but without the bright streaks of sun that Adam's had. He was shorter than Adam by an inch or so, but his shoulders were broad and he was narrow waisted and slender hipped, giving him the appearance of a heavier strength. Where Adam was quiet, Brian was given to streaks of mischief and occasionally narrowly escaped getting into trouble. Girls found him completely impossible to resist, so consequently, he spent much of his time fighting them off.

She sighed discontentedly, again threw back the covers and got out of bed. She washed herself quickly and dressed in a soft white blouse, long sleeved and open at the neck, and a dark riding skirt. With a last pat to her hair, which she had rebraided and wrapped about her head in a shining coronet, she left the room and went downstairs. There, she quickly gulped down a cup of hot coffee and much to Felicia's distress, prepared to leave.

Felicia had been a slave at Briar Hill for all the years that Deline could remember. She was a second mother to her and a close friend and confidante. This was one of the few times Deline could not confide her feelings to her, for she did not have the words to explain her emotions. She planned to escape as quickly as possible before unwanted questions came, for Felicia knew her much too well.

"Now you sit yo' bottom down, Missy, and yo' eat some breakfast. Yo' gettin so skinny, yo' gonna get sick."

"Felicia, I'm going riding with Dix and Graham. I'm late now, so I don't have time to eat."

"But yo' mama going be mad you ain't at the breakfast table with the family. Now yo' brother Adam's home, they want the whole family at the table."

"Just tell them I had to run an errand, Felicia," she called back over her shoulder as she left the kitchen and cut across the lawn to the stables.

Felicia shook her head and chuckled in distress. "That young'un sho is impatient," she thought, hoping such impatience in one so pretty was not going to cause her any trouble.

Deline reached the stables quickly and went inside the cool semidarkness. She ordered her horse saddled and waited while Jonas moved to comply. Once saddled, she mounted immediately and set off in the direction of Cross Oaks. Her horse hadn't been ridden for a while, and she was hard put to get him under control. He wanted to stretch out his legs and run.

After a while, she gave up trying to hold him back, and bending forward in the saddle, she let him have his head. Feeling the surging power of the stallion moving under her, they raced toward the covered bridge that separated the Forrester and Gilcrest property. They clattered across the bridge. She never knew what it was that spooked the horse when they reached the other side. Something dashed in front of him, and he leapt to one side rearing on his hind legs. Taken by surprise, she lost control, and the last thing she remembered was hitting the ground along the bank of the river and rolling down. Then her head struck something and blackness engulfed her.

Bram moved slowly along the road occasionally shifting the load of wood he carried from one shoulder to the other. Old Maddy who had raised Bram since birth, had wanted these special logs for burning because of the aroma.

Maddy was the closest person that Bram could think of as a relative, although she was not related by blood. It was impossible to tell how old Maddy was. She was small and very wrinkled, looking at least a hundred, but she had looked the same to Bram for as far back as he could remember. She had cared for him and loved him as her child all his life. He knew, that she knew the answers to his questions about his parentage, but after years of trying to get her to tell him, he finally realized that Maddy would never speak so he gave up asking. Bram had gone to collect the logs, mostly because he wanted an excuse for a swim in the river in the cool light of dawn. He had first chopped the logs for Maddy, then after bundling them, he had left them on the riverbank, stripping down and diving into the water, sputtering as the coolness of the river struck his body. He had floated on his back in the water, feeling it loosen the tightness of his muscles, and he gazed up at the early morning sky. He allowed the painful thoughts he usually kept under control to creep unaware to the surface.

"If I were only white instead of one-quarter black," he thought. Maddy had told him of his mother. She had been half-black and half-white and very beautiful. About his father, no matter how much he had questioned, Maddy had refused to speak. Bram knew that his father was white, and for years, had looked closely at every white man around to try to find a resemblance. After a while, he had stopped doing this, but deep in his mind, he would have given his soul to know who his father was.

Now he whistled gently as he moved along the road feeling the beginning heat of the day along his back and shoulders. The sound of a horse running brought his head up quickly as the riderless horse dashed madly past him.

"Somebody's been thrown," he thought, and dropped the logs on the ground. He ran until he came to the bridge but could see no one on the road. His eyes searched everywhere. Then suddenly, he spotted someone laying close to the water. It was a woman, and she was laying very still. He ran down the bank and knelt by her side, gently turning her over. Her eyes were closed, but she was breathing. There was a nasty bruise on the side of her forehead.

"Deline Gilcrest," he thought. "What should I do?"

A black could be hung for putting his hands on a white girl. But he just couldn't let her lie there. She might die before he could get back with help. He made up his mind and, putting one arm under her back and the other under her knees, lifted her in his arms and climbed the bank to the shade of a tree. There, he laid her gently on the grass. Then he took his handkerchief and going back to the

49

river, he wet it in the water.

Deline had just begun to regain consciousness when she felt strong arms lift her from the ground. Her head lay against a muscular chest, and she could hear the steady, strong beat of his heart. She kept her eyes closed, wanting, for some reason, to savor the feeling. Then she was being laid gently on the soft grass. She cracked open her eyes slightly and watched Bram walk away from her, his lithe body moving with the grace of a sleek animal. She watched him kneel by the water and wet the handkerchief, then she closed her eyes as he started back in her direction. She could sense him kneel beside her, then the coolness of the cloth against her face where her head hurt so badly.

Still, she kept her eyes closed. Now he really began to worry, and he lifted her hand in his and patted it briskly.

"Miss Gilcrest, Miss Gilcrest! Please wake up. Come on, wake up," he repeated.

Deline's eyes opened slowly and she smiled up at him, and he smiled in relief.

"Are you all right? What happened? Can you move? Is anything broken?"

"Which question do you want answered first, Bram?" she laughed, then winced as the pain flashed through her head.

His answering laugh made her feel warm, and she realized that she had enjoyed the feel of his arms about her. She looked closely at him, and another thing struck her violently. Although she knew he was considered black, he was as white-skinned as she, and also alarmingly handsome and virile looking.

"Just so you can get up. We've got to get you home," he answered.

Deline continued to look at him steadily.

"I don't think I can, Bram. You'll have to carry me.

50

Can you?"

He looked worried for a moment. Although he had never suffered punishment for this kind of transgression, he had seen many who had. The thought of it caused him to hesitate. He looked at her; her eyes were kind, but he had also seen kind eyes turn to something else when the white man was angry.

"I . . . I could go and get some help if you would be comfortable enough to wait for my return."

If she was surprised at his use of the language, she never showed it. Instead, she shook her head negatively.

"It would be better, Bram, if you carried me home. I don't think I could walk that far, and I don't want to stay here alone . . . and . . ." She smiled. "Don't worry, I will explain exactly what happened."

He looked steadily at her for a moment, then kneeling by her side again put his arms under her and lifted her easily from the ground as though she weighed nothing. She could feel the muscles of his back and arms against her skin and found herself enjoying it.

"My head hurts terribly, Bram. Do you mind if I lay it against you?"

"No, ma'am," came the soft, strangled reply. Her softness against him was causing him to react in the last possible way he wanted.

He moved down the road to Briar Hill, enjoying the feel of her in his arms but making a superhuman effort to control the thoughts she roused in him. Deline lay very still, listening to the insistent throb of his heartbeat, and in the age-old way of women, knew that the rapid beat of his heart signaled more than even he knew.

The pressure of his arms had brought the soft round curve of her breast against his chest. The rest of the walk was done in silence as both of them enjoyed the forbidden delights of something neither of them could have.

Chapter 6

Adam and Holly had been riding for over half an hour without too much conversation. Holly had the strongest feeling that Adam was holding himself in check with the strongest willpower. They were cutting across a field and had almost reached the center when Adam reined his horse. She stopped also and turned questioning eyes to him. He dismounted and walked to her side. Without a word, he lifted his arms to her. She gazed deeply into his eyes for a moment, then with a smile touching the corners of her mouth, she reached out both arms and put her hands on his shoulders. He lifted her gently from the saddle and slowly touched her feet to the ground, but he did not release her. Instead, he stood holding his hand tightly about her waist. Slowly, he lifted one hand and pulled the pins gently from her hair allowing it to drop about her loose and free. Then he pulled her into his arms and held her with his face pressed against the soft sweet-smelling hair.

"Holly," he said longingly, "I've dreamed of holding you like this for so very long. I never thought it could ever be."

She could feel the length of him against her, solid and warm, and a feeling of well-being overcame her. This was where she belonged; here was the haven she had longed for and needed. This was the man who could hold her heart and soul forever.

She looked up at him again and saw the longing for her in his eyes. Putting one hand on each side of his face, she pulled him down to her and brought the softness of her lips against his. Adam made a small sound deep in his throat as her cool lips touched his. Then suddenly, his arms were about her, and his mouth was parting hers, exploring, demanding, giving. He pulled her down with him in the tall grass, and they lay still together for a moment. Then very gently, he touched her, caressing her with infinite tenderness. Slowly, he undid the buttons of her blouse and dropped it off her shoulder. The straps of her chemise followed and she felt the tender strength of his hands against the soft flesh of her body. It was like a current moving from him to her as he kissed her again and again. First her cheeks, her throat, then the softness of her shoulders, then lightly the tips of each breast, touching them with his tongue until he felt them swell and rise against his hands. He removed the rest of her clothes and ran his hands over her, enjoying the warm feel of her body. Then he rose and removed his clothing. She watched him, enjoying the sight, absorbing everything about him. He was like a young god, she thought. His body, long, lean and with tightly pulled muscles. His stomach was flat, and the matted gold hair on his chest flowed downward to a long line that ran down his belly to the pubic hair. His manhood was large and throbbed with life of its own. The flashing pain of desire overwhelmed her, and she lifted her arms to him, whispering his name as he came to her. Now he gathered her tightly against him, and the years of hunger for her throbbed with every beat of his heart. Then he took her mouth again with his in a kiss that left her breathless and panting. His hands seemed to touch her everywhere and she began to ache with the wanting. Still, he did not enter her but continued to lift her passion with his mouth and hands until she wanted to cry out.

Gently, he moved between her thighs, and his body came against hers. She was moist and throbbing with desire for him. He held himself in check with only the greatest of command as slowly he began to enter her. She gasped and her body stiffened as she felt the first searing pain, and he held back again for a few minutes, kissing her lips and throat until he felt she was ready. This time, he could not control the desire for her and entered her fully, hearing her cry out his name as he held himself deeply inside her.

Then slowly, he began to move, and after a few seconds, he could feel her body pick up the tempo and respond to the rhythm of their song. Her dizzy world spun wildly, and the only realism was the feel of him deep within her. They moved as one now, each giving and demanding all. Her hands roamed over the hard, muscular frame of his body, pulling him even more tightly against her. Her long velvet legs were about him, and she almost sobbed his name as his lips caressed her shoulders. She could feel the hot sting of tears in her eyes and knew she was crying not for the pain but for the great sense of fulfillment she felt, a oneness with him that surpassed all her dreams. Great heaving waves of ecstasy washed over her as he dove deeper and deeper into her, moving with greater speed and harder thrusts until she thought she could bear it no longer. A voice whispered endearments and words of love and encouragement, and she realized the soft moaning words were coming from her. She wanted no end to this violent pleasure he brought to her as their bodies built together a fire that would last a lifetime.

They lay still together for a long time afterward, neither of them capable of coherent speech. His eyes were warm on her, and he smiled tenderly at her as she looked up at him. One finger brushed gently the tears on her face and lingered to trace a line down the corner of her lips to her throat and on down to caress her gently and pull her close to him. She nestled her head on his shoulder, and as the sun warmed her body, she felt a contentment creep over her that she had never experienced before. She dozed awhile, but Adam remained awake, savoring the reality of a dream he had carried for so long.

"Holly, Holly," he whispered gently against her hair.

"Yes, Adam?" came the murmured reply.

"Whom shall we tell first that we want to marry? Your parents or mine?"

His words brought back the harsh reality, and she sat up suddenly to his surprise. She turned and looked down on him and answered quickly his unspoken question.

"Yours, Adam, for I do not believe my father shall listen to us with any great pleasure. You see, he has planned marriage between Graham and me."

At these words, he also sat up.

"You and Graham? Never you and any other man as long as I'm alive!" Now his frown deepened. "You're under age, Holly. He could stop us, you know."

"No, Adam," she answered quietly. "He may not approve, but he will never stop me."

Adam drew her to her knees, and they faced one another. From around his neck, he took a chain upon which hung a plain golden ring.

"My mother's," he said. "She gave it to me for my wife."

He took the ring from the chain, and lifting Holly's hand, slipped it on her finger.

"I, Adam Gilcrest, take thee, Holly Jemmison, for

my wedded wife," he whispered, "until death do us part."

She repeated the words he had spoken so gently to her as tears fell unheeded down her cheeks. Then he lowered his head and kissed her.

They took as much time as possible riding home, stopping now and then when Adam would reach out and touch Holly or lean over and kiss her lightly. They were deeply in love and content to just share one another. He left her at her front door with a promise to be there for supper, then they would tell her parents. In the meantime, he intended to tell his parents as soon as he got home, enlisting their support for Holly.

He whistled as he rode toward home, never remembering a time in his life when he had felt happier. When he dismounted in front of the house, he handed the reins of his horse to a large-eyed boy who grinned up at him, then he took the front steps two at a time and swung open the front door to face confusion. Someone was shouting and his brother, Brian, was pulling on his jacket in preparation for leaving.

"What's going on?"

"Got to go for the doctor," mumbled Brian, struggling with his coat.

"Why? What's happened?" he asked in alarm. "Who's hurt? Where's Mother?"

"Deline. She fell off her horse. Bram just brought her home. He found her down by the river."

"How badly is she hurt?" shouted Adam at his brother's retreating back, but the slamming of the door was the only answer he got. He cursed to himself and took the stairs in a few short leaps and almost ran to his sister's door. When he opened it, Deline was sitting up in her bed with Dixon and his mother on either side of her. She was protesting but unable to do anything about the pampering she was receiving.

56

"What happened, Del?" he questioned harshly, his brows coming together in a deep frown.

"Oh, not you too, Adam!" Deline said exasperated. "I'm perfectly all right. My goodness, you'd think I'd never fallen off my horse before."

The bruise on the side of her head had turned several shades, ranging from deep black to a violent orchid.

Adam chuckled and reaching down, gave her hand a squeeze.

"You look all right with the exception of your multicolored skin."

"Good. Then tell Mother and Dix to let me out of this bed," she begged.

"Nope! You stay right there until the doctor gives you the okay."

"Oh, Adam, really!" she said in anger.

"Yes, really, little girl. I've got some good news for all of you, and I want you all together and in good condition when I tell you."

"What, Adam, oh what?" yelped Deline with delight.

"When the doctor says you're all right, I'll tell you all at the same time. For now, why don't you rest until the doctor arrives?"

Jessica and Dixon rose immediately, and no matter how Deline pleaded, they ordered her to stay in bed and left her to rest.

Deline lay back against the pillows. Her body relaxed, and she drifted off into a semisleep. Again, strong arms held her close, and she could still almost feel the throbbing beat of his heart against hers. She was determined to see him the next day to thank him for bringing her home. That's what she kept saying to herself, but the warmth that invaded her when she thought of him belied the reasons she tried so hard to cling to.

Chapter 7

The doctor came down the stairs and smiled at the group that awaited him.

"She's perfectly all right. Going to have some interesting bruises by tomorrow. And she'll be a little sore, but everything else is fine."

Jessica sighed with relief, and all three of the young men smiled with relaxing tension.

"Should she stay in bed, Doctor?" questioned Matthew.

"I really don't think you'll be able to keep her there," laughed the doctor. "In fact, I think she was dressing when I left the room. Well, I must go now. I hope the next time I see you, Matthew, and you, Jessica, that the circumstances are different." He smiled at Jessica.

Jessica took his arm and escorted him to the door.

"Thank you, Jim. I appreciate your coming so quickly."

"Any time, my dear."

She closed the door after him and turned to see Deline limping slowly down the steps. Adam moved quickly to her side and lifted her in his arms. He carried her into the drawing room and set her down gently in a chair. She grinned up at him.

"You didn't tell anyone your surprise before I got down here did you, Adam?"

He laughed aloud while Dixon and Brian simply threw up their hands and shook their heads in exasperation.

"Well, did you, Adam? If you did, I'll never speak to you again."

"No, I didn't, Del, so sit back and relax, all of you. I've some news I think will please you all. It's made me very happy, and I want the people closest to me to be the first to know." He paused for effect, and they watched him with silent, expectant faces.

"Holly Jemmison and I are getting married as soon as possible." He said the words slowly and quietly.

Jessica rose rapidly from her chair and threw her arms about Adam, laughing and kissing him.

Brian threw back his head and gave a roaring shout.

Dixon pumped his hand rapidly with a delightful grin, and Deline, unable to move rapidly, sat in her chair and clapped her hands together in delight. Adam turned to his father who had a worried frown on his face.

"Father?"

"Aren't you going to give your blessing, Matthew? Don't you think it's wonderful?" questioned Jessica.

"Have you told Holly's parents yet, Adam?" his father asked him quietly.

"No, we're going to tell them tonight at supper."

"Be prepared, son, for some strong opposition. Just last week, I was having a drink with Richard Forrester, and he was bragging about joining the Forrester and Jemmison property. Said he was going to announce the wedding of Holly and Graham real soon."

"He'll just have to understand Holly and I love each other," replied Adam.

"You don't know Richard Forrester, son. He doesn't have to understand anything except what he wants, and he generally gets it one way or another."

"Not this time, Father," Adam said firmly. "This is one thing he won't have his way about. No matter what

59

else happens, Holly is mine, and I'll fight anyone for her. Graham Forrester or her father, it doesn't matter."

Matthew looked at his oldest son, and the glow of pride in his eyes made Adam smile. Matthew realized what a mistake he had made when he had angrily sent Adam away. For two years, he had regretted it and had told Adam so on his return. Now he held out his hand, and Adam took it.

"Congratulations, son. You're getting a lovely lady. I hope you'll be very happy. How soon will it be?"

"Well, if I had my way, it would be today," laughed Adam, "but I suppose we'll have to ask Holly about the date. Now, if you all will excuse me, I'm going to take a hot bath. I want to look my best tonight."

He kissed his mother, accepted a few more hearty whacks on the back from his brothers, ruffled Deline's hair as he bent to kiss her and left the room.

"Do you think Adam's going to have a problem, Father?" Brian asked.

"Yes, son, more of a problem than he can imagine."

"Adam can handle it," Brian said confidently, and this was seconded by Dixon.

The two boys began to discuss the situation between themselves, but Deline watched her father's face intently. "He's really worried," she thought. She thought of her brother, Adam. What family wouldn't want their daughter to marry a man like him? He came from a family as wealthy or wealthier than hers, with a name as honorable as theirs. What then was the reason her father foresaw such problems?

Moving behind her father, she put both hands on his shoulders and bent her head to kiss him, then whispered in his ear, "Father, what's wrong? Why shouldn't the Jemmison's want Adam to marry Holly?"

"It's an old wound, Deline, better left to die," he said, more to himself than to her.

A quietness descended on the room, and for a time, everyone seemed caught up in their own thoughts. They were interrupted by Cornelia, Jessica's maid.

"Miz' Gilcrest, a message done come from Heritage. They want y'all to come to supper tonight with Mista' Adam. They' boy waitin' fo' an answer, Ma'am."

Jessica and Matthew exchanged glances, and Matthew nodded his head. Cornelia turned to leave the room.

"Cornelia, did they request the whole family?" asked Jessica.

"Yes'm."

"All right, Cornelia, after you've sent word, tell the boys to get ready, but I want Deline to stay home."

"Mama!"

"Deline, you will stay here. You're in no condition to go anywhere," snapped her father sternly.

"Oh!" Deline stamped her foot in exasperation and, with a swish of her skirts, turned toward the stairs. She tried her best to make a proud, angry exit but lost her body's cooperation. It rebelled firmly to any violent movements, and she had to cling to the banister to reach her room, where she half-satisfied her anger by slamming the door loudly behind her.

Meanwhile, when Holly had arrived at her house, she dismounted and entered the front door and went directly to her room where she stripped off her clothes and ordered a hot bath. Her heart sang as she sat back and let the scented water relax her.

"Adam," she whispered softly to herself, then laughed, remembering the day and delighted with the thoughts of all the days and nights to come safe in Adam's arms. It never occurred to her that there would be any real opposition to her marrying Adam. Her father would just have to forget the Forresters.

Her mother came in the room as she finished dressing. Odella Jemmison was a very gentle, quiet woman. Raised to be a lady, she never questioned the authority of her husband. She had spent twenty years doing everything in her power to make him happy.

She was a small, slender woman. Her eyes were hazel, and her hair was a deep warm brown. She was quick and intelligent and ran her household well. Her daughters loved her dearly. If her husband did not, it never was obvious to anyone else. Still, about her eyes lingered a look of sadness that Holly had noticed occasionally, as if she kept a secret deep within her and the keeping was painful.

"Holly, where have you been all morning?"

"Riding, Mother."

"Ah," her mother smiled, "and how was Graham this morning?"

"I wasn't riding with Graham, Mother."

"Oh? Who were you riding with?"

"Adam Gilcrest."

Her mother looked at her steadily for a few seconds, then repeated, "Adam Gilcrest."

"Yes, Mother, and there is something I would like to talk to you about."

Odella slowly sank into a chair and waited. Holly came to her mother's side and dropped to her knees in front of her.

"Mother, Adam has asked me to marry him, and I've accepted," she said, watching her mother's face.

For several moments Odella sat stunned, her mind wildly searching for the right words to say.

"The gentleman has a very poor reputation, Holly," she said lamely, and knew as soon as she uttered the words they were the wrong ones to express.

"Do you believe every bit of gossip you hear, Mother?" she asked coldly as she rose from the floor and turned away from her mother. "Adam is a wonderful man, and we love each other. I guess we have since we

62

were children," she mused and smiled to herself as she realized this must be truth, remembering all the times Adam had shown off in front of her. The time at the river when his gray eyes had spoken to her, and she did not hear.

"Why, I guess I've always loved him," she said in wonder.

"Holly, your father will be angry, and Graham's father . . . They've planned for so long for you two to marry."

Holly turned angrily to her mother and was about to say something when she realized how upset and frightened Odella was.

"Mother, would you want me to marry a man I did not love when I've found one who loves me and whom I love deeply? Mother, please," she said gently. "Remember when you were young? Didn't you love Father deeply? Wouldn't you have been upset if you had been forced to marry against your will?"

Odella let her mind drift backward, something she had not permitted herself to do for nineteen years. "Yes," she thought to herself, "it would be terrible to be forced to marry someone she didn't love and to lose someone she did." For that was exactly what had happened to her. Tyler Jemmison had been a friend of her brother's at school. He had met and admired Odella, more, Odella thought, for her inheritance than her beauty. Although she was attractive, she was not beautiful, and Tyler was a handsome man, very popular with the ladies. Her parents had thought it a wonderful match and had agreed to the marriage without even consulting her. She remembered also, very painfully, the dark-eyed boy whose father was overseer on the next plantation. They had met when she was visiting and had been drawn to one another. He was a gentle boy with a bright smile who quoted poetry to her and captured her gentle heart. They had laughed together and planned how they would marry and had promised undying love. They had not counted on her parents. Despite her tears and his anger, the young couple had been separated. The boy's father had been dismissed from his job and had taken his son away. Odella had been forced to marry Tyler. She would never forget her wedding night.

Brutally, he had taken his young, virginal bride without thought for her needs or her feelings. She had become pregnant almost immediately, and Tyler had turned from her to a string of dusky-skinned mistresses. Afterward, he returned to her bed with the same cold use of her body, and she had become pregnant with Steffany. Her will to resist him seemed to have died, and a series of still-born sons followed. For some reason, he blamed her for their lack of sons, and finally in anger turned from her completely. He now kept an octoroon mistress to fill his needs, and Odella continued as mistress of Heritage without love or thought from Tyler. She had forbidden herself the luxury of remembering Sean and had enclosed herself in a quiet shell from which she emerged rarely. She loved both of her daughters dearly but felt their disappointment in her and was unable to explain to them how she really felt.

Now she studied her daughter carefully.

"You really love him, Holly?"

"Oh, yes, Mama, so very much. No matter what Father says, I will marry Adam."

Holly was never more amazed in her life when her mother drew her into her arms and said softly, "Yes, Holly, I believe you do. Don't let anything separate you, my love. Cling to him no matter what the odds. I shall do everything in my power to help you."

She felt the deep pain in her mother and began to realize that she had never known or understood her mother, something she vowed to remedy.

Chapter 8

Tyler Jemmison, at forty-one, was still a handsome man. He had kept his body in good physical condition with much hard work. He was strong and muscular; his hair was a deep auburn color, waved back from a broad forehead to his shoulders with a vibrant life. He also had a short beard and a full mustache, through which his strong, white teeth gleamed.

He dressed slowly, relaxed and comfortable now, as he gazed back at the woman who lay on the bed.

Portia was amazingly beautiful. Her skin was the color of pale chocolate, and she had long, black hair that fell almost to her hips. She lay naked against the blankets, and he stared down at her in satisfaction. She was probably the best investment he'd made in years, he thought. The fact that she cared deeply for him and obeyed his every whim meant nothing to him, for he would have taken her under any circumstances. Her body was long and slender, her breasts high and full with dark rosy tips. He could still feel the velvet smoothness of her body against his, writhing under his expert passion. It pleased him that she enjoyed him as much as he did her, not like his cold-blooded wife, he thought.

Now he sat on the edge of the bed and ran his hand slowly and sensuously up the inside of her long legs letting his fingers caress her satin-smooth skin. She stretched languidly and smiled up at him.

"Goddamn, you're a beautiful wench, Portia," he laughed as he ran his hands expertly over her body. When he felt her stir under his hands, he laughed again and with a sharp smack on her bottom, he rose from the bed.

"I've got to get back to work, much as I'd like to stay for another romp. That damn overseer of mine can't seem to keep those niggers humpin' unless I'm right behind him."

"You comin' back to Portia tonight, mastah?"

"We'll see, Portia, we'll see."

"Yo' come back, mastah, I make you feel happy."

He chuckled, "You always do, girl, but Odella sent word she's invited the Gilcrests to supper. After they've gone, I'll probably be back for a visit."

He shrugged into his jacket and turned to give her one last, appraising look. Then he opened the door and closed it firmly behind him. She could hear the sound of his retreating footsteps across the porch of her small cabin, then they were gone, and it was quiet.

Very slowly, she rose from the bed and slipped her cotton shift over her head. Twisting her hair into a coil, she knotted it at the back of her head. She thought about the man who had just left her. Deep, warm stirrings began inside her at the thought of him. He had bought her at the slave auction in New Orleans and had made no excuses about the reason as most white men did. He had put her in his wagon and started home. That night he had taken her as easily as though they had been together always, making her body sing. She had begun to love him then, and now he was the center of her world.

Tyler strode across the porch and mounted the horse he had tied there. Swinging him about, he returned to the fields from which the urge for Portia had brought him.

Matthew and Jessica Gilcrest rode in the carriage while

66

Brian, Dixon and Adam followed behind on horseback. They were greeted at the front door by Tyler and Odella who gave the warm impression of genteel hospitality. Holly and Steffany had not come downstairs yet, so the family was invited into the drawing room where the men were offered drinks, and the two women sat side by side on the sofa and exchanged small talk.

Adam listened half-heartedly while his eyes continued to stray in the direction of the stairs.

"Bet you wish you were up there instead of Steffany, don't you?" whispered Brian, keeping his face straight while Adam almost choked on his drink, then glared stonily at him. He had to be nudged by Dixon when he realized a question had been directed to him by Holly's father.

"I beg your pardon, sir. I didn't hear you."

"I said," repeated Tyler, "you've been North for the last two years. What do you think of all this talk of war?"

"Frankly, sir it scares the hell out of me."

Both Brian and Dixon watched Adam closely, weighing with respect his words.

"Why, I'd never take you for a coward, my boy."

Adam gazed coolly at him, and Tyler's eyes were the first to drop away.

"It takes more than courage, sir," he said softly, "when the enemy you fight can outgun you and outsupply you in any battle that is prolonged any length of time."

"Length of time!" snorted Tyler. "I've never found the Southern gentleman who couldn't whip any two Yankees in no time."

Adam smiled with his lips, but his eyes still glimmered a cool frosty gray.

"I just don't think it would be that easy."

"We'd whip them good and send them home to Mama inside a month," repeated Tyler firmly.

"Mr. Jemmison, the North has three times the factories the South has, and access to more arms and ammunition than we do. All we have of any real value right now is cotton and courage."

"Enough, we can send our cotton abroad and buy all the arms and ammunition we will ever need."

"Unless they block our ports," replied Adam.

Jessica had been half listening to the conversation for some time and realized that Adam was getting himself into a serious position and would never back down. She rose and went to Adam's side and tucked her hand in his arm.

"You gentlemen must not discuss war. We just won't have it." She smiled up at Tyler Jemmison with all the charm she could muster. He, being a gentleman and also appreciating Jessica's rare beauty, chuckled and nodded his head.

Mother and son exchanged glances, and Adam's look told her he wasn't fooled for a moment. His mother was not the clingy, syrupy type. He smiled fondly at her, trying to protect him from himself as usual.

Jessica was never more grateful for anything in her life than the appearance of Steffany in the doorway. She smiled brightly at everyone, greeted her parents first and then her guests. Steffany had a charm and enthusiasm that included everyone in the room. This kind of excitement was what Steffany enjoyed most. She wanted always to live her life as she was now, surrounded by people who loved and admired her, wearing pretty clothes, dancing, laughing and being happy. Finally, her eyes settled on Adam and glowed with deviltry.

"Holly will be down in a few minutes. I guess she really wants to look special tonight for some reason." She smiled mischievously at Adam who returned her smile, unperturbed.

"I doubt Holly could look any other way," he

answered softly.

Tyler had been deep in conversation with Matthew and so had missed this exchange.

Steffany was watching Adam's face intently and knew without turning about, the moment Holly appeared on the stairs. She could hear Adam's indrawn breath catch and hold as his eyes seemed to devour her.

I wish someone would look at me like that. It's a good thing Papa isn't watching closely right now, she thought as she watched Adam's reaction.

Holly was wearing a plain gown of deep, emerald green. It was off her shoulders and cut low in front to reveal the soft, round curve of her breasts. There was no jewelry or adornments whatsoever. Her hair had been drawn back from her face severely, then a mass of deep, auburn curls fell almost to her waist. Because of the severity of her hairstyle, her eyes looked enormous and innocent. Slowly, she smiled at everyone and finally let her gaze come to rest on Adam, who hadn't taken his eyes from her for a moment.

Several things happened at the same time. Adam moved to Holly's side and lifted her hand to his lips and kissed it gently. At that moment, Tyler turned toward the door and looked directly at them. They stood close together, oblivious of all the others. Adam's family smiled in unison at the sight, and Odella watched her husband, pale faced. Tyler stood frozen, staring at the two.

They made a beautiful couple; his tawny head bent close to her brilliant auburn one, his large body making hers appear tiny and helpless. He still held her hand and slowly they pulled their hungry eyes from each other and turned to face the others in the room.

There were several moments of silence as Tyler collected himself. He had been struck with the deepest sense of rage he had ever felt in his life, but being the clever person he was, he masked his emotions well and presented a calm exterior while his brain spun busily. Adam and Holly, he thought angrily. No one was going to ruin his plans now. Not Adam Gilcrest nor his own daughter. There was too much at stake to let these young fools interfere. He smiled and moved to Holly's side.

"Well, it's about time you got down here, Missy. We're about to starve waiting for you."

He presented his arm to her and Holly automatically took it.

"Adam, would you please escort Odella, and we'll go in to dine?"

There was no other choice but for Adam to comply and he went to Odella's side.

"My pleasure to escort a lady as beautiful as you, Madam," he said gallantly, but caught Brian's glimmer of amusement and quick wink as they all went in to eat.

Dinner affected everyone differently. Odella could not eat but toyed with her food while she watched her husband closely. She had known Tyler Jemmison too long not to realize he was holding back violent anger. He was not used to having his will thwarted, and she was deeply afraid of the plans he might be formulating.

Tyler chatted with Holly and Adam who sat across from each other next to his seat at the head of the table.

Both Matthew and Jessica were aware of the sudden feeling of strain in the air, but Holly and Adam seemed not to feel the current as they smiled at one another. Neither was it missed by Brian and Dixon who exchanged worried glances, remembering their father's words. Brian and his brother did their best to bolster a sagging conversation. Finally, dinner was over and the men excused themselves for cigars and brandy in Tyler's study.

"Mr. Jemmison," began Adam hesitantly, after drinks had been passed around and everyone was seated, "I have

70

something very important I'd like to talk to you about."

With a deceptive smile and a gentle voice Tyler said, "Yes Adam, what is it?"

"I . . . we . . . I mean, Holly and I are very much in love, sir. We'd like to marry with your permission."

"Adam," Tyler began slowly as he rose from his chair and put his glass on the table, "I want you to know that I have the greatest respect for you and your family," he lied glibly. "And, under any other circumstances, I would welcome you into our family."

Adam's body became quite still as he watched Tyler.

"You see, Holly and Graham Forrester have an agreement which we approve of."

"And you don't really approve of me," finished Adam as his eyes chilled to a frosty gray.

Tyler looked away from him and chuckled.

"Now, my boy, most certainly I approve of you, but you see, the arrangements have already been made."

"Has anyone asked Holly how she feels about this?" Adam asked coldly.

"Holly is under age. She will do what I tell her to do," Tyler answered quietly.

"No matter how she feels?"

"No matter how she feels," repeated Tyler. "Sometimes, young people do not know what is best for them. Older, wiser heads must make the necessary decisions."

"I love Holly very much—" began Adam.

Tyler raised his hand to interrupt.

"I understand, but it cannot be helped. Holly will marry Graham Forrester, and that's all that will be said on the matter."

He started to move toward the door when Adam's cold voice stopped him.

"No, sir!"

"What?" Tyler turned to face Adam with a look of

complete surprise on his face.

"I said, no, sir. Holly loves me and I love her. I'm going to ask her to marry me, and if she accepts, I'm taking her."

"She'll never accept against my wishes."

"Is it fair to her, sir, to make her marry a man she doesn't love, to be miserable for the rest of her life? What good can that bring to anyone?"

Adam did not realize he had hit closer to the truth than Tyler liked. Tyler's face became red with anger, and he spoke through gritted teeth.

"Holly is my daughter. She is obedient. She will do exactly as I command." He was almost shouting when he added, "And I say she will marry Graham Forrester."

Adam walked toward the door. "We'll see!"

"Adam!" Matthew put his hand on Adam's arm, but he shrugged it away. He turned and went out of the door leaving the men watching him in amazement. They then all moved quickly to follow him.

When he walked into the room, Holly rose to meet him, the smile on her face dying when she saw his face gray with anger. He went to her side and stood looking down into her questioning eyes.

"Holly," he said softly, and he touched her face lightly with the tips of his fingers. Her eyes filled with tears as she realized the truth of what her father's answer must have been.

"Holly, I love you beyond all else. If you want me, I want us to marry right away. But if you agree, it is without your father's blessings." He held her eyes with his.

Odella gave a small sound and leaned back in her chair.

"He refused," Holly whispered.

Adam just nodded.

At that moment, her father walked through the door.

"Holly, go to your room at once," he said sharply. "And you, sir, will leave my home now and never return."

"Holly," Adam repeated, ignoring her father, "come with me, Holly. Come with me now," he pleaded quietly.

Holly was confused and frightened and almost prepared to refuse until a quiet voice from behind her said, "Go with him, Holly. Don't make a mistake you'll regret the rest of your life. You love him, go with him."

"Odella!" Tyler shouted in anger.

But she faced him with her head high and her eyes calm.

Holly placed her hand in Adam's and turned to face her father.

"I'm sorry, Father. I would rather have your blessing. But, with or without it, I will marry Adam."

Tyler Jemmison watched the two leave the room, and his anger struck fear in Matthew Gilcrest, for no one knew Tyler as well as he. Then he gathered his family together and they left.

Tyler turned to face Odella. Her face was serene, and she smiled at him.

"You shall regret this day, Odella," he said softly.

"If Holly is happy, there is nothing more you can do to me. For once, Tyler, you will not ruin someone else's life for your will. Go back to your mistress," she added softly, and with her shoulders straight, she walked past him and up the stairs, leaving him standing alone and watching her retreating figure.

Chapter 9

When her family had gone, Deline lay in bed fuming at what she considered very unfair treatment. She turned on her side and sighed deeply, allowing herself to relax and let her mind drift. Her eyes half closed in semisleep; she felt again the warmth of a pair of arms about her. The feeling would not go away, and she wondered how it would have felt if he had kissed her. Her body became warm with the thought, and she drifted off to sleep.

Bram was not as fortunate. Desired sleep would not come to him. Instead, a pair of soft, blue-gray eyes smiled up at him. Her slow smile lingered before his eyes no matter what he did. His body responded when he felt again the soft warmth of her body through the thin shirt she was wearing. He swore to himself and rose from the bed. Slipping into his pants, he walked outside. Bram, though a slave, was given privileges above a normal slave because of his closeness to Graham. Consequently, he had freedom to roam anywhere on the Forrester property. He walked slowly toward the river where he dropped his clothes and dove deeply into the cold water. He pushed himself downward until his lungs demanded air, then with a strong kick, headed toward the surface. He swam until he could feel the tired pull of his muscles, then coming out of the water, he fell down on the bank and stared up at the glowing stars against the night sky.

"She's white, and you're black," he said angrily at himself. "You'll be hanged if they just knew the things you're thinkin'."

He rolled over in the grass and felt the cool earth against his fevered skin.

"But I can't stop the feeling or the thinking. As long as I do nothing about it, no one will ever know."

With this thought, he drifted off to sleep and allowed the beautiful dreams of her to come as they did every time he closed his eyes.

Bram and Deline did not know that the wheels of fate were already in motion, and they would be together in a way neither of them could imagine.

Tyler Jemmison nursed his drink in the dark, shadowed study. He had sat there for a long time after Odella had gone from the room. There was some way to stop this marriage, he thought, and I will find it. His anger for Adam Gilcrest and his family grew, until he felt the throbbing blood in his temples and his hand clenched spasmatically on the chair arm.

"I can't let them marry. There's too much at stake. I'll not lose everything for that young bastard. I'll go see Richard tomorrow. Together, we'll find a way to stop this. He has as much at stake as I."

It was the wee hours in the morning when he left the house, saddled his horse and rode to Portia's cabin. She was asleep when she felt him slide under the blankets next to her, his hands reaching and drawing her close to him, and his hard lips descended on hers fiercely and passionately. He released all his frustrated anger on her, taking her forcefully, and afterwards, he fell into an exhausted sleep. She lay wide-eyed and suddenly frightened at the fierce and uncontrollable fury of this man.

Adam had watched Holly's tightly closed face all the

75

way home, and when they arrived, Jessica had taken her upstairs to show her a room in which she could sleep. There were no words of comfort Jessica could say. *What she needs most is Adam*, she thought.

After a few quiet questions, Jessica had left her and gone back downstairs. Joining her family, she smiled gently at Adam's worried eyes.

"Why don't you talk to her for a few minutes, Adam? She's frightened. She needs to know you're strong enough for both of you."

Adam needed no more encouragement than this. Without a word, he rose and went upstairs. He rapped gently on Holly's door, and when there was no response, he opened it and went in. She was standing out on the balcony looking up at the stars. He came up behind her and gently slipped his arms about her. His lips close to her ear, he whispered as he tightened his arms about her.

"I love you, Holly. I'll try to make you happy. I'll do everything in my power. Maybe someday when he sees how happy we are, he'll come around to forgive us."

She turned in his arms. There were tears in her eyes, but a tremulous smile on her lips. She raised both hands to his face and pulled it gently down to hers. As their lips met, he felt the depth of her love for him, and he held her, gently caressing her as his mouth devoured hers in a kiss that had suddenly become hungry and seeking. When they finally moved apart, she looked up at him and smiled again.

"Remember . . . with this ring, I thee wed?"

He nodded.

"Well, remember also the rest, Adam. Wither thou goest, I go. Thy people shall be my people. I love you so very much, Adam. Without you, I would never be happy.

I shall have no regrets. I only hope I can make you as happy as you have made me."

He felt a constriction in his throat that prevented any further speech, and his heart beat a rapid tattoo against his chest. He kissed her once again and then moved her away from him.

"Either we stop now," he laughed shakily, "or I'm not going to stop."

She realized that he was right and walked back into the room, away from him.

"I'll see you in the morning, love."

"Good night, Adam."

He closed her door behind him and went back downstairs. His mother and brothers had already gone to bed, but his father awaited him.

"Still up, Father? I thought you'd be in bed by now."

"I had to speak to you, son, just for a moment."

"Of course," Adam replied and preceded his father into his study where he dropped comfortably into a huge chair and stretched out his long legs in front of him.

Matthew looked at his handsome son and felt a surge of deep pride and affection. How could he have been stupid enough to have believed anything dishonorable about him?

"Adam," he began slowly. "This affair with Holly's family. I hope you'll be careful. Tyler Jemmison is a powerful man and a man who never forgets a grievance. You've hurt him where he's most vulnerable."

"Holly?"

"No, his pocketbook and his pride. Two very serious places to injure a man like him. Tyler, Richard and I came out here together. We worked the land together, and I feel I know him as well or better than anyone else around."

"Father, why did you three separate? I noticed for the

past ten years you drifted further and further away from them, but they became closer and closer friends."

"For the good of everyone, Adam, I think what happened would be better left untold. Suffice it to say that I could not nor would not be close friends again with Tyler or Richard. That is another reason why I ask you to be careful. I know full well what vindictive people they can be separately. Together, I have no idea what they might conspire to do. Richard wanted this marriage for Graham and Holly even more than Tyler did."

"But, why? Our family is every bit as good as the Forresters and every bit as wealthy. What is the real reason, Father? It's not just me, although that little fiasco with Diane didn't help my reputation any."

Matthew leaned back in his chair with a deep sigh. Adam could see the tired lines etched in the corners of his mouth and the deep furrows between his brows as he frowned.

"Adam, there is nothing more I can say about their reasoning. I just wanted to warn you to be on your guard. You've created two very bad enemies. Watch your back."

Adam realized that there were many things his father was leaving unsaid. He also knew there was no use in pressuring him, for Matthew did not intend to reveal whatever it was. And if Matthew had decided to continue to hold his secret, nothing in the world would pry it out of him.

Matthew stood up and moved to Adam's side. There he placed his hand on Adam's shoulder. "Did I tell you, son, how glad I am you're home to stay? And how sorry I am about misunderstanding you in the first place?" he said very quietly.

All the bitterness Adam had felt for the past two years melted away under the obvious love his father had for him. He smiled up at him, and Matthew responded. There was nothing more to be said. Slowly, Matthew left the room and closed the door behind him. Adam sat for quite some time, contemplating the past events. Then he rose also and made his way to a bed that seemed lonelier than ever when he desired Holly there with him.

The next day dawned clear and bright. The early morning mist from the river began to rise as the rays of the sun warmed it. One by one the people in the Gilcrest house stirred. Jessica, always an early riser, was already in the kitchen giving orders for breakfast and the daily housekeeping. She had awakened when the first streaks of daylight touched the dark sky. A dream she could not remember had lifted her from a sound sleep. Now she tried to shrug away the heavy feeling that held her as she moved about the kitchen giving orders for the daily work.

One by one, her family appeared. Strangely, all of them seemed quiet and reserved today. Even Brian, whose early morning cheerfulness had always put a smile on everyone's face, was still.

Adam rapped gently on Holly's door. A young, black maid opened it.

"Is she still asleep?"

"No, suh," she replied. "Miz Holly, she don't sleep much las' night."

"Adam?" Holly called from inside the room. "I'll be out in one minute."

He could hear her rustle about, and then she came to the door.

She had pulled her hair into a chignon at the nape of her neck. She was wearing a pale blue cotton dress that caressed her figure as Adam longed to do. She reached up on tiptoe and kissed him lightly. The soft scent of jasmine enclosed him, and he had the urgent desire to hold her.

Without another word, he reached out and pulled her into his arms. Holding her against him, he inhaled the warm fragrance and felt the softness of her body.

Finally, she stirred and moved away from him in a rather shaky smile. When he looked down at her, he could read the desire on her face. His gray eyes were softened and smiled into hers.

"Good morning," she said quietly.

"Good morning. I can't wait to be on the other side of that door when I tell you 'good morning,'" he replied with a laugh.

"We'd better go down to breakfast. From the look in your eyes, I don't put it past you to remedy the situation."

"I was so busy looking at you I didn't think of it, but now that you mention it . . ."

"Forget it, Adam," she giggled. "Would you want to shock the entire family?"

"At this moment, I don't really care."

"Come along, sir. Breakfast awaits," she said sternly.

Holly and Adam seemed to bring some brightness to the table, and the conversation became warm and friendly when the maid came to the doorway.

"Mistah Gilcrest, suh, they's a gennaman to see yo', suh, in the study."

Matthew was a little startled at the early morning visitor but rose and left the room. He was gone for almost twenty minutes when he returned, walking slowly, his face very pale.

Jessica rose slowly from her chair, her hand on her breast as her heart began to thump painfully.

"Matthew, what is it? What's happened?"

Matthew stared at his sons and said quietly, "Fort Sumter was fired on day before yesterday. Anderson may evacuate the fort. We're at war."

Chapter 10

As days passed on, word was awaited of the situation between the states. Young men waited impatiently and with vibrant enthusiasm. On April 12, 1861, the South Carolina forces became angry, charged bad faith and opened fire on Fort Sumter. Just as relief ships for the fort appeared. Major Anderson responded, and for two days, a hot fire was kept up, during which no one on either side was injured.

Fort Sumter, being only partially completed, suffered severely. The barracks were burned, and only salt pork was left for rations. Under these circumstances, Major Anderson surrendered on the fourteenth and hauled down his flag, and by agreement, he went North with his command.

The effect of this was electrical. It solidified the North and the South; the excitement was intense. The North became unanimous, the South likewise, while the border states tried to maintain neutrality but were really divided in sentiment.

Lincoln at once issued a call for volunteers. Five thousand men, to serve three months. It took only a few days to enlist them, but it took time to equip them, and few of them saw any active service until they reenlisted under the next call for three hundred thousand men for three years.

There was great difficulty getting guns and powder, tents, clothing and rations. There was even a greater difficulty in organizing and drilling regiments. The South was not well off except that it had begun to prepare earlier, but in equipment, it was worse off than the North.

The young hot-flowing blood of the South did not realize this. In their magnificent pride, they assured themselves of quick victory. Men joined the army in masses, while frightened women watched.

Bradley and Charles Gordon of River's End were two of the very first in the area that answered the call to arms.

In the Gilcrest home, there was silent tension, as Jessica realized deep inside that it would not be long before her sons would also be gone. Adam was completely torn apart. He did not want to see his brothers fighting this doomed war, but his loyalty to his home and state was just as strong.

The family was seated about the table for supper with the exception of Brian and Dixon who had gone into town to see what the latest news was. There was sporadic conversation, but no one's mind could concentrate on talking about trivial things and no one wanted to bring up the subject of the possibility of the family's separation.

The sound of the closing front door, masculine voices speaking in high excitement and approaching footsteps drew everyone's eyes toward the dining room door.

Adam knew what to expect when the door opened, so he kept his eyes on his mother. He watched her face drain of all color as she rose slowly, her hand pressing against her chest as though she could not control the beating of her heart.

"Brian," she whispered. "Dixon!"

Both boys moved quickly to their mother's side. There was no necessity for words to explain their late arrival. The gray uniforms they wore told the story.

With tears in her eyes, mingled with pride, she opened her arms to her sons, and they gratefully acknowledged her acceptance. But her eyes found Adam's, and he could feel the pain. Yet he knew there was much more to come for all of them, for he, at that moment, knew that he also would be wearing the same color soon.

Holly, who stood beside him, slipped her hand in his, and he held it tightly, not wanting to turn and look into her eyes at the moment.

Supper continued, and Brian and Dixon kept it as bright and cheerful as they could with their enthusiasm. Holly and Adam exchanged no words, but both knew the thoughts of the other. There had been no time yet to make wedding plans, and Holly was suddenly very frightened. She felt that some enormous black thing was going to separate her and Adam, and there was no stopping it.

The inevitable day came when Adam told her that he had signed up with the second call to arms. She tried in vain to keep herself under control and would slip away from Adam when tears threatened. Nevertheless, he instinctively knew how she felt. The day came quickly when he had to leave. He held her very close to him, her cheek against the rough fabric of his gray jacket. "I'll not cry," she said to herself silently.

He lifted her chin in his large hand and looked deeply into her eyes. The gray of his jacket deepened the gray of his eyes until they became slate colored.

"I'm sorry, Holly. I wish things had been different. I wanted things to be perfect between us. Just as soon as I get back, we'll be married."

She smiled up at him and made her voice as light as possible.

"Are you sure you didn't arrange this just to get out of marrying me, Adam Gilcrest?" Her voice caught in her throat, and tears came unwanted to her eyes. "I assure you, sir, you won't get away with it."

She felt control slipping from her grasp, and she wrapped her arms tightly about him and buried her head in his chest. He chuckled, and she could hear the deep beating of his heart.

"Why, no, Madam, you've caught me fair and square. I guess I know when I'm trapped."

She didn't answer; she couldn't. Her eyes were filled with tears and her voice seemed caught in her throat. Now he lifted her face again and kissed her gently at first. Her lips were moistened by the salty tears, and he felt them warm and soft against his; the kiss deepened. Slowly, her lips parted under his, and his arms tightened about her as she pressed herself against him.

"Adam, oh, Adam," she whispered.

"I know, Holly." He looked down at her. "Do you know, I think I've loved you since I can remember. I'm a very persevering man, Holly. I usually get what I want. You be prepared. This can't go on forever. I'll be back to claim you soon, and you'll never get away from me again."

He put both hands on her shoulders and pushed her gently away from him.

"I've got to go, Holly," he said quietly.

With his arm about her waist, they walked to the front porch and out into the drive where his horse waited. Deline and his parents were there. He shook hands with his father, kissed his mother and sister, then mounted his horse. Holly came to his side, and he bent down to gently touch her lips with a feather-light kiss. Then he was gone, and Holly, with the greatest sense of desolation and loneliness she had ever felt, watched as he rode away.

For a while, the war was a game for these fiery young men. There were parties and balls each time they came home on short leaves. Women banded together in groups to make bandages and apparel for their "boys in gray."

Brian and Dixon, never having had any trouble finding feminine company under normal circumstances, thoroughly enjoyed themselves. Adam concentrated on getting the men under his command in the best possible fighting order, for the cold hand of warning lay heavily on his heart.

And then it came; a forward movement was ordered on Manassas. The battle took place along a stream called Bull Run. The early part of the battle was favorable to the Federals, but the Confederate general, Thomas J. Jackson, made a strong defense.

Both sides were lacking in training. Young men, playing at war until now, tasted the bitterness of a bloody battle. The first fingers of tragedy reached out to touch the people of River's End. Charles Gordon, Jr. and his brother Bradley, both gave their lives in this conflict. At home, Jessica and Merilee, along with Odella, tried their best to comfort Martha Gordon while their heavy hearts thought of their own loved ones from whom no word had come.

A senseless panic followed the battle of Manassas and the whole Federal army fled in terror to Washington. The Confederates suffered heavily, but not until they heard of the flight of the Federals did they know the extent of their victory. Neither side was really prepared for war as the battle of Bull Run proved.

And then in April 1861, President Lincoln declared a blockade of the Confederate coast. Unable to trade their cotton with other countries, the South began to feel the pressure of deprivation. The women kept up their spirits, and their menfolk bravely laughed about the luxuries they were doing without.

The women didn't complain that there was not enough food to eat nor clothes to wear. The blockade of their coast that stopped them receiving these commodities also prevented them the medicines they so desperately needed. Hundreds of men died from the lack of treatment for their wounds.

Sheets of names were released of the dead and wounded. Daily reports came home, and each day Holly would scan the list, thanking God Adam was not among them.

Merilee Forrester sat in the drawing room with Holly, Deline and Jessica. She had brought the lists and given them to Holly. With a white face, she had declared she could not read another list. Holly ran her eyes down the names quickly; then suddenly her eyes stopped, and she turned very pale. She looked up at Merilee.

"Graham?" Merilee asked hoarsely.

Holly could only nod her head.

"Dead?"

Holly looked back at the name then across the page.

"Missing in action, presumed dead," she replied softly.

Merilee sat very still, slow tears falling down her cheeks. Then quietly, she rose and left the room. Jessica followed quickly to try to comfort her as best she could, but Holly sat quietly staring at the name on the list. Flashes of Graham returned to her. The lazy days they spent together as children, the gentleness of the man and the deep friendship that existed between them. Then slowly the tears came, and when they started, she could not stop. She shook with the agonizing grief of a world that was spinning out of control. Deline made no move but sat in frozen pain. There were no words that would be able to soothe this agony.

The juggernaut of war rolled onward collecting lives as violently as it came. The pressures of a superior-equipped army bore down upon the South. One black day followed another. One battle after another brought longer and longer lists of wounded and dead. Hospitals were filled to overflowing and became, because of the lack of doctors and medicines, hellholes of dying men.

All the women volunteered their help, but it was such a small effect on the great tragedy that was happening to them all. The dark clouds gathered, and as the South lay like a virgin bride, the groom came with the ultimate destruction. Sherman!

General Sherman sat in his tent, a bottle of whiskey in front of him, and glared balefully at the map spread out in front of him. He paid no attention to the man who entered and stood silently waiting to be acknowledged. Sherman spoke without lifting his eyes from the map.

"You have your men assembled, O'Brien?"

"Yes, sir."

"You've been given your orders?"

"Yes, sir."

Sherman looked up at the tall young lieutenant who stood at attention before him. For one moment, his eyes glimmered in amusement.

"O'Brien, I want you to get this through that thick Irish head of yours," he grinned, then placed his fingers on the map. "These three plantations are valuable to me. They'll be used as part of our supply line. We can't afford to lose any links in our supply line. I'm taking this goddamn army straight to the sea, and I don't want anything ruining my plans. Do I make myself very clear?"

"Yes, sir."

Sherman laughed, then stood up and clapped Lieutenant O'Brien on the shoulder.

"Then come and have a drink with me."

He lifted the bottle and poured two drinks, handing one to O'Brien. They both drank then Sherman said quietly.

"Nothing is to happen at these places, O'Brien, not to the plantations or to the people you find there."

"Yes, sir, nothing will go wrong, sir."

"Good, you're dismissed. I hope I see you again, O'Brien. You're a hell of an officer and a man."

"Thank you, sir," O'Brien said, turning to leave.

"Oh, O'Brien?"

"Yes, sir?"

"That means all the pretty girls, too," he laughed.

O'Brien smiled and left the tent to prepare his men to march toward Cross Oaks, Heritage and Briar Hill.

Lt. Devlin O'Brien rode at the head of his men at a slow pace. His orders were to secure the three plantations and set up a command post to use as a link in Sherman's supply lines.

O'Brien had come from Ireland ten years prior as a young man of seventeen. He realized immediately that his future lay with the Army. Here, he had some chance to advance himself. He had blue-black curly hair that sprang from his head with a life of its own. Contrasting this, his eyes were sky blue. His face was deeply tanned from being outdoors continually. One eyebrow cocked upward and gave him a devilish air. He laughed easily and enjoyed life to the fullest. He was a tall man but filled out well so he gave the impression of hugeness. He was respected by his men for his honesty and courage. They trusted him and would have followed him anywhere. Like the typical Irishman, he chafed under this kind of job. He wanted to be in the thick of the fighting. In future years, he would thank his guardian angel for putting him where he was at the moment.

Briar Hill was the first plantation in his path. He knew that the men were gone, but he didn't know who was still there or what kind of defense they could muster. He spread his men out then moved up the drive toward the big house. So far, there was no one in sight except a few blacks who offered no resistance but gaped at him in fright. As he moved closer, he saw three people standing on the front porch awaiting him. When he drew even nearer, he could tell they were all females.

"Some nice Southern beauties, Lieutenant," said one of the sergeants who was riding next to him.

O'Brien snapped his eyes around. "You keep these boys under control, Sergeant. I don't want any problems here."

"Aw, Lieutenant, the boys need a little fun. These ain't nuthin' but some—"

"Sergeant," O'Brien interrupted, "you keep these men under control or I'll personally nail your hide to the barn door. Understand?"

"Yes, sir!"

There was nothing more said between the two men as they moved closer to the house.

Holly and Steffany had been trying to organize some of their clothing to see what could be repaired and made wearable. Neither of them, as well as all the other women, had very little left that was wearable. They were piling up the worn clothes in groups of repairable and not when they heard Merilee call for them. Shouting was not Merilee's way, and they looked at each other in amazement. Then they both ran to the stairs. Merilee was halfway up. Her face flushed, she was breathing heavily, as though she had run a long way.

"Yankees!" she gasped. "Yankees coming up the drive!"

Steffany could feel her legs go weak, and even Holly became frightened. The stories they had heard of the Yankee monsters had struck fear deeply within them.

"Oh, God," whispered Steffany. "What are we going to do? We don't even have a gun in the house."

"What would we do with a gun if we had it?" Holly asked. "Hold off all Sherman's men with it?"

"Well, what are we going to do?"

Holly straightened her shoulders, and her eyes hardened as her chin lifted determinedly. "We're going out to show them we're not the least bit afraid of them."

"Maybe you're not, Holly," whispered Steffany, "but I am."

"They don't have to know that, do they, Steff?"

Holly's calmness and determination gave courage to the other two, and together they walked out onto the front porch to await the enemy.

Lt. Devlin O'Brien dismounted at the bottom of the steps and removed his hat. Then he looked up at the three women awaiting him. Not to be at the disadvantage of being looked down on, he mounted the steps.

"Lt. Devlin O'Brien, Ma'am," he said to Merilee. "I'm sorry, but I must take over your house."

Merilee looked steadily at him, then said coolly, "Welcome to Briar Hill, Lt. O'Brien. I'm sorry we can't offer you any refreshments. You see there's nothing here to offer you."

He gazed at her face then smiled his most charming smile that had melted the heart of many young girls.

"We won't inconvenience you in any way, Ma'am. You just go about your business as usual. We're going to use just a couple of rooms. My men can camp on the front lawn."

A small choking sound came from Steffany, and it drew his attention to her. Two bright spots of anger appeared on her cheeks, and her eyes were full of fury. He didn't believe he'd ever seen as pretty a girl in his whole life, and he wondered how she would have reacted to him if he had not been a Yankee.

"Yankees on the front lawn of Briar Hill," she said frigidly. "I just wish—"

"Yes, Ma'am?"

"I just wish our men were here. They'd shoot you and your men full of holes before they'd let you camp on our front lawn."

He grinned again and watched her with deep admira-

90

tion in his eyes.

"Steffany!" said Holly firmly. Then she turned to face him.

"Your sister?" he asked quickly, more as a statement of fact than a question. At her nod, he turned again to Steffany.

"Believe me, miss, I wouldn't disrupt your home, but I have my orders."

Steffany was silent, but he could still see the fire raging within her. For some reason, he wanted this angry young girl to understand. But before he could say another word, Steffany turned her back on him and walked away.

"Please excuse my sister's rudeness, Lieutenant," said Holly, "But—"

"It's all right, Ma'am. I understand. I'd probably feel the same way."

She nodded silently, then invited him into the house. Before entering, he ordered his men to set up camp. For one guilty minute, he felt as though he were using an army to lay siege to one small, auburn-haired, green-eyed girl.

Chapter 11

Graham regained consciousness slowly. For a time, he couldn't remember where he was or what had happened. Then it all flooded back into his memory. Graham had been serving under Brigadier General Bragg for over a year. Although he did not like the man personally, he tried his best to put his likes and dislikes behind him and serve as well as he could.

They had moved forward to Chickamauga on September 19, 1863. Graham remembered the crispness of the air and the brilliant shades of the trees. After all the things he had seen, he still wondered why men should be killing each other in a place as beautiful as this.

The first attack, on Saturday, September 19, was a complete failure for both sides. The Union forces under Brannan reconnoitered at Chickamauga Creek and encountered Forrest's cavalry, dismounted and completely unprepared. Forrest's men were driven back, and the battle lasted all day, with no appreciable success on either side.

That night, they sat around campfires and discussed the useless battle of the day and tried to ignore the fact that tomorrow would probably be much heavier and much bloodier. Graham moved among his men slowly, going from campfire to campfire. At each one, he spoke a few words to each man, and at a few, he shared a drink or two. It was a thing he always did before a battle, and he wasn't sure he did it for the confidence of the men and to bolster their courage, as much as to bolster his own. Despite the fact that his men respected him and were completely loyal to him, his self-respect and self-confidence were slow in building.

Because he was so large, he exuded self-confidence, and the men gravitated toward him. Behind his back, they called him "King" Forrester because one of the men at one time remarked how much he looked like a king.

Now he squatted down beside one fire and accepted a drink from one of the men; he smiled. "See you got a letter from your wife, Tucker. How is everything at home?"

"Fine sir. My oldest boy's fourteen and already has got the crop in. He's a good kid. Boy, I hope this thing's over soon."

"Yeah," one boy replied.

Graham looked at him. He couldn't be over seventeen, and looked a little frightened. Yet afraid to appear so in front of the rest of the men.

"We movin' out first thing in the mornin', sir?" he questioned.

Graham nodded his head. "First thing."

The boy gulped down his fear and remained silent. Graham accepted the jug of whiskey again and took another sip. The boy looked at him again across the fire; he said very softly, "Will we beat them, sir?"

"Shit," Tucker replied. "We'll chase those blue coats all the way back to Washington." A ripple of laughter went around the group, but Tucker's eye caught Graham's across the fire. For a few minutes, their eyes held; then Tucker looked away, and Graham realized he was just as frightened as the boy.

"You all better get some sleep, morning's goin' to come early," he said as he rose and headed for his tent.

93

Once inside, he sighed deeply and sat down on his cot. He stretched his hands out in front of him; they were trembling a little. If he hadn't known they were moving out early, he would have gotten completely drunk. He unbuttoned and removed his jacket, then lay back on the bed with his hands clasped behind his head. He remembered how his father had reacted when Graham had enlisted. Not too many words were said between the two men, but Richard's eyes had told Graham more than his words ever could. The first battle he was involved in, Graham had been so frightened he had become violently ill just before. But during the fight, he had performed well and kept his men under control. It was after this battle, when he had the chance to think it all over, that he took the first steps in becoming the man he wanted to be.

Now, remembering his father, he felt, for the first time in his life, the beginnings of a release from the hold Richard had over him. He didn't know how the war was going to turn out, but he did know that when he returned home, he was no longer going to be the boy Richard maneuvered so well.

He thought once of all the times that Richard had beaten down his courage, even from the time he was a small boy and slowly washed himself clean of Richard's negative influence. During the night, Graham and the other officers were called in to receive their orders for the battle to follow.

Graham was given orders to move his men in position under General Longstreet, who had arrived during the night to reinforce Bragg, and he was given the left wing of the army while Polk was given command of the right.

After orders were received, Bragg set about rearranging his position. It was early Sunday morning when Graham was roused from the shallow sleep he had just recently achieved.

"What time is it?" he asked his orderly.

"About six a.m., sir," he said quietly. Graham looked at him quickly. It was obvious the boy was frightened, but Graham couldn't console him; he was too busy fighting the fear that wanted to dominate him. Graham dressed and left his tent as quickly as possible; he didn't want any time to think. He looked about him. Most of the other officers seemed so calm to him, and he wondered if he was the only one who was afraid.

After his horse was readied, he stood by him and talked softly to him. He wanted to soothe him, but he also wanted something to do.

They were ordered into position, and Graham was surprised at his own commanding voice as he ordered his men to prepare to move out. Combined with Breckinridge, they attacked the Union forces at nine a.m. on Sunday morning.

The battle would have been a repetition of the day before if Rosecrans, the Union officer who led the opposition, hadn't made a serious mistake. Trying to strengthen the defenses on the right, he gave orders to close up and support Reynolds. Doing so, he created a gap in the defense lines and was promptly attacked by Longstreet in precise timing and in the exact spot. Union defenses shattered.

The broiling excitement caught Graham up, and without knowing he was doing so, he screamed encouragement to his men and urged them forward into the opening gap.

Without giving a thought that anything could happen to him and seeing the crumbling of the Union lines, he surged forward with a loud yell. Suddenly, he felt a sharp pain in his legs, and he looked down to see a bright spurt of blood stain the gray of his pant leg. He ignored the pain, gave a rebel yell as loud as he could and waved his men onward. Pandemonium and a confusion of men and horses followed. Then another searing pain caught him

95

in the left shoulder, and he felt himself lifted from the saddle. He struck the ground with such force that he felt he could never rise again. Slowly, with determined will, he pulled himself to his feet and staggered on. Then he felt the last sharp and final blow on the side of his head, and he tumbled down into a deep, dark tunnel of oblivion.

Now he tried to move and found he couldn't. Either something was lying on his legs or he had lost the feeling in them, for they would not respond. He realized that everything around him was quiet, and he struggled to a sitting position. His head pounded terribly, and when he raised his hand to touch it, his fingers came away sticky with blood. He gazed about him. They were in the outskirts of the woods, and soft, filtered sunlight came down through the tree branches in long, bright fingers. Then his eyes lowered to the ground about him. Bodies lay still in the soft grass. With a tremendous effort, he pulled himself to his hands and knees and crawled to the nearest one, turning him over on his back. He gagged and drew back quickly; the boy had no face, just a bloody mass where the face should have been. He choked and felt his stomach heave. When he got the spasms under control, he crawled away from the thing in the grass.

A soft moaning caught his ear, and he looked about for the source of the sound. It came to him again, and he finally noticed a man sitting against a trunk of a tree. Painfully, he dragged himself to his side. This man was older. He held both hands pressed against his abdomen. When he finally got to his side, he found Tucker.

"Let me see," gasped Graham.

"Forget it, Lieutenant. It's no use. There's nothin' you can do except sit by me for a few minutes. I don't want to die alone." The last words were in a quiet whisper as he slowly slid sideways, and his sightless eyes turned toward the bright blue sunny sky. He sat paralyzed, looking at the dead man, then around at all the bodies scattered over the battlefield.

"Such waste," he thought, "such a goddamn waste."

There was nowhere for him to go and no way to get there if he could. His leg pained unmercifully, and he felt the warm blood squish in his boot. His left arm would not respond, and he wondered if the bone had been broken by the bullet. He knew he had to do something, or he would surely die. With a strength he didn't even know he had, he began to crawl, dragging his wounded leg behind him. He couldn't have gone very far when he felt waves of blackness settling over him. He shook his head blindly to get the blood out of his eyes. It is no use, he thought, and he slowly sagged to the cool ground as a dark curtain lowered over him. It is good to rest, just for a moment, he thought, as his eyes closed and unconsciousness claimed him.

From somewhere vaguely came the sound of the jingle of horse harnesses. The wagon moved very slowly through the masses of fallen men. A man and woman sat upon the wagon seat scanning the mass of dead bodies for any sign of life. The man was slender, about fifty, with a wavy head of white hair. The girl who sat beside him was obviously his daughter, for she bore the same clear brown eyes of the man with her. Her hair was the color of burnished gold, parted in the center, it was drawn back in one long plait down her back that hung below her hips. She wore a faded blue cotton dress open at the throat to expose the long column of her neck. She looked intently from one body to the next. There were tears in her eyes. But her jaw was firmly set, and her hands were clenched together in her lap.

"I think they're all dead, Pa."

"Well, we better hurry out of here then gal, or them boys in blue will be back to check for prisoners."

Graham groaned and gave a slight effort to rise to his

knees again unsuccessfully.

"Pa! That one's still living."

The old man stopped the wagon, and they both jumped down and ran to Graham's side. When they rolled him over he muttered a curse, and his eyes cracked open slightly. Above him floated a vision, golden hair, brown eyes. It faded in and out of his consciousness.

The old man looked at his wounds quickly and shook his head. "This boy's in bad shape, and I don't know about that leg wound. Looks like he lost a lot of blood." Graham had lost complete consciousness again. Together, they lifted him into the wagon and left the woods. They traveled along a dirt road for almost three miles, then turned off onto a road that had all but disappeared in the underbrush. Another hour of travel brought them to a large wooden-frame farmhouse. The house sat against the side of a hill, and if no one had known it was there, it would never have been found.

Laboriously, they got Graham from the wagon into the house, and struggled up a flight of stairs to a small bedroom, placing him gently on the bed.

"I'll put the wagon away," the old man said. The girl just nodded, for she already was moving about, cutting away Graham's clothes in preparation for working on his wounds. When she had his clothes off, she washed away the blood from his body so she could tell just how bad the wounds were. The one on his shoulder was not the problem, the bullet had gone through and meant that she would only have to clean and bandage it. There were no broken bones. His head bore a deep cut as the bullet creased across his upper right forehead and along the side of the temple.

"An inch lower and you wouldn't have been alive, either," she said as she wiped away the dirt and blood from his hair.

He moaned softly under her ministrations, and she

looked at him with pity-filled eyes. Laying her cool hand on his head, she felt the beginnings of a fever.

Now she concentrated on his leg. Here, a worried frown wrinkled her forehead. It was not a bullet that wounded him but some kind of a piece of metal, most likely from cannon fire. She sponged away the dirt and examined it closely. Then she stood up and picked up a small knife from a table nearby. She went back to the bed. The old man reentered the room.

"Well?"

"You'll have to hold him down. I've got to dig that out of his leg."

"He looks pretty strong."

"Straddle him and sit on his chest. That way you can hold his body. I'll hold his legs."

Putting both of Graham's arms at his side, the old man straddled his body pinning them effectively. Then the girl did the same, sitting on both of his legs. Grimly, she picked up the knife and began to work. The pain reached Graham's mind, and he began to move about and mutter under his breath. Perspiration beaded the girl's brow as she bent over him and worked as rapidly as possible. Under her body, she could feel the thrashing of his muscles. Still, she clung desperately to him with her knees.

"There," she said triumphantly as she held aloft a bloody piece of metal. She washed and bandaged the wound, then covered his body and looked down on him. "Now we pray, Pa. Pray we helped in time, and he's strong enough to live," she said softly.

Several hours later, she came back in the room to check on his condition. Placing a cool hand on his head, she frowned. His fever was rising. As if to confirm her fears, he began to mutter under his breath.

Ann went downstairs and brought up a basin of cool water and a cloth. Squeezing out the cloth in the water, she placed it on his head. The hours grew longer and longer, yet she continued methodically to place the cloth on his head. Despite this, the fever continued to rage. He began to stir restlessly and to mumble. She sat through long hours listening, relieved only a few times by her father to let her rest for a while. It hurt her to see his big body so helpless and in such pain. At one time, he opened his eyes and looked at her. She thought, for a moment, he had regained consciousness, but bending close to him, she could see his eyes were glazed. He had no idea of what he was doing or where he was. Suddenly he reached out and grabbed her wrist in an iron-tight grip that almost caused her to cry out.

"Holly," he muttered. "Holly, I can't fight him Holly, I can't. . . . I can't. Forgive me Holly. Pa . . . Pa, please. Don't make it like this. Try . . . try to understand me . . . Pa . . . Holly, Holly!" Slowly, his grip eased as he tried to focus his eyes on her.

"You do understand, don't you Holly?" he smiled, and the grip on her wrist loosened. Then he reached up and touched her face and said softly, "I knew you would. You always do, don't you, Holly?" He sighed deeply and dropped his hand limply on the bed and drifted again into that restless mumbling fevered sleep.

She sat very still and listened quietly to the half-connected words. Always it came back to Holly. Whoever she was, she must have meant a great deal to him.

Days passed before the fever began to break, and then one morning he opened his eyes and looked about him in wonderment. He was completely disoriented, for the last thing he remembered was crawling through the grass.

He was lying on a large double bed. Beside it was a dresser and one straight-back chair next to the bed. The window was open, and a soft breeze billowed the curtains out into the room. He attempted to move, and a red-hot pain stabbed him in the thigh. He gasped and fell back against the pillows. This was the first time he realized several things. He was completely naked and well bandaged. "I wonder who I have to thank for this," he thought.

As if at command, the door opened, and the old man came in.

"Well," he smiled. "You're finally awake. I was beginning to wonder if you were ever goin' to wake up."

"Where am I?"

"My farm—about ten miles from Chickamauga Creek. You boys fought one hell of a fight down there. Chased them good you did."

Graham smiled. His heart filled with gratitude that they'd won the day with their sacrifice.

"Did you bring any other wounded here?"

"Son, you was the only one we found alive, and for a while, we weren't too sure about you."

"God," Graham said softly. "All those boys."

The old man nodded his head in silence.

"Do you know how far my outfit is from here?"

"Well, I know the Union has hightailed it back to Chattanooga, and as far as I can find out, Bragg has pulled back to Missionary Ridge."

"I've got to rejoin them as soon as I can," Graham said. Then he made an effort to sit up, which in his weakened condition he found impossible.

"You ain't goin' nowhere for a spell, boy. By the time you're well enough, you ain't goin' to be able to get out of this area without bein' caught. Son, you sure as hell don't want to end up in one of those prison camps. You'd have been better off dyin' on that field than endin' up there."

"But I just can't lay here and wait out the war," Graham said urgently. "There must be something I can do, some way to find a way out of here."

"You just lie still until you get well, and we'll find a way then to get you out of here." The old man said firmly.

"I don't mean to sound ungrateful, sir, but you can see, can't you, I've got to get back to my outfit."

"It's all right, son," the old man said calmly. "Rest easy. I guarantee you when you're well enough, we'll get you back."

"I want to thank you, sir, for my life and for doing all the doctorin' on me. I really am grateful, sir."

"Oh, you don't have me to thank for anything. I didn't do nothin' but sit on you and hold you down."

"Then just who do I thank?"

Footsteps could be heard running lightly up the stairs, then Ann pushed the door open. Graham stared in surprise as she slowly smiled at him.

"You're the vision I saw. I thought I'd died and gone to heaven."

The old man chuckled softly at the blush on his daughter's cheek.

"I'm glad to see you're awake. You had us quite worried for some time."

"I want to thank you for all you've done for me. I owe you my life."

"It's all right, you're very welcome. I'm glad Pa and I were around when you needed us." Again she blushed, for Graham's eyes were holding hers.

"We'd better go down and let you get some rest. You need all you can get if you want to recover. I'll bring you some food in a little while," she promised.

Graham closed his eyes for a moment, remembering the boys who had died in battle. He wondered at his luck at having been found as he was and nursed back to health instead of being left to bleed his life away beside that beautiful creek. He also wondered at another streak of luck. "Who ever had a nurse as pretty as he had," he thought, and he planned on enjoying every minute of his recuperation time.

Chapter 12

There were very few blacks left on any of the plantations. Most of them disappeared when Lincoln signed the emancipation proclamation. The few who remained were mostly old people who had nowhere else to go and no desire to leave the security of the places they had known all their lives. Devlin O'Brien had put several men in each house, but kept himself and two other officers quartered at Briar Hill. Still angry with Odella for backing Holly against him, Tyler Jemmison had spent his last three days at home with Portia. The results of that time together was the birth of Portia's child just four weeks ago. Odella, feeling a deep sense of shame, had abandoned her husband's home to the Union soldiers. Richard Forrester had also joined the Confederate army, sure that ultimate victory would be theirs and his property and the property he desired so badly would someday be his.

Bram squatted on his heels and examined the horse which Sergeant Taylor had brought to him lame. It had taken some time before any of the army men really believed Bram had been considered a slave or that his ancestry was partially black. No matter what he said, Devlin O'Brien and most of his men had tried their best to be friends with him. He had kept a wall of sorts between himself and them, mostly because he was afraid to let anyone too close. He divided his time between Cross Oaks and Briar Hill, trying his best to make the people on both plantations comfortable. He had watched Deline from a distance, being very careful not to be alone with her or let her see how she affected him. He spent his nights in restless dreams of her that roused him sweating and left him sleepless more nights than he cared to count.

"She's pulled a tendon, Sergeant. I'll take good care of her. She'll be all right."

"Boy, I hope so Bram," said Sergeant Taylor worriedly. "She's the best mare I ever had. Besides, Lieutenant O'Brien's gonna have my head on a plate if we have to do away with her."

Bram laughed. "O'Brien's tough, huh?"

"Naw, he's all right. Damn good officer." Sergeant Taylor laughed. "It's just he believes in rules and regulations. Lives by them himself and expects us to also."

Bram looked up into Taylor's lined and weathered face. "Don't you think," he said softly, "he'd do better to camp somewhere else instead of the big house. Surely the ladies must resent his presence."

Sergeant Taylor chewed his tobacco thoughtfully for a while, then spat. "Well, Bram, I'll tell you. In this man's war, I've seen a hell of a lot of rotten things, and I'm sayin' those ladies is safer with O'Brien there than if they was alone. You understand?"

Bram nodded and watched Taylor walk away from the barn toward the tents in which they camped.

Taking the horse by the bridle, he led her into a stall where he began preparations in caring for her. He removed his shirt and dropped it over the wall of the stall in which he was working. Bram had changed considerably in the past two years. Where he had been slender before, he was now filled out and muscular. Long sinewy muscles rippled under his tight skin as he stretched his

104

arm to stroke the horse's neck. Gently soothing her with soft words and gentle touches, he tended her leg. Finally he helped her to her feet and forked some hay into her stall. "You rest up and get fat lady," he laughed. "And then you can ride these Yankees back where they came from."

He had been concentrating so thoroughly on what he was doing that he did not hear the soft footfall until it was too late. He turned about and looked directly down into Deline's eyes. "You're very gentle with horses, Bram," she said very quietly.

If Bram had changed in the past years, Deline had changed even more. Her body had filled out, and though her waist was small, the rest of her was very much a woman. She wore a riding skirt, which hugged her waist and hips, and the white, long-sleeved shirt she had worn when he had carried her home injured near the river. Her hair had lightened with the summer sun, and she now wore it coiled about her head like a silken halo.

"D . . . Miss Gilcrest."

"Deline was right Bram."

"Now, Miss Gilcrest, it ain't right yo' bein' called by yo' first name by a black boy. No, Ma'am, t'aint right at all."

"Stop it, Bram! You don't talk like that, and you know it. You're as educated as I am."

"Yessum', as educated maybe, but not as white. You know what they do to black boys what pesters white women. They hangs 'em, that's what! Maybe it's better for both of us if we just stay in the worlds we belong in."

He turned his back on her before she could see the bitterness and the hunger in his eyes. He could feel that she was still standing watching him. Then she took a step closer and put out her hand flat against his back. He could feel the tingle of her touch clear down to his toes. He jerked around and looked at her.

105

"Don't do this to me Del," he almost begged. "I'm a man; I'm not made of stone."

She smiled at the use of her first name. "And I'm a woman, Bram, and therein lies the story does it not? Stop feeling sorry for yourself, Bram. You can reach out and take all the happiness you want. The only thing stopping you is you yourself."

Try as he would, he could no longer fight the magnetic pull she held over him. Very slowly as if he were afraid she'd fade away, he reached out one hand and laid it against the side of her face.

"Do you know what you're doin'? Do you know what you really want? Do you?"

"Why do you always ask the silliest questions in bunches, Bram?" She turned her lips against the palm of his hand and kissed it. He moved his hand to the back of her head and drew her slowly toward him, watching her eyes as he did. Then he lowered his head and took her upturned mouth with his. The world about them began to crumble away, and there was nothing in existence for them but each other. Slowly her lips parted, and his tongue lightly touched the soft moistness of hers. A trembling sigh escaped her, and she relaxed against him. He could feel the softness of her against his skin. Pulling her tightly against him, he ran his hands over her shoulders and down her back until they rested on her hips. Then he moved his body against hers until she could feel the desire in him. If he wanted to frighten her, he failed, for she wrapped her arms about his neck and pressed herself even closer.

When he finally released her, she took one step back from him. Then slowly mounted the ladder to the hayloft. Without a word, he climbed up behind her. They lay together in the semidark with the sweet smelling hay under them. His hands moved deftly to the buttons of her blouse, and he dropped it from her shoulders. He lowered

106

his head and kissed the throbbing pulse at the base of her throat and let his lips roam over her shoulders to the softness of her breasts that strained against the light fabric of her chemise. This he quickly removed, running his hands over her breasts lightly and gently until they swelled with passion, and the nipples rose hard against his hands. Then he bent his head to taste the sweetness of her with his lips. She was soft and warm and pulsing under him. He pulled the skirt free from her body, and the rest of her undergarments were followed by his. Now he lay against her body. Thigh to thigh, he held her for a few seconds while he kissed her again deeply. Soft sounds escaped her as he began to touch his lips to her body, to the small curve beneath her breasts, to the narrow waist then down to the softness of her belly. Moving her legs, his lips gently kissed the soft inner flesh of her thighs, then more intimately until she wanted to cry out with the ecstasy of his touch. Now he rose above her and knelt between her legs, looking down on the beauty of her pale body in the half light. He whispered her name softly as he lowered himself to her. He entered her quickly and stifled her cry with his mouth against her. Then he lay still for a moment until she regained the pulse of their desire. Then slowly, he began to move. Cradling her gently in his arms, he moved her in rhythm with him until she picked it up herself. Then her body came up to his with a passion to match his own. Her hands caressed the broad muscles of his back, and she strained him closer and closer. They moved together giving to one another, taking from one another. He held himself in check until he could feel her body tremble violently against his. Then he allowed himself to dissolve into the joy of her, deeply he thrust until she sobbed out his name over and over against his shoulder, and they reached the deep fire of their love never feeling the flame only the joy of oneness.

107

It was a long time later before she stirred against him. He'd held her close to him, and for a time, she had slept. Holding her, listening to her breathing, feeling her lying confidently against him, gave him a feeling of strength he'd never had before. She trusted him. She loved him.

"Somehow," he thought, "I'll make life as good for her as I can. I don't know how, but I'll find a way."

She moved her head from his shoulder and lay back on the hay looking at him. A slow, warm smile formed on her lips, and she raised her fingers and gently traced a line about his mouth.

"Happy?" he asked.

"Very," she sighed.

He lay back beside her, and they remained quiet for a time, contented with being together.

"Deline," he began.

"Not now, Bram, let me have this day before you present me with all the problems you think exist."

"Think exist! Deline, do you realize that what I've just done is a crime!"

She giggled and rolled against him. "Oh, I didn't think so, Bram. I thought you were quite good. Of course, I'm no judge. Are other men better?" she asked looking up at him with innocent eyes.

He had to laugh with her. He pulled her into his arms and then, reaching down, smacked her solidly on her bottom. She gave a little yelp and bit him on the shoulder whereupon he smacked her again.

"Your Mama should have done that a long time ago. Maybe you wouldn't have been here today."

She sat up and looked at him. "I'm so glad she didn't, Bram. I wouldn't have wanted to go through life having missed you. When will I see you again, Bram?"

"You'll see me every day for the rest of your life, Deline. Somehow, I'm going to find a way for us to be together."

She smiled at him, kissed him lightly on the lips and left the barn. In the yard, she passed Sergeant Taylor headed in the direction of the barn.

"Good afternoon, Sergeant Taylor," she called.

"It's a pretty day, Miss Gilcrest, almost as pretty as you, Ma'am," he answered.

The silvery sound of her laughter answered him, and they stood together talking for a few minutes. Then he turned from her and went to the barn where he questioned Bram regarding his horse. Just as he was about to leave, he turned to Bram.

"Bram, you're a damn good man, and I like you. What you plannin' to do when this thing is over?"

Bram shrugged, "I don't know exactly, Sergeant."

Sergeant Taylor studied him closely for a moment. "I'd give some consideration to movin' West, son. You see, out there nobody asks questions about a man . . . or his missus. Where he comes from or what he is is strictly his own private affair. Yep," he said slowly, "I'd give it some real close thought if I were you and had your chances."

Their eyes met, and Bram realized he knew about him and Deline and was encouraging them to find a new life for themselves.

"Thank you, Sergeant Taylor," Bram said softly, and for the first time in his life, he extended his hand to another man in friendship.

"Matthew," said the sergeant, as he took Bram's hand in a firm grip.

As Bram moved toward the house, Matthew called back softly. "Bram."

Bram turned to look at him. Matthew chuckled at what he thought was a great joke. "You could name your first son after me."

He turned away still chuckling to himself. And Bram watched him walk away with a smile in his eyes.

Chapter 13

Steffany studied the dress she held in her hand, looking closely at the frayed collar and cuffs. There had been a time, she thought, when she would never have even considered letting one of their black girls wear the dress she was holding. Now, it was the best thing hanging in her closet. Steffany, whose whole world three years ago had centered around parties and pretty clothes, was finding it very difficult to cope with this changed situation. But the biggest thorn that pricked her was the presence of Yankee officers in their home, and specifically, one blue-eyed Irishman who continually seemed to be laughing at her. She detested his presence in the house and the losses that he reminded her of. Somehow, in her mind, she put all the blame for their predicament on him. She thought violently how she hated him. No matter how often he made overtures of friendship, she could see the laughter behind his eyes and thought, wrongly, that it was directed at her. She could see in her mind's eye the clear blue of his eyes and the way they tried to hold hers when he was speaking.

She would not admit, even to herself, as the others had that his strong masculine presence made her feel safe. She put him quickly out of her mind, for continued thought of him made her so very angry!

She was standing in what was once the ballroom of

Briar Hill. Now it was occupied by the enemy. She had brought the dress down to repair. Holding it tightly against her, she let her eyes drift about the empty, massive room. Letting her mind drift back to the last party she had attended there, she closed her eyes and listened with her inner mind to the soft strains of the waltz. Slowly, as though drifting, she began to sway with the music.

She let herself float across the floor. Who had she danced the last dance with? Charles Gordon—handsome, dark-eyed laughing Charles—dead now on some godforsaken battlefield. The terror of her crashing world closed about her heart as she thought of the friends of her youth, and she buried her face in the tattered dress and cried. A gentle arm came about her shoulder. She leaned her head against it, and her body shook with grief. Then suddenly she blinked open her eyes and realized that the shoulder she was crying on was blue.

He had come through the door and watched her as she swayed gently to the music and had almost felt the pain in her tears as she cried into the ragged dress in her hands. He wanted to comfort her, for he understood the way she felt. And he walked quietly to her side and very gently took her in his arms and let her cry against his shoulder.

Now she leapt back from him as though she was burned, and the tenderness that was in his eyes was quickly masked.

"I'm sorry, but you looked so miserable, I thought maybe I could help."

"You! What do you understand about misery? You come in here and take what you want," she sobbed, she was so angry.

"You silly little fool," he said softly.

She opened her mouth to answer, but it was choked back when two hard arms grabbed her and held her fast against a chest as strong as iron. She tried to wriggle free,

111

but he held her as easily as he would a child. Then, just as leisurely, he bent his head and kissed her. Slowly, he savored the sweet taste of her mouth, unmindful of her writhing protest. When he lifted his lips from hers, she glared at him.

"If I wanted to come in here and take anything I wanted, I could have long ago. Do you think you could have stopped me? Stop living in the past, Steffany. You're young. You have a whole beautiful life ahead of you."

"You just don't understand. I don't even expect any of you Yankees to understand. You've destroyed a whole world." Her voice fell to a whisper. "You've destroyed all our lives. We have nothing left to live or fight for. Why? Why? For what? Why couldn't you all have stayed where you were and left us alone. Oh! I hate you—all of you. I hate you!"

He knew she was as close to hysteria as she could be.

"Listen to me, Steffany," he said in a quiet tone.

"No, I don't want to hear." She tried in vain to move, but she felt his arms tighten about her until she could barely breathe.

"You will listen! Years ago, when I was a small boy in Ireland, life for me was beautiful. My parents had a small farm, and we lived well. I had two younger sisters, and I was about as happy as a young man could be. Then the famine struck. Slowly, I watched our world crumble to pieces. I watched my father trying in vain to get the earth to yield enough to keep us alive, and when he couldn't, I watched his defeat turn to despair. I saw my sisters sicken for lack of food and die of a disease they were not strong enough to fight. I saw my mother slowly fade away from grief and follow them, then my father. You see, Steffany, you are not alone in grief. But life is very short. You have to pick up the pieces and start again, or you will die inside and that's the worst fate that can befall you."

Her world shook. She didn't want to hear, didn't want to understand that someone else knew and shared a grief as deeply as hers. But his blue eyes were soft and tender as they looked down into hers, and she could not doubt the truth in his words. Her lips began to tremble, and hot tears stung her eyes as she sagged against him and began to cry deeply, washing herself clean of all the past grief. Steffany was coming of age.

The room was almost dark now. Only the light from candles in the hallway illuminated them. He handed her his handkerchief without a word, and she wiped the tears from her face. She is a child, he thought, so young and vulnerable. She could be hurt so easily.

When she finally looked up into his eyes, she gave a little half smile. He grinned broadly back at her, and his blue eyes lit up with laughter.

"And now," he said with a very formal bow, "would you give me the pleasure of the last waltz, Miss Jemmison?"

She gave a delighted little laugh and lifted her arms toward him. Holding her gently by the waist, they began to move slowly about the empty ballroom.

"Forget just for now this uniform I wear, Steffany," he said softly. "I'm the boy next door, and this is your first Ball. You're wearing a white gown, and your hair is piled on your head. There are diamonds in your ears and on your fingers."

She smiled up at him, grateful for his knowing.

"I wish I'd seen you then," he whispered. Slowly, he gathered her closer in his arms until he held her against him. They moved as one about the floor.

They had reached the far corner of the ballroom, shrouded in early evening darkness, when he stopped. He found that after having his arms about her, he didn't want to let her go. He continued to hold her tight as she slowly lifted her face to his. Her response to his gentle

113

kiss this time sent fire through his body that shocked him. He had kissed many women and never felt as he did now. For the first time in Devlin O'Brien's life, he was unsure of himself. He put his cheek next to hers and gently kissed the tip of her ear, inhaling the clean fragrance of her hair.

"Devlin?"

He looked down questioningly at her, and he could see her eyes more contented than he had ever seen them since the first day he had arrived. "Don't rush things, O'Brien," he thought and held his natural instinct in check with difficulty. He didn't want to frighten her, but he was sure, if she knew how he felt at that moment, it would have scared her silly. With a great deal of difficulty, he dropped his hand from her waist and offered her his arm. She tucked her hand under his arm, and they walked to the bottom of the stairs together.

"Good night, Steffany. Sleep well."

She stood two steps above him and looked at him quietly. Then she put both hands on his shoulders.

"Thank you, Lt. Devlin O'Brien. I shall never forget what you've done for me."

Quickly she bent down and brushed his lips with hers then climbed the stairs.

He stood and watched her until he heard the door close, then he turned and walked outside. The night was warm, and a soft breeze whispered through the trees. The soft chirp of chickadees broke the night's silence. Then from the tents of his men, came the sound of a guitar and someone singing softly. O'Brien cursed himself for all kinds of a fool. The desire for her was so strong he could taste it. With her innocence and her sudden trust in him, he knew he could have gotten himself into her bed. Then he chuckled to himself, for he knew without a doubt that Steffany suddenly meant everything to him, and he wanted things between them to be perfect.

114

He sat down on the front steps and leaned his head against one of the large white pillars. He closed his eyes and allowed his thoughts to drift. From all the reports he'd had, the war would be over soon. He would be removed from Briar Hill and sent home. Home! Where was home? The small house in Pennsylvania he'd shared off and on with a string of different women. Home should be here, here with a woman like Steffany to bear his sons and help him rebuild an empty life.

His reverie was interrupted by the sound of footsteps across the porch. He turned. "What are you doing out here this time of night, Sergeant Taylor?"

"Jest checkin', Lieutenant. Makin' double sure none of our boys walk in their sleep. You did say you'd have my hide on a barn door, didn't you, sir?"

O'Brien chuckled. "Sit down, Sergeant."

Sergeant Taylor eased himself down on the steps and leaned back with a sigh. "Sure wish this damn war was over and I could go back to my woman and relax in my rockin' chair."

O'Brien snorted rudely. "You in a rocking chair, Taylor? I'll never live to see the day. You're too ornery a cuss to die in bed."

Taylor laughed. "Maybe, maybe, but still I sure get a hankerin' for home now and again."

Devlin reached across the space between them and patted Taylor's chest. "Is that a bottle?"

"Ah, yes, sir. Just a nip now and again makes a man sleep better."

"Well, now that you mention it," O'Brien laughed, "I'm having a little trouble sleeping myself."

Taylor pulled the bottle from under his coat and offered it to O'Brien who tipped it and took three good swallows before handing it back.

"God, that's rotten stuff," he gasped.

"Best I can come by right now, sir," laughed Taylor,

115

taking a deep swallow himself.

They didn't talk for quite awhile, but passed the bottle back and forth. Sergeant Taylor didn't drink much each time, but noticed that O'Brien took several healthy gulps. It was easy to see, for a man that knew O'Brien as well as he did, that there was something weighing heavily on his mind. He was not concentrating on where he was and what he was drinking, but his mind was caught up in his thoughts.

"Heard news the war might be over soon?"

"Just rumors, Sergeant. Nothing official yet."

"You gonna reenlist when this thing's over, Lieutenant?"

"No, I don't think so. I think it's about time I settled down and quit roaming."

The bottle exchanged hands again. "Ain't nuthin' wrong with that. You got some particular girl in mind?"

"Yep."

"Wouldn't be some pretty little Southern belle we both know, would it?"

O'Brien took a long pull from the bottle before passing it back again.

"You think our little rebel would marry the Yankee who took over her house and her world?"

"Lieutenant, you think a thing like that makes a difference to a gal when she's in love?"

"Don't you, Sergeant?"

"Hell, no. Beggin' the Lieutenant's pardon, but you ain't got the sense God gave a duck. That little gal needs a man like you. Take her and ask her questions later."

He passed the bottle back firmly as if he was disgusted.

"You boys make me mad as hell, you surely do. If I was your age, I'd take her away from you so fast your head would spin."

O'Brien drank deeply again then held the bottle up so he could see what it contained. "We're gonna kill your

116

bottle, Sergeant," he said lazily, as he was beginning to feel the effects of the liquor.

"That's what I brought it for," he answered, taking a small sip and passing it back to O'Brien who took another drink.

"What you gonna do about that pretty little gal? Just ride away and let some no good rebel boy come around and marry her?"

A doubtful hesitant look came over O'Brien's face.

"What if . . ."

"You know, Lieutenant, I've been with you since this thing started. We fought through a lot of battles, and I ain't never seen you afraid before."

O'Brien would never have talked like this if he wasn't on the verge of being drunk, and he definitely would not have listened to this kind of talk from the Sergeant. He contemplated the words in silence for several minutes, and then taking another drink, he held the bottle instead of passing it back.

"You know, you're right, Sergeant. I think the Union and the Confederacy should be reunited."

"Yes, sir," chuckled Taylor.

"And I think it should start here and now with one rebel girl and one Yankee boy."

"Yes, sir!"

"And I think I'm drunk, Sergeant."

"Yes, sir."

He stood up shakily, leaning against the pillar. Taking the bottle with him, he started back into the house to go to bed.

"Good night, Sergeant."

Taylor heard him stumble once going up the stairs, then the sound of his door closing. He sat back down on the steps, a smile of satisfaction on his face. He hoped the war was going to last a few more days, for he felt that was all O'Brien was going to need.

117

Chapter 14

There was such weariness in Holly's body that she felt she would never feel rested again. Constant worry over not having had any word from Adam in months, coupled with physical labor she was not used to, drained her completely. Each night she fell into bed sometimes too tired to sleep. These were the worst nights, for then her mind conjured up dreams of Adam dead on some battlefield far away or wounded with no one to care for him.

She had to admit that Lieutenant O'Brien tried his best to make things easier for them. The attraction he had for Steffany was obvious to her, and Holly watched the two circle each other like fighters. It amused her to watch his face whenever Steffany was around. He and three or four of his men would always be present for supper, and he would try his best to make Steffany participate in or at least laugh at some of his Irish tales. Steffany would remain cool and aloof, and Holly would catch the strange, hurt look in his eyes when he looked at her. She thought, he's falling in love with her.

"Well," she sighed, as she pushed back the covers and prepared to face another day, "that's between him and Steff. I can't interfere." Although the thought suddenly came to her that it might be good for Steffany for she knew Steffany could not accept the changes in their lives.

118

Dressing was a simple thing today. There were no choices to be made. She possessed two cotton dresses, both of which were faded from many washings. She washed and dressed, quickly combing her hair, braiding it and wrapping it about her head, then left the room. She hurried down the steps toward the kitchen to prepare breakfast. She smiled to think of the many times she'd had breakfast in bed without giving any thought of those who had risen so early to prepare it.

Early as she was, someone was in the kitchen ahead of her. Since there was no way for the women to handle three plantations at once, all of them were living at Briar Hill. She assumed it was either Merilee or Jessica. She walked into the kitchen and found . . . Steffany.

"Steff," she said in shock.

"Good morning, Holly," she smiled. "I've started breakfast. There isn't much, but I gathered what few eggs there were and dug some of the potatoes out of the cellar. There's no meat, but we'll just have to make do."

"Make do!" Holly repeated watching her sister, open mouthed.

"Bram brought some wood, so the fire's going good. The Lieutenant and his men should be down soon. We'd better get a move on."

Steffany had changed. Lying awake most of the night, she had thought deeply about her future. She had realized that she could never go on living a life in the past. She had decided to try to rebuild what she had almost destroyed. She thought of Devlin O'Brien.

"Holly, I'm sorry for the way I've been, a silly, little girl afraid to grow up. I know it's been hard for you doing all this work. I want you to know I'm going to help as much as I can from now on."

They worked together preparing the small amount of food they had. The household awakened slowly. One by one, she heard them come down the stairs. All the men

119

were seated at the table when Merilee and Jessica came into the kitchen. Both of them were as amazed to see Steffany as Holly had been, but they regained their composure quickly and helped with the preparations.

No one was half as startled as Devlin when Steffany placed his plate before him. He watched her silently as she put down her own plate on the table next to his. Then she sat down beside him and gave him a bright smile, lifting her green eyes warmly to his. "Good morning, Lieutenant O'Brien, gentlemen," she said softly.

Holly smothered a laugh. Steffany had been a definite expert in flirting with boys from the time she was fourteen. When she wanted to turn on some charm, very few males could resist her. As if to prove her point, the young corporal seated at the table next to Holly was about to slide his plate over and sit next to her when O'Brien's eyes caught him. The look froze him where he was, and he sat back down.

"Good morning, Miss Jemmison," he answered. She leaned toward him and touched his arm very gently.

"Steffany, please!" Then she turned toward the others. "I declare, Miss Jemmison is so formal, you all must call me Steffany." She again turned to smile toward Devlin.

Breakfast was one of the happiest meals they had shared together for months. Devlin was captivated by Steffany and couldn't take his eyes off of her. If he hadn't carried the rank he did, he would have been hard put to keep the others away from her, and he used his rank shamelessly.

For the next several weeks, Steffany made herself as pleasant as she possibly could. She had most of the men falling all over themselves to do any little thing she wanted. Much to Devlin's distress, he could never seem to get her alone, which is exactly how Steffany had planned it.

Then one morning they came to the breakfast table, she bubbly and filled with laughter, he grimly determined to get her away from the rest of them and tell her how he felt about her.

When breakfast was over, Devlin stood up.

"Would you consent to accompany me on a ride this morning, Steffany? I'm going over to Heritage and Cross Oaks. It would give me a great deal of pleasure if you'd care to ride along."

"I would love to, Lieutenant O'Brien. If you'll just wait a few minutes, I'll try to scrape up something suitable for riding."

"Of course," he said, his eyes soft upon her. He watched her retreating figure climb the steps. Then he turned to Holly and the others. "You men get about your duties," he said, then, "If you ladies will excuse me, I'll see about the horses."

He turned and left the room. Leaving the house, he moved rapidly across the road to the stables. He opened the door quickly and stepped inside the large semidark room. He moved quietly down the stall until he found his own horse. He wondered where Bram was; he was usually here at this time of the morning. Seeing the door to the tack room ajar he went over to it. He was about to push it open when the soft sound of voices came to him. His eyes widened as he listened and realized to whom the voices belonged. Walking lightly, he looked through the crack in the door.

Bram was holding Deline Gilcrest tightly in his arms, and she had her eyes half-closed in passion and her parted lips turned to his.

As quietly as he had come, he turned and left. Taking both horses outside, he saddled them himself and walked them both to the front porch where he awaited Steffany. It was only a short time later that she made her appearance.

He caught his breath at the sight of her. Since her riding habit was long gone, Steffany had improvised. Using parts of Dixon Gilcrest's remaining clothes, she had put together an ensemble that was meant to stir the blood of any man. A yellow, long-sleeved shirt was open at the throat revealing more than it was concealing. She wore black riding breeches that had belonged to Dixon, also with high black riding boots pulled over them. Her auburn hair, tied back with a ribbon, hung loose down her back, the morning sun catching sparks of fire from it. She walked to his side and spreading her arms out, she slowly turned about.

"Well, what do you think of my creation? It's what the best-dressed horsewomen will be wearing this year."

"You know what a position that outfit puts me in, don't you?" he asked seriously.

"Position? No, what?"

"I'm going to have to shoot someone just to protect my interests."

She laughed, delighted with his compliment. "Your interests?" she questioned mischievously.

He laughed and, reaching out, took her by the waist and lifted her into the saddle. Then he mounted, and they rode away from the house.

The day was filled with bright sunlight, and they rode in silence for a while enjoying the beauty.

One would never believe there was a war, she thought painfully, that her family had been torn apart, that her life had almost been destroyed.

He watched her closely and saw the fleeting look of pain cross her face. Then she turned to look at him, and he smiled at her. Her responding smile told him she again had herself under control.

"You ride well, Steffany," he said.

"I've been riding since I was a child," she answered.

"That's a long time," he chuckled.

"Are you trying to make me angry with you, Lieutenant? I'm not really much younger than you, you know?"

"Not in years, maybe."

"I'm almost twenty."

"Twenty years of protected, pampered life is different than twenty-seven years of fighting on my own."

She turned to him, her face stormy, and he laughed.

"I'm only teasing you, Steffany. You're really a very remarkably lovely lady."

"Thank you." Her answer was quiet, and she chewed on the corner of her lip.

"How far would you say it is from here to Cross Oaks property?"

"Well, I'd say it's another mile or so to the bridge and then five or six to the main house." She slapped her horse with the reins and dug her heels into his side causing him to charge suddenly ahead. "Race you to the bridge!" she shouted back over her shoulder.

"Hey!" he shouted, then when he heard her laughter he dug his heels into his horse's side and started after her.

She was an excellent horsewoman, and she flew ahead of him. But slowly he drew abreast of her, and they clattered across the bridge together. She reined in her horse laughingly, her hair blowing about her and her face pink from excitement. He jumped off his horse and went to her side. She slid down into his arms, and he was very reluctant to set her on her feet. They walked together, leading their horses so they could rest. It was a compatible silence as each of them were content just to walk together.

"Steffany?"

"Yes, Devlin?"

"I want to talk to you seriously for a moment. Let's tie our horses under the trees down by the river. They can rest."

They walked off the road and went down through the trees to the river where he took both horses and tied them. Then he took her hand, and together they walked along the shady bank of the river.

"Steffany," he began, "I know things have been very hard for you the past three years. A whole way of life you'd always known is gone. Things are going to get worse. I may have to leave here pretty soon, and I'm afraid of what will happen when I do."

"You think there will be trouble around here, Devlin?"

"There are men deserting every day, scavengers banding together to raid plantations."

"Raid? But we've nothing here to raid. We have no possessions, no valuables."

He turned to her, his eyes intent and serious. Taking both her hands in his, he held them tightly.

"I'm afraid for you, Steffany," he said softly. "You've become very valuable to me, and I don't want anything to happen to you."

He watched her eyes kindle with warmth, and he gently pressed his lips to her forehead, then to her cheeks, and finally, he brought his lips to hers. He kissed her deeply wanting to crush her to him and hold her forever. When he finally separated from her, it was not because he wanted to, but because he knew if he didn't, he was going to take her right there.

"Steffany, would you consider going with me? Let me take you out of here to someplace where I know you're safe."

She looked up into his blue eyes and smiled. "You of all people, Devlin, should know I can't do that. You told me the other night to grow up. Well, I have, and my responsibility is to my family right now. When this is over, we have will time for us. For now, we each must do what we know needs doing."

124

"You won't come?" he said softly.

"It's not that I won't; it's that I can't, Devlin. Would you want me to run away and be safe with you and leave Holly and the others to face the unexpected?"

"Yes!" he lied.

She smiled and moved close to him. Putting her arms about his waist, she tipped back her head and looked up at him.

"You lie," she said softly.

He sighed and surrendered to her logic. He had known he wouldn't be able to get her to leave, but he had to try. Now he wrapped his arms tightly about her and held her close to him.

"I love you, Steffany. Can you forget we're from opposite worlds and love me, too? Will you say you'll wait for me until I get back?"

"I'll wait for you, Devlin, no matter how long it takes. But wouldn't you rather have me wait as your wife than as your girl?"

"You'd marry me now?" he asked, a delighted smile lighting his eyes.

She nodded her head in silent acceptance. They looked deeply into one another's eyes, and he gently kissed her again. Then wordlessly, he led her to the shade of a great, huge oak tree where he pulled her down to the grass beside him and took her willing lips again with his, and her arms lifted to hold him close to her.

Chapter 15

She was frightened, and he felt her tremble under his hands as he caressed her. He kissed her eyes, her lips, her throat, soothing her fears and rousing her at the same time. He slipped back into the Irish brogue he always reverted to when he was emotionally stirred. "My darlin', darlin' girl," he murmured against her throat, as he slowly undid the buttons on the front of her blouse. He slid his hands against the warm, silky skin of her breasts and caressed them gently, then lowered his head to touch them lightly with his lips.

"Oh, Devlin," she sighed as she relaxed her body against him, moved by the gentleness of his touch.

He pushed the blouse completely away now and ran his hands lightly down the soft curve of her back to her hips. Tenderly, he brought her body against his, letting her feel the fire that was beginning to burn in him.

He leaned back from her for a minute while he shrugged himself free from the shirt he wore. Then reaching for her again, he pressed her body against the muscles of his chest until he could feel the fierce pounding of her heart. His lips were hungry for the sweet taste of her, and he moved them leisurely down the slender column of her throat to her shoulders, down the soft roundness of her breasts that swelled and throbbed against him. Very gently, he released the belt from the breeches she wore and slid them gently down off of her hips. Things were going fine as far as he was concerned until he got the breeches down to the tops of her high boots. He looked down at them, temporarily frustrated. She began to laugh silently, trying not to let him hear her, and he looked up into the wicked mischievous glitter of her eyes. He grinned in response.

"I'll get mine off before you do," she giggled.

"Uh, huh," he said, as he rapidly began to remove the boots and pants he wore. When he turned back to look at her, she was watching him intently, her gaze warm and filled with desire for him. He knelt beside her and looked at her, his warm gaze memorizing every inch of her.

"You're very beautiful, my lass. And you're all mine."

He lay beside her and, twining his fingers in her hair, brought her body against him with the other hand behind her hips. The response from her now surprised him and yet made him feel happier than ever before. There was a fire in her that only he could quench as her body arched against him and her hands clung to bring him closer and closer to her.

He whispered against her ear as he held her close. "I'm going to hurt you, Steffany, but just for a moment. The pleasure will be worth the pain. Trust me."

He pushed her legs with his knee until they separated, and his gentle hands moved up the inside of her thighs until, with the tenderest touch he could manage, he found the center of her need. Then he was over her, and he entered her quickly, catching his mouth against hers. She trembled violently against him, and he kissed away the tears that escaped from under her closed lashes.

"Now you are mine, and we begin to share the real pleasure of love."

Slowly, he began to move, and in a few minutes, her body began to respond to this new feeling. She felt him deep within her and knew the completion she felt was theirs alone. They were one. Soft cries of pleasure came from her, and she lifted her body to meet his deep thrusts. He felt her twine around him, and he rocked himself in the cradle of their love, listening to her murmured words of love as she sighed his name over and over. Together, they rose to a fiery completion that left them both weak and clinging to one another.

He rolled over on his back and pulled her against him feeling the silk strands of her long hair fall over his body. With one hand he caressed her gently. They lay together quietly listening to the soft ripple of the river and the breeze that made a whispering sound through the trees.

"I'm probably the happiest Union soldier in the whole South," he chuckled.

She could hear the rumble of laughter deep in his chest as her head lay against him.

"And I'm probably the happiest Confederate that's ever been captured," she answered.

He rose on one elbow and looked down at her. "Are you captured, Steffany? You meant it when you said you'd marry me now, didn't you?"

She raised both hands to the sides of his face and pulled him down to her. Her lips were soft, and the kiss was like a butterfly's wing.

"I meant it. You didn't think you were going to get away and go marry some horrible Yankee girl. You'll never get away from me."

He sighed deeply, then laughed.

"Get up and get your clothes on, woman. I'm anxious to get on with this wedding. I'll never be sure until I get a ring on your finger."

When Steffany smiled, a small dimple appeared on her cheek.

"Well, I never noticed that before," he said, and promptly kissed her there, then again and again until she became breathless.

"Stop, Devlin, stop," she said.

"Temporarily," he answered. "We'll find someone today to marry us. Tonight, I want you in my bed where you belong."

"But, Devlin, we have to go back and tell my mother and Holly first. They have to help me. Oh! Whatever am I to be married in? I don't even have a presentable dress. Oh, Devlin, I'll make the most horrible bride!" She looked so very distressed.

He captured her fluttering arms by simply wrapping his about her.

"Calm down, darlin'. You see, it doesn't really matter what you're married in. All I can see is your beautiful face. And afterwards, well, it won't matter what you're wearing."

"Oh, you beast. Don't you understand?"

"I do, Steffany," he said softly. "And don't you think I'd get you the most beautiful dress in the whole world if I could? When this is over, Steffany, I'll dress you like the lady you are. Until then, my love, I want you no matter what you wear."

"I'm sorry, Devlin. I'm being a baby again."

"It's all right. I guess every girl feels that way about her wedding. I'll make it up to you, darlin', I promise," he said, very gently kissing her again.

It began as a gentle kiss, but when he felt her lips part under his and her warm body stir in his arms, he forgot where they were going, and his whole being was centered on the beauty he held in his arms. It was almost an hour later that he lifted her gently back upon her horse and they went to Cross Oaks.

The deterioration of Cross Oaks since all the blacks were gone and Richard Forrester was away was remarkable. The lawns and gardens were overgrown, and everything gave the impression of neglect. Steffany felt the same tug of futile pain as she gazed about her. Some

129

of Devlin's men were occupying two or three of the rooms but the rest, everything was dust covered and filled with cobwebs. Her mind flashed back to happy memories of Cross Oaks, and she suddenly felt desperately angry at the wasteful war that had caused all this destruction.

She wandered from room to room while Devlin talked to his men and left orders. She was very quiet when they rode on and he understood how she felt, so he said nothing.

She was hoping against hope that Heritage would not have suffered the same fate, but she was doomed to disappointment on that subject. Heritage, if possible, was in worse condition than Cross Oaks.

She was glad Odella had not been back to the house since her father had left. She would have been brokenhearted to see the condition her home was in. She was walking through the rooms when Devlin joined her. She described how the house had looked before the war. Her description, filled with love, made him see through her eyes the loveliness that had existed there.

"Steffany, I sent one of the men into town to pick up the preacher and bring him to Briar Hill. I've also invited the rest of them to the party we're throwing tonight."

"Party!" she laughed, "with what?"

"Well, whatever we can scrape up, and you'd be surprised what Sergeant Taylor can scrape up."

When everyone at Briar Hill was told the news on their return, they greeted it with good will and wishes of happiness. Devlin was relieved for in the back of his mind, he harbored the idea they might not take to a Yankee husband for Steffany. He had been quite prepared to put up a battle for her.

Odella cried, but they were tears of happiness. She kissed Devlin and welcomed him to the family.

Devlin called in Sergeant Taylor who was also

delighted with the news.

"I've bragged about your particular talents in organizing a party, Sergeant," laughed Devlin. "Now don't make a liar out of me."

"Yes, sir. A party she'll be, sir," he said, and left immediately to get it prepared.

It was almost dark when the preacher arrived. He was a tall, skinny man who heartily disapproved of this marriage and kept asking Steffany if she was sure or if she was being forced in any way until Steffany became irritated, and, much to the hysterical delight of everyone present, she smiled innocently up at the preacher, batted her green eyes at him and said shyly, "Ah do believe it's best that my child have a father even if he is a Yankee, don't you, sir? After all, what's a poor girl to do if the man offers to make her respectable?" The man sputtered an agreement, then did not question her again.

The ceremony was short, and the preacher left immediately after giving the papers to Devlin who paid him in Yankee gold.

Sergeant Taylor had done exactly what Devlin had promised he would do. They had scavenged the countryside and came up with three chickens and a pig. These were roasted and the tables set up. Where he got the whiskey, Devlin never asked, but the party was a huge success when a fiddle was brought forward, and they all danced and sang together.

Holly stood and watched Devlin's tenderness with his new bride and Steffany's happy face as she looked up at him.

"Oh, Adam," she thought. "Where are you now?" Her arms ached to hold him again, and she cried silently.

Devlin whispered in Steffany's ear, and with a surprised look, she followed him to the stable. In front of it, he had a horse tied. He mounted and reached down to lift her into his arms.

131

"Where are we going, Devlin?"

"Wait and see."

She rested her head against his chest, and they rode in contented silence for some time. Finally, they came to the same spot they had shared that morning. Now a tent had been set up and he lifted her down from the horse. After tethering the horse for the night, he turned to Steffany. "Welcome to our first home, my darlin' wife."

She stepped inside. He had prepared the best bed he could, padding it with blankets collected from several of the men at Sergeant Taylor's request. She turned to him and smiled. He took her in his arms and for the rest of the night, they left the world outside and slept cradled in each other's arms with only the gentle sound of the river to break the beauty of the night.

Chapter 16

The boxcar kept a rhythmic motion, back and forth, back and forth. Adam was weighed in by a mass of men crowded together. It was semidark inside, just enough to make out the dark forms of the men around him. Thick black smoke from the engine found its way through the cracks into the boxcar along with the cold wind. Not only was Adam blackened and choked by the smoke, he was colder than he had ever been before. He admitted, only to himself, that not only was he dirty and hungry, he was also afraid.

The battle of Chattanooga was one of many Adam had been part of, but it was the one most memorable. He leaned his head against the side of the vibrating boxcar and closed his eyes. Memorable he thought. He remembered how, just before it he had listened to the men's enthusiastic conversation about how they would "whip the tails off the Yankees."

It had been several days, but he could see it in his mind's eye as though it had happened just that morning. His orders were to swing his men about and make a diversionary attack in the center of the lines. He still did not know, in all the fury and pandemonium of battle, how the order was misunderstood. Instead of making a swing about, his men had charged in a full attack. His shouts of anger and frustration had gone unheeded, and he rammed his spurs into his horse's flanks and surged ahead trying to head his men off and turn them about. He did so, in time for them, but not in time for himself, for he suddenly felt the horse jerk and fall, and he tumbled over her head and landed solidly on the ground. When he caught his breath and got up he was already surrounded by blue uniforms.

Less than two days later he found himself being herded into the boxcar, headed for a prisoner-of-war camp that he didn't even know the name of. He'd gotten a letter from Holly just a few days before the battle, and he wondered if she would ever got word of what had really happened to him and where he was.

He had no arms, since they had been confiscated first, but he had a heavy coat on and good solid boots. Most of the men in the boxcar when they had entered, did not look any the worse for wear than he. Some of them were equipped with blankets and canteens of water.

They had been traveling now in the same boxcar for four days. Sanitary facilities had been completely ignored by their wardens, and consequently, the closed car had a foul odor that made him nauseous every time he inhaled deeply.

He blinked his eyes open as he realized the car had come to a stop. Suddenly the doors were slid open. Bright sunlight, something they had not seen for days, blinded them all so that for some time they milled about in confusion.

Two planks were laid from the boxcar to the ground, and the men were forced down them and out into the raw wind. Adam pulled the coat tighter about him and thanked God he had decided to wear it the day of the battle.

Adam looked about him. They were on the outskirts of a very small town. They were forced into lines and marched away from the area of the town itself.

134

As they walked along, Adam looked up to discover that a Yankee was riding next to him.

"Where are we going?" he asked.

The man looked down at Adam. He was a tall man, Adam could tell by the length of his legs that hugged the horse, and he was thin almost to the point of emaciation. His face was all plains and angles: the nose, long and sharp, the cheekbones high and prominent, and deep-set brown eyes under blond-white brows, deep in contrast, looked at Adam with a look that suggested well-suppressed pity.

"Hell, rebel, hell," he said softly, then urged his horse forward to be away from Adam's questioning eyes.

Edward Franklin was twenty-seven years old and from Pennsylvania. He had often, during his life, done things quickly and then lived to regret them. Joining the army was one of them, he thought. Oh, it had been all right at first, listening to all the speeches and all the cheering and flag waving. It had not really been that bad when they had gone off to fight. Then he had been transferred here as guard at Chase Prison camp near a town called Columbus, Ohio. From then on, he had detested the war and all it stood for. Each day or so he would herd a new group of Confederate soldiers up the hill to the stockade. He had stayed as far away from them as he could, for he had a deep-seated sense of right and wrong that he had been doing battle with since the day he had arrived. The softly drawled question from the man walking beside him had upset him more than he cared to admit and caused a deep rush of pity for him. No matter how he tried to push it from his mind, he could remember his mother's teachings when he was a child.

"Do unto others as you expect them to do unto you, Edward. Then you have no cause to worry during your life. The Lord will reward you," she had said with her gentle slow smile. Well, he wasn't treating others as he

135

expected them to treat him, and he wondered what his punishment was going to be. In fact, he harbored a deep-seated fear of it and, in his nightly dreams, conjured up all sorts of punishments he would receive.

Adam and the group of men walked slowly up a hill. Almost at the top, the line of men began to slow, then finally came to a stop as the men had their first glimpse of the stockade.

A huge wooden stockade about fifteen feet high made of fresh cut trees embedded deep in the ground, extended farther than they could see. A balcony extended around the top part of the outside where the sentry walked. Two huge gates were slowly opening to accept the new sacrifices of war.

As they moved slowly inside, they seemed to huddle into a group as though their neighbor was going to tell them that what they were seeing, feeling and smelling was only a bad dream from which they would soon awaken.

The old prisoners were drawn to the gates to watch the newcomers. They were filthy scarecrows of men who eyed the new men to single out the weaker and more vulnerable men to rob. Two younger boys crowded nearer to Adam as though for protection and eyed the gaunt smelly men who began to close about them with unbelieving eyes wide with fear.

The gates closed loudly and firmly behind them, and Adam felt lonelier and more deserted than he had ever felt. One of the boys standing near him clutched a blanket close to his chest and watched the large evil-faced man who was slowly inching toward him. Suddenly, with a harsh laugh, he reached out and grasped one of the edges of the blanket.

"Let go, pretty boy," he snarled, "or I'll tramp you into mush right here, and you won't have to worry about being cold."

The boy realized, as did every other man with him, what was happening. The strong left inside were preying upon the newcomers, and the weakest would be left with nothing to help them through the winter. Adam admired the boy's bravery; knowing that his opponent was twice his size, he still clung to the blanket and pulled it from the big man's hands. Soft jeers and catcalls came from the crowd around the bully.

"You gonna let him keep the blanket, Jarrod?" one man laughed. "Maybe he's scared you so bad you're afraid to take it."

Jarrod's face became red, and his eyes narrowed as he reached out and gave the blanket another jerk and said in a deceptively soft voice.

"Now you let go the blanket," he chuckled evilly, "and maybe if you're good, pretty boy, I might just share it with you."

The boy's face turned gray, and he showed his fear for the first time. It brought harsh laughter from the crowd. The boy backed up until he was almost beside Adam. He did not say a word to Adam but kept his eyes on Jarrod, who eased step by step closer.

Adam felt a tiredness enclose him like a large fist. He knew what he was going to do, and he hated himself for it. He cursed himself, but as Jarrod's hand reached out again, he slapped it aside and took one step that put him in front of the boy.

"Leave the boy alone. The blanket's the only thing he's got."

Jarrod hesitated. Here was a more formidable foe than the one he was harassing. He could tell by the narrowing cold eyes that Adam would not be pushed or frightened like the boy was. He might even have backed off if it hadn't been for the laughter and encouragement of the men surrounding them.

"Hey, Jarrod. If you get those two pretty boys, I get to

137

share one."

"Hey, Jarrod, finally got someone your own size, that's new for you. Bet he knocks your ass off!"

Adam could not take his eyes off of Jarrod, but he realized through the sound of these voices and what they were saying that they were only encouraging Jarrod because they hated him and were just as afraid of him as Adam was.

Jarrod squinted at him with a half smile on his face.

"You're goin' to save yourself a lot of trouble if you just give me that blanket and get out of my way."

Adam remained silent, but he watched Jarrod's face intently. He knew Jarrod could beat him because he was bigger, but he felt he had a small advantage. Jarrod was angry, and anger made a man move often before he thought. He decided to galvanize him into irrational action if possible, so he grinned nonchalantly and reached out and took the blanket from the boy.

"Give it to a man," he smiled at Jarrod, "not this dirty pig. He can wallow in the mud to keep warm, where he belongs."

Jarrod gave a wild shout of anger and dove at Adam. At the last minute, Adam stepped aside, and dropping the blanket, he clenched both hands together and clubbed Jarrod as hard as he could on the back of the head.

Jarrod fell face down on the ground with a solid thump and remained there motionless. Adam looked up from Jarrod, but the boy who had stood beside him was gone.

"Where is he?" Adam demanded.

Blank faces of the men who had come in with him gave him no answer, and the knowing grin on the faces of the inmates made him almost sick with anger. While he had been concentrating on Jarrod, the others had taken advantage and attacked the boy, dragging him soundlessly away.

Adam stood glaring at them furiously, when suddenly

a heavy weight struck him from behind. The blow almost knocked him unconscious. He hit the ground, and before he could regain his feet, Jarrod kicked him on the side knocking the wind out of him. Another kick brought a cracking sound and a flash of agonizing pain. He knew if he didn't get up, Jarrod was going to kill him where he lay. Desperately, he rolled toward the foot that was coming toward him and in spite of the agony it brought he grabbed it and twisted with all his strength. A loud cracking sound came as Jarrod hit the ground again. He groaned in agony and rolled on his back. The fight would have been over then, but Adam was so angry that he wanted to kill him. He straddled Jarrod's body and doubling his fist and swinging with all his might, he struck him again and again. He was too blinded by his pain and anger to realize what he was doing. He took out all the frustrations of his fear and pain on Jarrod. Someone grabbed his arm from behind, and he looked up, his face twisted by a fury he had never before felt for another human. The man he looked at was one who had come in with him named Maguire. He was a gentle, bookish type of man, and no one could ever figure out why he had enlisted in the first place.

"Adam," he said gently. "It's all over. He's unconscious."

Adam looked down at Jarrod in shock. It was the first time in the last few minutes he had seen Jarrod at all. He shook his head negatively, as if he couldn't believe what he had done and tried to rise. The effort brought a gasp of pain from him, and for a moment everything spun before his eyes. Maguire helped him up, and they made their way to an empty area where he helped Adam ease his way to the ground. Under Maguire's arm was the trophy that had started the fight—the blanket.

Adam lay still, his eyes closed while Maguire knelt beside him and examined him.

"You've got a couple of broken ribs, and I doubt," he said slowly, "if there's a whole lot of doctorin' around here."

"I . . . I'll be all right. We've got to build some kind of shelter."

"We ain't goin' to do nothin'. Me and Rollins got a blanket apiece and with this one, we'll build something. You'd better lay still or those ribs could puncture a lung, then we'd really have a problem."

Adam nodded in agreement. Another man joined them and sat on the ground beside Adam.

"That was some fight, Adam. I thought for a minute there, you were plannin' to kill him."

"I was," Adam replied softly, his eyes darkening.

Rollins said no more, but he and Maguire began to build a lean-to for shelter against the raw, biting wind. After a while, despite the agony it caused him, Rollins and Maguire moved him under the shelter. He closed his eyes against the pain and lay still.

Maguire and Rollins reconnoitered the area and were gone for over two hours. Adam lay quietly thinking over what he had seen and what had occurred. They were only here less than a day and they were fighting each other like animals. What would happen to him, he thought wildly, if he were here for a long while. Would he let himself disintegrate to the type of man he had just fought? No! he thought violently, I'll not let it happen to me. He wanted to cry out, he needed something to fight against, and there was nothing there.

Maguire and Rollins came back, their faces long and miserable. Maguire sighed deeply as he sat down beside Adam.

"It's every man for himself, Adam. This place is like an animal cage," Maguire said.

"Yeah," Rollins agreed, "we get fed once a day . . . sometimes. From what the others tell us, they certainly

140

don't treat us with any great amount of care. There's no doctor, and there's no way to get any medicine for ourselves. I hate to say it, but I can understand why those men acted as they did today."

Adam stared bleakly around him, and a heavy flow of desperation almost overwhelmed him. He took hold of himself. I will survive, he thought. No matter what it takes, I will survive.

"What chance have we got, Maguire?" he asked softly.

Maguire shrugged his eyes looking off unseeing in the distance.

"'Bout as much as any of them, Adam. I guess it's a matter of the survival of the fittest in here. We've scraped ourselves down to the marrow. Now, I guess we find out what's in us."

There was a silence as each tried to gather from somewhere deep inside the strength to go into the hardest and most violent battle they would ever see.

Later that night, Maguire and Rollins built a fire, and they ate the small amount of cornmeal mush that had been passed out to them and had to pass as the day's ration of food.

Adam lay in the makeshift tent and was cared for until his ribs began to heal and he could begin to slowly move about. It was several weeks before he could be of any use at all.

The tent they were living in was very poor protection from the elements, as they discovered after the first rains. Rollins caught a bad cold, and they huddled together to keep him as warm as they could. All three were silently terrified of pneumonia. Instead, Rollins recovered, but they decided they needed more shelter. They scavenged around looking for something with which to build. In the process, Adam tried to measure the size of the encampment and to count the inhabitants to the best of his ability. From what he could figure, the area

141

was about six miles long and about four wide. What astounded him was the number of men they had enclosed. It was beyond belief that so many men could exist in an area so small.

Here and there, they found scattered pieces of tree branches and other odds and ends of debris. Slowly, painfully, they put together a lean-to that protected them a little better and used the three blankets to cover themselves at night.

At Adam's urging the three of them exercised daily and washed themselves in the upper area of the stream that ran through the middle of the camp. The lower area of the stream was used as a latrine.

The three men became good friends and worked together well. They pooled what food they could scavenge for so that all three received something to eat, not enough, but something every day. Adam's grim determination to stay alive rubbed off on the other two, so that they depended on each other to survive.

About four months later, Adam was lying in the lean-to with his hands clasped behind his head, contentedly dreaming the same dream he always had. Holly, beautiful Holly, with her auburn hair loose about her like it was the day in the field when he had first found her. Holly's soft lips against his, the feel of her velvety skin under his hands. His body hardened in reaction. He was so caught up in his dream that he didn't realize Maguire had sat down beside him.

"How you feelin', Adam?"

"Me? I'm fine Maguire, how about you?"

"Fine. I'm glad you're feeling well today. I got some news for you, and I want you in complete control of yourself."

Adam laughed, then when he looked at Maguire he could see he was very serious.

"What news?"

"Jarrod. He's pitched his tent right next to ours."

Adam said nothing for a few minutes, then slowly, he got to his hands and knees and crawled to the opening of the lean-to and looked out.

Jarrod stood beside a tent he had just put up next to theirs. He looked at Adam, and he smiled a cold-eyed smile.

"Why, Lieutenant Gilcrest, *sir*," he said, "I just want to keep an eye on you, *sir*, so I'll know where you are if I ever want to find you."

Adam could still hear his mirthless chuckle as he went back inside and lay back down. He had made himself a murderous enemy, and now that enemy was camped next to him. The test of wills had begun, and Adam knew he'd better win, for losing meant certain death.

Chapter 17

Adam sat cross-legged on the ground in front of the makeshift shelter the three of them had built. The lethargy of mind slipped over him again, the one thing he dreaded, the forgetting of things. Things like the exact date, how long he had been incarcerated here, the faces of people he had left behind. The only faces he could conjure up clearly were his mother's and Holly's. He found himself doing it often, too often for his mental health, sitting quietly straining to remember. He was doing it now, remembering Holly, dreaming of coming home to her, not looking as he did now, a filthy wretch of a man, but whole and well and anxious to share his love with her again. The dry chuckle he heard, broke through his thoughts and, as always, filled him with a burning anger, an anger he could control less and less as time went by. Stirring slowly, he turned to look at the man who stood in front of the tent that had been deliberately placed as close to his lean-to as the owner could place it.

"Daydreamin' again Lieutenant Gilcrest, *sir?*" the man asked softly. "Maybe if you do that often enough, you can forget that you're here at all. Maybe just enough so we could dump what's left of your body where it belongs—in the latrine."

His hatred burned deeply in him, and he was glad, glad of the emotion that stopped him from slipping away

144

mentally to that safe secure place. He did the one thing that angered Jarrod the most, he smiled that slow knowing smile.

"At least I've something to remember, Jarrod," he drawled softly. "I doubt if you could remember your father, of course," he added, "if you ever knew who he was in the first place."

Jarrod's face turned a mottled red, and he looked as though he would have liked to kill Adam. With a superhuman effort, he got himself under control. Adam couldn't help but wonder why a man with such a violent temper and evil disposition would even try.

"Why don't you move your tent Jarrod?" Adam asked with a half smile. "The air down on this end of the camp is bad enough."

"Talk away, Lieutenant Gilcrest, *sir*. The time will come when we'll—" he stopped, then he smiled and shrugged and walked inside his own tent.

Adam did not miss the "We'll," and he wondered just who the *we* were and what had been planned against him. There was no doubt in his mind that something was afloat, but what, and from what direction was it coming? It was also obvious that Jarrod had set up his own tent to be close to Adam to watch his comings and goings and to keep an eye on his possessions.

Slowly, pooling their efforts, Rollins, Maguire and Adam had made their small lean-to almost livable. Trading and selling anything they had or found, they found ways of acquiring some of the necessities to keep them alive. A small pinch of salt, a vegetable, another scrap of blanket to keep warm. There was never any meat unless a snake made the mistake of crossing the grounds or some other animal. Adam suspected rats and rarely took a bite of any type of meat for fear he was right.

As all the others, he was losing weight and strength daily. A thought was clear in his mind, he wanted to push

145

the fight with Jarrod before he lost the strength to fight back. No matter how he goaded him, Jarrod would not nip at the bait. Adam realized he was holding himself in control, because he thought that his plans were going to destroy Adam completely.

Rollins approached the lean-to with his odd walk. He was an extremely tall, thin young man. His arms were long enough to give him the appearance of a pleasant-faced monkey. He rolled forward, swinging his long arms and grinning from ear to ear. When he neared Adam, he held something aloft in his hand. For a few minutes, Adam could not make out what it was, then with a short laugh, he realized it was a carrot, a whole carrot. It had been so long since he had seen or tasted one. He remembered the sweet crisp taste. How he had always loved the way his mother had cooked them around a large roast of beef!

"Where did you find that?"

"Never question the source of our miracles, Adam, my friend," he grinned. "We'll chop it up and have a little tonight and save the rest for tomorrow."

"I was just thinking how my mother used to cook them about a roast of beef," Adam said softly.

"Yes," Rollins said quietly, "my mother used to put them in her stew, a nice thick brown gravied stew with big chunks of—" He stopped short and shook his head as if to wash away the thought. "Well, we're going to have it plain tonight. It's better for your health that way. You're getting fat."

He squatted down beside Adam after he had hidden the carrot safely.

"You tangled with Jarrod again today?"

"Not really," Adam answered. "I threw him a few insults, but either he's too ignorant to be insulted or he's saving up for something."

"Yeah, that's what I've been thinking, too."

146

"Why, what did you find out?"

"Well, I ain't found out nothing exactly, but every time we get near those two friends of Jarrod's, they shut up and watch us. But somehow, there's something about them that makes me get the shakes."

"They're planning something. That's obvious. Rollins, I don't want you and Maguire getting hurt because of me. I ought to take what I've got and move out of here. If they're planning to attack me, I don't want you two in the middle."

"Adam, this ain't a thing that means something just to you. The whole camp is divided. If we let Jarrod get away with this, he'll make himself king around here. How long do you think some of those youngsters just comin' in will survive with Jarrod in charge. It's everyone's fight. And for the sake of humanity, we'd better be on our guard against whatever he's plannin' for you."

Adam nodded; he couldn't think of anything appropriate to say. He knew deep in his heart that though the rest of the camp was mildly worried about Jarrod, sticking with him was something Rollins and Maguire were doing out of comradeship toward him. There was no way left to thank Rollins, so he said nothing at all.

The days passed slowly. The boredom and lack of food and clean water was taking its toll on all of them. Adam's clothes were worn and dirty; he had a beard which he had trimmed as often as possible by one man who had a pair of scissors in his pack and set up a place to barber in exchange for what he needed. He felt extremely dirty, for it was no longer possible to bathe in the stream that ran through the camp. It was filled with debris including human excrement that made a foul-smelling swamp. He could feel the vermin that made a comfortable home in his hair and beard.

The last few days had been dry and airless, as though nature was preparing for a great performance. Then just after dark, the low rumbling thunder was heard as the storm moved in their direction. A low wind began to build, and the lightning began to brighten the night sky. The men ran for all the shelters it was possible to find.

About midnight, the full force of the storm began. The winds lifted to almost gale force, and the rain fell in sheets that obscured vision, obscured it so well that no one saw the three men as they stealthily approached Adam's lean-to. Jarrod stood outside the front of his tent watching for them. As their shapes took form, he motioned them closer and leaning close so they could hear him above the thunder he told them, "I want Gilcrest dead. I don't care about the others. Beat them up and throw them out and divide their things up, but I want Gilcrest dead, do you understand?"

They nodded. To a man, they were the worst that the prison had bred. The condition of the men gave them a likeness of appearance so that even if they were seen no one could identify them.

Later in years, Adam would laugh at the thing that saved his life and probably the other two as well. It was Rollins' desire to eat another piece of the carrot they had hidden. It would be a constant source of amusement that his life was saved by a carrot.

Adam and Maguire were sound asleep, but Rollins lay on his back, his hands behind his head. Sleep would not come because he was hungry. Now, Rollins had been constantly hungry since the day he arrived at the camp and lived with it because he knew there was no source of food. But this was different, he knew the carrot was in the bottom of a rag sack that was hanging on the side of their lean-to, and no matter what he did, he could not get his mind off of it. Turning the matter over and over in his mind, he began to try and justify his intentions. Surely, he thought, Adam and Maguire would understand his taking just a small bite of the carrot. After all, he was the one who found it. He smiled to himself. I'll just sneak over and take one small bite. They'll never know the difference. His conscience set up a small discourse with him over what he was thinking, and he argued with himself for quite some time before the grumbling in his stomach won out over the possibility of the grumbling of his friends. With the promise to himself of taking only one bite, he moved toward the sack slowly and gently so he would not disturb the other two sleepers. He stood beside the sack, hunched over because the height of the lean-to would not permit his standing erect. He slipped the piece of carrot out of the bag and was prepared to take a bite when a brilliant flash of lightning illuminated the outside as though it were broad daylight. Rollins almost choked when he saw, distinctly outlined against the frayed blanket which covered the doorway, three figures brought in bright relief against the flash. Moving quickly but quietly he dropped to his knees and crawled toward Adam and Maguire. Putting his hand over Adam's mouth so he would not cry out, he shook his arm. Adam came awake fighting the hand that held his mouth clamped shut and for a few minutes, Rollins had a difficult time trying to hold him while he whispered what was happening.

"Shut up, Adam," he whispered. "It's me, Rollins. We got company outside."

Adam became very still.

"How do you know?"

"Seen 'em in the lightning a minute ago. We better get ready."

Adam nodded, and Rollins moved toward Maguire who was stirring awake at the movement.

"What's going on?"

"Company comin'," Rollins replied shortly. Immediately, Maguire was up and searching for something with which to protect himself. There was one breathless searching moment for them all before the blanket was yanked aside and the invaders prepared to kill what they thought were three sleeping unsuspecting prey. The first man found this out just one second before the club Adam was wielding descended on his head. He collapsed with a grunt and sprawled over what should have been the bed of the sleepers. It was all the warning the other two needed. One of them attacked Rollins and Maguire. In his hand he held a short length of metal. What it was or where he had gotten it neither of them knew, but they were hard put to protect themselves from it as they were backed away against the low, slanted wall. Lightning flashed again, and Adam's heart almost stopped beating as, in the flash, the bright glitter of a knife shone in the third man's hand. Adam was facing him alone and unarmed in darkness. Suddenly his mind became clear. He knew, without doubt, who was responsible for this. He crouched as low as possible, realizing it was just as hard for his opponent to see in the dark as it was for him. He heard the grunting and shuffling of Rollins and Maguire as they tried to find a way to subdue their attacker, and he knew it would be too late for him if he tried to wait for help from his friends. He sucked in his breath and with a mighty thrust of his strength he threw himself at the attacker. This was a completely unexpected thing. Judging for himself, he thought Adam would be crowded in a corner, afraid and awaiting death. The momentum threw them both backward, through the blanket and out into the rain and mud. The intruder fell with a solid thump and cursed as Adam's weight came down on him. Holding the arm which wielded the knife, he squeezed it and pounded it against the ground as hard as he could. He received several blows on the back and sides before he could feel the man weaken. The knife slipped from his fingers and fell in the mud. With a thrust, the man beneath him pushed him away and Adam fell on his back sliding several feet in the mud. He was so enraged now that he couldn't think of anything but getting another hold on him and pounding his face to a pulp. He struggled to his feet, and in his anger, he hurried too fast and his feet slipped out from under him several times before he could get to his opponent who was slipping and sliding just as badly in his effort to get away.

Adam leapt on his back, and they both fell to the ground, Adam cursing and pounding on him and the man making a desperate effort to get away. One lucky blow against his head, that set Adam's ears ringing, gave his opponent just the opportunity he wanted. Scrambling to his feet, he was gone in a few minutes. Adam sat for a moment until his head cleared. Rollins and Maguire came outside.

"These two are both dead, Adam. Where's the other one?" Rollins asked.

"The son of a bitch got away!" Adam panted. The other two looked at him in surprise as Adam got on his hands and knees and began to feel around in the mud.

"He hit you on the head too hard, Adam," Rollins laughed.

"What you doin' down in the mud, boy," said Maguire. "Come inside and help us dump these two where they belong."

Adam shook his head negatively and continued to search around in the mud. They watched him in amusement until with a yell, Adam held aloft the knife his opponent had dropped. Without saying another word, he rose to his feet. Anger swelled within him like a blazing fire, as he walked slowly to Jarrod's tent. He pushed open a flap and stepped inside. Jarrod had been sitting and waiting for word of Adam's death and his face was full of amazement as he recognized the black form silhouetted against the opening of his tent. Without uttering a word, Adam was upon him. Because of the

151

surprise and the feel of a knife edge against his throat, Jarrod was still.

"Your boys failed, Jarrod. I'm still alive."

"I don't know what you're talking about."

"You know, you lying bastard!"

"I don't know," Jarrod yelled. "If I wanted you dead, I'd kill you myself. I don't need any help. I'll get you before you leave this place."

"I should kill you right now," Adam snarled.

No matter what he was, Jarrod knew his men pretty well. He knew that Adam was not the kind to kill an unarmed man. Adam's sense of honor was the best defense Jarrod had.

"You won't! You ain't really sure I'm mixed up in this, and I ain't got no weapon. You goin' to kill me without me bein' able to defend myself?"

Adam remained quiet while the knife point pricked at Jarrod's neck. For a minute, Jarrod thought he'd made a mistake, then suddenly the knife was gone and Adam stood up. Jarrod couldn't see him clearly in the dark, but he heard him.

"Stay away from me, Jarrod. Keep your bullies away from me, or so help me God, the next time something like this happens, I'm going to kill you no matter what. I'll find you wherever you are in this camp, and I'll kill you."

There was silence for a few moments, and all that could be heard was the drumming of the rain on the tent. Then the flap was pushed aside and Adam was gone.

Once outside the tent, Adam stood still letting the violent emotions flow out of him. He put the knife in the waistband of his pants. Then he looked up toward the sky and let the rain wash away the mud.

Once free of the mud, he went back to the lean-to. He needed to get dry quickly before he became ill. He was trembling already, but he knew most of it was just the results of his fierce anger.

He stepped inside the lean-to and found the bodies of the other two men were gone.

"We dumped 'em," Maguire said.

"Yeah, down near the front gate where they'll find 'em in the morning," Rollins added.

"Adam," Maguire said quietly. "You kill Jarrod?"

"No, I guess I should have. He'll probably try this again."

Maguire smiled, "He probably will, but we'll be on the alert even more now, and, Adam, I didn't think you were really goin' to kill him. This place can't make his kind of animal out of you."

Adam dried himself off as best he could, then sat down in front of a small fire Rollins and Maguire had built.

"Mac, I wanted to kill him more than I ever wanted to do anything in my life," Adam said softly.

"Sure, you wanted to kill him." Mac smiled his slow understanding smile. "But there's a whole heap of difference between wantin' and doin'. It's the difference between you and Jarrod, and it's the difference between a man and an animal."

There was silence for a few minutes, then Adam turned to Rollins.

"I want to thank you, Rollins. You woke up just the right time. I owe you my life."

Rollins looked at Adam, then his eyes lit up with their perpetual humor. The corners of his mouth quirked, and when he could hold it back no longer, he broke into laughter. He lay back against his blanket and rolled with laughter until the tears came to his eyes as Adam and Maguire looked at him in stunned confusion.

"Mind tellin' us what's so amusing about saving another man's life?" Maguire asked.

Rollins finally got his laughter under control and sat back up. Wiping his tears away with the back of his hands he said, "Adam, I was only awake because I was so

153

blamed hungry I couldn't forget that piece of carrot we was savin' for tomorrow."

"What's so funny about that?" Adam asked.

"Well, I got up to snitch a little piece and saw the shadows of those men against the blanket."

"I still don't see what's so funny," Maguire said.

"Well, I really don't want to take credit that belongs to someone or somthun' else," he said as laughter began to build in him again. He could see by the dawning light in Adam's eyes he was beginning to get the picture. Maguire's face was still full of questions when Adam turned on him.

"Mac, I guess you might say my life got saved by a carrot!" Adam grinned.

The three of them looked at each other as the humor of the situation overcame them. Anyone passing their shelter just then would have been amazed at the unrestrained laughter from within.

Chapter 18

Adam stirred himself reluctantly awake and pulled the ragged remnants of a blanket over his body. He felt as though he had been cold for as long as he could remember. He had to think very carefully how long he had been in the prison camp. Trying to hold on to his sanity with the conditions they were living under was almost impossible. He was afraid that every day he was slipping backward. It had been fourteen months and six days since he had been taken prisoner. He had been living in hell since then. His clothes were ragged and filthy. He hadn't been able to wash himself, and he felt the vermin crawling in his tangled hair and beard.

He had come to the prison camp proud, but scrambling about in the mud and filth for his food had changed his attitude quickly. The first time it happened, he remembered painfully, he had refused to eat until hunger forced him to grapple with the emaciated men who fought for their daily food. He had been stronger then and had taken enough to fill his stomach. But watching some of the men move away with nothing had made him ill, and he shared what he had.

That had been the last time he had done that. From then on, Adam learned rapidly that he had to fight for every scrap if he wanted to remain alive, and he wanted desperately to remain alive. The last letter he had written to Holly was the day he was captured, and he thought she might think him dead as there had been no more word since then. He felt the sting of tears in his eyes and was ashamed but could not control them.

Confusion and loud voices brought him completely awake, and he sat up. From the shelter he shared with the two other men, he watched the gates of the camp open and a small stream of Confederate soldiers move slowly inside.

"God," he thought, "the camp could not support the men it contained now."

In the beginning, he noticed the men brought to the camp were warmly dressed and with good boots. He noticed now that some of them were in as bad a condition as the ones already inside.

The man in the tent next to his groaned and moved about, annoyed at the disturbance.

"What the hell's goin' on now?" one of them asked garrulously.

"More prisoners," Adam replied shortly. After all this time, Adam could still feel the hatred for Jarrod bubble through him. There had been no more attempts on his life, but he was constantly expecting one. There was no doubt in Adam's mind that Jarrod was a mortal enemy. Adam had been forced to fight him only once for the ragged blanket he held now about his shoulders and had nursed three broken ribs and almost died because of it. He had beaten him only because he was new and still had the strength to fight. Even at that, it had been a very close battle. Adam knew that Jarrod watched him daily for every sign of weakness.

The other two men were quiet and watchful. Outside of sleeping, they kept as much distance between themselves and Jarrod as they possibly could. Occasionally, one or the other of them would share a small portion of what they had with Adam, for it had now become a contest between wills. Would Adam be able to keep his strength up long enough to survive Jarrod, or would Jarrod finally take possession of everything Adam had and doom him to a slow death?

"Why don't you go out there and kiss their asses, Lieutenant Gilcrest, *sir?*" he said sarcastically. "Welcome them to their new home."

Adam turned to him and said coldly, "Why don't you ever shut your goddamn mouth, Jarrod?"

Jarrod's glare was murderous when Adam turned his back on him, and if it hadn't been for the presence of the other two, he would have attacked him from behind.

Adam sat and watched the new prisoners shuffle about uncertainly while they were eyed by the older prisoners to see what they possessed and what could be taken from them by force. Suddenly, he jerked himself alert. A familiar face, at least he thought he had seen it in the crowd. Adam watched intently. From the way they looked, they had been through a great deal. They moved hesitantly with wide unbelieving eyes. It was impossible for them to believe a place like this existed. Adam watched for a few minutes, then rose to his feet and moved toward the new men as quickly as his exhausted body would allow. He stopped beside a young soldier who stood with his head bowed. He looked completely beaten and worn. His hair was long and fell a little over his face. The shoulders slumped in dejection, but Adam could see he was clinging tenaciously to the blanket he had with him and holding tightly to the tattered gray jacket he had on.

"Brian?" Adam said hoarsely.

Brian's head came up, and he stared at Adam as if an angel from heaven had called to him.

"Adam? Adam!" Slowly, his eyes filled with tears, and his shoulders began to shake with dry, broken sobs. He moved quickly to Adam's side, and the brothers threw

157

their arms about each other.

When they finally had control of themselves, Adam led Brian away from the crowd of newcomers to his own lean-to.

Jarrod stood in front of his tent, a hard sneer curled his lips. "Find yourself a pretty boy, Gilcrest?"

"Shut up, Jarrod."

"Gonna share him with your bedmates, or keep him all to yourself?"

Adam had reached the end of his endurance. Not just of Jarrod but everything he'd gone through in the past year.

"This is my brother, Jarrod, and he's sharing my blanket and my part of the lean-to." Adam's gray eyes had chilled like frozen pieces of steel, and he said the words very softly.

The two men looked at each other, and Jarrod felt the sudden tingle of real fear, possibly for the first time in his life. For he knew, beyond a shadow of a doubt, Adam meant to kill him if necessary. He spat and turned his back on them, rolling himself again in his blanket and muttering curses.

Brian and Adam sat down side by side, and Adam introduced him to their other two companions. "Brian, this is Maguire and Rollins. They're both from down around our way. This is my brother, Brian."

Brian nodded to both the men, then turned again to Adam. Now he really looked at him, and the condition Adam was in disturbed him. "Christ, Adam, you look awful. Don't they ever feed the men here? You're so skinny."

"It's all right, Brian. We manage. We'll survive. Tell me about you. How did you get here? Have you been home in the past year? And, Brian, do you know if Holly is all right?"

"Ah, we got caught about two weeks ago," said Brian

angrily. "I got a letter here from mother and one from Holly. You can read them both. They're only about two months old now."

He handed both letters to Adam who grasped them as a drowning man would grasp for help. Brian watched his brother's face and felt the pain Adam must have been through lately. Adam opened his mother's letter first and read slowly the familiar beloved handwriting:

Dear Brian,

I miss you so very much, my son. I hope God watches over you and you remain well and come home to us soon. Your last visit home was too short. In reply to your question, no, we have had no news of Adam or Dixon. Dixon wrote to me just before you left. You remember, you read his letter, but it has been so many months since we've heard from Adam. I am near frantic with worry for him, and Holly is beside herself with fear.

Here Adam dropped the letter to his lap and wiped his eyes, then with a trembling hand he picked it up and read on.

Brian, there is some news I have to tell you, and I want you to try to understand. Several months after you left, Briar Hill fell in possession of the Yankees, who use it as a command post. The lieutenant who is in charge here is a wonderful boy named Devlin O'Brien. He was so much like you and your brothers we could not bring ourselves to hate him. He tried in his way to make things a little easier for us. To come to the point, Brian, he and Steffany Jemmison fell in love and were married. Please do not condemn Steffany. I know how it must seem to you, but wait until you come home to make any

159

judgment. The tearing apart of our country has to be mended, and maybe this is one small step in that direction. Devlin intends to come back here to live after the war. He had no family and would like to make our family his. Try to think of him not as the enemy but as the husband of someone we all hold dear.

There is no possible way for us to continue to keep up three homes, so Merilee and Odella have come here to spend the duration of the war. It is much better to put our food surplus together. Do not worry about us, son, we are doing well. There is enough to eat, and although not an overabundance of anything, we are getting along fine.

Nancy Summers, of course you remember her, came by to ask about you. In fact, my son, there have been quite a number of visits by young ladies asking about your well-being.

The one spot of bad news is that Merilee received word that Graham was reported missing—presumed dead over five months ago. I see her terrible silent mourning, and I understand how she feels. There is no way one can console someone who has lost her only child. Merilee is a strong woman, as all of us are. She will survive, but her world will never be the same again.

I don't know if it's possible for you, son, but is there any way you could find out anything about Adam. Holly and I pray each day for him. Holly is a wonderful girl, so helpful to me and to the others, in the meantime keeping her desperate fear for Adam to herself. We all know how she feels and admire her courage deeply.

The fields are empty now Brian, but we have planted a small garden beside the house—only large enough for us women to care for it. I am not the greatest gardener in the world, but Merilee seems to have a green thumb, and things grow well for her.

Dear Brian, how we miss your brightness and your laughter (and your mischief). I pray each day this war will soon be over and my sons can come home again. Take great care of yourself and write as soon as possible. I love you.

Affectionately,
Jessica Gilcrest

The reading of his mother's name made his eyes burn, and his hand trembled as he slowly folded the letter and handed it back to Brian, who put it safely inside his jacket. Then, very slowly, Adam opened Holly's letter.

Dear Brother,

I know the war does not go well for us. All I can find myself doing is praying daily that it will end soon, and you all will come back to us safely. Brian, I know this is not easy for you, but if you could find some word of Adam, some hope I can cling to? There has been nothing in over a year. I miss him so terribly. I would be very grateful.

We miss you very much, Brian. I suppose your mother has told you the news of Steffany's marriage. Brian, he is a wonderful man, and in many ways, he has the qualities I love so dearly in Adam. He is strong and kind and has given us the strength to keep our hopes alive when we were in despair.

If you do find Adam, no matter what condition he may be in, let him know I love him and I miss him. God bless you and bring you home safely, Brian.

Your loving sister-to-be,
Holly

Tears fell unashamed down Adam's thin cheeks as he folded the letter and put it back in the tattered envelope. He held it for a moment as if the pain of parting with it was more than he could bear. It was the only lifeline to home he had found, and it took a great deal of effort to hand it back to Brian. Brian shook his head, for his throat was constricted with pity; then he said quickly, "You keep it, Adam," he said.

Adam merely nodded, the tightness in his throat too strong to allow him to speak. He pushed the letter under his ragged shirt next to his skin where it seemed to warm him. The two brothers sat together quietly, each caught up in his own painful memories.

At the same time Brian and Adam were finding each other, the commander of the prison camp received a knock on his door. He opened it and looked coldly at the man standing outside.

"Well, it's about time you got here. You were to relieve me two weeks ago."

"I'm sorry," came the reply. "I got here as fast as I could after I received my orders. After all, I was quite a distance away when they came, and I must say, they came at the worst time in my life."

"Oh, really, Lieutenant! Well, I don't think the army runs on what is convenient for you. Come in, come in. We have to go over the papers. I have to leave in the morning."

The young lieutenant stepped inside the room and closed the door behind him. The officer sat down behind the desk. He pushed across a sheaf of papers to the Lieutenant, who sat down in a chair opposite him. He watched the officer's face. It was probably the tiredest face he had seen since the war began, but it was a different kind of tiredness. It was as though he had borne a burden too heavy for him, for too long. He was a square-built man with heavy features. His face was round, and the nose was rather large. His mouth, wide and full, was clamped firmly about a cigar. His eyes were black as were the fringes of hair he had that surrounded a round bald spot in the middle of his head.

"We've twenty-five hundred men here in a camp to hold one thousand. There's little food and no comforts at all. They survive, and that's all they do. I'm damn glad it's your problem now." He looked across at the young man opposite him.

"You're going to hate this job, Lieutenant. Thank God it's temporary until the new commander gets here. After you've been here awhile," he said softly, his eyes looking beyond the lieutenant, "the pain kind of gets to you. I'll be glad when this war is over. And, thank God again, I think that will be soon. Are there any questions?"

At the negative shake of the lieutenant's head, he stood up and held out his hand.

"Good luck, you'll need it, Lieutenant. What's your name?"

"O'Brien, sir. Lt. Devlin O'Brien."

Chapter 19

Graham stood up slowly. His leg pained him unmercifully, but he gritted his teeth and forced himself erect. He couldn't put any weight on his leg, but Ann's father had carved out a T-shaped piece of wood, and Ann had padded the top to make a rough kind of crutch.

It had been months, but the leg continued to give him a great deal of trouble. Occasionally, it would become inflamed and irritated, and after a great deal of pain, a small piece of metal would work its way out and Ann would have to lance it to bring relief. Graham began to worry about whether he would ever be able to walk on it again. Both Ann and her father had reassured him that once all the foreign matter was eliminated, his leg would heal as good as new.

"Maybe you might have a slight limp, boy, but it's sure as hell better than losing it."

Graham had found it impossible to go up and down the stairs, so finally they had made him a bed downstairs. He reached out now and took the crutch from against the wall. Tucking it under his arm, he made his way laboriously toward the kitchen door. He stood in the doorway and watched Ann walk from the barn toward the house. He enjoyed watching her walk with the free swinging stride. In fact, he enjoyed everything about Ann. She was the most natural and honest girl he'd ever met outside of Holly. He had tried more than once in the past few months to tell her, but there was something in her that withdrew whenever he tried to get too close.

She stepped up on the porch, then saw him standing in the doorway. Immediately, a bright smile lit her face. Standing aside to let her pass him, he smelled the fresh, clean smell about her. It made him respond more violently than usual. He laughed to himself. "Maybe I'm getting better quicker than I thought."

Setting her basket on the table, she began to transfer the eggs she had gathered from the basket to a bowl.

"Good morning. Feel like some fresh eggs for breakfast?"

"I feel like I could eat a horse," he laughed.

"Well, we've only got two of those, and we need them to pull our wagon, so you'll just have to settle for eggs."

"Speaking of the wagon, has your father come back yet?"

"No. He should be back soon though."

"I hope he can find out more than he did last time."

"Pa does the best he can without telling every Yankee in the area that you're here," she said coolly.

He felt immediately contrite. After all Ann and her father had done for him, he had no right to question them on anything. He felt lucky to have been found by Confederate sympathizers in Union territory. Without their help, he would either have been dead or confined to the horrors of a Yankee prison camp. "I'm sorry, Ann, I didn't mean to sound ungrateful, it's just that—"

"I know Graham. I didn't mean what I said either. I can understand why you're impatient for news."

He sighed deeply and sat down at the table. "You know I've got to get back to my outfit."

"How, Graham? When the whole area is overrun with Union soldiers."

Restlessly, he stood up again and walked across to the

165

door and stood looking out.

"I've been here for months now, Ann. My family probably thinks I'm dead. I hate to just sit here and do nothing to let them know."

She looked at his broad back, and her eyes clouded with sympathy.

"I know how you feel, Graham. You know Pa and I will do our best to get you out of here."

"I know, Ann. I know. I owe you and your father my life."

She moved to stand behind him. He turned from the door and stood looking down into her eyes. He had felt a deep attraction to her from the first clouded vision he'd had of her when they brought him to their house. Now she stood looking up at him with her clear, honest eyes.

"You don't owe us anything, Graham," she said softly. "What we did for you we did because we wanted to. I've never told you, I've a brother somewhere. If he were hurt, I'd hope for someone to help him like we did you."

"I see. Well, I'm very grateful nonetheless."

She started to move away from him, but he put out his hand and caught her by the arm turning her back to him.

"Ann," he said softly.

She looked up into his eyes, unafraid but aware of him. He touched her face lightly and drew his fingers across her cheek to her lips.

"You're lovely, Ann. Not just the way you look, but the way you are. I want—"

"What, Graham?" she asked softly.

"I want to hold you, Ann," he whispered.

"Do you think this is wise, Graham, I . . . I imagine there's someone else who's thinking of your return."

"No, no one special waits for me."

He felt her stiffen a little, then realized she thought he was lying to her.

"Then tell me, Graham, who's Holly?"

166

"Holly!" he said in surprise. "How did you know about Holly?"

"In your fever, when we just brought you home. You talked of her quite often. I realized she was someone very important to you."

He grinned, then reached out and put his arms about her waist. Quickly she pulled free and stepped back from him.

"I'm not someone you can play with, Graham, then go away and forget. When I say yes to a man, it will be because I know I'm the most important thing in his life."

"I can't chase you with this crutch," he laughed. "But if you'll stand still long enough, I can explain everything about my past life to your satisfaction." She was wary, but she stood just out of his reach. Slowly, he began to explain his whole life and Holly's place in it.

"So you see, as far as I know Holly and Adam Gilcrest are married by now, and," he laughed, "when I take you home as my wife, they'll be our neighbors. I'm sure you and Holly will be good friends. You have a lot in common."

"You presume a lot, Graham Forrester," she laughed and moved away from him. "We haven't known each other a long time."

"I'm not really capable of doing much more," he said seriously, "Ann, I just want to hold you, to feel you near me."

Never taking her eyes from his, she moved close to him and put both her arms about his waist. He wrapped his arms about her and pulled her against him. She rested her head against his chest, and he put his face against her hair, inhaling the soft, clean smell of her. They stood together for a few minutes. Then he lifted her chin with one hand, and cupping it about her face, he lowered his head and touched her lips with his.

The reaction startled him more than her, for from the

167

first minute she had looked at Graham, she felt that someday she would come willingly to him. Now he lifted his head and looked into the brightness of her eyes. There, he could see the willingness, and he pulled her back against him. This time, the kiss was different. His mouth, hungry for hers, seemed to devour her, and she allowed herself to be absorbed into it.

"Ann, Ann," he murmured softly against her throat, as he kissed her again and again.

Ann moved out of his arms before her emotions gained complete control. She was breathless, and in her mind, she knew she wanted nothing more than to continue, to have him make love to her.

They stood apart from each other, but both of them knew it would only be a matter of time. From that day on, Graham concentrated on getting better. Every day he exercised his leg, bathed it and tended to it carefully until the raw wound slowly began to heal. It was almost three more months before he could put any weight on his leg without pain and several more weeks before he could limp about with the use of the crutch. Night after night he dreamed of Ann, of making her his wife and taking her home to Cross Oaks. Their daily contact with each other only aggravated his desire for her. Then the day came when he could bear it no longer. He wanted her, but most important, he had to find out if she loved him as much as he did her. He watched her father climb aboard the wagon and leave for town to find out as much as he could about the war and if there was any possibility of Graham getting out of the area and home. He made his way toward the kitchen. Ann stood over the stove preparing what would be their one main meal of the day when her father returned. She turned when she heard him and smiled, her cheeks flushed from the heat of the stove. She had never looked lovelier to him. He grew warm at the sweetness of her smile and went to her side.

"You slept late, lazybones. Do you know it's after noon?"

"I always was a late sleeper," he laughed, then his eyes turned serious. "A few months ago, we discussed something important to us. It's time we discuss it again, Ann. I've got to know how you feel about me."

"Graham—"

"Let me say one thing, Ann. I've never ever lied to you or to anyone. I'm sure you know by now how much I want you. I've made no secret of it."

She looked up at him searching his face for something she seemed to find, for she took his face gently between her hands, and standing on tiptoe, she pulled his face down to her and kissed him. Graham could not control the groaning sound of relieved pleasure as he felt the moist softness of her lips part beneath his, and he knew her answer was yes.

He put one arm about her waist, and with the other, he lifted her from the floor. Without a word, he carried her to his bed.

He removed her clothes and looked at her slender loveliness. Then his fingers moved through the long braid she wore and loosened it until it fell about her in a golden cascade. She was so lovely it took away his breath, and he enjoyed looking at her for so long that she finally moved to him.

She worked the buttons of his shirt free, and he worked rapidly to remove the rest of his clothes. Then they were together on the bed, her body long and cool against him, moving first gently then with unrestrained fire as his hands and lips brought her body to a singing life.

Graham felt a wanting he had never felt for any woman before in his life, and he immersed himself deeply into her with her soft lips sighing his name against his neck. They moved together as though they had belonged to each other since the beginning of time. The age-old rhythm of the universe engulfed them and carried them along a molten river to completion that left them both breathless and contented.

Some time later, he rose from the bed and dressed, then he went back and sat on the edge of the bed beside her. She smiled up at him, and he took one of her hands in his and gently kissed each finger. She watched him.

"Ann," he began.

"Graham, before you go on, you made me no promises and I expect none."

"Promises are what I want from you. I want you to come back with me when it's safe to get out of here. Come back to Cross Oaks with me, Ann. I need you there. I'll need you for as long as I live."

Her hand was soft against his face and her eyes moist with tears.

"Not just because—"

He interrupted her. "Because I need you to make a whole man out of me. I suspect I've been looking for you all my life."

Before she could answer him, the thud of horses' hooves could be heard.

"Pa's back!"

He grinned. "You'd better get dressed, lady, or you'll marry me before you planned to."

She dressed quickly, and they were at the kitchen table when her father came in. They smiled warmly at him, but their smiles faded when he did not respond.

"Graham, I got some news for you, boy," he said quietly.

"Yes, sir?"

"The war's over, son."

"When?"

"Day before yesterday."

"Tell me," said Graham.

170

"Lee surrendered at Appomattox Court House. The North won. The fightin's done."

Graham sat back down slowly. "Then I've got to go home, 'cause I think the real trouble is just gettin' started."

"Yeah, boy, I know what you mean. They sure gonna need you now."

"Not just me sir. I want you and Ann to go with me. I've asked Ann to marry me, and she's accepted. Will you come, too?"

"I can't, boy, but I can join you two later. You see, I got to wait for my boy to come home. You two can use my wagon. But I think we better get Graham some other clothes."

They spent the rest of the afternoon making preparations, and by nightfall, everything was ready. They planned to leave at dawn. With a smile he kept well hidden, Ann's father excused himself and went to bed. Within a few minutes, Ann was in Graham's arms.

They left at dawn the next morning. Ann kissed her father and made him promise to join them as soon as Robert came home.

The trip was slow, and they were often stopping to pick up others headed home. War-weary men with ragged clothes and sometimes bare feet struggled back to what was left of the homes of their birth.

Graham looked at the misery and destruction he saw all along the way. The beautiful plantations were burned and gutted. Land, once flourishing, now lay in waste or was overgrown and uncared for. His heart became heavy with what he was afraid he might find at Cross Oaks.

Then they crossed the border into Georgia, and Graham began to point out familiar things to Ann. Familiar, yet unfamiliar because of the condition they were in. Homes Graham had visited as a boy and young man were now empty shells with broken windows.

When they crossed into Forrester property, Graham became silent. Ann simply held onto his arm and watched his face as he neared the home of his youth. And then they were turning in under the crossed oak trees and going down the long drive toward the main house. It rose in front of him, the most beautiful sight he'd ever seen in his life. It was intact. It was whole, he thought happily. He jumped down from the wagon and helped Ann down.

"Go on, Graham," she smiled.

He smiled at her like a young boy again and turned and took the front steps two at a time and threw open the door.

"Mother!" he shouted. "Pa! Where is everybody?"

The house was deathly quiet, and then for the first time, he noticed how uncared for it looked. Merilee would never let it get this way unless . . . He couldn't allow himself to think that way. But where was his mother? There was no one in the house at all. His mind shook under the idea. Merilee, Mother. She wouldn't have left the house if she hadn't been made to.

He came back outside feeling numb and not really knowing what to do. Ann watched his face, "Graham?"

"Everyone's gone, Ann."

"Take it easy, Graham. Maybe there's a good reason. Maybe they're nearby."

"Nearby? Maybe . . . Briar Hill or Heritage. Those are the only other places they could be. Are you too tired to go on, Ann? Maybe we could try Briar Hill first, spend the night there and go over to Heritage in the morning, okay?"

"Of course, Graham. Come on," she smiled.

They climbed back onto the wagon and urged the horses forward.

It was just growing dusk when the weary horses pulled the wagon up the front drive of Briar Hill. Slowly, Graham led Ann up the steps and to the front door of

172

Briar Hill. He raised his hand to knock, then hesitated. Ann watched his face and knew he was afraid. Afraid of what he would find behind the closed doors of Briar Hill. Ann lifted her hand and knocked firmly at the door. Jessica Gilcrest stood in the lighted doorway.

He and Ann entered.

"Wait here, Graham," she said softly and then turned and went into the parlor.

"Merilee, there's someone at the door to see you," she said.

"Me?" said Merilee questioningly. "Who ever at this time of night?"

She rose and came to the parlor door. She froze in the doorway at the sight.

"Mother," said Graham softly.

With a sob, Merilee threw herself into her son's arms, crying his name over and over again. He lifted her against him. Laughing and crying at the same time, he swung her off her feet. When he put her down, she looked up at him, reaching up to touch his face as though she couldn't believe he was there.

"Oh, Graham! You're safe. You're home!" Suddenly, she covered her face with her hands and began to cry. He held her against him.

"It's all over, Mother. It's all finished. I'm home to stay. We'll rebuild Cross Oaks. We'll be happy again . . . Where's Pa?"

"He's gone since right after you left. I haven't had too many letters, but he's alright. Now that it's all over, we'll be together again, Graham."

Now Graham reached his hand out to Ann who went to his side.

"Mother, I want you to meet Ann Somerfield. She literally picked me up from a battlefield and gave me back my life. We're going to be married, Mother. Soon."

"Welcome to our family, Ann Somerfield."

Chapter 20

Devlin lifted Steffany laughing from the cool water of the river where they had spent the early morning swimming. He held her wet, wiggling body against him and kissed her thoroughly. They had spent over a week in their tent by the river. They had swum and talked and made love. They spread a blanket under the oak tree, and he pulled her down beside him where she lay with her cheek against his chest and his arm encircling her. For a long time, they lay together listening to the call of the birds and the soothing sound of the river.

"Devlin?"

"Mm?" he said drowsily.

"Do you think it's wrong for me to be so happy when everyone else is so . . ."

He rolled on his side and lay facing her. Very gently he ran his hand down the length of her body, causing her to shiver with pleasure.

"Everybody has a right to happiness, Steff. When it comes, you're supposed to grab it and hold on to it for as long as you possibly can. That's just what I'm going to do. I would never sacrifice the joy and happiness I've found with you no matter if the whole world burned around me."

"I do love you so, Devlin," she whispered softly.

Raising her arm about his neck, he brought her close to

him and kissed her, running his hands over the velvety softness of her body.

Much later, they saddled their horses and rode back to Briar Hill. There, they joined the rest of the family.

Life proceeded there at a slow, steady pace, each person working daily trying to scrape together enough food to sustain them. Bram carried a considerable load for the women, keeping them in firewood, hunting whenever he could or fishing to help keep the table supplied.

Holly realized she had come to depend more and more on Bram, and he never let her down. He whistled as he went about his work repairing what he could and making everyone's life more bearable. The nights that she could slip way, Deline came to him, and they shared their love together, never knowing how long it would last. Devlin, one of the few who knew of them, understood when he saw them slip away together, but he was worried about how the others would take their affair. He should not have worried, for when he finally told Steffany, she realized that Deline must feel for Bram what she felt for Devlin.

"What are they going to do, Devlin? If people around find out about them, they'll never be free again."

"I think the best thing for them to do would be to join a wagon train headed West. Out there, no one would know, and they could make a new start. But Deline won't go until the war is over and her brothers are back and she knows they're safe, especially Dixon. There's been no word from him for weeks."

"Oh, Devlin, I wish this horrible war was over and I could sleep at night knowing that we were all safe, and someone couldn't come along and take you from me at any minute."

"Shh, love . . . no one will ever take me away from you. Wherever I have to go, I'll be back. You see, the best part of me is here."

He was almost certain from reports he had been receiving that the war was nearly over. The Confederacy was on its knees, and the death blow would soon be felt. He was also very sure he would receive orders to leave Briar Hill soon, and he enjoyed each day with Steffany as much as he could. He wanted to have every minute with her to help carry him over the long days until he could return. And finally, as he felt it would, it came. He held the papers in his hands for a long time. He was not surprised that he was ordered to leave; he was just surprised at where he was ordered to go. He was to temporarily relieve the commander of a small prison camp until a new commander could arrive to take over.

He broke the news to Steffany as gently as he could. Still, she cried, and he held her and tried to give her as much comfort as possible.

Ordering his men to pack up, he took Bram aside. "Bram, I'm worried about what might happen around here from now until I can get back. Up in the barn, under the hay, I've left three rifles and some ammunition. There's not much else I can do. I'm not allowed to do even that, but I just can't leave you defenseless. Take good care of them until I get back here, will you, Bram?"

"You know I will, Lieutenant O'Brien. They're as much family to me as to you. Thank you for the rifles. I was wondering where I might get a hold of one. I don't suppose there's too many left in the whole South."

"No, I don't suppose there are, and the scavengers coming back through here are going to count on that."

He reached out his hand to Bram, who took it with a strong grasp. The two men had come to have a great deal of respect for one another. Then he turned and walked back to the front porch and called to Sergeant Taylor.

"Order your men to mount up."

"Yes, sir!"

The women stood silently watching as the men

176

mounted, realizing that outside of Bram, there would be no one else on which they could depend until their men came home.

Devlin walked over to the group.

"Mrs. Gilcrest, Mrs. Forrester, Mrs. Jemmison," he said softly. "I'm truly sorry I wasn't able to stay here until you were better prepared. There's not much more I can do right now but follow orders."

It was Holly who reached out and put her hand on his arm with a warm smile.

"Lieutenant O'Brien, you have done a great deal for us, and we appreciate it. We understand that it is impossible for you to stay."

"Thank you," he answered.

"Lieutenant, you could do one last thing if you would?"

"Anything I can."

"If there is any way you could find word of any of our men. Maybe they're in this prison you're going to. Just let them know we love them and we're all right."

"Of course, I'll do anything I can."

He turned from them to Steffany, and taking her by the hand, they walked around the side of the porch out of sight of the others. Without a word, he took her in his arms and held her. She clung to him, and they stood together silently for a moment.

"Steffany, I'll be back just as soon as I can." He tipped up her chin and looked into her tear-filled green eyes. "I love you, Steff. Take good care of yourself for me, will you?"

She nodded her head, unable to speak. Then he took her lips in a gentle kiss. He could taste the salty tears on them as they gently parted under his, and he wanted to draw her into himself and never let her go.

Then, putting one hand on each shoulder, he gently moved her away from him. For another moment, they exchanged unspoken promises with their eyes, then she smiled tremulously.

"Come back to me soon, Devlin," she whispered.

There was no necessity for him to answer her, so putting one arm about her waist, he walked with her to his horse. Mounting, he leaned down and again brushed her lips lightly with his. Then suddenly, he was gone, and she felt as desolated as though she were alone in the world.

Holly moved to her side and put her arm about her shoulder.

"Come on, Steffany. If we keep ourselves occupied, maybe the time will go a little faster."

Keeping herself occupied is exactly what she did. In fact, the family became worried about the way she insisted on working, trying to exhaust herself so that she would sleep at night.

Devlin pushed himself and his men and still did not reach the prison camp on the day he was expected. Even temporary duty here was repugnant to him. He had been a soldier for ten years and accepted the fact that men lived or died in battles. But holding men in pens like animals upset him, and when he saw the conditions of the camp, he was enraged and sickened.

He went immediately to the commander's quarters and knocked at the door. The greeting he received was cold and inhospitable. After being reminded that he was late in arriving, he was offered a drink and invited to sit down. It did not take him long to realize that the commander was not the hard man he had thought him to be but rather a man who hated the job he was doing and was bitterly disillusioned with the great art of war.

"What's your name?"

"O'Brien, sir. Lt. Devlin O'Brien."

"Well, Lieutenant O'Brien, we have a list of names of all the men here. The new ones brought in this morning

178

and the dead ones removed last night."

"Sir?"

"Oh, we have a great turnover in clientele in this establishment, Lieutenant. Of course, they keep me balanced well. They send me about as many every week as we manage to bury."

"They die that quickly, sir?"

"Quickly, Lieutenant. No, no, never quickly. It would be better if we shot them. No, instead, we feed one thousand of them. Of course, there are twenty-five hundred here. So only the strong survive. If you go in for coarse amusement, Lieutenant, you should watch at feeding time—if you can stand it," he added softly.

Devlin watched his face and felt a weariness overtake him. Goddamn, would this war never end, he thought. How could decent men survive under these conditions and come out whole men?

He thought of Steffany's and Holly's family and hoped against hope they were not in this hellhole. But if they were, he thought, he would do everything in his power to get them out.

Chapter 21

Carl Brenner sat his horse on a ridge overlooking Briar Hill with two other men. Carl was a large, red-haired man. His eyes were narrow and hard as, in the distance, he watched Holly walk from the barn to the house. He couldn't tell yet how many people were there, but he licked his dry lips at the sight of Holly. He hadn't had a woman for two weeks, since that last house they had raided, and she hadn't been much. She had whimpered and cried and begged him not to take her, but he had and brutally. Then, tired of her crying, he had shot her.

"She looks like a nice little piece," one of the men, named Parks, said hungrily.

Carl nodded and nudged his horse gently forward. They moved slowly and silently to the back side of the barn. There, they dismounted and tied their horses. Carrying their guns, they went in the back door of the barn and searched stealthily about them.

Holly and Deline had been in the barn collecting the few eggs that were left by their chickens, which they had managed to accumulate about the countryside. Holly had gone back in the house, but Deline had made an excuse to stay since she wanted to wait for Bram. She waited, unsuspecting their presence, until a sound behind her made her smile to herself. "Bram?" She turned and found herself looking up at the cold, hungry face of Carl

Brenner. The scream froze on her lips as he held a gun against her side. Her whole body shook with fear, and she managed to ask hoarsely, "Wha . . . what do you want? We haven't anything here. There's no food, no clothes, no money."

He just grinned at her, and her heart began to thump fiercely against her ribs. She tried not to look afraid, but she knew she failed.

He reached out his huge hand and touched the length of her hair that hung over her shoulder. "Beautiful, beautiful," he said.

She pushed his hand away, and he chuckled. This one was going to give him a fight, and he loved a good fight from a woman. It made taking her more fun for him.

"How many people in the house, little gal?"

"Ten!"

"Ha, ha, don't you jest wish they was!"

She looked with disdain at the remnants of their gray uniforms. "Scum! Preying upon your own people. Maybe if you'd fight the Yankees we might win."

"Guess you don't know, lil' gal. The war's over. Lee done surrendered."

"Over?" she repeated.

"Yep, over. We're on our way home. We just need some provisions, and maybe just a little lovin' to make the travelin' easier."

Deline had never been so afraid in her life. She watched the man closely, and she knew he spoke the truth.

"We'll give you all the food we have," she said chokingly, "just leave us alone."

"Aw, you're just too pretty a little gal to leave alone. I'll bet it's been a long time since you seen a man." He licked his lips again. "And I'll bet from the looks of you, you ain't never had one. Watch her, Jake," he said, and Jake pulled out his gun with a lascivious grin.

181

"I'm next after you're done, Carl."

Carl moved toward her, and when he was close enough, he reached out both hands and grabbed her to him. She could smell the foulness of his unwashed body, and it nauseated her. She fought with every ounce of her strength, but she was like a child in his hands. Holding her against his side by reaching around her body, she was powerless to move. Slowly, he pulled apart the front of her dress, and she cried out as she felt the heaviness of his hand squeezing her breast. She writhed and fought his embrace, but he simply laughed.

Bram had been cutting wood for the stove. When he had as much as he could carry, he headed back to the house. He was supposed to meet Deline in the barn, and the thought of her lent him considerable speed. He stacked the wood outside the kitchen door and headed for the barn. With a chuckle, he slipped around the back and crept inside. The sight before him froze him in his tracks.

Deline struggled in Carl's arms while the other two men watched, enjoying the scene. Her dress torn off to her waist, Carl was fondling and caressing her roughly.

Bram's first instinct was to attack them but he knew he would be shot down before he got two steps. Although he hated to let Deline suffer in Carl's embrace any longer than she had to, he eased himself toward the ladder that led to the loft and the three rifles hidden there. He gritted his teeth as Carl's hands freely handled her body. Forcing her legs apart with his hands, he touched her with probing fingers.

"No virgin here, boys. She's been had, but I'll bet not by a man like me."

The other two men laughed and encouraged him with obscene remarks.

Bram felt the rage boil up in him, and when he reached the ladder, worked his way up slowly. Crawling through the hay, he felt desperately for the rifles. Where the hell

182

did O'Brien hide them, he thought wildly. Deline's moaning cries and Carl's chuckles of enjoyment spurred him on. Ah! Finally his hand came across the rifle and the pouch of ammunition. Quickly, he shoved in a bullet, then went to the edge of the loft and aimed the rifle at the three men.

"Take your hands off of her, you filthy bastard!" he shouted.

All three men turned on him with open-mouthed surprise. A man was the last person they expected to find here, and an armed man astounded them.

"Bram!" Deline sobbed, her strength almost gone.

"I said take your hands off of her," he repeated coldly.

Carl dropped his hands from Deline who staggered away from him.

"Get their guns, Deline," Bram said slowly.

With shaky hands, Deline wrapped her dress about her as best she could. Then, moving slowly, she took the guns from all three of them.

"Come up here with them, Deline," Bram said softly.

All three of the men could see death plainly written on Bram's face.

After Deline had climbed to where Bram was, he took one of the guns from her. Then, with slow, cold deliberation, he aimed the gun at Carl and pulled the trigger. The bullet caught him just below the ribs in the stomach. It lifted him off the floor and slammed him against the stall where, with eyes full of amazement, he grasped his stomach and slowly collapsed on the floor.

The other two men gaped at him in fear. "Jesus Christ, mister," one of them moaned, "let us go. We didn't touch her."

"But you would have, wouldn't you, you filthy animals?" Bram snarled. "Get out of here, and remember, we're here to defend ourselves. If I see any sign of you in this area, I'll shoot you on sight. Understand?"

As fast as they could move, the two of them scrambled for the door. Soon the sound of the retreating hoofbeats could be heard.

Bram turned and took Deline in his arms, and she collapsed in tears. He held her against him, gently rocking her in his arms while he caressed the top of her head that lay against his chest. When her trembling eased, he lifted her chin and looked into her eyes.

"It's all right, now, Deline," he said softly.

"Oh, Bram, if you hadn't been here . . . Where did you get the guns?"

"O'Brien left them for me."

She turned and looked down at Carl.

"I'm glad you shot him," she cried softly.

At that moment, the barn door opened and Holly came running in, white faced. She stopped abruptly when she saw Carl and then raised her head up to Deline and Bram. Bram was still holding Deline in his arms, and he did not drop them when he and Holly's eyes met.

Holly was a very intelligent girl. For some time, she had carried a suspicion in the back of her mind. Now she knew the truth and slowly she smiled.

"Is Deline all right, Bram?"

"She is now, and I intend to see she stays that way."

"Of course you do," she answered quietly. "Bring her down so we can calm everybody's fears at the house. Then we'd better get all this out in the open so you two don't have to sneak around anymore."

"O'Brien told you?" he questioned.

"O'Brien knew?" she asked and he nodded.

"What are you going to do, Holly?" Deline asked.

"Try to help you as much as I can."

"Thank you, Holly." Deline's grateful tears touched Holly deeply.

"Oh, my God!" Deline exclaimed. "I just remembered what that that man said—the war's over! The war's over!"

184

Chapter 22

"Are you sure that's what he said, Deline?" Bram asked quickly. "Maybe he meant it was over for them."

"No, no, Bram. He said Lee surrendered. The war's over."

"The war is over," repeated Holly numbly. Then the full realization hit her. Adam . . . Adam would be coming home. For the first time since it had begun, Holly allowed her emotions to control her. She swayed on her feet and covered her face with her hands and allowed the tears she had held in check for so long to fall. Bram moved to her side and laid a comforting arm about her shoulders. She got herself under control in a few minutes and wiped the tears from her face.

"We must tell the others," she said.

"You take Deline to the house, Holly," Bram instructed. "Tell the others. I've got a job to do right here," he indicated Brenner. "Take her in the back door. I'll bury him. It's best if they never know what happened here today."

Holly nodded agreement, and the two women left the barn. Bram turned to look at Brenner. He was not sorry for a minute that he'd shot him. The sight of him pawing Deline had enraged him so that killing him was the only thing his angered brain could think of.

Slowly, he went to Brenner's side and knelt beside

him, then he reached out and went through his pockets. If he had anything of value, it would be of more use to the living than the dead. He was amazed to find a small bag of gold pieces and several pieces of jewelry. He hated to think of where the jewelry must have come from. He pocketed the money and the jewelry, then grasping Carl by both feet, he dragged him out behind the barn. He dug a deep hole and pushed him into it; then he filled the grave. Leading Brenner's horse around to the front of the barn, he unsaddled it and put it into a stall. Then he washed the blood from the floor as best he could. The stain would remain forever. Scrubbing himself clean, he went to the house.

The women were so excited at the news; they were laughing and talking all at once, with the exception of Merilee, whose smile was tightly drawn. Bram knew she was thinking of Graham. They had never confirmed Graham's death, but the last word had been missing in action—presumed dead. Bram also knew that Deline was worried about the fact that there had been no word about her three brothers for months. Even though he was upset about the situation between him and Deline, he still had not pressured her to go away with him until she knew for sure about her brothers, especially about Dixon who was as close to her as her own heartbeat. She had told him with deep assurance that she knew Dixon was alive, for she felt that if he were not, she would have known. In some mysterious way, she and Dixon had been tied together by more than just a brother-sister tie as she and Adam or Brian were. It went beyond that.

They had a small celebration that night with what they had to celebrate with. Then when the house had been darkened for the night, Bram went to Deline's door and knocked. He stepped inside the door and took her into his arms and kissed her until she clung weakly to him.

"God, Deline, do you realize I almost lost you? I don't

186

think I could live without you," he whispered against her hair. "Come with me, Deline. Let's go West where we can start a life together."

"Oh, Bram, there's nothing I want to do more than that. Do you think I want you to leave me before daylight every morning? I'm so empty when you're not beside me. But I've got to know that Adam, Brian and Dixon are safe. Please understand," she pleaded.

He held her even closer, for no matter what he said, he did understand.

For several weeks, there was a kind of tension in the air. An expectancy hung over everyone. Then slowly, the area was filled with men—ragged sick, wounded men, some even dying, trying desperately to get home. Each new person that crossed Briar Hill property was watched closely, but no familiar faces were among them.

It was several weeks later that the women, exhausted from nursing sick men who were passing through, were sitting together in the parlor enjoying a few minutes of quiet rest before going to bed.

A knock sounded at the door, and for one surprised moment, they looked worriedly at each other for Bram was not in the house. Jessica rose and, taking the gun Bram had left, held it down in the folds of her dress. Then as calmly as possible, she motioned for the rest to remain seated, and she left the parlor.

They heard soft voices from the hallway; then Jessica reappeared at the door. "Merilee, there's someone to see you."

Merilee was surprised, but she rose and came out through the door.

Graham stood before her. Taller and filled out, he seemed suddenly so strong and mature looking. She felt almost a deep, unbelieving pain as she cried out his name and felt his strong arms lift her against his hard body while his voice, suddenly more gentle than it had ever

187

been, murmured, "Mother, Mother," over and over again.

The happiness that welled up in her left her unable to speak, and suddenly she could no longer control the tears that had stored themselves within her for the months she had thought him dead.

He reassured her and comforted her, then reached his hand toward the young girl who was standing quietly at the door watching, with a look of deep happiness, the reunion between mother and son.

"Mother, this is Ann Somerfield," he said, and went on to explain what Ann had done for him. When Merilee looked at Ann, she realized from his words and the way Ann looked at her son that she truly loved him. She welcomed her with joy in her heart. They were talking and laughing at the same time when again the door opened and Bram walked in.

For several minutes, a thick silence hung in the air, then Merilee and Jessica, both with the same thoughts, moved to Bram's side and faced Graham.

"Graham?" Merilee said, watching Graham's face closely for some sign of how he felt. "Bram has been our lifeline for so long. You owe him a great deal, for without him, we might not have been here."

Bram felt it was going to be impossible for Graham to extend his hand to a man who at one time had been his slave, to a man whom he had trained from his youth was inferior to himself. That was the reaction Graham would have taken four years ago. Bram did not know the changes four years and the love of one girl could do for a man. He was prepared to be told to leave the house, and was taken completely by surprise when Graham offered his hand to Bram, his eyes never faltering. Bram took it, and the grasp was strong and firm.

"I guess I do owe you everything. This war has changed things so much, it's going to be difficult to pull everything back together. We're all going to have to help one another if we're going to be survivors, and I intend to be a survivor."

Bram grinned. "That's what we've all been doing up to now. It can't get any harder than it's been."

There was such a sense of relief in the air that everyone began to talk at once, except Deline, whose eyes caught Bram's across the room. Graham had accepted Bram's being there to help, but would he ever accept the fact that she and Bram loved each other or that they intended to marry. Bram gave a slight, negative shake of his head. There would have to be time spent together, he thought. Maybe after a while, Graham could be taught to realize that a man was no less a man because he carried in his blood a few drops of the wrong color.

Merilee was happy that Graham was back, but she still felt for Jessica and Holly. It seemed to them that there had been enough time for the others to have returned . . . if they were coming.

Graham and Bram worked well together, and after a time, Graham did not give a thought of Bram's past. Slowly, things around Briar Hill seemed to improve. The women improvised and changed the house, never back to the sparkling showplace it was before the war, but to a warm, comfortable home filled with love.

Bram and Graham built furniture, plowed fields and planted what seeds they could manage to get, borrow or steal from other farmers in the country.

Ann and Graham were married quietly, and before long, Ann's father arrived with her brother, Robert. The house was filled to overflowing, and yet the emptiness caused by the absent members was felt. Being so happy with Ann, it took Graham no time at all to figure out what was going on between Deline and Bram. He kept it to himself and tried to sort out in his own mind how he felt before he confided in Ann.

189

Now that the house was in good repair and the family was beginning to reorganize, Graham suggested to Merilee that they go home. She agreed that it was about time to start working on Cross Oaks. Bram offered to come and help, and his help was readily accepted by Graham.

Merilee and Graham, along with Ann, her father and brother, gathered together their few possessions and headed for Cross Oaks. As soon as they arrived, the women set about immediately cleaning the house and rescuing anything that was usable or could be repaired. The men began examining the barn, stables, fences and fields.

The days drifted slowly by, rolling into one another, and slowly, the house became alive again with laughter and happiness.

Bram came over to help repair a wall in the parlor. He and Graham and Robert worked together laughing at stories Ann's father told. Ann carried a pail of cool water in from the well and handed a dipper full to her father who drank and handed it to Graham. Graham was about to hand it to Bram when a cold, familiar voice stopped him.

"You go outside and drink from the trough, Nigger."

The voice was bitter and brutal. Graham whirled about. In the doorway stood Richard Forrester and Tyler Jemmison.

Chapter 23

"Did you hear what I said, Nigger? You get your black ass out of my house!"

"Pa!" Graham tried to explain. Then he looked at his father's face, and he knew that it would be impossible to explain anything to him. Another realization came to him at the same time. He was no longer afraid of his father. Richard ignored him and continued to glare at Bram who returned his gaze with no fear, only a look of contempt which outraged him even more. Richard withdrew his gun from its holster and aimed it directly at Bram.

"Richard." Merilee's voice came from the kitchen doorway. "Put that gun away. Bram is a friend who has done more for us than anyone in the world."

"There's no black bastard going to have free run of my house just because we lost a war. I want him out of here."

"If he goes, Richard," Merilee replied softly, "Graham and I go also."

He stared at her in open-mouthed disbelief, and then at his son whose eyes returned his look without the fear they used to hold but instead with a cold look of defiance.

"Richard, I want to talk with you privately," Merilee said, pointedly looking at Tyler Jemmison. "Mr. Jemmison, Odella is at Briar Hill if you care to call. If not, Portia still lives with your son in the slave cabin at Heritage."

It was said with cool disdain and achieved the effect

191

she desired. His face reddened, and he spun on his heel and abruptly left the room.

"Now, Richard, I would like to speak to you . . . please," she added, almost as an afterthought.

Richard could not believe that the people he had dominated so well before had become strong enough to defy him, and he turned and followed her into the kitchen, closing the door behind him.

Bram turned to Graham. "I'd better leave."

"Bram, I'm sorry about this," Graham said miserably.

Bram just smiled and shrugged his shoulders. "Graham, you can't change the thinking of a whole generation in one night. It's going to take a lot of time. People like your father will never see below a man's skin color. We don't get by with people like that; we get by in spite of them. Don't worry about it. Come on over to Briar Hill and visit soon."

Graham smiled with gratitude and watched him leave the house and mount his horse, turning him toward Briar Hill with a wave to Graham.

Richard faced Merilee, after an absence of almost two years, with no sign of affection. In fact, his face was blazing with anger.

"Why did you speak to me like that in front of my son and that, that—"

"Richard, Bram is a man, a better man than most I've met in my lifetime. He stayed here and protected us when he could have gone to safety. He supplied us with food and moral support when we needed it most. Do you really think I could treat him any other way than as a friend? I might add, a very dear friend."

"I won't have my son in his company. Graham was raised a gentleman. He'll do as I say."

"I'm grateful to say Graham has changed since he went away. He is also a man of whom I'm very proud. You'll not rule him again, Richard. I won't allow it. He's happy

192

with his new wife. Leave him be."

"I'm not afraid, Merilee. I'll handle Graham. He'll do as I say in spite of what you think you 'may allow.'" He laughed.

"Richard, I'm warning you—"

"Warning me!" he said in amusement. "What could you ever do to stop me?"

"If you, in any way, try to do Graham any harm or his wife, if you try to spoil the friendship he is developing with Bram, I'll be forced to tell the world a story that I'm sure you'd rather I'd keep a secret."

"Merilee, don't threaten me," he warned.

"I'm not threatening, Richard," she answered softly. "I'm making you a promise. I will tell the truth not only to Graham, but to Bram and everyone else concerned. Do you want that to happen?"

"You would do Graham more harm than good," he answered belligerently. But his eyes were unsure, and she knew she had won temporarily. She went to his side and gave him a light kiss on the cheek; then she promptly turned from him and walked to the door. "Welcome home, Richard."

He fumed with impotent rage, most of which was directed at Bram. "Damn black bastard," he muttered. "I knew I should have gotten rid of him when he was born. Well, it's never too late to remedy a situation."

The Richard that came out of the kitchen was a different man than the one that had gone in. As the days passed, he appeared to have changed. He was friendly with everyone, even Bram, to his amazement. But Merilee watched him closely, for she knew this side of Richard, also. And then, his opportunity came in the most roundabout way.

He was talking to Deline, who was charmed by his beautiful manners and kindness. In a considerate, thoughtful method, he had led her to feel open and friendly with him. Eventually, the story of Bram's defense of her came out. Richard held his enthusiasm in check with difficulty. Now he could get rid of him without anyone being the wiser. He sat back and waited for the opportune moment to present itself.

Tyler Jemmison had ridden to Briar Hill and received a blow of his own. When he came in, Odella had received him with a cool smile but no sign of the former affection she had felt for him. He bent to kiss her, she turned her cheek, and after he had touched it lightly, she drew away from him.

"I'm home to stay, Odella. You can get ready to leave here. I'm taking you back to Heritage."

"To share you again with your mistress and your son? No, I think not, Tyler. I have been told I'm welcome here at Briar Hill, and if Jessica and Matthew will allow me, I shall stay until you decide what you really want. I do not love you, Tyler. I never have, and I will not allow you to use me any longer. Maybe there might come a time when we can share the balance of our lives together, but for now, I cannot. I simply cannot."

He watched her, amazed at the courage he never thought she possessed and the beginning of respect he never felt for her before. Then he turned away and went back to Heritage alone.

The destruction he saw as he went from room to room made him think back over his life. He remembered the reasons he had tried to force Holly to marry Graham, knowing that Graham was not Richard Forrester's son but Charles Gordon's son. The marriage when Charles had been told the truth would have united three plantations instead of two. They would have owned one quarter of the state of Georgia.

Greed and pride had driven him. For what? Now he had lost both his daughters, for Holly was waiting for Adam and Steffany and Graham were already married. He

194

began to see what he had lost, for with the loss of Odella and both his daughters, he was left with the empty shell of a once beautiful home and a woman he had bought and paid for. He sat down in an empty room on the sad remains of a chair and watched the bright square of sunlight from the uncurtained window slowly darken.

It was totally dark outside before he rose from the chair. He went outside and mounted his horse. Then, instead of going to Portia's, he headed back to Briar Hill. It was not going to be easy, but he wanted to regain the love of his family and rebuild the wreckage of their lives and his. He prayed all the way back that one day Odella would forgive him and that his daughters would learn to love him again.

Now, again, the waiting became an unbearable strain on everyone. Surely they could have reached home by now. Even Steffany began to worry about Devlin. "What if something has happened to him and no one knew to send me word?" she thought painfully. Each person was caught up in their own grief and thoughts.

Bram and Deline lay side by side in the hay, neither desiring to speak. He had held her and made love to her, but he felt there was something different about her. Some subtle change he could not put his finger on. "What if she was tired of him?" he thought. "What if she had decided she'd made a mistake?" Dear God, he didn't know how he would face the balance of his life without her. His arm tightened unconsciously about her, and she looked up at him.

"What's wrong, Bram?"

"I was about to ask you the same thing."

"When I'm with you, nothing is wrong," she murmured. "But when you're away from me, I become scared, Bram. What's going to happen to us?"

"We don't have a lot of choices, do we?"

She shook her head. "I guess not, especially not now. I

195

guess we've narrowed it down to one."

He looked down at her, and she gazed steadily at him. Then slowly, he sat up. She did not say a word as he gently touched her.

"Why didn't you tell me?"

"You had enough problems for a while."

"Do you honestly think they're any more important than you? You're carrying my child, aren't you, Deline?"

She nodded, searching his face. "Don't you want it, Bram? It's not too late—"

"Deline, for Christ's sake, don't say a thing like that. Our child. Of course I want it. Nothing could make me any happier. I'm just worried about you."

"Don't worry, Bram, for I want your child more than anything else in the world," she said softly.

His hard face softened when he looked at her moisture-filled eyes. He knew that he loved this woman beyond anything else in the world. Slowly, he touched his lips to hers and drew her body gently against him. His touch, infinitely tender, made her want to cry.

"No matter what anyone in the world says, Deline, tomorrow you're going to become my wife. If we have to go to the end of the earth we will, but tomorrow you will belong to me."

She gave him no argument, just lifted her arms about him and surrendered to the warm wash of his love that flooded over her.

Chapter 24

Devlin slowly sat down in his chair. He had just finished making his inspection of the prison camp. His stomach was nauseated, and his head throbbed painfully. He had never seen so much human misery in his life.

The camp was large, covering over a five-mile square of land, fenced in by a high, wooden fence, along which, at regular intervals, guards were placed outside for their own protection also. Inside, the prison contained no shelters at all. Men who came here erected what protection they could from the elements with what they had. Lean-tos made of anything that could be found, were erected by the prisoners themselves and guarded jealously. The prisoners slowly became like caged animals fighting for the smallest morsel of food or piece of clothing. The wounded stayed that way until they either died or recovered. Dying was taken as a blessing for both the wounded and the men around him, for it meant they could divide his possessions.

Devlin had tried to look closely at the men as he moved through the camp, but the conditions were so bad that he couldn't. It wouldn't have mattered, for by now, all of them looked the same. They were ragged, filthy scarecrows of men who were either too weak to look up as he went by, or those who did glared at him with a hatred that washed over him like a black wave.

Slowly, he pulled from the desk the list of names of men imprisoned here. His hands trembled as his eyes came down the pages over the names and ranks and ages of the men. There was the hot sting of tears in his eyes as he read.

Andrew, Baylor, Collins, Davidson, Davis, Eppley, Farmer, Farrington, Gilcrest—Gilcrest, Adam and Gilcrest, Brian, ages twenty-six and twenty-three. This had to be them, he thought, as he threw the papers back on his desk and shouted for Sergeant Taylor. Taylor came in slowly, his eyes weary and his face gray.

"Yes, sir?"

"They're here, Sergeant," Devlin answered. "At least, two of them are."

"Christ, sir," Taylor said weakly. "I was hopin' they wasn't here."

"From these records I'd say Adam's been here almost a year and a half. His brother arrived with the ones that came the day we did."

"A year and a half? Here! How did he ever manage to stay alive?"

"I don't know, but I want to go in and find them and bring them to my quarters."

"Yes, sir."

Taylor left and Devlin sat staring at the door he closed behind him. A year and a half in this place would ruin the sanity of any human being. He wondered how he would find Adam. Remembering Holly's worried eyes and pleading voice, he determined that one way or another he'd get Adam out of here, no matter what it cost.

The heavy shuffle of feet outside his door brought him back from the depths of his thoughts. A light knock and Taylor stepped inside the door.

"They're here, sir," he said softly, but his eyes were clouded and his voice shook slightly. Going down into the camp had so unnerved him that he strongly desired to get drunk, give up his career in the Army and walk away from this hole of living death, and he didn't care in what order he did it.

"Bring them in, Sergeant."

"Yes, sir."

Adam and Brian moved slowly, neither of them having the strength for anything else. They did not know what the new commander had in store for them, nor did they care. Nothing but Adam's grim determination kept them alive at all, and the only thing about him that was really conscious were his eyes. Smoky-gray eyes watched Devlin closely, but he remained quiet waiting for the commander to speak.

"Adam Gilcrest?"

"Yes."

"This is your brother, Brian Gilcrest?"

"Yes," he repeated.

"You're from Georgia, Crawford County, Briar Hill?"

Now Adam was alert. His gray eyes watched this man closely and waited.

"Yes."

Devlin came around the side of his desk and stood beside Adam. Then very quietly he said, "I'm Devlin O'Brien. I'm your fiancee's sister's husband. I married Steffany six weeks ago. I'm going to get you out of here."

Adam weaved on his feet as though he had been violently struck, and Brian's head came up. Adam's body began to tremble violently, and the tears he could no longer contain fell helplessly down his face.

"Oh, God," he moaned and began to sag. Devlin reached out his arms and caught him before he could fall.

"It's all right, Adam," he said softly.

Adam's body was wracked with sobs, and he clung to Devlin weakly. When he could get some control of himself, he straightened and looked at Devlin.

"Holly? How is she?"

"Fine, Adam. She's quite a lady."

"My mother and father?"

"Your mother's fine. The last letter she got from your father while I was there, he was well."

Devlin turned to Sergeant Taylor who had been watching, his eyes filled with pity.

"Take these men to my place, Taylor. See they get a bath, a haircut and some food."

"Yes, sir."

Adam felt no guilt for the other prisoners. He had been fighting for his life for too long to care anymore. He and Brian staggered after Taylor, and Devlin watched them leave, feeling slightly better than he had when he first arrived.

Neither Adam nor Brian could eat much; their stomachs, not being used to the food, had rejected it violently. But the hot water soaking the filth and tiredness from their bodies was welcome as it soaked away layers of grime. Adam lathered his hair and beard washing away some of the crawling objects nested there. He felt alive for the first time in over a year. After reluctantly leaving the tub, Sergeant Taylor chopped away most of his beard and hair. Clean and warm, Adam dropped on the bed beside his brother and fell into a deep sleep.

When O'Brien came back to his house that night, they were both still asleep. He and Taylor, who had agreed to come back to Briar Hill with him when the war was over, sat and talked and waited patiently for them to awaken. But at midnight, they showed no signs of wakening, so Taylor left and O'Brien made himself a bed of sorts on the couch.

Adam stirred and came slowly awake. He didn't know for a few minutes where he was, but he was sure it was a dream. He was lying on a soft bed instead of the ground. The blankets were warm, and he felt clean. It had to be a dream.

Slowly, reality came back to him as he felt Brian stir beside him. Soft moonlight sifting through the window laid a bright path across the wooden floor. He lay very still, savoring the warmth and cleanliness of the blankets and remembered the man who had brought him here. He recalled his mother's letter to Brian and laid his hand over Holly's letter that was worn and faded but which he kept under his shirt next to his body.

Steffany was married to this man. He remembered Devlin vaguely in a dream. Very quietly, so as not to wake Brian, he eased himself from the bed and stood up. He looked at the door and wondered if it was locked. He wrapped a blanket about himself and went to the door. Slowly, he turned the door knob, and it opened. Just the pleasure of opening an unlocked door tightened his throat and made him quiver with pleasure. Never again would he be ungrateful for the small pleasures in life, he thought.

Opening the door completely, he stepped out into the parlor. Devlin had not been fully asleep as he half-listened for movement from the next room. He heard the click of the door latch and sat up. Then he rose to his feet. Striking a match, he lit the lamp on the table beside him and turned to look at Adam.

Adam was very thin from the lack of food, but he still gave the impression of strength. His tawny, sun-streaked hair and beard gave him the look of a thick-maned lion. His gray eyes were calm but filled with questions as they looked into Devlin's blue ones.

201

"Sit down, Adam," Devlin said quietly, watching Adam move from the door to the couch where he sat down slowly.

"Would you like a drink?"

"I don't think I could handle it," he replied.

"Do you feel like talking?"

Adam nodded his head. "Tell me about home, everyone there, everything. It's been so long. . . ."

They talked for the remainder of the night. Adam, hungry for every bit of information, listened avidly to every word Devlin spoke. He described the conditions and every event that had transpired. Adam even laughed at his description of the preacher at Devlin and Steffany's wedding.

Adam watched Devlin as he talked. He had been sure before, in his own mind, that he would never be able to sit in the same room with a Yankee without the anger and frustration he had felt over the past years controlling him. But he listened to Devlin talk of his home and his family, and he realized that his man loved them also. Steffany loved him, Holly's sister. How things must have changed if Steffany was as Devlin described her.

He asked Devlin one question after another, hanging on every word he uttered, and Devlin patiently answered, giving every detail he could remember. Then suddenly, the conversation seemed to fade and both men sat in silence, allowing their thoughts to drift.

"Would you like that drink now?"

Adam nodded and Devlin poured them both a glass.

"Devlin, what are you going to do with us now?"

"Well," Devlin sighed deeply. "I've been giving that a lot of thought. Whatever we do will have to be before the new commander gets here. I'm only a temporary replacement. But rest assured, Adam, that one way or another, you and Brian are going home."

202

Chapter 25

Time pushed the days into one another, rolling along rapidly, too rapidly to suit Devlin who could not think of a way to get them safely away from there. He had tried his best to alleviate some of the suffering he found in the camp. He sent for a doctor from the nearest town and had a rough wooden shed built for his use. Then he separated the sick men from the healthy, or reasonably healthy ones. He put the ones that could respond to work cutting down trees which they fashioned into small log houses, ten men to a house. He rode into town and made arrangements for some extra food, taking his own money to pay for it.

It was a drop in the bucket, and he knew it, but his conscience would not let him rest. Perhaps it was Adam and Brian's treatment or the efforts he was trying to make at the camp, but slowly, he could feel the atmosphere change when he came out for inspections. Men who had glared at him in hatred did not smile yet, but they looked at him with grudging respect.

Late in the evenings, Devlin, Taylor, Adam and Brian would sit on the front porch of Devlin's cabin, nursing drinks and talking. They were doing so one night when the sound of hoofbeats filled the night air. Devlin rose quickly and motioned Adam and Brian back into the house. Then he stood on the porch and watched the rider approach.

"Lieutenant O'Brien?"

"Yes?"

"I've a message for you, sir."

The soldier handed Devlin a packet of papers, saluted, and when Devlin returned his salute, he turned his horse and left. Devlin was sure the papers he held were telling him that the new commanding officer was on his way, and he would soon be replaced.

"I'll read them in the morning," he thought, and put the papers away in his coat pocket as Adam and Brian came back out.

"If these are what I think they are, Adam, I've got to get you and Brian out of here as soon as possible."

"The new commander?"

"Yeah, I imagine."

"Devlin, there's no way for you to free us without destroying your own career. Brian and I are grateful for what you've already done, but we just can't let you jeopardize yourself."

Brian nodded agreement. "Adam and I will be all right now. Maybe this thing'll be over soon, but either way, you've given us enough to keep us going and we're grateful."

Devlin shook his head stubbornly. "You think I could face Steffany again if I let you two go back into that place? No, there's a way; I just have to find it."

Taylor chuckled. "When this Irishman sets his mind on sumthin' they ain't no use arguing with him. If he says he's gettin' you out of here, he will if he has to turn the world upside down to do it."

"Well, if you do have to send us back," Brian said quickly, "Adam and I would understand."

They sat for a while longer, sipping their drinks, each one contemplating their future. O'Brien was first to rise.

"Well, I've got to get up at daylight. You two can sleep

all day if you want. I've got to get some sleep."

Taylor said good night and left. Both Adam and Brian went inside to the small back room they shared.

"You think Devlin will find a way for us to get home, Adam?"

"I wouldn't put anything past his capabilities," Adam said. "From what Taylor says and the way he's worked around here, I think he could probably do anything he wanted."

Devlin lay sleepless for a long time, but no constructive ideas would come to him. He finally pushed them out of his mind and let his thoughts drift back to Steffany. She was the only anchor Devlin had in the past ten years, and he enjoyed the thought of having a home and a woman like her waiting. He finally drifted off to sleep with her face floating before him, vaguely feeling in his dreams her warm body lying next to him.

At daylight, Sergeant Taylor knocked on his door, and he stirred reluctantly awake. "All right, Sergeant," he said as the insistent knock came again. "I'll be right out." He rose from the bed and splashed water on his face to help him wake up. Then he reached out to lift his jacket from the chair. The rustle of papers reminded him of the papers he had put there late last night, and he withdrew them from the pocket, tossing the jacket on the bed. He opened them slowly and began to read. His eyes slowly widened, and he began to smile. Then he threw the papers down and, grabbing his pants, hastily pulled them and his boots on. Shirtless and unshaven, he looked like a huge bear. Throwing open the door where Adam and Brian slept, he shouted, "Get up! Hurry up!" They stared in amazement as he slammed their door behind him and they could hear him shouting at the top of his lungs.

"Taylor, Taylor, you ugly bastard, where are you?"

Taylor ran to the door, his mouth open in surprise. He'd never seen Devlin act like this.

205

"Yes, sir?"

"Get me about twenty men with sledge hammers. Hurry up! Don't just stand there."

Taylor rushed to obey as Adam and Brian came out of the bedroom.

"Come with me," said Devlin and threw open the door. They followed him rapidly as he crossed the hundred feet or so that separated his house from the camp. Taylor awaited him at the door of the camp with the men, who all gaped open mouthed at a man they thought had lost his mind.

"Open the gates," shouted Devlin to the guards. They threw open the gates and Devlin led his parade of frustrated men inside. The occupants of the camp stirred awake at the unusual racket and came out to see what was going on. In as loud a voice as he could raise, which was considerable, he shouted, "Sergeant Taylor, tell these men to swing those hammers and tear down this fence."

Taylor just stood still for a few minutes, then it suddenly came to him what the reason must be. He gave a loud shout of pure joy as Devlin threw back his head and laughed.

Adam and Brian exchanged doubtful looks, wondering if they had both lost their minds. Devlin turned to Brian and Adam. His face was so filled with happiness that he was actually laughing and crying at the same time.

"The war's over! The war's over!" he said to Adam.

The word spread through the camp like a raging fire. Men staggered from the cabins trembling with excitement. The twenty men Taylor had brought were soon joined by twenty more, then twenty more as Confederates and Union men alike ripped wildly at the fence.

Only Adam did not move. His face was still and filled with sadness. Devlin went to him, understanding the unspoken thoughts in Adam's mind.

"When?" he asked quietly.

"Two weeks ago. Lee surrendered at Appomattox."

"We've destroyed ourselves," Adam said. "We've torn apart our way of life, our homes, the lives of our boys. For what?" he whispered the last words.

"Adam," Devlin said quietly. "We'll rebuild. We'll work together. We're one country again. It's up to people like us, you, Brian, me and our women, to put the pieces back together again, to heal the wounds, to start a new life. We're not beaten unless we let ourselves be beaten, and I, for one, don't intend to be. I've got Steffany and, for the first time in my life, a home and a good future. You, you've got even more. You've got Briar Hill and Holly and your damn rebel pride. With all those things, we'll put our world right again."

Adam looked into the quiet, blue eyes of Devlin O'Brien and acknowledged his truth. Slowly, he extended his hand and O'Brien grasped it firmly.

The fence that had held them in bondage for so long was torn apart and men flooded over the remnants toward freedom and home. Adam, Brian, Devlin and Sergeant Taylor walked back to Devlin's house.

"I know you're in a hurry to get home, Adam, but it will only take me about two weeks to get out of this man's army. I'd like to go back with you if you'll wait."

Adam grinned. "You think I could face Steff after what you've done for us and tell her we left you behind?"

"Christ," Devlin laughed. "I don't think I've been so happy since Steffany said she'd marry me."

They spent the next ten days waiting for Devlin to wind up his affairs and get himself mustered out of the army. The day they were ready to leave, he discarded his uniform and bought a pair of dark pants, boots and a white shirt. Then he sold all his property and gathered all the money he had.

"We can use this to help us get started with seeds for planting."

"You're going to be a regular country farmer, aren't you?" laughed Brian.

"Yep." Devlin smiled. "I can't wait to bounce my sons on my lap."

"Boy, Steffany really domesticated you," whooped Brian gleefully.

Devlin joined in his laughter for a moment, then his face became serious. "I intend to build a good future, for myself and for my country. I want to give it the kind of sons who will never let this kind of injustice happen again. The kind who love their homes and their country too much to ever let her suffer like this again."

Adam nodded in agreement silently, his mind going back to Holly. It seemed so many years since he'd held her in his arms. He remembered exactly the soft color of her eyes as she'd smiled up at him and the velvety feel of her in his arms. Adam knew firsthand of man's inhumanity to man, and he felt when he got home, he was going to immerse himself in Holly's love and never leave her again.

The day finally came when they were prepared to leave. Devlin had bought a wagon and stored in it the things he wanted to take along, including gifts for everyone. The one package that he stored very gently, he wouldn't even tell Adam and Brian what it contained.

As the sun rose over the horizon, the wagon creaked along the road toward home.

Chapter 26

The days seemed interminable to Adam, and watching the destruction about them as they traveled, made things worse. Occasionally, they passed men singly and in groups headed for what remained of their homes. The wounded staggered along in silent desperation. Often, they gave rides to some who were very badly hurt and took them as far as they could. On two occasions, they buried an unknown soldier who had dropped along the way.

Mile after mile fell behind them. Nights were spent around a campfire discussing plans for their futures. All of them seemed to gather fresh enthusiasm when they crossed the border into Georgia. Even Devlin felt a strong sense of coming home.

They were seated now around a dying campfire, for some reason, reluctant to roll in their blankets and sleep. If they could keep up the pace they had been making, they would be home by this time tomorrow night.

Adam had changed a great deal in the past two years. He had gained a maturity and strength. There was no bitterness in him now, thanks to Devlin, but instead there burned a great determination to erase the past and put together a new future. Slowly, he was regaining the weight he had lost in prison, and his body filled out and regained its strength. The bright Georgia sun turned his skin to bronze and lightened the streaks in his tawny hair. He had kept his beard and mustache. His smoky-gray eyes had developed a cool, calm look which lent him an air of solidity and power.

Brian had also changed. The laughing, mischievous boy had developed into a man. Although flashes of his brilliant wit and humor would burst forth occasionally, he was much calmer and quieter than he had ever been. He had grown a full mustache, mostly because he wanted to copy Adam. It gave him an older look. His hair had been bleached almost blond by the sun, and his body had filled out from the slender form of a young boy to the hard, muscular form of a grown man.

He had picked up, to Adam's amusement, an old guitar in one of the towns they had passed through. When they had finished eating, he pulled it over onto his lap and began to strum it gently. Adam looked at him in surprise, and he chuckled.

"I've developed a lot of talents you didn't know about, Adam. I've heard this is a very useful thing in courting young ladies, and I intend to do some fancy courting when I get home."

"When haven't you done a lot of courting, Brian?" laughed Adam.

Brian's eyes twinkled with amusement. "Adam, you remember the time Deline dressed up like Dixon and serenaded Selena Mitchell?"

Both Adam and Brian laughed and then told the story to Devlin who enjoyed it as much as they had.

"I wonder if Selena's married? She was sure one pretty girl. For a while there, I thought Dixon was gonna propose to her. I wonder if Barbara ever got married either? And I wonder—"

"Brian," Adam laughed, "you gonna try to collect every unmarried girl in the county?"

"The way I feel right now, I'd collect every married

one too if they give me half a chance."

They all got a laugh from this, and they leaned back in comfort and listened while Brian's deep voice sang *Lorena*. After a while, Devlin's strong tenor joined in, and they sang together.

When they finished singing the song, the crackling of the fire was all that could be heard. Without a word, Brian put the guitar aside, rolled in his blanket and went to sleep. In a few minutes, Devlin followed his example. Adam sat and watched the embers die away, feeling a peace and contentment close about him. Tomorrow he would be home.

It was the dusky, half-light before dawn that saw them up and packing. By the time daylight came, they were well on their way. Now a feeling of urgency struck them all. It was all Devlin could do to keep from slapping the horses into a run. Familiar sights now began to appear. Places they had hunted, fished and swum, homes they had visited, some of which stood deserted and over-grown. Some had strangers living in them.

They traveled down the main road to Briar Hill. At the beginning of their property, they began to see signs of repairs. A few squares of the fields had been plowed. They moved slowly on, then the solid sound of someone chopping wood rang through the air. The heavy, solid whack of the ax against the wood told them immediately the wielder was a man. But who? They topped a small ridge in the road. There, several feet in from the road, was Bram. His back was turned to them, and he was swinging the ax with a mighty heave. He didn't hear the wagon approach or stop. Adam climbed down and walked to where Bram stood.

"Workin' hard, Bram?"

The ax froze in midswing, and Bram whirled about. His face broke into a wide grin, and he was about to extend his hand and welcome him home when he realized that

211

Adam might not consider that appropriate. Adam read his thoughts like a book and took the extra step himself putting his hand out to Bram.

"Welcome back. We thought you were dead. We haven't had word of anybody for months."

"We're far from dead. In fact, Brian is with me, and so is Devlin O'Brien."

"It sure is good to see you. There's going to be some mighty happy ladies up at the house tonight."

"C'mon back with us now, Bram. You can chop wood later."

Bram stared at Adam with doubt in his face. He hesitated to tell him about him and Deline. Maybe it would spoil his coming home. But if he didn't tell him, what then?

"Bram, we've been traveling for a long while. In all that time, me and Devlin and Brian have had a lot of time to talk."

"You know about me and Deline?"

"Yes."

"Where do you and Brian stand, Adam?"

"Well, at first it was hard for us to accept," he answered honestly. "But Devlin told us how you stayed here when you could have gone and how happy Deline is with you. Devlin's a pretty persuasive fellow. He's got us convinced you're doing us the greatest favor of our lives getting us into your family."

The relief he felt turned Bram's legs weak, and he leaned for a minute against the tree he'd been chopping. He realized he'd been clutching the ax so tightly his fingers were numb. He expelled his breath in a sigh.

"You've got no idea what that means to me and what it will mean to Deline. You see, we were married last week in Delaware County. Deline is expecting a child. We've been packed to leave since then, but she had to see that you and your brothers are home safe, even if you

212

wouldn't have anything to do with her after this."

"Not have anything to do with her! Bram, Deline is blood of our blood. She's family. I don't care what she had or had not done, Deline is our sister. Her child is my nephew, and I'll not let you take my nephew away where I won't get to see him."

Bram smiled widely, and together the two men started to walk back to the wagon. Then Bram stopped and turned to Adam.

"One more thing I have to tell you, Adam. Graham and I have become good friends. In fact, he's given me his name. Deline is now Mrs. Abraham Forrester."

Adam began to laugh heartily. "Boy, I'll bet that went over good with Graham's father."

"Well, I wouldn't exactly say that. He's disowned Graham. He's living alone at Cross Oaks. Merilee came with Graham to stay at Briar Hill with us."

"How's Graham taking all this? From what I remember—"

"Don't judge Graham on what you remember. He's a completely different man. He came home after being badly wounded. Brought home the prettiest wife you've ever seen. They're so happy with each other, it's great just to watch. Graham simply told his father he'd live his own life, and there was nothing he could do about it."

"How's Richard taking that?"

"Sits up at Cross Oaks and don't say nothing. I think he's losing his senses. Sits there like an old spider and waits to catch someone in his web. I got a feelin' it's me he'd like to catch. I don't think there's anything he can do, but it still makes me nervous sometimes, him waitin' and watchin' like he does."

"Well, you've sure as hell developed enough friends to help you. Including me, Brian and Devlin. I don't think old man Forrester is going to get at you, Bram."

"Thanks, Adam."

"Let's go home. I don't think I can stand it much longer."

They went back to the wagon, and Devlin again urged the horses toward Briar Hill. The yard was deserted when they pulled in. Brian and Adam almost fell over each other in their haste to get off the wagon and to the front door. At that moment, the door opened and Jessica stepped out. Her face went from a tired, strained look to amazement and joy in a few seconds.

"Adam! Brian! Oh, my sons," she cried and extended both arms. Brian reached her first and swung her up into his arms laughing. He whirled her about and set her down in front of Adam who put both his arms about her and held her close. She simply repeated their names over and over.

"Mother, where's Holly?" Adam asked.

"She's out in the barn, Adam."

Adam was about to turn away when Deline came to the door. Her face was white, and he could see her hands clenched tightly at her side. Her body was still slender. It was not obvious she was pregnant, but she seemed to be very frightened. He held out his arms to her.

"Come, let me kiss the bride, Mrs. Forrester," he said softly.

"Oh, Adam," Deline moaned softly as she threw herself into his arms and began to cry. He held her tight for a minute, then lifted her chin and smiled down at her.

"Well, baby sister, you've gone and grown up on me when I turned my back. Going to make me an uncle, I hear?"

She nodded, her eyes bright with happiness as Bram came up beside her and put his arm about her waist.

"Congratulations, I hope you two will be very happy— and speaking of happiness, I've got to see Holly."

He kissed Deline again and his mother. Then he walked around the side of the house toward the barn.

Holly had just come out the door with a basket of eggs on her arm. Her back was to Adam as she latched the door. He watched her hungrily, taking in her slender body, her long, bright hair, hanging loose down her back.

"Holly," he whispered.

She froze, then turned slowly; her eyes widened, and the basket fell unheeded from her hands. Then suddenly she flew to him and he gathered her close with a cry of sheer joy.

"Adam, Adam, Adam," she was crying until he stopped her mouth with his. He felt he could never hold her close enough. He wanted to devour her. He held the back of her head with one hand twined in her hair, the other arm strained her to him until she could barely breathe.

He felt the world spin as the softness of her flowed against him. This was his haven. This was home!

Chapter 27

Steffany, working in an upstairs bedroom, heard the commotion outside. Pulling aside the curtain, she looked down in time to see Devlin climb down from the wagon. Her breath caught in her throat, and she spun from the window and ran to the bedroom door and flung it open. They arrived at the top of the stairs together, and she flung herself laughing, into his arms.

"Ah, darlin', darlin'," he murmured against her hair as he held her tight against him. He held her away from him for a minute and smiled down into her eyes. Then slowly and leisurely his mouth captured hers.

That night they were all gathered together in the parlor. There was not much conversation. Adam could not keep his eyes from Holly, and they followed her hungrily every time she left his side. Now, Brian's pure mischievousness was showing; he could not resist a few amusing remarks at Adam's expense.

"Mother," he said, nonchalantly, "if I wasn't so blasted tired from Adam's draggin' me home so fast, I'd ride into town and bring the preacher out here." He chuckled heartily. "Guess Adam'll have to wait awhile since tomorrow's Sunday and the Reverend is probably too busy for a wedding." He clucked his tongue. "Too bad, old man, guess you'll have to sleep in the barn for a few nights."

The last remark was accompanied by a yelp of surprise from Brian as Adam threw the first thing his hand connected with, which was a book from the table next to him. Trying to dodge the book, Brian tipped back his chair and promptly fell backward on the floor. Now Adam grinned at him. "Since you're down there, Brian, you might as well stay. Holly has my room, so I'm using yours. Sorry, little brother, but it looks like the floor for you."

Everyone laughed, including Brian. As he picked himself up, brushing off his clothes, he grinned wickedly at Adam, then turned and said, very seriously, to Holly. "My dear sister-to-be, despite the crudity of the uncouth gentleman over there, I am going to take myself to town and bring back the Reverend." He bent down and kissed Holly's cheek. "I'm anxious to have a new sister as pretty as you."

"You're anxious to have your bed back more, though, aren't you, Brian?" questioned Deline. Brian chuckled, delighted with his maneuver.

"Well, I could stay here and tell Holly all of Adam's little secrets from when we were boys," he offered.

"On second thought, Brian," interjected Adam, "why don't you get going before I have to take you out and tan your hide like I used to?" They all laughed uproariously. Then Brian picked up his jacket. Ann's brother, Robert, offered to accompany Brian, and he accepted. Robert was a quiet, likable boy of nineteen. He resembled Ann in many ways. He was considerate, and his shy smile and thoughtfulness had made him a very welcome addition to the family.

After Brian had gone, Devlin rose from his chair. He went to Steffany's side and whispered something in her ear. She smiled up at him before he turned and left the

217

room. The sound of the door closing left everyone in silent surprise. After a short time, the sound of horses' hooves could be heard. Steffany got up and turned to the others in the room.

"Good night, everybody," she said, amused at the surprised looks they tried to keep under control. She turned and left the room as, outside, the noise of retreating hoofbeats broke the air.

Steffany sat in front of Devlin. She leaned back against him as they rode, feeling the welcome strength of his arm about her. When they reached the river, he dismounted and lifted her down beside him, taking the opportunity to kiss her as he did. Then he reached up to untie a bundle from behind the saddle. They walked to the large oak tree that carried the memory of their first togetherness and spread a blanket out on the ground. Turning to face Steffany, he held out his arms. She smiled and stepped into their enclosing circle and lifted her lips to meet his.

It was a long while later when they lay contented side by side. Her face was absorbing the firm warmth of his shoulder, his arm holding her close to him, when suddenly he stirred.

"I forgot to give you your present."

"Present?"

"Yep." He moved from her and reached out to pick up a package from the bundle he'd brought with them, and he handed it to her. Then she undid the strings that secured the wrapping. Her face beaming with anticipation in opening the package, she found a lovely white dress trimmed with ribbons of soft, green velvet.

"I hope it fits, I just used my hands to show the girl what size I wanted."

Tears formed in Steffany's eyes and fell unheeded as she reached out her hand and smoothed the delicate material of the dress.

"Oh, Devlin, it's so lovely." She began to cry as he pulled her close to him.

"Remember me?" he said softly. "I'm the boy next door and this is your first party dress. I want to see you with your hair all bright and shiny and stars in your eyes."

She lifted her hand and gently caressed the side of his face, her eyes glowing with love.

"You are wonderful, Devlin O'Brien, and I thank God every day I had the good sense to marry you."

He brushed her lips with his.

"Put it on, darlin'. I want to see if I remembered the size."

She laughed, but rose swiftly and lifted the dress from the package. Slipping it over her head, she let the white ruffles cascade about her. He reached around to lace up the back, then stepped away to admire her. The moonlight bathed her in a pale, golden glow. Her hair fell loosely and full over her shoulders in a bright red-gold haze. She looked like a vision, and his eyes told her as much.

"God, Steff," he whispered, "you're the most beautiful thing I've ever seen in my life." She smiled proudly and swished the full skirt of the dress about her.

"It's as lovely as a wedding gown," she said, happily. Then slowly she became motionless and gazed at him.

"What's the matter, Steff?"

"A wedding dress," she said quietly.

"Steff, I wish you could have had this when we got married. Maybe we should have waited." He stepped close to her and put his arms about her. "But I couldn't stand the thought of going away and maybe losing you. I'm sorry, Steff, I really am."

"I'm not talking about our wedding, my love," she said with a smile. "It was the most beautiful time of my life,

219

and I wouldn't exchange it for anything in the world."

"Then, what are you talking about?"

"Holly's wedding."

"Holly?"

"Devlin, would you be angry with me if I let Holly wear this when she and Adam get married tomorrow? They've been apart for so long, and Holly's sacrificed so much for us." She watched his face anxiously.

He pulled her gently into his arms and kissed her tenderly; then he smiled down into her questioning eyes.

"I'm so proud of you, Steff. My lady's really a great lady. Let Holly wear the dress if she wants to. She could never be as beautiful to me as you are."

He enfolded her in his arms again, and while he kissed her thoroughly, his hands loosened the laces at the back of the gown and, slipping it down off her shoulders, it fell in a white cascade at her feet. He picked her up from it and held her against him. Time drifted by them unheeded as they blended together in a sharing of love and contentment.

It was daylight when Steffany slipped quietly into Holly's room and shook her awake.

"Holly, wake up."

"Steff," Holly said sleepily, "what time is it?"

"Daylight."

"Daylight! Ohhhh," she groaned, "go away, Steff. I'm not getting up at daybreak on my wedding day."

"I've got the greatest wedding present for you that you've ever seen. But, of course, if you don't want to see . . ." She shrugged nonchalantly and pretended to leave.

"Steff, you come back here. What do you have?"

"Look, Holly," she said, and slowly lifted the dress and held it before her. Holly gasped and just sat, stunned at the sight of the lovely billowy garment.

"Where—" she began and looked closely at Steffany.

"Devlin brought this home for you, didn't he, Steff?"

Steffany nodded.

"But I want you to wear it, Holly, I really do."

"What does Devlin think?"

"He wants you to wear it also."

Suddenly Holly burst into tears. Steffany sank to the edge of the bed and took Holly in her arms. It had always been Holly who had comforted her when things went badly; now she felt contented to return the love when Holly needed her.

Adam paced the parlor in nervous tension, while all the others seemed to flutter about with things to do.

"What's the matter, Adam?" questioned Brian gaily. "Getting cold feet?"

Devlin laughed and turned to Brian. "If you stand on one side and me on the other we can hold him up."

"Yes, and keep him from running in case the urge strikes him."

"Why don't you both quiet up before I knock your heads together?"

Everyone waited patiently for Holly's appearance. A door closed, drawing all eyes upward to the stairs. Steffany descended slowly and placed herself next to Devlin. As he leaned close to her ear, he whispered, "You look like the cat that just swallowed the canary."

"Just wait, Devlin, she's so beautiful and so happy!" She squeezed his hand. "I love you."

Then all eyes were riveted to the staircase as, slowly, a radiant Holly appeared. Soft exclamations of surprise and delight came from the woman as Adam stood paralyzed. Her eyes held his as she moved to stand beside him. There were no words for him to say; his face told her everything she needed to know. Gently he took her hand, his gray eyes smiling into hers as they turned together to face the preacher.

Chapter 28

The war's end had left the South destitute. Rapidly, the wolves closed in on her. Land was bought for nothing, mostly taxes that had been raised exorbitantly by Union tax collectors. This land and houses were the best in the South. If it had not been for the money Devlin had, the Forresters, Gilcrests and Jemmisons would have lost their homes, for there was no money to be had between the three.

Adam, at one point, tried to thank Devlin, and he never tried again. Devlin turned to him, his face clouded, and said, "Adam, I know you Southerners have a great deal of pride, but is it too strong to let an outsider share it. After all, Steffany is my wife, and I consider all of you family. As part of your family, I expect to share the burden of rebuilding our home. If it can't be that way, then . . . then I guess Steffany and I will have to leave."

"Devlin, we could never consider you an outsider, and I deeply apologize if I've offended you. The last thing any of us would want is for you and Steffany to ever leave us." He grinned and held out his hand. "Am I forgiven for my lack of manners, suh?" he asked as he magnified his already slow Southern drawl.

From that day on, Devlin's money was used for seeds for planting and for repairs. With their combined efforts, for the first time in three years, there would be enough food to supply them. And the houses were made livable. Although they lacked all their past elegance, they were comfortable.

Still, a feeling of pain hung in the air. Daily, Jessica watched the road, but there was no sign of Dixon nor had they had any word from or about him.

"He's alive, Mother," Deline said positively. "I know he's alive. I feel him. I would know if he were not."

"How can you be so certain, Deline?" Holly asked.

"Don't doubt her for a moment, Holly," Adam said. "Those too have always lived inside each other's minds. It used to cause Brian and I no end of grief, believe me," he laughed.

The conversation gradually became lighter, and they launched into some earlier escapades involving Dixon and Deline, told comically by Brian.

Slow summer days eased along. The war had been over for almost three months. The men who passed Briar Hill became fewer and fewer, and finally there were days when no one passed at all. Still, Jessica watched and waited.

Steffany and Devlin had begun construction of a small house along the riverbank that Devlin claimed was his favorite spot on earth.

Deline blossomed under loving care from Bram and days of deep contentment were shared by Graham and Ann.

As for Adam and Holly, they had eyes only for one another. When their gaze met or the hands touched by chance, they would smile the knowing smile of lovers. Adam could not seem to get enough of her, seeking her out on any pretense at all for a moment to kiss her or simply to hold her close to him. Nights were spent in his arms, assuring him that he possessed all of the love of which he had dreamed when he was in his deepest despair. They had spoken of it one night, and, in a deep,

223

quiet voice he had tried to tell her how it had been. It was nearly impossible for him to use words to describe it, but she could see the pain in his eyes. Kissing him tenderly, she whispered, "Let us heal the pain for you, my darling. You're with those who love you. Let's begin now and we'll never look back again."

He drew her close to him. "You're my life, Holly. I never would have survived if it hadn't been for the memories of you and the plans I made for us." He cupped her face in his hands and looked deeply into her eyes.

"Take all my love for as long as I live, my darling wife. Let me hold to you and give you my life, for you are what my world consists of."

Filled with his gentleness, she wept until he held her, and they made love, so infinitely tender that she felt she became truly a part of his body. He seemed to absorb her as their hearts blended to one beat.

Hope began to wane for everyone except Deline, that Dixon would ever return. Brian's attempts to comfort his mother were made difficult by seeing Deline every day.

It was very early in the morning when Deline climbed up to the wagon seat. She had promised Steffany her help in putting the finishing touches to her home in preparation for moving in. They had decided to have a small party, partly for the new house and partly to try to cheer up Jessica. The baby stirred within her, and she smiled, resting her hand on the growing part of her body. Bram stood by the wagon, and their eyes met. He grinned up at her.

"Now, don't do too much. You got to take good care of my son, lady."

"Or our daughter," she chuckled.

"Why don't we compromise and make it both?" he laughed.

"Don't laugh, or I might just do that to teach you

a lesson."

"Guess you would," he chuckled. He placed his foot on the wheel and, rising up beside Deline, kissed her firmly, then dropped back down to the ground.

She slapped the reins against the horse and moved slowly down the driveway. Bram stood and watched until she was out of sight.

Brian came outside, musing at the look on Bram's face.

"Damn, you almost make me wish I were happily married."

"Almost?" said Bram, cynically.

"Well," sighed Brian, "I feel it's my patriotic duty to care for the unmarried ladies in the area since all the boys aren't home yet. After all, Bram, somebody has to do something to ease their loneliness."

"And you feel you have to keep them all happy?"

"I'm trying, Bram, believe me, I'm trying!"

They walked, laughing, together to the fields to start the day's work.

Deline rode slowly along, enjoying the warm breeze and the brightness of the summer day. She felt a deep contentment steal over her and began to muse thoughtfully over her life. Five years ago, she had been a little girl who expected so much from life, without realizing the value of the little things. She knew in that past world she would never have been married to Bram, and suddenly she felt very grateful for what she had. She must have been watching the man approach her long before it registered in her mind. She was far enough down the road that she could barely make him out. She pulled the wagon to a stop and stood up, shading her eyes with her hands.

The way he walked struck a familiar memory deep within her, and her heart began to throb. She sank back into the seat and slapped the horses into movement, never taking her eyes from the approaching figure. He walked slowly, as though he were traveling a road strange to him.

As she drew closer, the beloved figure became clear to her, but she could not understand the unfamiliar way he walked or what seemed a lack of recognition on his part, for surely he was close enough to see who she was.

Deline stopped the wagon when he was almost beside her. He approached the wagon slowly. Her heart twisted with pain as she looked down at him. Her eyes caught the empty left sleeve of the man's jacket and rested on the scar on his forehead that traced a path across the left eyebrow and ran in a slanted line to his left ear.

As he stopped, he looked up at her with a steady, silent gaze, as if his mind were straining to materialize some familiar face. Shaking his head, he said, questioningly, "Deline?"

Shaking and weak with disbelief, she almost stumbled from the wagon to get to him. He extended his arm and held her tightly as she went to him.

"Oh, Del," he choked, "I knew if I looked for you long enough I'd find you. You're the only memory I can seem to keep hold of for a few minutes at a time." His eyes were full of apprehension as he held her away from him.

"Am I home, Del? Am I really home?"

"Oh, Dixon," she sobbed, clasping his thin frame against her. "You're home, Dix. We'll care for you. We'll make you well again."

He was pale, and his eyes wandered about in fear as if he were lost in a world filled with unfamiliar people and places.

"If I could only remember," he said softly.

"Dixon, how did you manage to get this far without help? Why didn't someone tell us you were wounded?"

"I remember off and on. Every day I would wake up with everything clear in my mind, where I was going and why. But then it would just fade away, and I'd have to

226

wait for it to come back. But you, Del, there was always you. I knew if I found you I'd be back home."

The hot tears burned her eyes, and she kissed him gently. He clung to her as if he were a child.

"Come with me, Dixon, I'll take you home. Mother's been living in hell every day, waiting for you. Rest easy, Dix, we'll help you. Everything will be all right."

"Mother . . . Del, I can't . . . Oh, Del!" he sobbed, shoulders shaking with his fear. "I can't remember."

"Don't try to force it. Mother will understand. Just as long as you're home safe."

She helped him climb into the wagon, gripping her lips with her teeth to keep from crying out at his helplessness. Dixon, the person who was half of her body, always alive, filled with wit and good humor. She was almost overcome with the anguish of seeing him like this.

Slowly, the horses made a wide turn and started the wagon back toward home. Deline could see, as she watched him closely, that his eyes held a painful lack of recognition.

Brian and Bram were busy in the lower field when they saw the wagon returning. They exchanged a questioning look.

"Oh, God, the baby!" Bram exclaimed and took off at a dead run toward the road with Brian hard at his heels. When Deline saw them coming, she stopped the wagon. Bram, oblivious to her passenger, came, panting, to the side of the wagon.

"Deline, what's the matter? Are you alright?"

But Brian stopped fast in his tracks. "Dixon."

Dixon stared at him through eyes clouded in doubt. Brian was stunned at his lack of acknowledgement until a closer examination hit him with reality. Noting the empty sleeve and the scar on his face, Brian's eyes turned questioningly to Deline, who gave an almost imperceptible negative shake of her head.

"Dixon's having a little difficulty remembering a few things, Brian," she said, with a choked voice. "I told him as soon as we get him home and rested up it would all come back."

Brian moved to the wagon and climbed aboard, sitting beside Dixon.

"I'm your brother, Brian," he said softly.

"Brian . . ." The trembling began again and Dixon's eyes filled with tears. "Brian . . ."

Brian was unable to control the emotions flooding his body. He held Dixon close in his arms, making soothing sounds as he would to a baby. Tears fell unashamedly down his face as Dixon clung to him.

"Bram, go on ahead across the field to the house. Tell Mother we're bringing Dixon home."

Chapter 29

When the wagon pulled up the driveway, Jessica was standing on the front steps waiting. Bram had told her everything, but still she was shocked to see Dixon's condition. He climbed slowly down from the wagon and went to her. Her eyes misted with tears, she put out her arms to him and held him tightly against her.

"Oh, my son, my son," she murmured. "You're home!" He looked down at her, searchingly. Gently she touched the scar on his forehead, "It's alright, Dixon. From now on, you're safe. You're home."

Slowly, the clarity of recognition crept into his eyes.

"Mother," he moaned. It was a sound so filled with anguish that those around him could feel the wrenching pain possess him. "Mother, I'm home. I'm home."

She assisted him to the house and up the stairs to his room, where she bathed his face and comforted him until he fell asleep. Then, with slow, contemplating steps, she went back down to join the others.

Holly and Adam had been told and were waiting for her return.

"Mother, how is he?" questioned Adam.

"Oh, Adam, he's so hurt, so terribly hurt." She wiped the tears that were streaming down her face. "But he's alive and home. It's up to us now to help him."

Dixon slept for several hours, while the family talked together and agreed to make life about him as normal as they could.

When he awakened, Deline's was the first face he saw. She kept a vigil, sitting in the rocking chair beside his bed, watching him toss in restless slumber.

"What kind of hell are you remembering?" she thought painfully. "If I could just reach inside you, Dixon, let you know that you are not alone. You'll never be alone again." Absorbed by her own thoughts, she didn't realize he was awake until he whispered her name.

"Deline."

She rose and went to the bed. Sitting beside him, she took his hand in hers and smiled at him.

"How do you feel?"

"Hungry." He laughed shakily.

"Good. That's a marvelous sign. I'll just go get you something to eat."

"Del," he said hesitantly as she rose from the bed, his hand still clinging to hers, "you won't be long, will you?"

"No, Dix," she said quietly, "just a few minutes. Just long enough to get you something. I'll be right back, I promise."

She bent and kissed him, then left the room quickly, before he could see the tears in her eyes. "He doesn't need my pity; he needs my strength, and he'll have it," she thought, determined.

She went downstairs and prepared him a tray and carried it back to his room. His look of relief at the sight of her made her weak with pity, though nothing showed on her face. She sat down beside him and chattered away at everything she could think of while he watched her and listened contentedly for the moment.

She told him that Graham and Ann were married, knowing that inside him there was no memory of Graham

230

at all. She tried other subjects, but nothing reached the blank look in his eyes.

"You get some more rest, Dixon. I'll be back very shortly."

"You won't—"

"No, Dixon, I'll be back soon, I promise. Now you rest and get your strength back. We need you around here, and the sooner you get well the better."

She blew him a kiss and left the room, closing the door behind her. Outside his room, she leaned her head against the wall and cried.

When Dixon was strong enough, they helped him downstairs, and slowly he began to drift around the house. Some days he would sit on the porch and look about him for hours. Often, he walked from room to room, touching here and there an object from his past.

Jessica had called in the doctor, and after he had examined Dixon, he said that plenty of good food, love and rest were all her son needed. She went back to her son's room a little more at ease.

The doctor called Adam aside, and they walked together to his buggy.

"Doctor, is Dixon going to get better, or will he stay this way for the rest of his life?"

"Adam, I haven't seen too many cases of this, but for what it's worth, I want to give you my opinion."

"And that is?"

"Dixon is deliberately forgetting."

"Deliberately? Why?"

"Something he's lived through is so bad that he's blocking it away from him. In the process, other things are automatically blocked out."

"You mean like home and his family."

"I mean possibly everything that came before the incident, whatever it was."

231

"But what about Deline? He remembers her."

"Deline is something extraordinary in Dixon's life, a part of himself. You might say she's his anchor on sanity."

"What can we do? How can we reach him? Is Deline the answer?"

"No, Deline is his comfort and his haven. I may sound brutal, Adam, and I don't mean to, but you—you've got to make him remember, the pain and the suffering. You reach beyond that horror and find out what happened. Deline can never do that."

"And what if I fail?"

"You could possibly push him over the edge and never get him back."

"Christ, that's some choice."

"It's the only one you've got. I know how hard this sounds, Adam, but you've got to do it soon before he builds a wall you may never get through."

"Thank you, Doctor."

"For what, Adam? I haven't done anything but patch up the boy's outer shell. Someone stronger than me is going to have to reach in and make him whole again."

"Thank you for telling me what to do. I'll try my best. I can't stand to see him like t...s. One way or the other, I've got to at least try, for his sake."

The doctor reached out his hand, and Adam took it silently.

"Good luck, my boy," he said softly. Then he turned and climbed slowly into his buggy. Adam watched until the night swallowed up the sound of the horse's hooves. For a long time, he stood staring inwardly at his thoughts. Then, with a determined straightening of his shoulders, he reentered the house.

The next morning, he had his horse saddled early and rode into town where he collected some valuable information. He came home in time for supper. Then he called Brian aside and asked him to find Devlin and Bram and meet him in the barn. When they all arrived filled with curiosity, he began to explain what the situation was and what he was going to try to do.

Devlin spoke first. "What if it doesn't work, Adam?"

Adam's gray eyes softened to an almost blue gray.

"Then I've got to live, for the rest of my life, with the fact that I destroyed my brother. Don't you see, Devlin," he added gently, "if there's the smallest chance I can reach him, I've got to try. He deserves a better future than he has now."

They nodded in silent agreement, and each of them went back to the house.

The next morning, on one pretext or another, each one of them maneuvered the women away from the house. As the door closed behind the last of them, Adam turned to face the stairs. Then, with a straightening of his shoulders and tightened lips, he climbed the stairs to Dixon's room. Opening the door, he stepped inside. Dixon sat on the edge of the bed trying to put on his boots with one hand. Perspiration covered his brow, and he cursed mildly under his breath. He looked up when Adam came in, and the cloudy look reappeared in his eyes, as though he was trying to put a name to this tall stranger.

"Good morning, Dixon. How are you feeling this morning?"

"Quite a bit better, thank you," he said, as formally as though he were a house guest. "I think I should be up moving around."

Adam nodded and sat down in the chair opposite him.

"You could take it easy awhile longer. You've been through a lot, haven't you?" He added the last sentence quietly, watching Dixon closely.

"I—I really don't remember," Dixon replied in a

233

shaky voice. Adam noticed that his hand on the top of his boot shook slightly.

"Oh, I think you do," Adam replied gently.

Dixon looked up, startled. The brothers' eyes met and Adam's gaze held him.

"Gettysburg—early morning. Your outfit was the first across the cornfield to attack the Union forces."

"No—No, I don't remember," he said frantically. There was a flickering in his eyes. Adam could feel the force as he fought the memories that crowded toward him. The tremor that started at his fingers went up his arm. There was stark fear on his face as he stared across at his brother.

"I don't know where I was or where I got wounded. I don't remember."

Adam stood up and looked coldly at him. What he wanted was to hold him and tell him not to worry, it didn't matter. But it did. He wanted Dixon to have his life back, and if he had to hurt him to do it, he would.

"You remember. Are you a coward, Dixon? I don't think so. You were there, you saw your friends die there. You almost died there yourself. They left you wounded on that field for hours, didn't they? You heard them all around you, crying, moaning, dying. You prayed to die, didn't you?"

Dixon whimpered, "Deline, where's Deline? I've got to get back to Deline."

"Deline can't help you, Dixon," Adam said brutally. "Only you can help yourself."

"I can't," he was crying now. "I can't remember."

"You don't want to remember!" Adam shouted.

"Go away, Adam, go away!"

Adam felt his first hint of success. He had called him by name! Dixon knew exactly who he was fighting.

"No, Dixon, I'll not go away. I'll remind you over and

234

over. I know the pain, Dixon, I felt it, too. Don't be ashamed of being afraid. We were all afraid, and some never went through what you did. You lay on that field, bleeding your life away while your friends died around you."

"No!" Dixon panted through the dry sobs. "I don't know what you're talking about. I can't remember."

"You can, and you will."

"Let me alone!" Dixon screamed at him, backing away until he was against the wall.

"So you can crawl back in that black hole you live in? No, brother. Come out of there; come out into the light where you can live again. You're not a coward, Dixon . . . or are you?"

"Adam, please," he begged, his eyes wide with fear. "Please leave me alone. I can't—"

"Coward!"

"No, no!"

"Coward, you're a coward! Did you run away that day, too, Dixon? Did you run and find a hole to crawl in like you are now?"

Dixon's eyes flashed, his body trembling with violent anger.

"No! No! No! No! I fought! It was useless. Sending us across that field with no protection. They sat up on that hill and picked us off one by one!" He was sobbing, but glaring at Adam furiously. "When I got shot I just laid there for a while, bleeding. I called for help, but nobody came. I watched. I watched them all die. Steve Miller got his legs shot off. He laid there and cried until he died. There was blood, blood all over that field!"

He leaned his head back against the wall and cried out loudly, his eyes squeezed shut, his face bathed in tears and sweat. "I couldn't stand it, Adam, I couldn't. Boys I knew, friends I'd slept with, ate with, lying in pools of

235

blood, crying their lives away. And then when it was over, I was hoping someone would come for me. I could feel the blood soaking my clothes, but no one came, Adam, no one came. Hours went by. I was afraid, so afraid, Adam. They were going to leave me to die there. When daylight came, they finally found me and took me to the hospital." Here, his voice became silent. His eyes saw a distant horror no one could share with him.

"At the hospital," he said very quickly, "the doctor said, 'I'm sorry, boy, that arm has to come off.'" The cry of pain was ripped from Dixon as he relived the violence. "There was no morphine, Adam—nothing." Here he laughed a dry humorless laugh. "Not even any whiskey. They held me down, Adam. Held me on that table while they sawed off my arm. Oh, God, I begged. I begged. Don't, don't! Let me die! But they didn't listen. They didn't listen."

Adam could feel the hot sting of tears in his eyes as he watched his brother writhe in a torment he was unable to do anything about.

"For days I lay there. No one came; no one cared. I prayed to die. I prayed over and over, but not even God was listening. Then one day I woke up, and the pain was gone. I couldn't remember how I'd gotten there or how I'd lost my arm. Funny, all I could remember was Deline. I needed to come home. Part of me was somewhere, and I had to find it. I had to find it." He began to cry, as a hurt child cries, and Adam went to him, holding him closely.

"You are home, Dixon. There will be no more pain." He eased Dixon down on the bed and began to talk to him. Finally Dixon slept, but it was a resting sleep.

Adam left the room, drained of all his energy, but proud of the strength of the boy who had become a man. He felt as though he had fought himself. But he also felt contented. Dixon was finally home.

Chapter 30

Everyone was seated about the table at suppertime, but no one even showed a pretense of having an appetite. Occasionally one or the other would watch the door, hoping that Dixon would come down but afraid of how he would be when he did.

Adam was more frightened than anyone. Would Dixon be able to survive what he'd just been through or would he slip back to what he had been? If he did, Adam knew there would be no way of his making contact again. The first time he had caught Dixon unprepared and vulnerable. He would not catch him that way again.

A door closed upstairs, startling everyone, and slow footsteps came down the stairs. Then Dixon stood in the doorway. He stood taller than ever before, his back straight. There were lines etched in his face that told of suffering. And the scar on his head was prominent, but his eyes held a peace they had not had for a long time. Deline was the first to recognize this and rose from her chair with a smile to cover the tears of happiness.

"Welcome home, Dixon," she said softly, and went to him. He held her against him with his face against her hair.

Jessica sobbed and, pushing back her chair, ran to her son's side.

"Mother," he laughed shakily. "It's impossible to hold

two beautiful ladies with one arm. You'll just have to take turns!"

Brian gave a shout of pure joy and slapped Adam so hard on the back he began to choke.

Suddenly everyone was laughing. Dixon was thoroughly kissed by the women and pummeled by the men until he shouted for help.

"First you starve me to death; then you try to beat me to death."

Amid the pleasure and the laughter, Dixon closed the link and brought the family together again!

Late that night when he thought everyone else was asleep, Adam slipped from the house. He stood on the porch for a few minutes, then slowly walked down the steps. The night was clear. Millions of diamond-bright stars lay against the black-velvet sky. He stared up at the heavens.

"In case no one has thought of it," he said half aloud, "I want to thank you for giving Dixon back to us. I know without your help we never would have made it, and thank you for letting me be the instrument."

"Adam."

Adam turned about to see Dixon standing on the porch.

"Who are you talking to?"

"Just thanking the proper party," Adam laughed.

Dixon looked up. "Yeah, me, too." He sighed and sat down on the top stair. Adam came and sat beside him. They did not speak for quite some time.

"Everything's the same, and yet everything's changed," Dixon said quietly. "Where do we go from here, Adam?"

Adam contemplated his question. "Well, Dixon, we're all here. We've all survived. That's a lot to be grateful for. I guess we all pull together and put the pieces of our lives back together as best we can."

"I didn't say it would be easy. I rode over to see Charles Gordon at River's End a few days ago. Since Martha died, he's like a ghost. Both his boys were killed at Manassas. The house is empty, and so is he. So you see, Dixon, you've got a lot to give. Just the happiness of having you here has changed things for Mother and Deline. Give what you can, Dixon. Look inside yourself, and you'll find a strong man who doesn't need anything to lean on, who has a lot to contribute to those around him."

"Are you sure, Adam?" he asked softly.

Adam turned to him and smiled. "I'm sure, Dixon. I'm sure."

They sat together for a while longer, enjoying the peace and quiet. For the first time in a long time, Dixon felt full contentment and the happiness of coming home.

The days were warm and filled with the small pleasures that made up their lives now, things like the first successful field of cotton they were able to produce, having food stored from a good harvest and finally when Deline went into labor with her child.

Bram carried Deline upstairs to the bedroom and was quickly pushed out by Jessica and Merilee.

The men had been working in the fields, and Deline had carried them some water. Although she had not felt well since the morning, she had said nothing. Now as she lifted the dipper toward Bram the sudden pain caught her in the middle of the back. She gasped and dropped the dipper, staring wide eyed at Bram, who stood frozen.

"Deline?" he asked. "The baby?"

She nodded, placing her hand against her body. Then she smiled at him. "I think I'd better get back to the house. Bram, your daughter is calling for attention."

He laughed nervously and, reaching out, lifted her gently in his arms, kissing her lightly on the lips.

"My son, you mean?"

239

"I told you," she giggled, laying her head against his shoulder and wrapping her arms about his neck, "be careful or I'll have two just to spite you."

He hugged her against him as he walked. "Just take care of you, Del. It would be a damn hard world without you. I don't think I could manage it alone."

She sighed contentedly, remembering how long ago it was that he'd first carried her this way. Another spasm of pain struck, and she clenched his neck tightly. He could feel the hard contraction of her body against him and the child that stirred within. When he reached the house, he kicked the kitchen door and it was thrown open by Merilee.

"Bram, what?"

"Send for the doctor," he said as he passed her. "The baby's coming."

Merilee sent someone for the doctor, then called Jessica. They went to the bedroom where Bram had laid Deline gently on the bed. He was sitting beside her, holding her hands, kissing her fingers gently and watching her with a worried frown.

"Bram," Deline laughed. "I'm not the first girl to have a baby. I'm strong and healthy. I'll be just fine."

"You're the first one to have my baby," he said gruffly, "and I'll worry about you if I please."

"Well, you'll worry downstairs, Bram," said Jessica firmly. "You can't do anything here except get in our way."

"I'm staying right here," he answered determinedly.

Jessica gave an exasperated look at Merilee, who smiled.

"Bram, you could help us."

"What? What can I do?" he asked anxiously.

"Go downstairs and gather what blankets you can find; get some wood for the stove, and set some water to boil."

He nodded and, with a last parting look at Deline, turned and left the room.

"What did you need all that stuff for?" asked Jessica.

"To keep him busy, of course," laughed Merilee.

"Now close the door and lock it, then find some string and a pair of scissors. We're going to deliver us a nice healthy baby," she smiled down at Deline.

"You rest, honey. Sometimes the first one takes a little time."

Jessica bathed Deline's face and braided her long hair. Then she removed her clothes and covered her with a sheet.

Bram was downstairs busily moving about when the truth hit him. He laughed aloud, then stopped what he was doing and went into the parlor to join Adam and Brian, who'd been called in from their work.

Adam was pouring himself a drink but, after taking one look at Bram, he handed him the drink instead.

"Boy, did you ever feel so damn useless in your life?" Bram said.

Brian chuckled. "What happened, Bram?"

"I just got thrown out of my own bedroom. My baby's being born, and I get tossed aside like an old shoe."

"Maybe you'd just be in the way, Bram." Adam grinned as he poured himself another drink.

"Yeah, maybe."

The three of them sat without speaking for a time, then, Bram rose and walked to the bottom of the steps as though he were contemplating going up. He turned and walked to the window where he stood looking out as a muffled cry from upstairs made him start, and he turned around. As the hours passed, he was first patient, then nervous, which deteriorated rapidly until after almost six hours he was pacing the floor. He flung himself into a chair only to rise again in a few minutes and pace some more.

241

"Why is it taking so long? Do you think something's gone wrong? She's awfully little."

"Don't worry, Bram," said Adam. "I'm sure everything's all right. These things take a lot of time."

Bram muttered something incoherent under his breath and sat back down. He put his elbows on his knees and cupped his chin in his hands and stared morosely at the stairway.

Slowly, the clock in the hallway ticked away the minutes which turned into hours. Bram was beside himself with fear.

"Nine hours! Adam, something's wrong. I know it is. I'm going up there."

Before they could stop him, he was mounting the stairs two at a time with them right behind him. When he arrived at the door and was about to push it open, the knob turned and Merilee stepped out. She smiled tiredly at Bram's anxious face.

"Bram, she's doing beautifully, and the reason it took so long is . . . well, we had a little difficulty handling two at a time."

"Two at a—"

"Yes, Bram, twins. A boy and a girl. Beautiful children."

"And Deline? Is she all right?"

"She's fine. I don't know if she's asleep yet. She's been waiting for me to get you. Said something about having the last laugh. What did she mean, Bram?"

Bram chuckled to himself but did not answer her. Instead, he moved past her and slipped into the room, closing the door behind him. Jessica stood over the crib, and he went over to her. He looked down at the tiny features of his son and daughter in awe. They looked so much alike.

"Congratulations, Bram. They're beautiful," Jessica said. She kissed him on the cheek and left the room.

He turned to the bed and, walking over, looked down at Deline. He thought she was asleep and bent down slowly to kiss her.

"I told you what I'd do if you got too sassy, didn't I?" she whispered.

"I'll never get sassy again, lady. You scared the hell out of me, and you sure took your sweet time doing it, too."

She was too tired to laugh, so she just smiled up at him as he sat beside her and lifted her hand to his lips, kissing it tenderly. Then slowly her eyes closed in contented sleep.

He continued to look at her; then gently, he brushed some hair from her forehead and caressed the side of her face with his hand.

"I love you, lady," he whispered. "I'll love you till the day I die."

Chapter 31

Jessica ripped open the letter that had just arrived. She read the pages swiftly:

Dear Wife,

I hope this letter finds you well. We will be starting for home soon, now that the conflict is finally over and we have seen to the final details of reuniting our country. I feel only the urgent need to see you again, my love.

I have heard no news about the boys. I pray to God they're safe and find their way home.

This letter must be short, my dear, as the carrier is waiting. Expect me in about three weeks.

Your loving husband,
Matthew Gilcrest

She felt a peace of mind she had not felt since this horrible conflict began. For the first time in four years, her family would be whole again. She thought of Richard and Merilee. Richard had become worse and worse as the time went by. He refused to let any of them visit him at Cross Oaks but sat there nursing the hatred for those whom he thought had destroyed his life. After a while, the hate began to center on one person. Bram. When he had heard from Deline about the death of the soldier at Briar Hill, he watched until he figured out how and when Bram had disposed of the body. Then, steathily, one night he had gone and dug up the remains of the body, taking the identification from it and carefully reburying it. Then he waited and watched for the time when he would strike them down. ·

The arrival of Matthew Gilcrest was what he waited for. He wanted to hurt every one of them at the same time.

When Matthew arrived, he was warmly received, and Jessica decided then to have their first party since the war began. The excitement caught hold, and everyone poured all their enthusiasm into it.

Gone were the crystal chandeliers and lace tablecloths. Gone were the beautiful ball gowns and sparkling jewels. In their place rose the strength of a people reunited after a holocaust that had threatened to destroy them.

The table was covered with a plain cotton tablecloth. The women wore their faded cotton dresses, but the laughter was warm and friendly.

Brian had brought a girl he had met in town. She was very pretty and instigated immediately a laughing competition between him and Dixon. The friendly rivalry went on all evening to the delight of everyone. Even Brian was secretly filled with elation at Dixon's reaction.

Brian watched from the edge of the floor as Dixon swung Amanda about the floor in a slow waltz.

"Amanda, you sure are the prettiest girl in this room," he said, his eyes on her. With his one arm tight about her, she rested both her hands on his shoulders. It brought her closer to him than it would have normally. A situation of which Dixon took full advantage.

She blushed but smiled. "And you, sir, are the most

charming liar I've ever met."

"I, Madam? Never! I am a connoisseur of beauty."

"I'll bet," she laughed. "I've heard quite a bit about you, Dixon Gilcrest."

"All lies, I assure you," he grinned.

"Oh, really?" She tipped her head to one side and looked mischievously up at him. "And I heard you were such a wonderfully sincere person. But if it's all lies—"

He laughed aloud. "Trapped by my own mouth, as usual!"

She laughed with him, and he pulled her a little closer as they whirled around.

Brian and Adam stood sipping a drink with Matthew, as they watched the two young people.

"God, it's good to hear Dixon laugh again," Brian said softly.

Matthew had been told about Dixon and watched his son as he smiled down at the girl in his arms. "It's good just to know you boys are here, whole and safe again."

He turned and raised his glass with a wide smile. "Let's have a toast. To Briar Hill and all the family that lives here. May they live in peace and harmony from this day on."

"Amen," Adam replied quietly as they touched their glasses together.

The party increased in gaiety as Brian and Dixon competed for Amanda's attention and the others danced, laughed, ate, and completely enjoyed themselves.

Charles Gordon had been invited, and, to everyone's surprise, except Merilee's, he accepted.

He and Merilee were dancing together.

"You're as lovely as ever, Merilee. Time simply stands still for you."

"Thank you," she said softly, but her eyes were down and would not meet his.

"Have you been happy, Merilee, over the years since—"

"Don't Charles. Old wounds should never be reopened. What's past is past."

Charles was still a very handsome man. He was forty-five years old. The dark, wavy hair was lightly tinged with gray, and his hazel eyes looked tired. The grief he had felt in the past four years showed plainly in them.

"I want to talk to you Merilee, just for a minute . . . please?"

"All right, Charles." They walked from the floor to a corner of the room.

"Merilee . . ." he began, hesitantly. "You know I would never do anything in the world to hurt you . . . but . . ."

"But what, Charles?" she asked inquisitively.

"Both my sons are dead, Merilee. My wife never knew I didn't love her. Over the years I tried to make her life as good as possible."

"What are you trying to tell me, Charles?"

"I have all this property and no sons to leave it to," he said, a faint tinge of pain in his voice. "If my boys had come back, I would have let the past die, Merilee."

"Charles—" she began.

"I have to know, Merilee," he whispered desperately, "I have to know and only you can give me the answer."

"No!"

"Merilee, please. I want to leave my property to someone, someone of my own blood."

Merilee shook her head, her eyes filled with torment.

"You know I've always loved you, Merilee. We should never have let what happened between us come about. Why did you marry Richard? Why didn't you wait for me to come home?"

"What's the point of all this, Charles?" she said quietly. "There's nothing we can do about any of this."

He looked steadily at her. "Graham is my son, isn't he, Merilee?" he asked, his voice gentle and filled with love.

Her lips trembled, but she gathered control of herself. Lifting her eyes to meet his pleading ones, she listened.

"Please, Merilee, just tell me. I will never let anyone else know, no matter how badly I want to. I've felt it over the years. I knew the way Richard treated him, but I felt you knew what was best. I loved the boy, Merilee. When he would come to our home to share time with my boys, there was an attraction between us. I never said a word, for I thought it was what you wanted. You never gave me the reason for not waiting for me. You never told me you were pregnant with Graham before I left. Do you think I would have gone away and left you to face that alone?

"I accepted everything you wanted for I loved you then, as I love you now. But time is passing us by, Merilee. I want to give Graham something for all the years I missed out on. I want my own son to inherit River's End."

Merilee sighed deeply and placed her hand on Charles' chest as her clouded eyes looked into his. "Yes, Charles, Graham is your son," she said softly. He expelled the breath he had been holding as he awaited her answer.

"Merilee, leave Richard. Come to River's End with me. We could be happy. We could share these last years, make them the best years of our lives."

"I can't do that, Charles. Why should I do anything to harm Graham? He's so happy with Ann. I don't want to stir up old pain and make him pay the price."

"What about us, Merilee? Don't we deserve some happiness, too? After all the pain and wasted years, don't

248

we deserve something?"

"Life has taken a certain toll on everyone," she answered slowly. "Graham is happy. No matter what it costs, I'll not do anything to jeopardize that. As for Richard, I will never go back to Cross Oaks again, and he knows that."

"And us?" he said quietly, but he knew the answer before she spoke.

"There is nothing left for us, Charles, but to make the best of the lives we've got."

"I'll never give up hope, Merilee. If anything ever happens and you need me, remember I'm here, and I love you. I'm going to name Graham in my will. I'll never tell him why, but I want him to have River's End. It will help keep him away from Richard and give him something of his own!"

She nodded her head sadly and moved away slowly. He watched her walk across the room, her head held proudly. If only she hadn't always been so proud, he thought bitterly. They could have been together, and Graham could have been his son for all the world to know. He had been a hellion when he and Merilee had first met and fell violently in love. Their parents had felt he would never amount to anything and forced him to take a tour about the world, trying to get the wildness out of his system. When Merilee found she was pregnant, she had panicked and agreed to marry Richard Forrester, because she felt that maybe Charles would not come home. And if he did, he might be changed. He had cursed his young foolishness a million times since then as he watched Merilee turn into a lovely woman and Graham into the tall, handsome son he'd always wanted. He allowed the despair to wash over him for a moment before he got control of himself. He was going to leave the party and started across the room to the door. Because he was watching the door, he was the first to see Richard Forrester enter, accompanied by two men.

They stood looking over the room full of merrymakers. The gloating look on Richard's face sent a chill through Charles, for he, too, knew what had become of him.

Slowly, as the people spotted them, they stopped dancing, and finally every eye in the room was on Richard. The music died and everything was quiet while a heavy feeling of disaster hung in the air.

Finally, Jessica came forward.

"Richard, gentlemen, what can we do for you? Would you care to join the party?"

The constable was nervous and very upset. Richard was unshaven and tousled. He turned to the constable and, in an angry voice, snarled, "Do your duty. Arrest that man!"

There was an instinctive tightening in Bram's stomach, for he surmised that the problem was directed at him.

The constable cleared his throat and, in an embarrassed voice, said, "Bram, I have to arrest you for the murder of Carl Brenner, a soldier in the Confederacy."

There was a loud gasp that echoed throughout the room and a soft sound from Deline, who moved rapidly to Bram's side.

"This is ridiculous, Constable," Matthew said firmly. "Bram couldn't murder anybody."

The constable removed from his jacket the identifying papers. "These here papers belonged to Carl Brenner. My men are outside by your barn right now diggin' up the body," he said wearily.

Graham had come to Bram's side and put his hand on Bram's shoulder. He smiled grimly at the constable, "I'm afraid you have the wrong man, Constable. You see, it was me that killed Carl Brenner!"

Chapter 32

Richard jerked, as though someone had struck him and said, "That's impossible, Deline told me—" He glared wildly at the group of people clustered in front of him.

"What are you all trying to pull? Bram murdered him. Deline said so."

Matthew grinned. "Well, Constable, until we get this cleared up, I'll vouch for Bram. He'll stay here with us, and we'll get to the bottom of this."

The constable nodded with relief. "Mr. Gilcrest, I'll expect you in my office with Bram tomorrow."

"We'll be there, sir, along with my lawyer. We'll defend Bram," saying the last words with a cold look at Richard.

The constable nodded and turned to leave.

"Where are you going? You arrest that man! Put him in jail where his kind belong!" Richard shouted.

The constable had taken just about all that he could from Richard. He had not liked the man's attitude to begin with, and he knew and respected the word of Matthew Gilcrest.

"Mr. Forrester," he said, exasperated. "If Mr. Gilcrest says he'll bring Bram in the morning, I believe him."

The constable turned away with a last disgusted look at Richard and left the house. Now the group watched Richard. Slowly, the man deteriorated in front of their eyes. Wild eyed and close to madness, he ripped a gun from beneath his coat.

The group of onlookers held their breath.

"Step away from them, you," he snarled at Bram as he waved the gun at him.

"Richard!" Matthew began.

"Shut up! Bram, move away from them."

Slowly Bram stepped out of the crowd, his eye on the weapon in Richard's shaking hand.

"I'm going to kill you, Bram," he whispered hoarsely.

"Richard!"

Merilee came warily across the floor until she was about four or five paces from Bram.

"Stop there, Merilee, don't go near him."

"Richard, you're sick. Let me take you home," she said, inching her way a little closer to Bram.

"I said stop, Merilee." His voice sounded frozen. She knew he meant what he said. "Don't do anything stupid, Richard. Believe me, you will regret it."

"Always threatening me, Merilee. Well, this time it won't do you any good. I'm going to kill him, and you and Graham are coming home with me. Things will be like they were before."

"Things can never be like they were before, Richard. There's no way to turn back time. I wish there were."

Richard was shaking his head negatively, trying not to hear her voice. "No, I'm going to kill him and take you and Graham home," he smiled, chilling her to the heart, for she knew he was completely mad and intended to do exactly what he said. She became desperate.

"You can't kill him, Richard," she said softly.

"Can't?" he chuckled, with a harsh, rasping sound.

"But I can. I can," he said and raised the gun, pointing it straight at Bram.

"No, you can't. You see, Richard, he's your son."

The barrel of the gun gave a small jerk, but remained

aimed at Bram, who had turned with the others, to face Merilee.

"You lie!" Richard grated.

"No, he's Jennie's son. You remember Jennie, my half sister. Pretty Jennie, who died giving birth to Bram. Died of a broken heart because of your lies. He's Jennie's son, Richard, and yours."

Richard glared at her with a hatred that could be felt by everyone in the room. He looked indecisive for a minute, watching his eyes freeze into an insane glare. The gun lifted again toward Bram's heart, and she knew this time he meant to shoot. A small cry came from her, and she threw herself between them just as Richard fired. She felt the heavy blow as the bullet struck, and a bright red stain flooded her dress just under her left breast. Bram caught her as she fell. A cry of rage left Graham as Richard turned and ran from the room, with Graham and Adam right after him.

Richard slammed through the front door and ran across the yard toward the barn with an enraged Graham behind him. At the barn, he pushed through the door and locked it behind him, feeling the weight of Graham's body against it as he pushed the lock home.

Years of pent-up hatred bubbled up in Graham as he pounded his shoulder against the door. He felt it begin to give under the force and, just as the wood splintered, another shot rang out.

When Graham and Adam finally broke through the door, Richard Forrester lay in a spreading pool of blood. He had put the barrel of the gun into his mouth and pulled the trigger.

Graham took only one look at the man he had known as his father for so many years, then turned and left the barn. They ran back across the yard and into the house.

Bram had lifted Merilee in his arms and taken her to her bedroom, placing her gently on the bed. Her eyes were closed, and her face was drained of its color; the front of her dress was soaked with blood.

"Mother," Graham whispered as he sat beside her and lifted a cool hand in his. "Someone get a doctor."

"We've already sent for a doctor, Graham," Holly said quietly.

Ann came to stand by Graham's shoulder, and Charles stood directly behind her, his face gray with fear.

Slowly, her eyes fluttered open, and she tried weakly to smile at Graham.

"Bram?" she questioned softly.

"I'm all right, Merilee," he said.

"Richard?"

"He's dead. He shot himself. If he hadn't, I would have. I would have killed my own father just like a mad dog."

Charles and Merilee's eyes met above Graham's head, and she knew now that Graham must be told the truth.

"Oh, Graham," she let the tears slip down her cheeks, "he was not your father."

He looked at her, knowing deep inside somewhere that she spoke the truth and that maybe he had even felt it many years before.

"Not my father?"

"No, Graham. Your father is Charles Gordon."

All eyes turned to Charles, who watched Merilee with a look so filled with love her words could not be doubted.

Graham turned back to Merilee. "Don't talk now, Mother," he said gently stroking her hand, "Wait till the doctor comes. When you're well we can talk about it."

She shook her head. "I've got to tell you now, Graham, in case—I've got to tell you now."

"My father had an affair with an octoroon woman after my mother died. He loved her very much, and when she gave birth to a daughter, the baby, Jennie, was brought to live with us and was raised as my sister. We loved each

254

other. After Charles had been sent away and I found I was pregnant with you, Graham, I agreed to marry Richard. I didn't know that Richard had already seduced Jennie. She adored him, but he used her and discarded her. When she died giving birth to Bram, I allowed him to be kept and raised as a slave even though he was less than an eighth black. She told me on her deathbed. No one knew but me, and I made sure Bram received every bit of help I could give him."

Bram realized now that his being educated with Graham was not an accident, nor the way he had been treated by everyone except Richard. Although he tried to control it, when he looked at Charles Gordon and the woman in bed, he felt a deep hatred for the man who had sired him.

Merilee saw the look on his face.

"Don't Bram. Don't let the hatred control you. Look what it did to Richard. You have all the things that matter in life. Don't let hatred take it away from you."

Bram realized how true her words were when he felt Deline's hand slip into his and her head against his shoulder. He smiled at Merilee and gave her a small nod of agreement.

"Where the hell is that doctor?" Graham said, his voice heavy with concern, for Merilee's eyes had closed and her hand lay limp in his.

Finally the doctor arrived and everyone, except Jessica, were made to leave the room. They gathered together in the parlor. The strained silence remained unbroken. Each person enclosed in his own thoughts. Devlin and Steffany tried to console Graham, who sat in dejected silence. Holly and Adam stood together in one corner of the room.

"Oh, Adam, what if she dies?" Holly whispered.

"We have to pray she doesn't," he answered quietly.

Ann sat close, holding Graham's hand while Bram and

255

Deline, gray-faced, prayed silently.

The clock ticked away the minutes slowly. It was the only sound in the room.

Charles stood looking out the window, seeing nothing but the face of a woman he had loved for most of his life.

Graham rose and went to stand beside him.

"Did you know?" he asked.

"I suspected, I hoped, but I didn't know for sure."

"You and Mother loved each other very much?"

"Yes, Graham. If—If everything is all right I want your mother to marry me." He turned to Graham, and his eyes were clear and proud. "We deserve some happiness, too. We've spent a lifetime apart so that others could be happy. Now, if God is willing, I intend to make her as happy as I can for the balance of our lives."

Graham looked at him, reading his soul through the clear mirror of his eyes. Then he extended his hand.

"You have my blessing . . . Father."

Charles ignored the hand and stepped closer to embrace the son he had never been able to acknowledge.

The time dragged slowly until fear silenced any conversation. Then the footsteps brought them all to the doorway.

The doctor entered the room, his face unrevealing.

"Doctor?" Graham asked apprehensively.

"She's going to be all right, Graham. It was touch and go there for a while, but she's going to make it."

Graham breathed a sigh of relief and pulled Ann close to him as his eyes filled with grateful tears.

"You can go up to see her, Graham, if you like."

Graham turned to Charles and smiled. "No, I think there's someone else who should see her first."

"Thank you, Graham," said Charles softly. Then he turned and walked up the stairs to Merilee.

Chapter 33

Bram stopped the seeding he was doing and watched Deline walk across the field toward him. She was wearing a blue gingham dress and a bonnet tied under her chin to protect her from the heat of the early afternoon sun. Walking, she swung the bucket of water she was carrying slowly back and forth to match her steps. She smiled when she saw that his attention was on her.

"You look so hot, Bram. I've brought you some cool water."

He took off his wide-brimmed straw hat and wiped his forehead with the sleeve of his shirt.

"You're right, I'm boilin'." Taking the dipper from the pail he drank deeply, then dipping it back and refilling it, he poured it over his head. Shaking the drops free, he laughed. "That feels so good. Wouldn't it be nice to go for a swim in the river?"

"Mmm, that would feel so good," she said looking toward the river. When she looked back at him, her mouth turned up at the corners in a suppressed smile as she saw the wicked gleam in his eye.

"Where's Jennie and Jeremy?"

"Jessica took them with her. Merilee and Charles are moving back home today."

"Well," he grinned, "Looks like we're all alone."

Deline couldn't resist the infectious grin and the look

of warm wanting that brightened his eyes when he looked at her. She set the bucket down, took the hand he held out to her, and they walked toward the river.

Once at the river, Bram enjoyed watching Deline remove her clothes. Then he hastily removed his. The river water was cool to their overheated bodies, and they swam and played in the river like two children until Deline claimed she was tired. Climbing out of the water, she stood on the bank and smiled down at him.

"You look like the river goddess," he grinned.

"Well, come mortal, lie beside me," she laughed. He did not hesitate to climb from the water, and they lay side by side together in the tall grass.

"Oh, Bram, it is so peaceful and beautiful here. I hate to leave it."

"Deline, we don't have to leave it."

"But you said we'd have to go away for fear anyone should find out about us."

"I've been thinkin' on that. Things have changed a lot around here. All of the people who know about us are family. Since Graham gave me his last name and Cross Oaks, there's no one who knows that neither the name or the place are rightfully mine. To everyone, I'm Abraham Forrester, master of Cross Oaks, and you're my wife. I'm thinkin' we'll stay and bluff the world."

"What if someone should come back who knew you before the war, who knew you were a slave?"

"It would be their word against the Forrester and Gilcrest families."

He watched as her eyes shone with happiness.

"Then everything in the world is perfect. I've got you and the children and the home I love."

"Yes, I guess we have everything thanks to Devlin O'Brien. If it hadn't been for his money payin' the taxes and buying the seed and equipment, we would all have been homeless a long time ago."

"We'll pay him back someday. Wait until we get a good crop, one we can sell."

"Yes, the way those Northerners are movin' down here, I guess they'll be people to sell to. But it kind of upsets me to do it. The way they bring their money down here and buy off the best property for practically nothin'. Why, you know McAfferty's place?"

"Yes, the big beautiful place along the river?"

"Well, some uppity carpetbagger came in and bought the place just for back taxes, and then he had the nerve to offer McAfferty a small piece of land and tell him he could sharecrop it, sharecrop it! Can you imagine?"

"What did McAfferty do?"

"What choice did he have? No place to go and a family? He couldn't let them starve to death, so he took the offer. Farmin' a small piece of land that should be his and then givin' that thief half the profits, it's unbelievable, but it's happening all over the South. We're the luckiest people in the world to have some one like Devlin in the family. His federal money buys things."

"Do you know who he is?"

"Who? The man who took over McAfferty's property? No, and I don't want to know him. I know his kind, and that's enough for me; besides," he said as he rolled on his side and slipped his arm about her, rubbing his fingers up and down the smooth curves of her back, "I find it a lot better keepin' to myself. I've got too much here to enjoy without sharin' it with anyone."

Deline smiled a slow half smile that always intrigued him and put her arms about his neck.

"You're right, Bram," she said, as she pulled his lips to her warm waiting ones. "I would never share you with anyone."

She could hear the chuckle as he pulled her into his arms, and gently claimed her body in the same magical way he had done so often before.

It was over two hours later that Bram picked up the discarded seed bag and he and Deline walked slowly toward home. They walked across the fields hand in hand. Ahead of them loomed Cross Oaks. The large haven had not been damaged during the war, because Union soldiers had been stationed there. The house stood tall and proud. Bram looked at it and was overwhelmed by emotion he could never explain. Having spent the first twenty years of his life as a slave, not owning anything, not even knowing his parents, Bram still found it hard to think of himself as a free man and owning property like Cross Oaks.

They approached the house from the back, walking through the area that was now empty slave cabins. Bram went to the barn to take care of the early evening chores, and Deline continued into the cool kitchen. At the stove making preparations for supper stood Felicia. No matter what the world situation had become, Felicia had stood solid and unmovable. She had practically raised Deline, and she intended to stay with her as long as she had life in her body.

"My, my," she exclaimed knowingly. "For such a hot day you sure look nice and cool."

Deline grinned at her, as she dipped the spoon to taste the stew Felicia was cooking.

"Mind your own business, Felicia."

Felicia chuckled.

"When they bringing them babies home? It'll soon be gettin' on their bedtime. You know you puts them to bed past their bedtime they get fretful."

"They'll be home soon, Felicia. You know Mother and Merilee will take good care of them."

Before Felicia could speak again, the sound of wagon wheels could be heard in the front drive.

"I imagine that's them now."

Deline left the kitchen and walked to the front door.

260

Opening it, she stepped out onto the porch. Expecting the wagon carrying her mother and her children, Deline was surprised to find a buggy with just one occupant. For a minute, she did not recognize who it was. Then she remembered the girl Brian had brought to the party, Amanda Merriweather. She recalled at the same time that Dixon had been seeing a great deal of her since then. Amanda smiled shyly at Deline.

"Deline, I know it's almost suppertime, but could you spare me a few minutes? I would like to talk to you."

"Of course, Amanda. Please come inside."

As Amanda climbed down from her buggy, Bram came out on the porch and stood by Deline. He cast her a quck questioning look, but Deline only shrugged and mouthed the words silently, "I don't know." Bram greeted Amanda; then, knowing she wanted a private conversation with Deline, he made his excuses and left them alone.

"Maybe you'd like to sit out here on the porch, Amada? I could have Felicia fix us a cool drink."

"Thank you, Deline, that would be fine."

When Deline had returned from the kitchen, she paused at the doorway for a minute and watched Amanda's face. The girl was looking out across the lawn, but it was obvious to Deline that her mind was far away.

"Well!" she said brightly as she joined Amanda. "Felicia will bring us something in a few minutes."

She sat down on the chair next to Amanda and waited quietly for her to tell Deline whatever it was she came to say.

Still, Amanda remained silent until Felicia had served them cool drinks and then returned to her kitchen. Amanda sipped her drink absently. Deline watched her over the rim of her glass and wondered what could trouble her so deeply that she couldn't find the words to tell her. Somehow she knew instinctively that what-

261

ever she was going to say had something to do with Dixon, and she was prepared, as always, to defend him in whatever way was necessary.

"How is your family, Amanda?" Deline said in an effort to make it easier for Amanda to relax.

"Oh, we're doing quite well now. Father misses the plantation very much. It almost broke his heart when the Yankees burnt it, but maybe it was for the best. The store he started in town is doing well, and the house is quite comfortable."

"I'm happy for you. I guess it's time we all started picking up the pieces and learning to make do with less than we had before."

Amanda nodded.

"Deline, you know that the McAfferty place was sold for taxes."

Deline nodded. Now they were finally getting to the reason for Amanda's visit.

"Did you know that the new owner has cut the property into small pieces and is letting them be sharecropped?"

Again Deline nodded. She could not see what any of this had to do with her family or Amanda.

"Well, across the river from these small farms has sprung up a group of shanties and is housing some of the laziest, dirtiest scum of the earth. No one has been able to stop them from building on this land, for they have the money from somewhere to pay the taxes on it."

"I don't understand what this has to do with any of us. We're far enough away that they can't cause much trouble, and we have enough men to protect us."

"I thought the same until recently. They have begun preying on the small farmers and their families. They pillage their farms and terrify their wives and children. Someone is leading them and supplying them with money and weapons."

"Can't anyone find out who it is and why he's doing such a thing?"

Amanda gave a negative shake of her head.

"The situation is getting progressively worse. The last place they attacked was Monroe's farm. He tried to protect his crop and his family. They shot him, and they attacked his wife and daughter. I've been told the wife died later and the daughter—well, I heard she was in such a state of shock she might never regain her senses."

"What are they trying to accomplish?"

"They want to run the sharecroppers out so they can get their hands on the big plantations cheap. It's not going to stop at McAfferty's place. It'll move downriver. I don't think it will be stopped until someone, whoever he is, can get his hands on the largest piece of property around here."

"Amanda, I don't think you came here to tell me this. There's more to it, isn't there?"

"Yes, Deline. About two weeks ago, the raiders were attacking another home, when suddenly, as if they sprung from out of the ground, two men attacked and drove them off."

"Good, who were they?"

"No one knows."

"What do you mean no one knows?"

"Just that. They drove the attackers off; Then after seeing that the family was all right, they left. Both of them were dressed in Confederate uniforms and had their faces well covered and cloaks over them."

"Well, I think it was wonderful."

"It isn't the only time. It's happened three times since then. People are beginning to refer to them as the night riders."

"Very romantic," Deline chuckled, but she could see Amanda didn't share the amusement. "Deline, they left a message the last time. They warned the scavengers that if

263

they attacked anyone again, they were going to punish them severely. The scavengers are searching for any clue to the identity of the night riders. They're going to kill them if they can." Amanda wrung her hands in distress and her eyes had tears in the corners.

"Amanda, why are you so upset? I'm sure the night riders know of this and will be very careful."

"Oh, Deline. You have no idea how upset I've been for the last three weeks. I just know something terrible is going to happen. You see, I—I believe I know who the night riders are."

"You do?" Deline asked in an excited voice. "Who? Who are they, Amanda?"

"I'm not really sure, Deline, I just know a few things that make me believe I might know who they are."

"Well, who, who?"

"I just don't know what to do," Amanda said softly. Deline could have taken her shoulders and shaken the words from her she was so impatient.

"Amanda, did you come here to tell me that you knew who they are or to drive me crazy with curiosity?"

"Deline, I must tell someone, I'm so beside myself with worry, but I must tell someone that I know will understand."

"Well, I can't understand unless you tell me."

Amanda's eyes searched her face intently. Then she said in a small whisper, "Dixon and Brian."

"Dixon! That's impossible Amanda. You know how sensitive Dixon is about having one arm. Why, he hardly ever goes out socially, and he can't do so many jobs about the house. It takes all we can do to get him to join in the family functions. He's gotten quite reserved, and sometimes I feel he's beginning to feel sorry for himself. I could believe Brian, but I can scarcely believe Dixon."

"I wish that it wasn't so, but, Deline, I'm almost positive."

"How do you know, Amanda?"

"Well, it goes back to the first time it happened. Late that night, Dixon came calling. We invited him in, but he insisted I come out on the porch. It was dark, and I could barely make him out. We talked for a while, and he asked if he could come calling often. I said yes; then when he went to leave, I stood in the shadows and watched him walk away. I know he did not consider the bright moonlight, but I saw him so clearly, Deline. He was wearing a Confederate uniform."

"That's hardly enough evidence, Amanda."

"That's not all, Deline. That's just what made me a little suspicious. Then I noticed that every time the night riders were out, Dixon came calling late."

"That could be coincidence."

"Of course, it could, but I don't think it is. One of the farmers who was being attacked was talking to my father, and one of the things he recalls is that the bigger of the two night riders said something to the scavengers. He very clearly said, 'tell your coward of a boss to come out and fight like a man. Tell him Lee may have surrendered, but I never have.' It's something that Dixon said to me when I first met him. I was clearly defeated and to encourage me he said, 'remember, Amanda, Lee may have surrendered but it doesn't mean we have.' Taken singly, Deline, I know it doesn't prove anything, but putting them all together with the fact that the other night rider is obviously younger and rather reckless. I know who it is, Deline, and if you want to be honest with yourself you do, too."

Deline was silent for a few minutes contemplating all that Amanda had told her. Then she turned to Amanda and said quietly, "Now tell me the real reason you're telling all this to me."

Amanda said nothing for quite awhile then in a soft voice she replied.

"Deline, I love him. I love him more than I ever thought I could love anyone in the world."

"Does he know?"

Amanda shook her head negatively. Now she was crying softly.

"Why don't you tell him?"

"I'm afraid."

"Afraid, why?"

"Deline, what if he's only coming to my house to create a story to cover up his comings and goings? What if I'm just someone he's using as a coverup? I just couldn't stand it, to be so foolish to tell him how deeply I care for him only to have him turn his back on me; I couldn't bear it. I would rather have him near me no matter what."

"Amanda, I don't think Dixon is the kind to use anyone like you. Dixon and I have been too close for too long, and I know him as I know my own self. If he comes to your house, believe me, he comes to see you. Maybe he's afraid you would turn him down."

"Oh, I wouldn't; I wouldn't. I love him, Deline. To me, he is the most perfect of persons. I care about nothing else as much as I do for him."

"Then what you really came for is for me to find out what the truth is."

"No! Oh, no, Deline. I would never ask you to betray your brother. I only want him warned. They're getting together a group of men who will travel in separate parties. One will attack the farmers and one will wait in hiding until the night riders come. Then they will catch them. Deline, they plan to hang them. You've got to warn him. You've got to stop them. I could not live if they caught him and—Oh, Deline."

"How do you know this is true?"

"I overheard a conversation. No matter if it is true or not, we can't take the chance. Dixon and Brian have to be warned."

They were interrupted by the sound of a wagon approaching. Amanda looked up in surprise.

"It's Mother and Merilee. Merilee and Charles have moved into his home today. They wanted to take the children with them. I suppose the little devils are filthy and quite ready for bed."

Amanda stood up and turned to Deline.

"I'll be on my way. Will you warn him, Deline?"

"Don't worry any longer, Amanda. I'll make sure Dixon is warned."

"Deline, you won't—I mean—"

"No, I'll not say a word about you, but I truly think you should. You never win anything in this world, Amanda, unless you go out and get it."

Amanda bent and gave Deline a quick kiss on the cheek.

"Thank you, Deline. It's quite a relief to know he won't be walking into danger."

Amanda's buggy passed the arrivals in the long drive. When they arrived at the front of the house, Charles was driving and Merilee and Jessica were both carrying a sleeping child. There were quiet whispers and laughter as they put the children to bed. After they were gone, Deline joined Bram for their supper. Once supper was over, she explained Amanda's visit and told him she was going to see Dixon. Bram agreed. Leaving Felicia with the children, they rode over to Briar Hill. When they arrived, Jessica was surprised to see them after having just left them.

"Deline, Bram, is something wrong?"

"No, Mother," Deline laughed. "I just have to see Dixon for a few minutes. Is he home?"

"Yes, dear, he's upstairs. I'll go call him."

"No, Mother, if you don't mind I have to talk to Dixon alone. I'll just go on up and see him."

She ran up the stairs before a surprised Jessica could reply. Jessica turned a questioning face to Bram who shrugged his shoulders, but Jessica noticed he did not hold his eyes with hers. At the top of the stairs, Deline paused for a moment. Then she walked to Dixon's door and knocked. Before he could answer, she turned the knob and walked in, closing the door softly behind her. If she had been doubtful of Amanda's suspicions before she no longer was. He stood before her in full Confederate uniform, holding the long incriminating cape in his hand.

"Going out, night rider?" she asked softly.

Chapter 34

Dixon was the kind of man who found it almost impossible to lie to a stranger, and to bring himself to lie to Deline was something that never entered his mind. He looked at her for a few minutes, then grinned. "How'd you know?"

"A friend told me, a friend of both of ours. What are you trying to prove, Dix? I presume your accomplice is Brian. Don't you think this is rather a foolish thing to do, taking the law into your own hands?"

"Whose law, Deline? Look around you. You and Bram are happy and secluded over at Cross Oaks. You can't see what's happening. There is no law but Yankee law. They're stuffing their law down our throats, and there's nothing we can do about it. Adam has planned on parceling out some of our property to some sharecroppers, friends of ours whose land has been taken away from them by your "law." What chance do you think those people have if we don't put a stop to these raiders?"

"Do you really think you and Brian can stop them all alone?"

"No, but we do believe we can instill a little more courage in the farmers, maybe make them fight back on their own. At least someone has to do something."

"Dix, you and Brian could both be killed," she said quietly.

Dixon turned his back on her and replied in a hushed voice, "When we went to war Deline, we could have been killed. In fact, we came close to it, but we could not in good conscience back away from defending our states, our cause. Well, we can't back away from defending our homes and our friends when they need us the most."

There was no argument Deline could present against this, so she remained silent. Dixon turned around to face her again.

"What are you trying to accomplish, Dix?"

"We've got to flush out the man who's organized this group of thugs. We've got to get him out of Georgia and make it safe for our friends to sleep at night."

"You've no idea where or who he is?"

"None at all, but I know we're making him angry. Word has gotten out that they would pay anyone a tidy sum for turning us in or even naming who we are."

"God, Dix, how long will it be before someone finds that reward too inviting?"

"No one knows who we are. How can they turn us in when they don't know how to find us?"

"Someone came to me tonight, and that's the reason I'm here." Deline explained what Amanda had told her without naming her, and without mentioning his relationship with Amanda.

"So you see, Dixon, someone has a pretty good idea who you are and where you are."

"Who told you, Deline?"

"I'm sorry, Dix, I promised not to mention names."

"Amanda," he stated softly watching her closely. She said nothing. "I know it's Amanda. She's bright. She would have caught on quick." He went to Deline and took her shoulders in both hands.

"It's Amanda, isn't it, Deline?"

"Yes, Dix, it is."

"I knew I should have stayed away from her," he

laughed rather shakily. "But I guess in this case it's almost impossible."

"Dix, I think it's shameful what you're doing to Amanda," Deline said. She deliberately made her voice sound angry with him. She wanted to laugh when she saw the stunned look on his face. It told her as no words could have that Dixon was not using Amanda.

"Me? Amanda? What am I doing to Amanda? I think she's the nicest girl I ever met. Did she tell you I did something to her?"

Now Deline smiled brightly, and as he realized how he had tumbled into her trap, he chuckled.

"She's under the impression that the only reason you're calling on her is to create a story."

"She thinks I'm using her! Oh, my God, what ever gave her that idea?"

"Well, as you said and as I agree, Amanda is smart. She figured out quickly who the night riders were. So she also figured out that every night you rode you stopped to see her, consequently jumping to the obvious conclusion you were coming to see her just for an alibi."

"It isn't so, Del. Do you honestly believe I'd do a thing like that to a girl as be—well, as nice as she is?"

"I think you ought to go to her and tell her the truth. Skip what you were going to do tonight and ride in to see her, and Dix, wear something other than your old uniform."

Dixon stood quietly; Deline could see he was contemplating a very unpleasant thought.

"I—I can't Del," he said quietly.

"Can't. Why? Don't you care for her?"

"More than I could tell you," he answered. "But I can't ask a girl as beautiful and popular as Amanda is to tie herself down to—to half a man."

"Oh, Dixon!" Deline exclaimed, this time truly angry. "How marvelously proud you men are! You just take for

271

granted how a woman feels without even taking the time to ask her. You make me furious, brother. If Amanda loves you, she loves you as you are. If the loss of your arm meant that much to her, then she wouldn't have come to me to warn you about what you were involved in. That is absolutely the most unfair and stupid statement I've ever heard you say."

"Deline, try to understand. It would be unfair to Amanda. She deserves the best."

"Up until this minute, I agreed with her, I thought you were the best. In fact, I don't remember a time in my life when I didn't think you were. This is the first time I've ever been disappointed in you, Dix."

He turned away from her again.

"You don't know, Del."

"Oh, don't I? Do you think it wasn't hard between Bram and I? Do you think we don't live afraid that someone will find out about us? It would have been so much easier for both of us to walk away from this situation, but we love each other, Dix. If you truly love someone and they love you in return, there is no obstacle that is too big for the two of you together to overcome."

"Del, I'm sorry. I never think of Bram as anything but a brother-in-law. The circumstances just never occur to me anymore. He's a good friend."

"Dix," she said softly. "Don't let yourself be hurt by false pride. Don't let something you want badly slip through your fingers. Reach out and take it before it's too late." She put both hands on his arm and gave it a little shake to punctuate her words; then she walked toward the door, and with her hand on the knob, she turned to face him again. "Knowing you as well as I do, I know better than to ask you to stop what you're doing if you believe in it, but please, Dix, please be careful with your life and with Brian's. I couldn't bear it if anything happened to either of you."

Dixon watched without saying a word as she left the room, closing the door quietly behind her. He paced the floor for a few minutes in deep thought, then as if he had made a sudden decision, he began to remove the uniform he was wearing. In a few minutes, he was redressed in dark pants, a white shirt and a dark jacket. Quickly he pulled on his boots and left the room.

Deline and Bram were gone by the time he came down. He told his mother he was just going for a ride and would be back soon. He left the house and walked to the barn. There, he found Brian waiting for him.

"You're not in uniform, Dix, what's the matter?"

"We'll have to cancel tonight, Brian. I have something I have to do that's very important."

"But Dix—"

"Please, Brian, trust me. It's important, or I wouldn't put this aside. We'll talk when I get home. I'll try to explain everything to you then."

"Sure, Dix," Brian said. "If it's that important, I'll see you when you get back, and we'll talk. We've some plans to make anyhow."

"Thanks, Brian," Dixon said as he was mounting his horse. "See you later."

Brian stood and watched him ride away, curious about what could be more important to Dixon than the cause they had in common. He slipped back into the house without being seen and immediately changed from the uniform hiding it well so that his mother couldn't find it. He had too much respect for his mother's intelligence not to know she would figure things out quickly. After changing his clothes, he started down the stairs. He met Holly coming up. A deep friendship had developed between Brian and Holly. They had become as close as brother and sister. Often it was Holly who came between Brian and the results of some of his escapades. Brian found Holly easy to talk to, and more and more often, he

273

came to her with his problems, to get her advice or just to talk to someone who seemed to understand. As yet, he had not told her what he and Dixon were doing, not because Holly wouldn't understand, but just because he felt she might worry about him, and he didn't want her to do that.

"Not going out tonight, Brian?"

"No, I want to talk to Adam about the way we've been planning to parcel out the land down by the river."

"My, my," she teased. "All the girls in town will be destitute tonight."

He smiled. "If I could find another girl as pretty and as wonderful as you, I'd snatch her up and settle down, but," he sighed and shrugged his shoulders holding both arms out as in supplication, "Adam found you first, so what's a poor man to do but keep on searching?"

"Oh, Brian, you devil, no wonder the girls fall all over you. You're such a wonderful liar."

They laughed together.

"Where's Adam?"

"He's in the study. He's been working over those plans for most of the day."

"He's been so busy rebuilding this place and trying to make it pay, now working with these small farmers. I don't think he's paying you the attention he should. You don't see a whole lot of him, do you, Holly?"

"No," she said softly, her eyes shifting from his. "But Brian, he's trying so hard for all of us."

"Holly, no matter what we have or what we've lost, we've always had each other. Adam should do nothing to jeopardize that. It's more important than anything in the world."

"I know you mean well, Brian, and I love you for it. But I don't want you to say anything to Adam. We'll work out any problems. Adam is a wonderful husband, and I love him more than my whole life."

"I know you do. That's why I'd never want to see anything happen to it. Why, Holly," he grinned, "who'd straighten out my life if I didn't have you?"

"One of these days, Brian Gilcrest, some girl is going to come along and take you by surprise, and confidentially, I can't wait. I want to see the girl who catches you. She'll have to be some lady."

"Not for me, Holly, I think I'm a confirmed bachelor. I'm having a great time just as I am. Stop trying to marry me off. Now let me get in there and see if I can offer Adam some help, maybe give him a little time for himself."

She nodded and watched as Brian continued down the stairs, went to the study door, knocked and entered.

Somehow, Holly suddenly got the feeling that Brian was not at all as happy as he pretended to be. There was a deep unanswered question in his eyes, some spot that she could not reach. Often she caught him, when he thought no one was watching, in deep thought as if he were looking inward and was not content with what he was seeing.

She thought back over the past months since the war's end. Things were very difficult for the entire South. Since Abraham Lincoln's assassination, the gentle hand of mercy had been lifted from the Southern states, and they were left to the invading profit makers that swarmed over them. Penniless Southerners had lost their homes and their property to the tax makers. Confederate money being useless, the only people who had Federal money to buy with suddenly became rich. Holly was grateful for Devlin O'Brien. It was his money that paid the taxes, not only at Briar Hill, but at Cross Oaks, Heritage and River's End. Overcoming the pride of the Gilcrests and the others, he swore the money was only a loan, to be repaid as soon as the plantations were on their feet and producing again.

Adam had thrown himself into trying to make Briar Hill productive. There was no more slave labor, and Adam adamantly refused to let Devlin loan him enough money to hire help. Instead, with help from his father, Brian and as much as Dixon could do, Briar Hill was slowly rising from the dust of destruction and beginning to stand on its feet again.

Of course, it kept Adam busy day and night. She knew the struggle that was going on inside him as no one else did. His confinement in the prison camp had damaged Adam in a way only Holly knew. He was afraid, afraid he would lose Briar Hill and that the people he loved the most would suffer as others around him were. Often Adam had fallen in bed beside her so exhausted that he could not remain awake. Holly knew how much Adam loved her, and she also knew he considered her his rock of strength. She also knew, as no one else did, of the nights when he held her close to him, and they talked of what he was trying to do. She did her best to instill in him the confidence he desperately needed. His lovemaking was a thing of remarkable gentleness as if she were fragile porcelain and breakable. The touch of his hands on her body, seeking the center of her being, was a joy that made Holly cry. After he had made love to her, she would lie close to him and listen to the deep steady beat of his heart.

The decision to parcel out some of their land to sharecroppers was a hard one for him. Giving away one inch of Gilcrest land hurt him, but he realized that no matter how hard they tried they would never make Briar Hill what he thought it should be. He had talked the matter over with his father for weeks before he finally made the decision. Now they were marking out the places on the map and deciding just how much property they would give and more important . . . to whom.

Brian closed the door softly behind him, then walked

across the room to Adam's desk. On the desk was a huge map of Briar Hill Plantation, and on it were several small square blocks marked off in pencil of the small farms he had planned.

"How are things going, Adam?"

"Oh, fine, Brian." Adam stood up and stretched. "You can take a look at the map. I think I've got the four parcels figured out pretty well."

Brian looked at the map, then at Adam. "That's some of the best land we've got."

"What use is it to give a nonproductive piece of land to a farmer? He's got to have something useful to work with."

"Yes, I guess you're right. When do they arrive?"

"Well, Brian, that's a little problem I wanted to talk over with you."

"Oh? Something you wanted me to do?"

"Yes. As you can see, I've got each block of land named with the new tenant. Some of them are coming from Lester County. I was supposed to meet them next week and take them to their new homes, but I'm really busy. I'd like it if you'd ride over and guide them here."

"Sure, I'd be glad to."

"And I wanted to talk to you about something else."

Brian stiffened. What did Adam know? Was he aware of what he and Dixon were doing?

"What do you think about these scavengers who're preying on the sharecroppers?"

"I think they're a bunch of animals that ought to be eliminated," Brian replied.

"What's your idea on what they're really after, Brian?"

"Well, I don't think it's random raids. They have a definitive object in mind, and I think it's to run off the small farmers so the owners of the big plantations will have no money to continue working their land and will be forced to sell. Then it could be bought cheap."

"Then you think they're really well organized?"

"Of course they're organized. Somebody's pumping in some money."

"Have any idea of who it might be?"

Brian shrugged angrily. "Not one, but I sure wish I did."

"We've got to protect the people we bring in. We have to ask the law for some kind of protection."

"Law! Christ, Adam, where have you been? Sticking your nose in those fields, you don't seem to realize we've got no law down here to protect us anymore. It's every owner for himself, now."

"Then if it's that bad, we'll have to find some way of protecting them ourselves. We'll get the group together we're bringing in and tell them what the situation is, that they'll have to help protect the property if they want to farm it."

"Well, I hope you have better luck than the others had. The farmers seem to be looking to them for protection."

Adam ran his hand through his hair in a gesture of frustration.

"Well, we'll solve the problems when they get here. For now, we'll concentrate on getting them settled on the land."

"Yes," Brian said grimly. "I think some form of protection will present itself."

"Well, I'm going to bed. I'm so tired, I'm seeing double."

Brian fought a valiant battle with his conscience and lost.

"Adam, can I say something to you, something I consider very important, without you getting angry?"

Adam watched Brian curiously.

"Of course, you can. You always have, haven't you?"

278

"I want you to try to understand that I only mean to have your welfare at heart."

"Brian, I'm too tired for games. Say what you're going to say."

"Well," Brian said slowly. "It's about Holly."

"What about Holly?"

"You know that we all love her here, and, well that she's one of the greatest things that have happened in the family."

"Brian, I know how everyone here feels about her. How about telling me what's on your mind."

"Holly would never complain of anything you ever said or did, you know that, too."

"Brian, if you don't get to the point very soon, you're going to be talking to an empty room."

Brian gulped, then stated firmly. "You're not home very much. You're out in those fields until dark, then bent over this desk until the wee hours of the morning. I know you've got an awful lot on your mind, and things are getting more difficult day by day but," he paused then stated bluntly, "I don't think Holly should be paying the price for all of this. I think she deserves to be treated better. I just don't think she deserves to be lonely."

Adam watched his brother in amazement of this type of emotion from a man who had always treated women as if they were not important to him.

"Did Holly tell you she was lonely?"

"No! God, Adam, she'd kill me if she thought I ever said a word. I trust you not to mention it to her. It's my own observation, that's all. I think you have the greatest woman in the world, and you should take good care not to let anything happen to damage what you've got."

Adam stared at Brian, making him decidedly uncomfortable; then he smiled. The smile developed into a chuckle and the chuckle into a deep bubbling laugh.

"You're right, Brian. I realize it now."

"Then what are you laughing about?"

"That it's you who's telling me how to treat my wife. I always expect the unexpected from you Brian, and you never fail me."

"Why, I'd say you were in love with her also."

"Everybody around here is," Brian answered. "It's not love, Adam, it's something special. You two sort of mean everything to us all. Your Briar Hill and all the other Briar Hills' that suffered—you're sort of a symbol of strength to us. As for me," he added in a quiet voice, "Holly is someone I'd die for if I had to."

Adam reached out and clapped Brian on the shoulder.

"I'll never tell her what you said Brian, but I'm grateful for your mentioning it."

"That's great, Adam," Brian smiled in relief.

"Now, let's go to bed. There's a lot of work to do, and since I made the mistake of doing too much, I guess it's up to you to do more."

Brian groaned. "I knew I was talking too much."

They laughed and walked toward the door of the study. Before they reached it, a knock came. Brian opened it. Their father stood there, his face showing signs of anger.

"What's the matter, Pa?" Brian asked.

"I've just had a message delivered to me, or should I say to us, for it concerns us all."

"What does it say?" Adam questioned.

"Here, read it for yourself," Adam unfolded the paper and read aloud:

Don't bring any sharecroppers on your place or we'll burn them out and maybe you, too.

It was unsigned. Adam and his father exchanged angry looks, but Brian was grim faced, as he contemplated the use he would be making of the gray uniform folded in the box in the bottom of his closet.

Chapter 35

Dixon moved his horse at a slow walk down the road toward town, trying to formulate words in his mind. Words that would tell Amanda how he felt. The deep insecurity of the loss of his arm had been kept a dark secret in the recesses of his mind, even when he had fallen in love with Amanda at their first meeting. He remembered so well the party when Richard Forrester had shot himself. He had danced with Amanda as often as he could, watching in fascination as her cheeks pinkened when his eyes held hers. He remembered also the feel of her in his arms. He had flayed himself with the memory of it for many lonely nights afterward. He thought of every possible excuse to see her after that. Even on the nights that he and Brian were out trying to look out for the interests of the small farmers, he found time to stop and see Amanda even if only for a few minutes. He knew that Amanda was a very intelligent girl, and that he was playing with fire stopping to see her dressed in the gray uniform. He knew, but he also knew he could not miss an opportunity to talk with her, to absorb the calm beauty of her. She had a way of relaxing him, of making him feel confident and worthy.

Not once, in all the times he had called on her, did he say one word about how he felt toward her. It was the terrible certainty that she would refuse him, and it would be impossible for him to see her again. He preferred the security of being able to spend time with her, to share his thoughts and ideas with her. He found her quick of mind. In fact, it was an idea of Amanda's that he and Brian had expanded on that started their night riding. She had exclaimed angrily of the shabby treatment of the sharecroppers and how she thought it would be wonderful if someone could find a way to take a little revenge on the scavengers. The use of the Confederate uniforms had been Brian's idea. He thought it appropriate that they should use the idea of Southern justice being dealt out to the leeches who were feeding off their blood.

Now he could hear the echo of Deline's words in his mind: "If she loves you, she loves you as you are." His heart thudded painfully with the thought that Amanda might really care for him. It was an agonizing thought, for despite his need for her, he could see no reason for her to have any need for him. He warred with himself and, at one time stopped his horse completely, almost losing his nerve and turning around to go home.

The Merriweather house stood almost in the edge of town, so there weren't too many homes close to it. From what he could see as he drew nearer, there was a small light burning in the parlor and one in an upstairs bedroom. A dark shape walked between the light and the bedroom window and from the height and the obvious feminine shape, he knew it was Amanda's room. Edging his horse around to the back of the house, he dismounted and tied his horse out of sight. Then he walked around and contemplated the bedroom window. If he knocked on the front door, he knew he would be admitted happily, but all conversation would be suppressed by the presence of her father and mother. He had to talk to her alone. He reached down and picked up a small handful of pebbles. Then glancing around to make sure he was unobserved, he threw one against the window. Nothing happened. He threw another and another. Then suddenly, the light in the bedroom went out and slowly the window was pushed up. Amanda appeared, searching the darkness.

"Amanda," he said softly.

"Dixon, is that you?" she asked.

"Yes, Amanda, I have to talk to you."

"I'll come down and let you in."

"No, I've got to talk to you alone. Will you come out in the back garden? Please, Amanda, it's important."

She hesitated only a moment; then Dixon heard her whisper, "Wait in the garden for me. I'll be right down." Quickly, the window was pulled shut, and the blackness enveloped her. He walked quietly around the back and waited. It seemed like hours to him before he heard a soft click as she closed the door behind her. He couldn't see her in the shadow of the porch.

"Amanda?"

"Shhh, Papa's reading in the parlor, and we don't want to disturb him. Mama's asleep."

Her shadowy figure left the concealment of the porch, and in another minute, she was by his side. It was just bright enough from a three-quarter moon to make out her face.

"Dixon, what is it? What's wrong?" Her voice was quiet but strained with worry.

"Nothing's wrong. I just had to see you for a few minutes. I—I have something I had to tell you. It just couldn't wait."

"You're not in any kind of trouble are you?"

"Would you help me if I were?" he asked gently.

She could barely see his face in the deep shadows, but his voice was so different from any time before. She remained silent for a moment as she tried to figure out what the difference was. Then she found it. There was no undercurrent of half amusement in his voice as there

283

usually was. Suddenly she was very calm, and if he could have seen her face clearly, he would have seen the small smile that touched the corners of her full mouth.

"Of course," she said very softly. "You know I would help you."

"Yes, I guess I do know . . . now."

"Dixon, you said there was something very important you wanted to say to me. What is it?"

"You know, all the way in here, I thought of a million fancy ways I could say this to you, along with telling myself a million ways you would answer. None of the ways seem right at this moment. I guess there's only one way that I'll be sure and that's to tell you straight out and ask you to answer me straight out." He paused for a moment. "I love you Amanda. I want you to marry me."

She was quiet for so long that Dixon suddenly became afraid.

"Amanda, did you hear me?"

She reached out and placed her hand on his shoulder, and in a voice thick with tears, she answered softly. "I've wanted to hear those words from you. I've dreamed of them, and now that you've said them, all I can do is cry. Oh, Dixon, do you really love me, or is this a dream I will wake up from and find you gone with the morning mist?"

His fingers found the tears on her cheeks and gently brushed them away.

"Amanda, you've got a lot of things to consider. There's so much I'd like to give you, and I can't. Even myself, I'm—well, I'm not exactly what every young girl wants in a husband."

"You're all I've ever dreamed of since I met you, Dixon. You're all I've wanted. There has been no one but you. The idea of becoming your wife fills me with more happiness than I've ever known before."

"Then—then you'll marry me?"

"Oh, yes, Dixon, soon my love." The last words were

smothered as he pulled her against him and caught her mouth with his. His arm was like an iron hand about her waist pulling her so tightly to him that she was breathless. She wrapped her arms about his waist and pressed herself against him, her lips as searching and as hungry as his own. For Dixon, it was like being filled with a flame in all the empty spots he had carried within him since the war. He wanted to pull her deep inside him, to hold her, to tell her in every way the love he had for her.

Slowly their lips parted, and they stood together in the darkness and clung to one another. Neither of them wanted to part, and neither of them knew exactly what to do.

Dixon's hand discovered quickly that Amanda was wearing only a robe over her nightgown. His hand caressed her slender waist and slid down to the soft rounded curve of her hip. The urgent need for her made him curse softly for not finding a better place to tell Amanda how he felt.

He whispered against her hair, "Amanda, I love you, and I want you more than I could ever tell you. But not like this. You are more than just a woman. You are my woman, and between us, I want it to be perfect." He chuckled dryly, "I'll wait, but not patiently, so make the wedding as soon as you can, will you?"

He could feel her trembling body relax against him, and he squeezed her tightly. Just feeling her close and knowing that she wanted him as badly as he did her was somehow enough for now. He released her and stepped back from her. She was a shadow before him, and although he could not see her face, he could feel the warmth of her happiness like a live thing reaching out to touch him. The feeling also gave him a sense of inner release, as though something solid and hard within him began to crumble and leave bare for the first time in his life the inner core of the real man. Only with Deline had

Dixon ever been open enough to share his innermost being, and sometimes there was a time of darkness even between them. But this was more, so much more. Amanda held within her the key to his soul. She was the missing half of him, and he had searched for so long, the one who could make him whole again.

"Do you have any idea how much I need you, Amanda?"

"Dixon—"

"No, listen to me. At this moment I want you so badly I could tear that gown away and take you here on the ground under the stars. I could fill myself up with you and never have enough. I'm so hungry for you that I dare not touch you again or I would be lost to all reason."

"Don't you know, love, I want you as much as you do me?"

"Yes, that's what makes it so wonderful, just to know that you do, just to know I have the promise of you for always."

"For always."

"I'm going to leave, before I do something I will regret. If I come back tomorrow, can we ask your parents for permission to marry immediately?"

"Yes, Dixon, come early tomorrow. Each minute we waste is a minute less I have to share with you."

He reached out and touched her tear-stained face just for a moment; then she was gone. In another moment, he heard the soft click as the door closed behind her. He stood in the dark garden for a while listening to the night sounds about him. He was overwhelmed with a feeling of peace and inner contentment. It was the first time since he came home from the war that he realized just how unhappy he had been and how much he needed someone to share his life with.

He was mounted and on his way home before he realized that neither of them had said anything about

286

what he and Brian were involved in. The thoughts of her were agonizingly sweet as he realized that no matter what he did or what he was involved in she would stand with him. Although, from what she had told Deline, Amanda knew what they were doing, still she voiced no objection, no upset, only love for him.

He whistled under his breath a rather off-key version of Dixie as he let his horse pick its way home slowly, allowing his rider to lose himself in pleasant dreams.

Adam took the steps two at a time, then paused in front of the bedroom door while he stuffed the letter deep in his pocket. It was something he did not want Holly to see. He opened the door, and stepped into the darkened room. The pale path of moonlight from the half-open window cut across their bed. Holly was curled into a small ball hugging his pillow close to her. It gave him a sharp pang of remorse and guilt to think how many nights she had slept alone waiting for him. He was angry with himself, not because he had finally realized how much he had neglected her, but because it had taken his young unmarried brother to bring him out of his narrow world and back to his senses. Nothing was more important to him than Holly's happiness, and he couldn't remember where he had slipped away.

He walked across the room and sat down on the bed gently. Holly stirred in her sleep but did not waken. He reached out gently and brushed away a strand of her hair that fell across her face, feeling the silken strands of it between his fingers and remembering the times he had buried his face in the soft scented mass of it. Such a strong desire for her welled up in him, it was almost like a blow leaving him short of breath with his body wet with perspiration. He gently picked up her hand, and holding it, he touched his lips gently to the long slender fingers. He remembered, in the prison camp, how memories of Holly day by day kept him from that blank world. Just

287

remembering the silken smooth texture of her skin, the way her nose wrinkled when she laughed or the bright smile that warmed him. He was lost in his memories for some time before he realized that Holly's eyes were open, and she was watching him intently.

When their eyes met, a million unspoken words passed between them. Forgiveness was asked for and given; guilt was washed away with peace, and all that was left was the reality of the love that existed between them. He bent toward her, touching her lips very gently with his. A soft-whispered sound escaped her as his lips drifted across her cheeks, and he bit gently on her earlobe, then ran his tongue over it. His hands slid under her back and pulled her up against him. He kissed her throat and her shoulders, pushing the nightgown slowly down as his lips followed.

Holly wrapped her arms about his neck holding him close to her, running her hands over the hard muscles of his back.

"Holly, Holly," he whispered. "I'm sorry, I'm so damn sorry."

"Oh, Adam, you needn't be sorry. You're here. That's all that matters. I need you to hold me, to love me."

Adam rose from the bed and removed his clothes; then he slid down beside her, pulling her close to him, feeling the touch of her cool body next to his. Somehow there was something special in the way she felt in his arms tonight. Her body seemed softer as she clung to him. He closed his eyes and enjoyed the feel of her love surrounding him. Burying his face against her neck and feeling the soft flow of her about him, he moved inside her slowly and gently enjoying the burning need of her and savoring every touch. It was different from any time he had ever made love to her before. Her whole body seemed to close around him, holding him inside her, draining every other thought from him except the miracle of loving her. Her body ached against him, and he could no longer restrain the thrusts as he dove deeper and deeper within her.

"Oh, Adam, Adam, Adam," she moaned softly. His hands slid beneath her again. Grasping her buttocks, he pulled her up from the bed to meet him. He was whirled into a soul-rendering storm that contained only Holly as he felt her tremble beneath him. They lay still. He did not want to leave the sanctuary of her body. His face against her breasts, he could feel the gentleness in her hands as she caressed the back of his head and shoulders like a mother caressing a child.

"Holly, there is nothing in the world that I do that has any purpose but you."

"I understand, Adam," she whispered against his hair.

"Of course, you do," he sighed contently. "You always do. You're my peaceful island in this world." He looked up into her smiling eyes. "If I hurt you, if I ever forget again, remind me."

"Just what do you suggest I do?" she said with a hint of laughter in her voice. "Maybe I shall brazenly chase you into the fields and seduce you for all the world to see, or maybe beat down the door of that terrible study, where you work so long and so hard, and demand my pleasure there and then."

He laughed with her, and rolling on his side, he drew her against him.

"Maybe that has some possibilities. I don't think I'd mind being seduced by you in the fields or anyplace for that matter. So, Madam, you have your will with me anyplace and any time you desire."

"I'm afraid, Adam, that my ability to chase you into the fields can only last for a short while."

"And why is that?"

"I'm afraid," she whispered softly against his ear, "that in a few more months I shall be too big to do any chasing!"

He lay still for a moment, half dozing, before the impact of her words came through to him. He blinked open his eyes and sat up abruptly looking down into her amused face.

"Holly, I don't know if I really heard you right. You did say we're going to have a baby?"

"Yes, we're going to have a baby," she laughed.

"When?"

"In about six months."

"Then, how long have you known?"

"For about a month."

"Holly, why didn't you tell me before?"

"Well," she chuckled, "since you weren't paying too much attention to me, I was being perverse enough to see if I could waddle around here like a big balloon without you noticing."

"Now come on, Holly, that's not so damn funny."

"Oh come now, Adam, I'm only fooling you. I had planned on telling you tomorrow anyway."

Adam ran his hand over her gently. He felt the small rise in her stomach. "This is the reason she felt so different tonight," he thought. He let his hands move up to cup her breast. They were heavier and fuller. He always felt confident that he knew every part of Holly there was to know. He was surprised that the difference hadn't been spotted by him long before. He began to suspect there were facets to Holly he had not yet explored. The idea thrilled him.

"What shall we name him, Adam?" Holly said softly. Adam was so preoccupied with his thoughts and his gentle exploration of her body, he was taken by surprise by her question.

"Name him?"

"Yes, I do think he ought to have a name, don't you? Or should we just call him boy?"

"What, Mrs. Know-it-all, makes you think it's going to be a boy? I think maybe I'd like a girl first. One that looks as beautiful as her mother."

"No," Holly said determinedly. "It's going to be a boy first. I was an older sister. I've decided all girls need an older brother instead."

"Well," he sighed in mock dejection, "I guess you'll have your way. After all, what does a father have to say about the whole thing anyway? Look how you had your way with me."

"Oh, poor Adam," she giggled, "You've been so abused. How can I ever make it up to you for seducing you in all your innocence?"

"Well, now that we're on the subject," he chuckled, "You might just try it again and see if I've developed any resistance to your evil charms."

Holly pulled his head down to hers. Her warm, moist mouth found his, and her tongue flicked lightly against his lips. The kiss was long and lingering, and he was amazed at the demand of her passion. Lying back against the pillows, he pulled her over on top of him. Astride him, he felt the warmth of her over him. Running his hands down the curve of her back, he pulled her down tightly, thrusting his body up to meet hers. He was enclosed in her completely. His hungry mouth found a soft breast, as her hair fell over them like a silken blanket.

"No resistance at all," he murmured against her throat and heard the soft sound of her laughter as he let his senses go and closed his eyes to enjoy more fully, the feel of her body as she moved in a slow rhythmic motion above him. All thoughts were obliterated now, and they were both caught up in the deep all-consuming pleasure of each other.

It was some time later, when Holly slept against his shoulder, that Adam lay awake thinking. Outside of a few problems, he felt that Briar Hill was beginning to come

291

back to life again. He felt a deep sense of gratitude for all that he had been given, starting with Holly. Now she was to give him a child.

"My child," he thought, "the only link that offers man immortality." He wondered, as he drifted off to sleep, if there was another man who was as happy as he was this night.

Another mind shared the same thought. As Dixon stabled his horse, his mind drifted in the same direction. He left the dark barn and walked toward the house. He was on the porch before he realized that someone was sitting there. The black figure rose quickly as Dixon strained to see who it was.

"Dix?"

"Brian, is that you?"

"Yes, where have you been?"

Dixon walked over slowly and seated himself beside the chair Brian had slumped back down in.

"You've been waiting up for me?" chuckled Dixon.

"I have a message you've got to know about, or I wouldn't have been sitting here twiddling my thumbs all night."

"Message from who?"

"You know, we only have one informer in that bunch of riffraff. The little weasel wants more money, too."

"What did he tell you?"

"They're plannin' a raid on Kensey's farm tomorrow night. I think this time they're getting serious. They're plannin' on burning them out whether they're inside the house or not."

"Well, I've got more information," Dixon began.

Then he explained what Amanda had told Deline about the scavengers traveling in two groups, one to burn the farms and another to catch the night riders. Brian grinned broadly. This was the kind of excitement he liked. The danger of getting caught sometimes meant more to him than the work they were doing.

"We'll give them a surprise they haven't counted on."

"Just how do you plan to do that?"

"Well, before we go any further, I think we ought to enlist a little help and divide into two groups ourselves. That would sure scare the hell out of them if they found our number increasing."

"Just who do you think we ought to enlist in our endeavor?"

"Who else can we trust? Graham, Devlin, Adam and Bram."

"Brian, we can't do that. What if one of them should get killed. I'd never be able to face Holly, Deline or Steffany. We have to find another way."

"There ain't no other way. If those scavengers run out all these small farms, then it ain't going to be too long before we follow them, like a kicked dog with his tail between his legs. I'd rather go down fighting, and I'm sure the others will feel the same way."

No matter how he hated to admit it, Dixon knew that Brian was right. He sighed deeply and stood up.

"Maybe you're right, Brian. I'll talk to Adam tomorrow."

"Good, and I'll ride out in the morning and talk to the others."

"Good night, Brian," Dixon said quietly, and walking to the door without another word, he went inside. Brian watched him go and wondered at the difference in Dixon from last night to this one. Brian sat on the porch for a long time thinking. He had become restless a long time ago and considered traveling for a while. What he was in search of he didn't know, but it didn't seem to be here. He would never go away while his family was in trouble, but once it was over, he planned on maybe taking a wagon train and traveling West to unexplored country. Maybe that would cure the tense, almost strangling feeling he sometimes got as though there was something he needed or needed to do.

"Well," he thought as he rose to go to bed, "I'll ride over in the morning and talk to the others. Maybe we might be lucky if we got together and found out who the boss of that scum was. Once we found him out, this whole thing would be done, and I'd be free."

It would not occur to Brian, until a long time in the future, that the word "free" entailed a lot more than he thought.

Chapter 36

Adam rose quietly from the bed so that he would not wake Holly. Dressing as quickly as possible, he found his way to the door in a room that was dark since the early morning sun had barely rimmed the horizon. Usually he was the first one up and ate a hasty breakfast of coffee and a slice or two of bread before he headed for the fields. This morning he found, to his surprise, Dixon seated at the kitchen table.

"Coffee's on the stove, Adam," Dixon spoke softly so that their voices would not carry to the sleepers above.

Adam went to the stove and poured a cup of the hot black coffee, then returned to sit opposite his brother.

"You're up awfully early this morning. There's not much to do in the fields today. I just want to check. We need to do some repairs on our equipment."

"Adam, if you don't mind, I have something I have to do this morning that's extremely important. I'll be back by lunchtime."

"Sure, go ahead."

"Adam—" Dixon hesitated, searching for a way to tell his brother about the night riders and their need for him. "There's something important I've got to talk to you about. Could you spare me a few minutes?"

"Is there something wrong, Dixon?"

"Well, not really wrong, at least I don't think so, but

maybe you will. I want you to listen without interrupting until I'm done, Adam. Then I'll listen to whatever you have to say, agreed?"

"Agreed." Adam nodded wondering what could be so serious to make Dixon so intense.

"These sharecroppers on the other plantations are having a lot of trouble. I know you received an anonymous note warning you not to put any on our property. I also know that without their help, we can't expect to raise enough crops to pay the debts for Briar Hill. Three of the families on Cross Oaks have come close to being burned out, the same over at Heritage, and I heard Charles Gordon at River's End is having the same problem."

"What's all this leading up to, Dixon?"

"Just hear me out, Adam, please. I'm sure you've heard of the night riders?"

Adam laughed. "I sure have. I admire their courage, but two men alone can't accomplish protecting all the sharecroppers around here."

"That's what I want to talk to you about. The night riders have discovered another attack is due to happen tonight."

"How do you know that?"

"I have ways of getting information. But that's not what's worrying me. What's worrying me is the scavengers have decided to split into two groups, one to attack the farmers and the other to hold back until the night riders come to trap them."

"So?"

"We figured that if there were two groups of night riders, the tables could be turned on them. We might even scare them into not attacking for a while, at least to give the farmers enough time to join together."

"What you're saying is you want to join the night riders, and you want me to come along, too?"

"That's about the size of it."

"And," Adam said, his piercing blue gray eyes watching Dixon narrowly, "who else do you expect to get tied up in this?"

"Devlin, Bram, Brian, Graham . . . all of us. We fought long and hard and suffered a great deal for our state. It's about time we did the same for our own homes."

He watched Adam closely as he thought about what Dixon had just said. Dixon was tense and worried as he watched Adam thinking the words over, for if he didn't agree to join them, how would he feel when he learned that Dixon and Brian were the two original night riders.

"Adam, you know the law around here is almost all made up of Yankee carpetbaggers who are just waiting to pounce on us. There's no way we can turn to them for protection. Why they'd just as soon help the scavengers. The night riders would be killed if anyone knew who or where they were."

"Yes, I'm afraid you're right. I was contemplating writing some letters to Washington to try and get us some protection."

Dixon made a small cluck of his tongue in disgust.

"You know our new president has no great love for the South. He won't raise a finger to help us."

Adam set his cup down; his face was hard.

"I see you're right again, Dixon. But how long can this thing go on? Soon they'll have a small army organized. Bloodshed always leads to more bloodshed. Are we going to put our families through that again?"

"It's either that or pack up and run, Adam." Dixon replied softly, "And I, for one, am tired of running. I'm tired of these bloodsuckers thinking they can walk in here and take everything we have away from us without a fight. We may have lost the war, Adam, but we're still men. Men with homes and families that need protection as much now as they did when the war was going on."

There was a stillness in the room as the two brothers watched each other across the table.

"All right, Dixon, I agree you're right. I'll join you."

Dixon wanted to shout with happiness, but he still had something to confess to Adam yet.

"By the way, Dixon, now that I'm with you, why don't you tell me how you and Brian thought up this thing in the first place?"

"Huh?" said Dixon in shock.

"Now, how long did you think it was going to take me to figure out where you and Brian went every night the night riders rode?"

"You've known from the beginning?"

"Almost."

Dixon laughed. "Brian and I could never fool you on much of anything could we? Brian will be shocked to hear this. He thinks we've got everyone fooled."

"Speaking of Brian, what's been botherin' him lately? I've never seen him so quiet and so closed in on himself."

"I don't really know. He doesn't talk much about how he feels about anything other than family. He's furious that someone would try to get their hands on Briar Hill, and I think he's kinda' restless, after all the rest of us are married and have families of our own. Brian is kinda' at odds with himself now."

"What about you? You're not married."

Dixon grinned broadly. "Last night Amanda said yes. Now all I have to do today is convince her parents what a great fellow I am, and we'll be married as soon as possible. Sooner if I can arrange it." —

Adam smiled and held out his hand. The brothers clasped hands firmly across the table.

"Congratulations, but you've got a problem," Adam said seriously.

"What? What problem?"

298

"How are you ever going to convince Amanda's parents you're a catch for their daughter? Have you practiced any of your pretty speeches on parents before?" Adam laughed.

"Well," Dixon replied with a wink, "we'll never let them know what an obnoxious critter I am until it's too late."

"Seriously, Dixon, I think it's wonderful, and I'm sure you'll make Amanda happy."

"I'll sure try."

"Speaking of congratulations, I think Holly and I have some coming too. We're going to make you an uncle in a few months."

"Oh, Adam, that's great. It's the best news I've heard since the war was over. We're going to have a Gilcrest heir to Briar Hill. That kind of makes everything even more worth fighting for, doesn't it?"

"It's what I had in mind when I agreed to come in with you. Briar Hill's ours, and I intend to see it stays in Gilcrest hands. Whatever you do, don't let any word of this get back to Mother and Father."

"What do you think they'd do?"

"Well, knowing them like I do, Father would insist on joining us and Mother would wish us Godspeed."

They laughed together, then Dixon rose from the table, Adam following him.

"Well, I've got to go over to the Merriweather's," Dixon said. "Maybe if I'm lucky, Amanda will already have told them. Then if I get fired on as I approach, I'll have time to retreat."

"Never retreat, Dixon. That's a Gilcrest motto. Remember, 'faint heart never won fair lady.' If you want her as bad as I think you do, go and get her and don't let anything stand in your way."

"Yes," Dixon sighed, "it worked for you. Maybe I'll be lucky, and it'll work for me."

Adam stood on the porch and watched Dixon walk toward the stables. He was proud of Dixon, of his courage and his fight to stand alone. Learning to work with one arm had been hard for Dixon, but Adam noticed he never shirked any job and went at each one as though it was a personal vendetta. He won most of his battles, but he learned an even greater lesson, that the ones he lost had to be accepted and put in proper perspective. He had developed into a strong, capable man, and Adam thought, if the Merriweathers didn't see that, it was their loss, not Dixon's.

Adam was still standing there when Dixon walked his horse from the barn and mounted. He watched him ride away with a silent prayer for success.

They had agreed to meet after dinner in the barn when Brian had come back from talking to the others. Adam watched as Dixon disappeared. Then stood listening to the peaceful quiet, his mind deep in thought, he did not hear the door open and close behind him until his mother's voice came softly from behind him.

"Adam, where is Dixon going so early?"

Adam jumped a little at the sound of her voice, then turned around.

"Good morning, Mother. It's a beautiful day, isn't it?"

"Yes, it's lovely. Now where is Dixon going?" she smiled.

"Well, Mother, I'm sorry I can't tell you. That's up to Dixon when he's ready."

"All right, all right, I'll not interfere," she laughed aloud now. "Would you like me to fix you some breakfast?"

"Yes, I don't want to wake Holly so early."

"She's already up. Holly is never one to sleep late. You should know that. I heard her coming down the stairs as I came out."

Adam laid his arm across his mother's shoulder, then

300

bent and kissed her cheek as they walked back into the kitchen. Holly had already begun making breakfast, and she turned and smiled at Adam. They looked across the room at one another and Jessica got the feeling she always did when she was with them, that they seemed to be able to reach out and touch one another without moving.

"I'll go wake Brian and your father while you get breakfast started," Jessica said. She left the room and made her way to Brian's door. One quick knock and, to Jessica's surprise, she received an answer. Brian the proverbial late sleeper was already up. She was even more surprised when he opened the door and joined her in the hall fully dressed.

"Mornin', Mother," he smiled as he kissed her on the cheek.

"Brian, good morning. I'm surprised I didn't have to shake you awake as usual."

"Got to bed early last night. We've a lot of work ahead of us, and I wanted to catch up on my sleep. Is Adam up yet, or Dixon?"

"You know Adam's always early, and Dixon is gone. Brian, what's going on?"

"Going on?" he said innocently. "Mother, I don't understand what you mean. There's nothing unusual going on around here that I know of."

"Oh, you boys are exasperating," she said. "Go on downstairs while I go to wake your father. I can see you're going to tell me nothing."

Brian chuckled but did not deny her words. He walked down the hall away from her whistling softly under his breath. As she watched him leave, Jessica suddenly got an instinctive feeling that not only were they up to something, it was something they were doing their best to keep her and their father from knowing about. It gave her the uneasy feeling that whatever it was, it just might be a danger to her family.

Adam went to Holly and put both arms about her, pulling her close to him. For several minutes he held her without speaking. Then he tipped her face up and brushed her lips with his.

"You know, you took my mind off the subject last night, so we never did decide what to name the baby."

"Did you think it over and decide on something you like?"

"Well, I thought if it was a boy, we'd name him Brandon, and if it's a girl, we'll call her Leah. What do you say?"

"I think both names are beautiful, Adam."

He kissed her again this time slowly and thoroughly. They were both flushed and bright eyed when the others arrived for breakfast. It was a lively and happy breakfast, and soon they were ready to go about their day's work. Adam sent Brian on an unnecessary errand, to give him an excuse to ride to the other plantations and tell the others their plans. Then he set about work himself.

Dixon arrived at the Merriweather's home by the time their breakfast was over. He tied his horse and walked to the door. He took off his hat as Amanda's mother answered the door.

"Good morning, Mrs. Merriweather."

"Good morning, Dixon."

"I would like to talk to you and your husband, Ma'am."

"Of course, Dixon, do come in." She stepped aside and let him pass her, then closed the door.

The Merriweathers had owned a lovely plantation before the war. After her husband and son had gone off to fight, she had decided, instead of staying alone, to spend her time at her sister's home in town. She never returned home. The house was burned to the ground and all their possessions with it. Then she had the news of her son's death. When her husband returned home, they lived together in her sister's small house and slowly they started a small store. As time went on, the store prospered a little, enough to give them a decent living and buy her sister's home. The sister had gone with her husband to live in Mississippi. It was a comfortable home, and they were happy there. If she ever regretted the loss of what they had, she showed no signs of it.

"My husband is in the parlor, Dixon. It is almost time for him to leave for the store. He always has one last cup of coffee there."

"Is Amanda up, Mrs. Merriweather?"

Selina Merriweather could see Dixon's nervousness, and her eyes twinkled merrily. "Just as I'm sure you've been, Dixon, Amanda's been up since dawn."

Dixon flushed a little and cursed himself for being so obviously nervous. He felt himself shake inside and wondered if she could see it also.

"You go in. I'll go call Amanda."

He nodded and walked toward the parlor door, as Selina thought, like a doomed man going to his hanging.

Amanda's father rose from his chair as Dixon walked into the room. He extended his hand with a friendly smile.

"Good morning, Dixon. What brings you here so early?"

"Mr. Merriweather, there's something very important I want to discuss with you, sir, if I may?"

"Of course, Dixon, sit down, please."

Dixon sat, uncomfortably on the edge of the couch.

"What is it, my boy?"

"If you don't mind, sir, I'll wait until Amanda and your wife are here. It concerns all of us."

Axel Merriweather and his wife were both well aware of Amanda's feelings for Dixon. For some time, they had tried to dissuade her from thinking of him. But Amanda had firmly stated she would marry no one else if Dixon didn't ask her. Amanda had confided in her mother about Dixon's proposal, and she had promptly discussed it with her husband. Both of them had agreed that, despite his physical impairment, Dixon was a good, hard-working man. He had a reputation for honesty and loyalty. To Amanda's father, these were two of the most desired qualities to look for in any man. He had agreed with his wife and daughter that Dixon Gilcrest was a good catch. None of this was known by Dixon, who felt her father was looking at him like he would have liked to see him on the other side of the world. Dixon began forming arguments in his mind on why they should give their one and only daughter to him. The welcoming sound of footsteps and the arrival of Amanda were a great relief to Dixon, who rose and smiled at Amanda. "She's so beautiful," he thought wildly, "Why in God's name would she ever want me?"

Amanda was lovely. Her happiness glowed in her eyes, and her cheeks pinkened with excitement. She did not hesitate for a second as she walked immediately to Dixon's side and tucked her hand through his arm holding it close to her.

"Well, Dixon?" Axel asked quietly.

"Mr. Merriweather, sir . . . I . . . well Amanda and I . . . I mean. Amanda and I would like your permission to marry, sir."

"I see," Axel replied. He looked very thoughtful and leaned back in his chair crossing his fingers over his rather large stomach. "I see."

"I can take good care of her. We've got the plantation almost on its feet. She'll not be in need of anything, I promise you, sir. She'll have a good home and all that I can get for her."

"Well, so far, Dixon, you've offered her everything she needs except the most important thing."

"Sir?" Dixon was dumbfounded at what he could mean.

"You haven't said anything about loving her, son," Axel said softly. For the first time since his arrival, Dixon could see the smile in his eyes. He was filled with relief as he said firmly to her father, but he looked at Amanda, "I love her, sir, more than anything in this world, more than my own life."

"Good, good," smiled her father. "On that basis and considering all the other 'extravagant' things you've promised, her mother and I give our permission and our blessing."

Dixon saw clearly the glow of delight in Amanda's eyes as she squeezed his arm again.

"When do you two want the wedding?" Selina asked.

"Next week," Dixon said without thinking.

Her father broke into a hearty laugh as Amanda flushed furiously.

"Well, we'll leave you two to discuss the date. I must be off to work." He rose from the chair and went to Dixon and extended his hand. "Welcome to the family, son, I wish you all the happiness in the world."

"Thank you, sir," he gulped.

Selina walked out with her husband, and before Amanda could say a word, Dixon's arm was about her and his mouth searching for hers. She surrendered at once to his need to hold her and melted against him, her arms about his neck and her willing lips opening under his.

"God, Amanda," he whispered, "I was afraid he was going to say no. I was prepared to grab you up and run."

"You know, Dixon. I'd have gone with you anywhere, anytime."

He held her against him, his hand pressing on the middle of her back. He could feel the softness of her pressed against him and the smell of the light scent she wore. Her arms were still about his neck, and her hands

305

caressed the back of his head.

"Make the wedding as soon as you can. Will you, Amanda? I don't think I can stand it. I want to take you home. I want to know you belong to me."

"It will be soon, darling, soon."

He smiled down into her eyes, reluctant to let her go, but hearing her mother returning, he brushed his lips against hers and dropped his arm.

On the ride home, he tried to put his mind on the plans for tonight, but his wayward thoughts continuously went back to Amanda. Giving up any other thoughts, he relaxed and let himself enjoy thoughts of the near future.

His news was received with a great deal of excitement at home. Deline had accompanied Bram, and Steffany had come with Devlin, neither of them knowing the real reason for the visit. Deline was overwhelmed with happiness when Dixon told her of his and Amanda's plans to marry soon. Her eyes began to sparkle with familiar signs of mischief, which Dixon caught immediately. The old comradeship was there again. He winked at her from across the room, giving her a lot of credit for the happiness he had found.

The dinner was the gayest they had spent since they had all been safely reunited at the end of the war. Dixon suffered some good-humored jokes from Brian and the others. No one but Jessica and Matthew realized that this sudden get-together of the family meant anything else but a celebration of Dixon's future marriage.

After dinner, Adam and Holly broke the news that they were expecting their child in a few months. This called for more drinks and many blessings and good wishes.

It was long after dark that night, as the women were sitting in the parlor chatting, that the men took the opportunity to slip away to the barn. They discussed in quiet voices how they would proceed.

"You know how Kensey's house sits, right between

those two hills," Dixon said, as he sketched a map on the dirt floor. "Behind the house is that large stand of trees. It's the only place from which they could come or else ol' man Kensey would see them. We've got to have all but me and Brian stay on the other side of the crest of the hill. As soon as they attack, Brian and I will be right behind them. I don't suppose it will take the rest of them too long moving in on us thinking they've got us trapped. Adam, Bram, Devlin, Graham, we're counting on you riding in fast. There won't be much time for me and Brian if you don't come down on them quick and hard."

"This is dangerous for you and Brian," Graham said. "What if they shoot before we can move?"

Brian's teeth flashed in a bright smile. "They're not going to. We have complete faith in you, Graham."

"Thanks a lot," Graham replied grimly.

"I'm bringing Steffany over to your place, Bram. I don't want her home alone," Devlin said to Bram.

"Good, because I was afraid for Deline and the kids, too. It will do them good to be together. You know it's not going to take them long to figure out what we're up to."

"Yep, we're going to get more fire from home than we will tonight." Bram laughed.

"If we could catch one of them and find out who's behind this and why, maybe we could put a stop to it," Adam replied.

"If possible, we'll try to get hold of one of them," Brian said. "We'll meet back here. If anybody can capture one, bring him here. Maybe if we scare him enough, he'll tell us who's behind all this."

"Agreed," said Bram. He stood erect. "I suspect we'd better get back to the house."

They all agreed to this and left the barn, walking together toward the house. Brian and Adam fell a little behind the others.

"Brian, if we get through this tonight, you have to go

307

up to Taylor County and guide the farmers here. I've set out enough property for three of them for now. With a half of their combined crops and mine, we'll see our way clear for this season."

"Good idea having only three. That way we're not giving away too much of our property either. Where do I pick these people up, and what are their names?"

"They should be all packed up and ready to travel. Their names are Grayson, Beauregard and Stoddard. All of them are good reliable farmers with families. I checked them out before I offered any of them land. All of them are in the same boat. Burned out by the Yankees, they've been living pretty bad until now. You'll find them all collected at Grayson's old farm outside of Sutterville about three miles. I don't think you'll have any trouble finding it."

They walked along in silence for another minute.

"Brian?"

"Uh, huh?"

"You got something on your mind you'd like to talk about?"

"Who me?" Brian laughed, but the laugh was hollow. "You know ol' Brian, Adam. I got no problems."

Adam was silent. He knew Brian was lying, but there was no way he could do anything unless Brian wanted to tell him.

Brian couldn't, for he could not put his finger on what was bothering him. Brian, who had been happy-go-lucky all his life, was having a hard time recognizing loneliness when he saw it.

Chapter 37

Though the day had been warm, by dusk, black clouds skittered rapidly across the moon and the low rumbling sound of thunder could be heard in the distance. A cool breeze blew across the river and put a slight chill in the air.

Beneath the dark clouds, the five shadowy figures sat their horses in the deep shade of the trees and watched the house at the foot of the hill. No light could be seen through the windows, but they knew that no one was inside except one man. He had sent, at Brian's warning, his wife and children to a friend's house, and as they waited outside, he waited inside.

They sat motionless, watching closely down the hill to a patch of dark woods directly across from the house about two hundred feet away. This is the direction from which they expected trouble to come.

One of the dark forms stirred, and spoke in a whisper. "I imagine it's about time, Dixon. You and Brian should move down closer."

There was no sound from the two in question, but they slowly edged their horses forward and moved like two silent ghosts down the hill. They stopped at the edge of the trees and remained motionless. It was almost midnight, and as Brian's informant had told him, midnight was the time they would strike. Neither Brian nor Dixon spoke; both were tight with nerves. They knew that four or five mounted men would be on them as soon as they were spotted. It was up to Adam's timing to keep them from getting killed. The breeze began to mount a little, and the temperature began to drop. Dixon was grateful for the long cape he wore over the uniform. It not only hid the fact that he only had one arm, but it protected him from the bite of the chill wind. He tried to relax his tension by concentrating on Amanda, but when he did, he only realized how upset she would be knowing where he was tonight.

The thudding of horses' hooves brought them both alert. Breaking from the far edge of the woods came five riders. They were bearing down on what they thought was an unsuspecting farmer. They were less than forty feet from the door when the farmer fired on them. They broke ranks and began to circle the front of the house. Dressed in dark clothes, it was not possible for the farmer to see them clearly, and he fired again in panic random fire.

"Ain't no use farmer," one of the men shouted. "We warned you once to pack up and clear out of here. You don't take our warnin', we'll have to show you we mean business."

Suddenly a torch flamed, then another. It was obvious to Brian they meant either to kill the farmer when he came out or to burn him with the house.

Brian and Dixon were no more than twenty feet behind the scavengers, but they were just within the shelter of the woods. They knew they could be heard but not seen. Brian raised his voice just enough so that he knew it would carry.

"If ah was you gentlemen, I wouldn't try lighting anything on fire with them torches."

There was no doubt in either Brian or Dixon's mind, from the reaction of the scavengers, that they were expected. There was no excitement among them as they turned in the direction of the voice.

"Well, well," the leader of the scavengers said. "If it ain't our night riding friends."

Dixon and Brian urged their horses ahead so they could be seen clearly. By the light of the torches, it was impossible not to identify the Confederate uniforms.

"You rebels can't seem to learn when you're licked, can you?" one man sneered.

"I've told you before," Dixon said softly, "Lee may have surrendered, but I have not. This is my county, and I want you scum out of it, one way or another."

A ripple of suppressed laughter flowed through the group.

"What you goin' to do, Reb? You two goin' to chase us all by yourselves?" He looked around him as he spoke to see if his witticism amused his partners. It did, and he swelled with confidence, knowing there were four or five others in the woods prepared to capture the night riders. Dixon spotted his false confidence immediately and singled him out for capture if possible. He knew that a mob was not courageous and that usually the loudest among them was the most cowardly when faced with a real opponent.

"You boys ought to go home and bury those uniforms."

Brian chuckled, but it was not a very humorous sound as he edged his horse closer to the group. He also had singled out the speaker, and he stopped his horse just a few feet from him, with his pistol pointing directly at him. Even though he knew the others were out in the woods, he felt a chill of fear as he looked into cold blue eyes that held no sign of fear or compassion. He began to perspire, hoping that the men with him did not recognize his fear and wondering where the men were who were to come in and catch the night riders from behind. But

311

he wasn't the only one wondering.

"Don't make the mistake of dropping those torches. We want a good look at your ugly faces. This time we've decided not to just run you off," Brian said softly, "we think it would be more permanent if we just hung you from one of those trees to sort of show as a warning that we're through letting you Yankee scum walk on us."

If the leader had been frightened before, he was more so now, and very grateful that he had the reinforcements in the woods. It gave him just enough courage to reply.

"You ain't gonna do nothin', Reb, 'cuz by the time the sun shines tomorrow, you'll be a dead man."

"I doubt it, friend," Dixon replied. "My friend here is going to pass among you and relieve you of your guns. I do hope you will sit still and not do anything foolish. I'd hate to pop one of you off," he chuckled. "I think I'd rather see you hang."

They had no way of knowing that Dixon didn't have a gun on him. With one hand, just holding his horse motionless was a chore. Brian nudged his horse with his heels to close the distance between them. This is the moment the others in the woods made their presence known.

At the same time they burst from the woods, the air was filled with a loud rebel cry. Brian could have shouted with laughter as he realized, Adam had been clever enough to split up. Roaring down through the trees they sounded like a small army.

The reserve force was so astounded and so sure they were being attacked by a large group, they wheeled their horses and ran.

Brian pushed himself forward in a dead run straight at the leader. His gun held butt first, he struck him on the side of the head before the man knew what was happening. He slid slowly from his saddle and fell with a solid thump on the ground, lying still.

The men holding the torches dropped them in all the confusion and all light was extinguished. In a moment, they were broken up as each man for himself ran for the woods. Loud crackling lightning and rolling thunder accented the surprise of Adam and the others. Several loud shouts and a few shots from their pistols in the air finished the rout. Brian was laughing heartily by the time the others returned.

"Christ, Adam, you sounded like the whole army comin' down through those trees."

"Did sound rather impressive, didn't I?" Adam grinned. "Unless I miss my guess, they'll run all the way home thinking the whole Confederate army is on their tails."

"Well," Devlin said, "let's get this one inside and see if we can get him to tell us what we want to know."

Rollins Mueller was a large man, and it took the combined efforts of Graham, Devlin and Bram to lift him from the ground and carry him inside. Once in the farmhouse, they tied him to a chair.

"Put out all the lights and just light one candle, so he can't see too well," Adam ordered. They did as he asked. Adam dragged a chair in front of the tied man with its back to him, then he straddled it, and with the light behind him, he looked like a huge black shadow. They sat quietly and waited for the man to wake up.

Mueller stirred, then blinked his eyes open. He was a large man, but most of his muscle had long ago turned to dissipated fat. He took one look at the dark figure seated before him, and his face turned gray; his body began to tremble, and large beads of perspiration broke out on his forehead.

"Wh—what do you want with me? Who are you?"

"We want," said Adam in a deep, cool voice, "a name, my friend, only a name."

313

"What name? I don't know what you're talking about."

"The name of the man who organized you and tells you what to do."

"I still don't know what you're talking about. We just all got together. There ain't no boss."

Adam didn't move, but continually stared at the man before him, who would have given anything to see behind the scarf that covered the lower part of Adam's face.

Brian walked toward them slowly from the opposite side of the room. In his hand, he held a thick coil of rope which he slapped lightly against one leg as he walked.

"He ain't goin' to say anything. He's too dumb. Dumb enough to give up his life for someone who don't care if he lives or dies. Let's hang him right now. He probably don't know anything anyhow."

Brian reached out and began to fumble with the bonds that held Mueller to the chair. If the man had been frightened before, now he was clearly terrified. His eyes widened in fear.

"God," he whimpered, "you ain't goin' to hang me. I ain't done nothin, and I don't know nothin. I swear to God I don't know any boss's name."

"Oh, well," Adam said softly, "since you are so loyal to him and value your life so little . . ." He shrugged and rose from the chair. With slow casual steps he walked to the door and pulled it open slightly. "Bring him along. I'll find a nice sturdy tree." He pulled the door open and began to leave.

"Wait!" gasped Mueller, as Brian again began to fumble with the ropes that bound him.

"What for? For the things you've done to the people around here, you deserve just what you're going to get. I've no time to waste on a stupid puppet who doesn't realize he's being tossed to the wolves."

"Please, wait! The only name I know is Jessie Colton.

314

He's the one who knows what the boss's name is. Honest to God, that's all I know."

Brian turned to Adam who continued standing by the door watching Mueller. Then slowly, he walked back toward Mueller. As he came, he withdrew the pistol he had tucked in his belt. Kneeling by Mueller, he put the barrel of the pistol to Mueller's temple.

"There is nothing your group does that we don't know about. Now I know your name, and you would find it very hard to hide it from me. Outside is your horse. Leave the county. Leave the state. For if I ever see your face around here again, I'll kill you. Do I make myself clear?"

Adam punctuated his speech with little nudgings of the pistol barrel against Mueller's sweat-soaked face.

Mueller nodded violently, his throat so constricted with fear he could not talk. Once his bonds were released, he leaped to his feet as though shot from a cannon and bolted for the door. Within minutes, the receding sound of a rapidly running horse could be heard.

"What now, Adam?" Graham asked.

"It's too late tonight to do anything, and I seriously doubt if Colton will see our friend again. I'll ride into town tomorrow and find out what I can about him."

"I think it would be wise right now if we all headed for home," Brian interjected. "We'll wait for a while to catch Jessie Colton at just the right time."

Devlin shook his head slowly, "I know Colton, Adam, and he's not a smart enough man nor does he have enough money to be behind this."

"I agree," Adam said, "and he's probably the only one who knows who the real boss is. Somehow I don't think he'd be fooled as easy as this one."

"Well, let's head for home and make our plans tomorrow," Brian said. "I'm tired."

"Tomorrow you've already got a job to do," Adam replied.

"Oh, that's right. I've got to ride up and guide those farmers down here. After that note you got Adam, we're leaving ourselves wide open for an attack."

"What note?" Devlin said sharply.

"I received a warning not to put any sharecroppers on my place or else," Adam answered.

"Then we'd better question Colton soon, Adam," Devlin said. "Maybe we could find the boss before he gets a chance to do you any harm."

"We'll give it a few days," Adam said firmly. "I'll check around, and Brian can bring the new people in. If I don't find out what I want to know, Brian can contact his informer and find out as much about Colton as he can."

They all knew that there was no point in arguing with Adam. He was the chosen head of the group by unanimous consent.

The farmer whose house they were in had sat in complete silence watching the scene before him. He liked Brian because he knew him so well, but he had now developed a respect for Adam's caution and deep thought before he attacked a problem. Now, for the first time, he spoke to them. "You're right son," he said to Adam. "Don't go off half cocked. You boys got the safety of a lot of people around here resting on your shoulders. I know it's best that not too many people know who you are, and no one will ever get a word from me. But keep in mind that we farmers aren't a spineless lot. If worse comes to worse, we'll unite and stand behind you."

"With no guns and no protection for retribution on your families? No, we've got the best plan so far. As long as they don't know who we are and how much we know, they'll be a little more cautious about who they attack. In fact, I think it will be a while before we see them again. I want to bring my people in and get them organized. I think if we do this right, we'll make these people strong enough so they won't need the night riders any longer.

316

They'll be able to stand alone like they should."

The farmer nodded. "Anything I can do for you, son, you just send the word."

"Well, I guess that's settled," Devlin said. "Let's go home."

They left the house together and rode along in silence. The storm that had been hovering all evening built in strength, and they wanted to get home before it broke.

"One consolation," Brian said, "they won't be able to follow any footprints after tonight. If this storm gets as bad as it looks, there won't be any trail left."

They passed the boundry to Gilcrest land and Adam, Brian and Dixon separated from Graham, Devlin and Bram and cut across the outer fields to Briar Hill. The other three continued along for a while without speaking.

"I hope Adam isn't goin' to get hurt by his waiting," Devlin said thoughtfully. "He's always so busy worrying about someone else, he doesn't think of himself. If these men we ran across tonight get mad enough, like a cornered rat, they're going to spring on someone and really bite. I'd just hate for Adam to be the one who gets bit first."

"They haven't really attacked any of us directly yet," Brian said. "They're cowardly. They only attack those they think can't fight back."

"They'll get at us either way," Graham added. "If they get us through the small farmers or in a direct attack, they'll get the same effect. You know we can't survive without help from the sharecroppers. We can't afford to hire help, and with no slave labor, there's no way of running things without working together."

"Well, I'm for sticking by Adam whatever he decides to do. I guess I'll wait until Adam says move. He's always done what he thinks is best for us all," Bram said softly.

"I never said he didn't think of our benefit all the

317

time," Devlin answered. "I said I'm worried that when they do get pushed into a corner and decide to turn on someone, I'm afraid it might be Adam."

"You're right. Maybe we'd better keep closer contact than we have been. We've been so busy trying to get our places going, we don't realize how vulnerable each of us is by himself," Bram answered.

"Anyway, could you talk to Steffany about staying at Cross Oaks with Deline until this is all over?"

"I could try, Bram, but I certainly wouldn't count on too much success. You know Steff as well as I. She isn't exactly the type to run scared. She's more likely to pick up a gun herself if she thinks someone is threatening our home. She wouldn't even leave home tonight no matter what I said."

They all laughed realizing that Devlin's statement covered their wives as well.

They reached the river, and Devlin left them. Turning downstream, he followed the river until, under a great oak tree, he could see the lights of his home reflecting through the now-beginning drizzle of rain. By the time he reached the barn, it was pouring, and the thunder rolled loudly followed by fierce flashes of lightning. He unsaddled his horse, rubbed him down and led him into his stall. Bolting the barn door behind him, he ran across the yard to the porch. He pushed open the door and had to lean against it to get it to close against the rising wind. Taking off his hat and coat and shaking loose the water, he hung them on a rack behind the door. Then he walked to the doorway of the parlor; it was empty. Crossing the parlor, he walked through the dining room to the kitchen. There, he found Steffany sitting at the table. There was an untouched cup of coffee in front of her, and she was reading a piece of paper she held in her hand. When she finally noticed him at the doorway, she rose from the chair and ran to him. Throwing her arms about his neck, she cried his name softly, "Oh, Devlin, I'm so very glad you're home."

He instinctively knew something unusual had happened, and he had a suspicion it had something to do with what she had been reading.

"Steff, you're shaking all over. What's the matter?"

"Not long after you left tonight, I was working upstairs. I heard this terrible crash. I ran down to see what had happened, and I found this tied to a rock and thrown through our front window. Whoever threw it rode away quickly before I could get out to see who it was."

"Who it was! You never should have even thought of going outside. What if someone intended you some harm instead of just throwing this. Steff, don't ever do that again."

Steffany stepped back from him.

"And just who intends me any harm, Devlin O'Brien? You'd better sit down and tell me exactly what you've been up to staying out so late and just exactly what this note means."

Devlin went to the table and picked up the note. He was almost sure he knew what was written on it already, but he read it more to take the time to think up what to say to Steffany than anything else.

"Get off Gilcrest property. You're being given one warning. The next time there will be more broken than a window. O'Brien, if you value your life and your woman's, you'd better plan on sharecropping somewhere else. This land is not safe for you."

It was unsigned as Devlin expected it to be. He was angry. Yet he was afraid for Steffany. Then he thought of something and read the note over. It occurred to him

319

then. They did not know that Steffany was a Jemmison and belonged there. They thought that she and Devlin were sharecroppers. They were successful in one thing. Devlin was afraid enough for Steffany to get her out of here as soon as possible. The best place for her now, he thought, was if she would go back home. But would she go? Somehow he had to find the words to make her. "Sit down, Steff. I'm going to explain to you just what's going on. Then you'll understand that temporarily we have to leave here and go to where it is safe for you."

Without an argument, Steffany sat down at the table. Devlin sat down opposite her and took her hand in his. Then slowly, he explained exactly what was going on and what they had done that night. When he finished, he said softly, "Now you see why I have to get you out of here for a while?"

"No, this is my home. No cowardly Yankee is going to drive me out of it," she stated angrily.

He grinned. "All Yankees aren't cowards, Ma'am," he said. "Don't you remember the Yankee who had so much courage he captured a houseful of rebels single handed?"

"Oh, you're different," she laughed. "We've changed you from your terrible Yankee ways."

He stood up and pulled her up into his arms, kissing her so firmly and holding her so tightly she was breathless when he released her lips.

"Let me put it to you another way. Steff, you're everything I've got in this world. I want to help Adam and the others, but I can't. I can't because I won't leave you alone here. I couldn't stand it if anything happened to you. There would be no use in my trying. So you see, my lovely, if you want us all to be able to stand together, you've got to do your share by giving me the freedom to help."

Steffany smiled up at him, and he could see that all

argument was gone from her eyes.

"My mother should have warned me about you Irishmen and your magic tongues. I'll bet you could talk the saints right out of their silver slippers, Devlin O'Brien."

He laughed with her. Then his eyes became serious as he slid his hands gently over hers.

"If I could talk the saints out of their silver slippers," he said with a suggestive leer, "what are my chances of talking my wife out of a few pieces of clothing that stand between me and something I want very much."

Steffany cocked her head to one side and contemplated him very seriously, as though making a great decision.

"Well, I don't know. Suppose you give me a few samples of your argument and let me decide."

Devlin pulled her tight against him. She could feel the hard pressure of his desire. His mouth sought hers in a kiss that sent her world spinning and left her breathless and warm with the need for him.

"Well," she said softly. "There go my silver slippers."

Devlin threw back his head and laughed, then scooped her up in his arms and carried her to their room where they put aside all other thoughts but each other and their continual renewal of their promise of love.

Chapter 38

Jessie Colton was not a coward, but he was not necessarily a brave man either. To him, the matter of bravery or cowardice depended entirely upon the situation in which he was involved at the moment. When he had waited with his three accomplices in the woods for the night riders to appear, he considered himself quite brave. When the surprise attack came from behind them, he considered it wise to desert rapidly in the face of an overwhelming number that he would have to face. This, of course, was not cowardice; it was wisdom. Now he was faced with an even bigger test.

He pulled his horse to a stop and waited for the others to gather near him. He spoke shortly and angrily to the men around him.

"They were expecting us, goddamn it! They were expecting us."

"How could they know, Jess?" one of the men spoke up. He was a rat-faced man with his long pointed nose and protruding teeth; his bald head made him appear more rodentlike along with the continual blinking of his expressionless black marbled eyes.

"Some son of a bitch in our group has told him, that's why. We've a squealer in our midst. And after I tell the boss, we'll find out one way or another who he is and he'll be a dead man, quick!"

The rodent-faced man's nose twitched alarmingly like a rat sniffing out something edible.

"Want me to try and find out who it is, Jess?"

"I don't need any help from you, Zekel. You mind your business and just do as you're told."

"Okay, okay, Jess. Don't get mad at me. I'm only trying to help."

"You men go back to the cabin. Stay put until I ride over and see the boss and find out what he wants us to do."

He watched as the men rode away from him. He was upset, but not because he had to face the boss and tell him about it. He turned off the main road and cut across the country. At the edge of the group of cabins that formed the riffraff of Northern army deserters that had come down to try and make a killing, stood a small cabin a little away from the group.

There were at least twenty cabins strung out along a recently cut dirt road. It was an area unsafe for anyone to travel.

Colton walked his horse slowly to the front of the cabin, dismounted and stood beside his horse for a moment, trying to figure out just how he was going to break the news to the boss. Then slowly he walked up on the porch and knocked. A muffled, "Come in," and Jess lifted the latch and walked in closing the door softly behind him.

"Evenin', boss," he said.

"Colton, you're back early."

"Well, boss—" he began.

"Not only," the smooth voice said, "are you back early, but my lookout says there is no sign of fire from Kensey's way. Run into trouble, Colton?"

The voice was smooth and deceivingly soft. The man who sat in front of the small fireplace was a big man. Across his forehead was the band of a black patch that

323

covered his left eye and extended behind his left ear. His hair was thick and black and a little long. He had the broad, deceiving smile of friendliness that extended no further than his lips. His one eye was cold and expressionless, and Colton got the same eerie feeling that he was pinned down and about to be taken apart piece by piece.

"I have to explain to you, boss," he muttered.

"Please do, Colton, I'm waiting with what I consider a great deal of patience."

"They was expecting us."

"Two men were expecting you, two men! And you six or was it eight, and these two men probably fought their way out, right, Colton?"

"It wasn't like that, boss. The way I figure it, we got an informer here. Someone told them we were comin, and they got help. Just when we got those two night riders, about forty of them attacked from the woods. We was outnumbered, so we got outta there."

"An informer? Who?"

"I don't know."

"Well, we've got to find out."

"Boss, wouldn't it be easier to hit all those little farmers down along the river than the ones on Gilcrest, Forrester or Jemmison property?"

The boss rose from his chair and walked slowly toward Colton who began to shake with fear. He stood close, and Colton was sure he was looking into the cold eye of death.

"Colton," came the soft easy voice, "I'll tell you once, and I'll never repeat myself again. I came here and invested my time and my money for one purpose, and I won't let any stupid jackass like you stop my plans. I don't give a hoot in hell about those other small farmers, but there's three places I want to own, and one man I want to see dead . . . Adam Gilcrest. Not only do I want him dead, I want him to do a lot of suffering before he goes. Now he's got two brothers and a sister, and before I own Briar Hill, they're all going to feel my touch. I promise you, Briar Hill will be mine, and Adam Gilcrest will crawl on his knees to me before I kill him. Now," he tapped Colton on the chest and accentuated his words, "you find out who the informer is, and you get the men together and hit those other three farmers Gilcrest has coming, just as soon as they get their houses up and their crops in. Do I make myself clear?"

"Sure, sure, boss, I understand," Colton said rapidly.

"Get out of here, Colton, and get your business done or you might find yourself replaced . . . permanently."

Colton nodded rapidly and backed toward the door as anxious to get out of the room as the boss was to see him go.

After Colton closed the door behind him, the large man went back to the chair and sat down. His face was grim. Pure undiluted hatred coursed in his veins, hatred for one man. It was the kind of hatred that controlled him day and night. Dreams at night and the urgent necessity for revenge by day. It occupied his thoughts always. He, of all people, knew how dear to Adam's heart, Briar Hill and his family were. He knew also that the best way to destroy Adam Gilcrest was not to kill him, but to take away from him the things he cherished most.

Jess Colton was so relieved to be out of the house, he stood by his horse and leaned against the saddle for a moment too weak to mount. Then, after he was sure he was safely away from the danger, he became angry. It took him some time of furious thought before his singular intelligence leveled his anger at two people. The informer who made such a fiasco of tonight's attack and Adam Gilcrest, who caused the boss to be so upset with him.

Determination set in, and he promised himself that he was going to find the informer, whoever he was, and was

325

going to kill him personally. He went back to his own cabin. Inside, he was greeted warmly by the woman he kept. Stella was a prostitute at the age of thirteen. One of nine children who were born to a couple of illiterate cotton pickers who traveled from place to place. She was never sure who her father really was, for her mother spent more time making money flat on her back than picking cotton. Raped by one of her mother's clients at thirteen, it was not long before Stella realized that she could make enough money to eat by the use of her body. From there, it was man to man constantly changing and constantly worse. She hated Jessie Colton, but for now, he provided the food she ate and the clothes she wore.

She greeted him warmly because it was what was expected of her. She was thirty now, and she knew it would be harder and harder to find a man to take care of her. Stella had given birth twelve years ago to a son. Because Stella was in such poor physical condition and did not have the help of a physician, she had a difficult time giving birth, and her child, a boy, was born mentally slow. Now, he had the blank look of an infant. If Stella spoke slowly to him, he would obey her promptly. In his own way, he adored her and would have done anything to keep her happy.

Stella kept the boy out of Colton's sight. She had insisted that she bring her son with her and Colton had agreed as long as he was kept away from him. In return for cooking his meals, caring for his clothes and the use of her body at his will, she received shelter and a place to keep her son.

Up until a few weeks ago, Stella had kept her side of the bargain. Then one night, Colton had come home exceedingly drunk. As it happened, Stella's son was there, for she fed him and cared for him before Colton could get home. Finding the boy there, Colton had become unreasonably furious and beat the boy badly.

Then he had thrown her on the bed and taken her in front of the boy. That was the beginning of a simmering emotion Stella did not even understand. From that moment, she began to search for a way to find some money to escape Colton. She found it; the only thing she was afraid of was that Colton would find out before she had enough money to get away from him. Hidden in a black box under the wood stove was all the money she had saved, except what she gave to Zekel for being a go between, for she was the informer Colton was so hungry to find.

"Are you hungry, honey?" she asked.

"Yeah, what you got to eat?"

"I got some of that stew you like, and I baked some fresh bread today."

"Good, put it on the table."

He sat down at the table and watched her as she dished up a bowl of stew, sliced some bread and put it on the table before him. Along with this, she set before him a bottle of whiskey and a glass. Then she sat opposite him and watched him wolf down the food.

He leaned back in the chair with a glass of whiskey in his hand and belched. Then he reached for her.

"Come here, baby, set on my lap."

She moved obediently and sat on his lap, smiling although she hated the feel of his hard hands as he fumbled about her body carelessly. She moved as she knew he wanted to feel her move.

"You been out late tonight, honey," she said softly.

"Yeah," he muttered.

"Are you tired?"

"Not too tired to take care of you," he laughed and began to pull away her clothes.

"Where you been all night?"

He was so preoccupied by his need for her he gave no thought to her questions and as his lust increased so did

327

her questions until she had the whole story out of him before he pushed her to the floor and took her violently and carelessly, unmindful of her feelings. Satisfied he got up, and with his bottle, he staggered to the bedroom. In another hour, the bottle was empty and Colton was snoring heavily in a deep sleep.

Stella stood over him and watched him sleep. Then throwing a coat over her shoulders, she slipped out of her cabin and walked around back. She stood in the shadows of the tree until she heard a small whistle. Soon she was joined by Zekel.

"Did you get the money?" she asked.

"Sure did. Told him we needed more too," he laughed.

"Zekel, are you crazy? We need Brian Gilcrest, you damn fool. If he gets mad and cuts off our money, we're done."

"He ain't gonna. He agreed and gave me ten more dollars, and it's in gold, too."

"Let me see," she said anxiously.

She held out her palm and felt the good feeling of the sack of coins he dropped into it.

"You get the same as before. I get the extra ten."

"What! Why you sneaky little—"

"You shut up, Stella. I take almost all the risks and you get most of the money."

"I find out all the information first."

"Yeah, but it's me that takes the chances on deliverin' the information. You think it's easy to get out of here and back without anyone knowing?"

"All right, all right," she said in angry disgust. She was prepared to leave when Zekel grabbed her arm. She jerked free and turned to glare at him. Then Stella made one of the greatest mistakes of her life.

"What do you want, Zekel?"

"You wanna have that extra ten, Stella?" he asked slyly in a soft whining voice.

"What you talkin about, Zekel?"

"All you have to do is come over to my cabin for a little while. I bet Colton's already had his, and he's so drunk he's sleepin' it off."

"Come over to your cabin!" she said, as if she were stunned by such a suggestion. "Why you crawling little rat! I wouldn't come to your cabin if you was the last man in the world. Sleepin' with you is more worth ten million than ten dollars. Go back to your hole, rat, and leave me alone."

He glared at her. Then he spat noisily on the ground. "Come to think of it, I don't think you're worth layin' for the ten dollars. I got better places to spend it."

Stella laughed. "There ain't any woman that would let you have it for ten dollars, Zekel. I bet you ain't had any woman that would lay with you unlessin' she was blind or so old she couldn't run away fast enough." She laughed again and headed back to Colton's cabin.

Zekel stood and watched her walk all the way back. The name "rat" had been flung at him just one time too often. He quivered with rage as he watched the sway of her hips. His eyes burned brilliantly, and he suppressed the urge to follow her and beat her until she submitted. Instead, the seed of an idea came to him and he smiled. Stella would pay, he thought. Oh, yes, Stella would pay.

Stella slipped back into the cabin soundlessly and stealthily hid the money with the rest of her cache. How she longed to spill it out into her lap and count it, but she knew it was impossible. If any sound in the world brought Colton awake, even if he were drunk, it would be the clink of one coin upon another.

When Colton was wakened in the morning by the sound of Stella moving about, he was surly and hungover. She was used to him being this way, so she stayed out of his reach and did not speak to him. After he had his coffee and then some breakfast, his mood seemed to improve, at least to the point where he would talk.

"You goin' out again tonight?"

"Mind your own business, Stella. Where and when I go ain't none of your concern."

"I just wanted to take a run over to see my boy," she pleaded. "Ifin' you don't need me, I could visit him a while."

"Yeah, go on ahead. I gotta go check around. See if I can get any clues to our squealer. Then I got to watch and see if the Gilcrests try movin' those three farmers in after we warned them."

"That Adam Gilcrest, he's really somethin', ain't he? I bet he ain't afraid of anything."

"Well, if he ain't, Stella, he sure as hell should be. The boss is out to get him, and it ain't just to kill him either. He must have done something terrible to the boss. He's goin' to take it out on all them, especially Gilcrest's family. No, sir, I wouldn't be in their shoes for nothin'."

"The boss," she said, "doesn't he have a name?"

"Sure he does," laughed Colton, "but you or nobody else but me is goin' to know what it is. That's one thing he'd kill me over for sure, if they found out who he was before he wanted them to."

The boss's name was something she had been trying to get out of Colton for weeks. But no matter how drunk he was, the fear of the boss stayed his tongue. Stella felt that name would be worth the money to the Gilcrests to get her and her boy as far away from here and Jessie Colton as she could get.

Colton spent the next week with a close eye on all his men and watching Adam's property. He brought home the news a week after the aborted raid that Brian Gilcrest had guided in three farmers who were in the process of building their homes. He was surprised when he brought the news to the boss that he didn't seem angry. Instead, he smiled and told Colton that he would let them build.

Colton was told to stay away from them until their houses were up and the families in. "Then," he promised Colton, "we're going to hit them when they least expect it. Yes, sir," he laughed, "we're going to give them a big surprise."

Obedient to his every command, Colton told his men to relax; there would be no action for a while. Time went by. The farmers on the surrounding plantations relaxed, too. Since there were no more attacks by the raiders, they were under the impression that the night riders had put a stop to them. Both Adam and Brian knew they were wrong, but Brian could get nothing more from Zekel than that the raiders had no immediate plans to do anything.

It was several weeks after Colton had reported that all the farmers had their homes built and were preparing to plow that the boss called him in. He came immediately and stood across the table from him as he was given definite instructions on what to do. Then he went out, gathered his men and told them of the plans.

Stella, watching him approach the cabin, knew something important was about to happen. She was wondering if she would be able to get the information out of Jessie.

He ate hastily and didn't speak. No matter how she tried to get the conversation around to his plans, he would say nothing, giving noncommittal grunts for answers. She was so busy trying to get him to talk to her that she did not realize he was watching her closely under black brows drawn together in a heavy frown with his head lowered.

He listened to every word she said despite the fact that he acted as though he only partially heard what she was saying. He was thinking, as he watched her move about the room, of something Zekel had said to him. He told Jessie that he had to talk to him later, that he had to tell him something important, and it had something to do with Stella.

Although Jessie Colton had never loved anyone or anything in his life, he was attached to Stella in some way. She gave him some of the comforts of life without asking much from him, and that was a satisfactory situation for him. Now he was harboring a small suspicion that Stella had a deeper motive for staying with him than just for the safety of her son. Something in the way Zekel had said those words made him begin to wonder if there was some connection between Zekel and Stella. He could not really believe this, but he knew there was something he did not understand. He was going to talk to Zekel soon and find out.

He finished eating and rose from the table. Picking up his heavy coat, he prepared to leave the cabin.

"Another raid?" she asked, watching his face, for it was Jessie's eyes that told her most of the things she wanted to know. They shifted away from her, and he did not answer. A feeling of deep uneasiness struck her for a moment; then she shrugged it aside. She had to have some information to sell Brian Gilcrest. She needed just a little more money, and she would be able to pick up her boy and get away from this part of the country for good.

"Jessie?"

"Leave me alone, Stella," he said harshly, "I've told you a million times, it's not any of your business when I'm goin' or what I'm doin'."

She watched him leave the cabin and closed the door solidly behind him. Some kind of alarm rang deep in her mind, a note of warning. For the first time, she ignored her natural instincts. She was determined to find that one piece of information she needed.

It was only about a half-hour after Jessie had left the cabin that she heard a light knock on the door. Opening it, she found a grinning Zekel on the doorstep.

"What you doin' here?" she demanded.

332

He looked about him as if afraid someone would see him. Then he put his fingers to his lips.

"Shh, Stella. I gotta tell you some news I found out. It's important. I think Brian Gilcrest would pay a lot for it."

"Then, why don't you meet him," she asked suspiciously. "Tell him and get the money."

"That's the problem, I gotta go with Jessie right away. I was supposed to meet Gilcrest tonight, and I can't. You'll have to go in my place."

"Me! I can't do that. What if Jessie comes back?"

"Jessie's going to be out all night. It only takes a few minutes to meet Gilcrest. You'll be back before Jessie has any idea you're gone."

Stella eyed him nervously, and prepared to refuse again.

"Look, I found out the boss's name. I was listenin' at the window tonight while they was talkin'. This information could get us all the money from Gilcrest we want. Now, I can't go. If I ain't with Jessie, he'll get suspicious. You got to go."

Stella hesitated for another minute. Then she sighed disgustedly and pulled the door farther open so Zekel could slip inside.

"What's the name, and where do I meet Gilcrest?"

Zekel leaned close to her and whispered the name he had heard in his spying and the instructions on where she could meet Brian.

"Okay, now, get out of here, Zekel."

He nodded and slipped out the door. Outside he stood still for a minute. Then grinning broadly, he could barely contain the excitement bubbling up inside of him. He had no love for Jessie, and after her blunt refusal of him, he hated Stella, too. Well, he thought gleefully, tonight he would fix them both.

He made his way to where Jessie was saddling

his horse.

"Jessie, I gotta talk to you."

"I'm busy, Zekel, talk to me later."

Zekel was angry, and he would love to have had the courage to attack Jessie and beat him until he begged. He knew it was an impossibility, so he settled for what he considered the next best thing.

"I know who the informer is," he said in a whisper. Jessie's head snapped around, and now he gave Zekel his undivided attention.

"Who?"

"Stella."

"Stella! You're crazy, Zekel."

"Crazy am I? Well, you follow her later tonight, and you'll find her meeting Brian Gilcrest, setting you down the river for some money."

Jessie became coldly angry. "Stella, huh? Where and when, Zekel?"

Zekel told him when Stella was meeting Brian, then left him standing there. He knew Jessie would follow Stella and most likely kill her when he found out the truth. He was going to find himself another source of money for information. Possibly Dixon Gilcrest, he thought happily. He wondered just how Stella was going to feel when she found herself trapped. He wished he could watch as Jessie made her pay.

Chapter 39

Brian came awake suddenly. He'd been feeling that way a lot lately, and he hated the feeling. It was as though his mind and body were going in opposite directions. He lay still with his hands folded behind his head and listened to the birds sing in the crisp predawn air. The house was still. It was still early for the women to be up to prepare breakfast. He wanted to be dressed and gone before they were up. He found it more and more difficult talking to Holly now. She was too perceptive and asked him too many questions that probed places that were too sensitive to touch. How could he tell her what he felt when he couldn't even understand himself? He remembered the evening before. It was one of those nights that he felt exceptionally unsettled. They were all sitting on the porch after a late supper when Holly turned to Brian. "Brian, you haven't played your guitar and sang for a long time."

"I got rid of the guitar, Holly," he lied. Then he wondered why he had lied to her.

"Oh, Brian, you shouldn't have. You played and sang well. Especially love songs," she teased.

He did not rise to her humor as he usually did.

"Reckon it's about time I put those kid things behind me, isn't it?" he said a little sharply.

Holly was surprised at the tone of his voice, as were the

335

others. She laughed a little to cover up the surprised silence that followed.

He felt rotten, and he rose from the bed, washed, then dressed rapidly. Leaving the house as quietly as he could, he walked toward the barn just as the first rays of the morning sun lifted the heavy blanket of night.

Saddling his horse, he let him walk slowly away from Briar Hill. It was his job today to ride up and guide the farmers in, so he decided since it was going to take most of a day and a half to get there he may as well start as soon as possible.

He rode along easily. Brian was a natural born horseman and he rode without thought. His mind drifted from one subject to another. He wondered why, when everyone in the family seemed so organized and happy, did he feel as if he was going off in all directions all the time. He needed some goal, something to aim for to make all the living and doing worthwhile.

The road took him along the river for several miles. There was a fresh breeze blowing in softly from the river, bringing with it the soft scent of blooming wild flowers. The sun became brilliant, and the air heavy with the sounds of the awakening earth. Birds called from tree to tree. Often he would watch one lift gracefully from a tree and, with a flutter of wings, soar free and uninhibitedly through the bright sky.

He could hear the rush of the river as it twisted and rushed toward its destiny, the ocean. He felt a oneness with this hidden life. The urge for free flight, the desire for a promised destiny. The grass along the river and the trees beside it seemed greener than every other place, so he eased his horse off the road and down to the riverbank. After letting him have a cool drink and a short rest, he mounted again. Instead of going back to the road, he followed the edge of the river under the cool shade of the trees.

He traveled several miles until it came time for him to sever himself from the river and cut across country. He did this reluctantly, for he enjoyed this cool green world. Now, he came to the edge of a ridge of foothills and decided to stop and have lunch before he crossed them. He had planned to camp for the night on the other side of them. He unsaddled his horse and hobbled him to crop a patch of green grass. Spreading out a blanket, he sat down and undid the bundle he had brought for lunch. He had two large pieces of fresh-baked bread from the day before which he spread thickly with butter, a large piece of cheese and an apple. These he washed down with water from his canteen. Satisfied, he lay back against the blanket and watched the random patterns in the white clouds overhead.

He dozed for an hour or so, and then gathering his things, he resaddled his horse and resumed his journey.

He let his horse again pick his own way, for now he was no longer following a road. There was not even a path to follow. He could see why the farmers would have a hard time finding them if they had never been this way before.

The hills were the complete opposite of the riverbank, where it had been clear and clean in the morning air; the hills were deep shadows under tall trees that clasped hands over him occasionally letting a strand or two of sunshine slip through and find its way to the forest floor. He traveled upward through these for over three hours before he felt the ground begin to grade downward. Suddenly he broke from the edge of the forest into a grass-filled meadow with patches of yellow flowers scattered about it. It was a lovely scene, and he stopped to enjoy it, chuckling to himself for his sudden romantic interest in the beauty of the meadow.

Cutting diagonally across the meadow, he reentered the trees on the other side. Again, the arched green shadows covered him and the coolness was more tangibly felt after the bright sunshine of the meadow.

Resting his horse several times, he made his way slowly through the trees and emerged at the top of a high bank that led downward and met again the traveled road.

By this time, the sun was nearing the horizon. Brian decided that he would camp here for the night. Half a day's travel on this road would take him to Sutterville. From there, he knew he would have no trouble finding the Grayson farm. He just hoped they were all packed and ready to leave. He didn't like to be away from home too long with the kind of trouble they'd been having. Adam and Dixon might need him, and he wanted to be there if they did.

Getting the horse readied for the night, he took his gun and, in a short while, was cleaning and skinning a rabbit. Building a fire, he manipulated the rabbit on a stick, added a little salt and suspended it close to the fire to roast. Using his saddle to support himself, he leaned against it and watched the yellow flickering flames. This was the time that was the worst for him. He felt uncared for and the deepest sense of loneliness. He tried to search his mind for good memories and dig them out and wave them in the face of his misery to dispel it. He remembered women he had known, and suddenly discovered that they blended together until he could not put a definite name or description to any of them. Brian had always been laughingly assuring himself that he loved easily. Now he bitterly discovered he had never loved at all.

Angry with his own self-pity, he flung the memories aside. Sitting up, he took the roasted rabbit from the spit and ate it. Then taking his saddle blanket, he rolled in it, and using his saddle for a pillow, he lay down and went to sleep.

By dawn, he was again mounted and on his way. It was just before noon when he reached the outskirts of the

338

town of Sutterville. It was a very small town that consisted of two winding streets that crossed each other and, in the center, stood a large white church with a tall narrow steeple. There were several houses bordering each street, most of which were very old and had been there since the town was started over eighty years before. The houses were small but looked comfortable. Between them, here and there, were the small businesses that kept the town alive. A blacksmith, a milliner, dress shops and a general store were scattered haphazardly throughout the town as each one who owned a business usually lived in the house next to it. Trees lined both streets, and the brilliant green leaves heightened the bright white of the houses. The two streets that crossed each other meandered lazily out beyond the houses and twined and turned through the countryside. From the hill overlooking the town, Brian could see the small farms dotted here and there about the countryside. This was the source of the food supply that kept the town alive.

He drifted into town, listening to the signs of life pick up as he neared it, the shrill laughter of children and the bustle of the inhabitants going about their daily affairs.

Brian went first to the blacksmith who kept a large barn for boarding the animals of town visitors. Stopping in front of it, he stepped down and approached a large man, stripped to the waist and working diligently over the brightly fired forge.

"Good afternoon, sir." The man spoke pleasantly to Brian with a welcoming smile.

"Good afternoon," Brian replied.

"Something I can do for you?"

"Yes, could you direct me to the Grayson farm?"

"Of course. If you follow the west road," he said pointing, "about three miles down, there's a small road that cuts off to the right. Take it and go on a ways and you'll run across Grayson's place. You can't miss it; it's

339

burnt most ways to the ground."

Brian smiled, "Thank you, sir."

"You be Brian Gilcrest?"

"Yes."

"Ol' man Grayson told me he got a piece of property from your family in return for workin' it for five years."

"That's right."

"You're gettin' a good man, son. Grayson family had been farmin' around here for almost eighty years. Helped build the town to what it is today. Hate to see him go."

"Why doesn't he stay, then?"

The big man spat, then said quietly, "Lost his place. Yankees burnt it, and then the Federal taxers came in and taxed him right out of it. They got a prime piece of property for nothin'."

"That's too bad. Maybe things will be better now if he works ours for five years. It'll be his, and he can start all over again."

"Yep, that's how he figured it."

"You seem to be doin' all right," Brian said.

The man smiled, and Brian noticed the fine lines at the corners of his eyes that gave the impression he smiled often.

"Well, son, I work with my hands, so I can work anywhere I can build a fire and set up an anvil," he laughed. "They ain't found a way to tax that yet, but I reckon they will someday."

Brian laughed. Then the man reached out a large hand toward Brian.

"My name's Gifford, John Gifford."

Brian shook hands with him and was relieved to retrieve his in one piece. Gifford's hand smothered his in a handclasp like iron.

"Want to come in and set a spell, have a cold drink?"

"I'm tempted, Mr. Gifford, but I can't. You see, we got our own troubles at home, and I got to get back."

"Well, you tell Grayson I wish him good luck. Same goes for all the others, too."

"I will, sir."

Brian mounted and headed his horse down the west road and past the outskirts of the town. He found the rutted road that turned off the main one and followed it for almost three miles before he could see the half-burned remnants of what had once been a beautiful home. It sat on the top of a hill and commanded a majestic view of the valley below. Brian tried to visualize how it must have looked before the war, and found the old sadness tugging at him when he thought of the great beauty that must have been there.

Assembled in the front yard were four large wagons, loaded to capacity and a group of people standing about obviously waiting for his arrival. As he rode up, one man left the group and took a few steps in his direction. He waited until Brian came up beside him and dismounted. Then he extended his hand with a broad smile.

"I'm Howard Grayson, sir, and I believe you are Brian Gilcrest."

"Yes, sir, I am," smiled Brian. He took the offered hand and felt the hard strength of it. Their eyes met, and Brian felt an immediate liking for the man.

Howard Grayson was a tall man, he stood an inch or so over Brian's six foot one. He gave the first impression of extreme thinness, yet later Brian revised the idea to wiry, for he was strong and had long tightly pulled muscles. He had deep gray eyes, and a nose that took command of his rather long, pointed face. His thick, black, wavy hair was cut short and seemed inclined to leave his head at any moment.

"Let me introduce you to the others," he said, as he touched Brian's elbow and led him in the direction of the group.

Howard motioned to the closest man of the group, a

341

rather small man with slightly rounded shoulders. He had deep intelligent blue eyes and a warm smile.

"Mr. Gilcrest, this is Nathaniel Beauregard and his wife, Rachael." Brian bowed slightly toward the woman and extended his hand to Nathaniel.

"Mr. Gerald Stoddard and his wife, Cora, and the three young people behind are Nathaniel's daughter, Sarah, and Gerald's two children, Samuel and Gaylord."

"I'm happy to meet you all and be the first to tell you how happy my family and I are to welcome you to Briar Hill. We've already cleared the land for each of you and have made as many preparations as we could. We'll help you build and get your first plowing done. I'm sure we can work together for the benefit of all of us," Brian said.

They thanked him and began to ask him some questions about Briar Hill.

"I'll try to fill you all in on the way home. With all this equipment, I think it will take us at least three days, so if you all are ready, we'll get started. That way we can cover as much ground as possible before dark."

"Well, we're almost ready," Grayson replied.

"Oh, I forgot, sir, is your wife inside?"

"My wife died two years ago."

"I'm sorry, sir, is it your children we're waiting for?"

"My daughter-in-law. She's finding it rather difficult to leave. You see my son's buried in our family plot out back. He came back from the war wounded and died right after he got home."

His voice was gentle, and Brian could see the deep clouded look in his gray eyes. For the first time, he realized how bad it must be for these people to leave behind their homes and roots and move to a strange place among new people. His voice was much gentler as he spoke again to the older man. "Does she know we're ready to leave?"

"Yes. She's out back saying her goodbyes. If you would like to walk back, son, and I'll introduce you to her."

They walked away from the group and around toward the back of the house, through high grass and debris. The back yard was overgrown also. It was edged by an unattended garden that had a profusion of flowers growing carelessly. A wooden fence surrounded it. Walking to the fence, Grayson opened a gate and held it as Brian passed through.

About fifty feet away, a figure stood with its back to them. Grayson slowly led Brian in her direction. She stood very erect, yet her figure gave him the impression of terrible sadness as if it carried a weight far beyond its capabilities. They stopped within two feet of her, but she was obviously so engrossed in her thoughts, she did not hear them coming.

"Samantha?" Grayson said softly.

She turned and Brian saw the hastily brushed away tears.

"Mr. Gilcrest, this is my daughter-in-law, Samantha. Samantha, this is the man on whose land we will build our new home."

She took the two steps that separated them and extended her hand to him.

"Mr. Gilcrest," she said in a soft musical voice.

Brian took her hand in his and looked down at her. She had soft blue eyes, rather gentle and shy, set in an oval face; she had a small straight nose with delicate nostrils; her lips were full and wide. She was slender, almost tiny. The thick black waves of her hair fell about her face in tiny curls and was tied back with a ribbon. "She is," he thought, "one of the loveliest women I've ever seen."

"My name is Brian," he said quietly. There was never a time in Brian's life that he lost his charm and ability to talk with pretty girls. But it happened, now. There was an aura of sadness about her that made him want to reach out and comfort her, to say something that would ease the pain he felt emanate from her.

He looked down at the two headstones that stood side by side. "Amalie Grayson" was the name on one and "Daniel Grayson" was on the other.

"Tragedies of war," Grayson said. "They died close as they lived."

Brian watched the girl's face as she looked at the older Grayson. Pity flickered in her eyes, and she reached out and gently touched his arm. He looked at her, and some of the sadness left his face. It was as if they drew strength from one another. Without a word, Grayson turned and walked away from them. She watched him go and then turned to look at Brian.

"It is so very difficult for him to leave them both here."

"And you?" he said gently.

"I? I have lost a husband, but his grief is so great, for he has lost both a wife and a son." She looked up into Brian's eyes and could see clearly the sympathy and gentleness there. They were two emotions she could not yet bear; the grief was too fresh, too deep. She shied away from it. He watched in admiration as her shoulders stiffened and her chin tipped determinedly.

"Shall we go, Mr. Gilcrest?"

He noticed that she did not use his first name as he offered. He offered his arm, and she took it, lifting her skirts a little as they walked through the tall grass and back to the wagons without exchanging another word. He handed her up to the wagon seat beside Grayson, then mounting his horse, he rode back to Grayson's side.

"Ready, sir?"

Grayson clucked to the horses, and they were on their way. Brian noticed that neither of them looked back.

He rode along beside them, but with only supreme self-

344

control could he keep himself from looking at her. Again, the surge of admiration hit him. To be widowed and homeless was a terrible thing for a girl as young as she to bear. Yet she showed more pity for her father-in-law than for herself. Brian chastised himself for all the self-pity he had been wallowing in for a few hours before. What he had experienced was nothing compared to what she was living through. He had a home and a family who cared deeply for him. He felt small and weak in comparison to these people, and a small touch of ingratitude for all that he had. It gave him the urge to hurry home, just to kiss his mother and sit and talk with his father, to enjoy the comradeship again of his brothers and sisters. He only wished that there was some way he could share what he had with Samantha and her father-in-law. Maybe fate had guided him to their side to lead them back among friends and to a new life. Sometimes it is better to leave old memories behind, as they were, and begin anew.

He promised himself he would do whatever he could for them as soon as they got home. He never realized, until many weeks later, that it was at that moment he had completely abandoned any thought of ever leaving Briar Hill again.

Chapter 40

Steffany reluctantly left her home. She and Devlin had built it by themselves, and it contained the sweetest memories she had. She made it unquestionably clear to Devlin that she was only leaving for her family's sake. They went to Heritage, where her mother greeted her warmly. Since the war was over, Tyler Jemmison had been a completely changed man. He had finally convinced Odella to move back to Heritage and try to begin their lives over. Odella had misgivings for the memory of his affair with the slave, Portia, and the birth of a son was still a raw wound in her heart. Tyler knew this, but he tried in every way possible to make Odella comfortable and happy.

When the war was in its death throes, the Yankee army had lived at Heritage. Portia and her son had disappeared. If Tyler ever wondered where they were, he gave no sign to Odella of his thoughts.

He greeted his daughter with a warm smile and welcome arms, for he thought her arrival might make Odella a little happier.

Devlin rode over to Briar Hill to see if Brian had returned yet. He had not, so Devlin returned to Heritage. Steffany helped her mother around the house, but with two of them, it made less work, so to Devlin's delight it gave Steffany more time to spend with him. They took

346

long walks together, sometimes with a picnic. He would use any excuse he could find to get her away from her parents. The time was good for them, and they found a bright new depth to their love.

The days drifted on uneventfully, and slowly everyone began to relax and hope that the raiders were gone for good, had given up on the sharecroppers and decided to leave them alone.

It was Dixon who really never relaxed his vigilance. He visited with Amanda as often as time would allow and urged her at each meeting to rush the plans for their wedding. She would laugh at his impatience, but she knew deep inside she was as impatient as he was. Each evening, he left her more and more reluctantly, held her more and more tightly and kissed her more and more hungrily. Finally Amanda told him that all the preparations were done, and they would be married the week after Brian came home.

No one heralded the day Brian arrived with the farmers more enthusiastically than Dixon did. His enthusiasm left Brian dumbfounded until Holly whispered in his ear what the reason was.

Holly could see quite clearly that the trip had changed Brian somehow. It was not until she met Samantha and watched Brian's face as he spoke of her that she realized what was happening. After being told Samantha's story, she wanted to sympathize with her and her father-in-law until they made it clear that pity was one thing they didn't want or didn't need. They were starting a new life, and they intended to put forth every effort to make it a good happy one.

The farmers' houses and barns were erected by the entire family. They would get together at one place, and as all the men worked on building, the women would cook. After the sun went down, they would build a fire and enjoy the food, then, as the fire died, they would sit around the red embers and sing. It was then, to Holly's amusement, that Brian's guitar was suddenly resurrected. The three houses and barns were up in two weeks, and Dixon invited all three families to the wedding.

"It's going to be the grandest bar-b-que since the war," he stated firmly.

Brian had taken to dropping in on the Graysons often, checking up to see no one was causing them any trouble was his excuse, but seeing Samantha was his real reason. This was something that was observed and understood by only two people, Holly and Howard Grayson.

Howard Grayson had loved his wife and only son as dearly as possible. When his boy had first brought Samantha home, he was delighted, for he could see that she made him completely happy. Then the war struck, and his son had gone off to fight only to come home so seriously wounded that, despite Samantha's nursing, he had died. They had buried him in the family plot, but that was not enough tragedy. Two weeks later Amalie Grayson followed her son. Samantha could have gone away then, back to the family from which she had come, but she chose to stay with him. She wanted him to know that because of his son she loved him and wanted to try to ease his grief if she could. Howard and Samantha sat in the comfort of their small parlor. With much help, what furniture they had was arranged by Samantha. The room was plain and simple, yet held all the charm of a comfortable home.

"Samantha, is Brian coming over tonight?"

"I don't know," she said softly, her eyes intent on the sewing in her lap, they conscientiously avoided his. "I really don't see why he should be. Our house is completed and the fields are plowed and ready for seed. There's nothing more for him to do here."

"Now, Samantha, you and I both know that's not the reason that boy comes around. I suspect that Brian doesn't really know yet. I don't even think he realizes, he's in love with you."

"Don't," she said in a choked voice, and stood up from the chair and walked to the door and looked outside. The night was warm, and a soft breeze blew in from the river, lifting the night sounds and carrying them. Millions of stars and a huge golden moon lit the night sky.

"Papa," she said. She had called him so since she and Daniel were married. "I don't want you to say that again. I never intend to love anyone again," she whispered softly.

"That's not right, Samantha," he said gently. He rose and went to her. Putting one arm about her shoulder, he drew her against him. "Daniel would have been the last person to want to hear you talk like that. You're young and alive. You need love, as everyone needs love."

He could feel her shoulders quiver, and he knew she was crying silently.

"Let me tell you something, Sam," he said with a smile, reverting to his name for her. "Love is one of the most beautiful things in the world. Given enough time, it can heal the most damaged heart. You, for some reason, seem to think that finding another love should make you guilty of something. That's not true, and it's not natural. That boy had been hurt, too, Sam, and he's looking for someone to help heal his wounds."

"I can't, Papa, I can't!"

"Maybe not right now, but let time heal. Open up to the world again, Sam. You've got a long and, I hope, a happy life ahead of you," he said softly, then kissed her forehead gently.

Brian rode along slowly, whistling gently under his breath. The old Brian had returned with a vengeance, he was happier than he'd been for a long time. He didn't know why, but he suspected it had something to do with seeing Samantha.

349

Although neither of them had spoken of love for each other, he realized that what he felt for her was different than anything he had felt for any other woman.

There was a softness, a gentleness about her. When he was in her presence, he felt comforted and at home.

"She was so beautiful," he thought. The way her eyes softened as she looked up at him, and despite the fact that she had been married, she had an innocent air about her, a trusting air, and it made him want to hold her and protect her from any other sadness that might come into her life.

Suddenly his thoughts were jolted alert, someone—or something—was behind a tree that was about twenty feet ahead of him. He had seen a stealthy movement. Pulling the pistol from the holster at his side, he rode to within three feet of the tree, then said calmly, "I'd suggest you come out of there with your hands in the air, my friend, or I might just be forced to blow your head off."

The figure hesitated for a moment, then stepped out from behind the tree. It was a woman with a dark shawl wrapped about her head and shoulders. She took a few steps, then motioned him to come to her. Brian looked about him carefully, but she seemed to be alone. He urged his horse forward until he was beside her. Her face was a pale shadow under the shawl, and he could barely make out her features.

"You're Brian Gilcrest. I've watched you ride this way before. I had to be sure."

"I'm Brian Gilcrest. What business do you have with me that you couldn't come up to the house with it?"

"I'm the one who sent Zekel to you."

Brian looked at her. He had to be careful of any kind of a trap, but what reason would a woman have to be out on a dark road, on foot, at this time of night?

"Where's Zekel?"

"He couldn't come, and I had to get this information to

350

you and tell you one more thing."

"What is it?"

"First, I'll tell you the information you're paying for tonight, then," she said pointedly, "we'll discuss the price of the rest of it."

"What do you have to tell me?"

"Your brother Dixon is gettin' married day after tomorrow, right?"

"That's right."

"Well, the night after that, when you all are relaxed and not expectin' anything, they're goin' to hit two farms together. They figure you both can't be in two places at one time."

Brian chuckled. "Maybe they'll get a surprise and find out that we can be. Which two farms is it?"

"Grayson's and Beauregard's."

"You got a lot of others workin' with you now, don't you?"

Ignoring her question, Brian asked, "What other information do you have for me?"

"Something I think you'll be willing to pay double for."

"Double! Money isn't that easy to get a hold of today, woman. We have to pool our resources to get the money to pay you now."

"Well, then," she said quietly, "you pool your resources because I'm askin' double for what I know. After that, I have to get out of here or my life won't be worth a dime."

"What do you know?"

"The boss's name," she said softly.

There was no sense, Brian knew, of trying to bargain with her. The name of the boss had been something he'd been after from the beginning, and he had made that fact clear. Now that she had it, how could he pretend it was unimportant. In fact, he was relieved that she had not

351

asked for more.

"All right," he said. "Double. When will you meet me and tell me his name?"

"How soon can you get the money?"

"Couple of days."

"They're plannin' something else, maybe I can find out for you. You meet me here three days after the raid. Bring the money, for I'm not goin' back there after I give you the information."

"All right, I'll be here three days after the raid."

She nodded her head without speaking again, then turned and melted into the woods. Brian, whistling absently through his teeth, rode slowly toward the Grayson home.

The trail was quiet in the pale moonlight. It was serene and peaceful. Then, two figures could barely be seen from their vantage point.

"Ya see, didn't I tell you," whispered Zekel.

Jessie Colton nodded his head, and his wicked cold eyes gleamed brightly in the moonlight.

It was Howard Grayson that answered Brian's knock and greeted him with a friendly smile of welcome.

"Good evening, Brian."

"Evenin', sir," Brian answered, but Howard watched with amusement as his eyes fled past him in a search for Samantha, then brightened as they found her standing quietly at the fireside.

"Hello, Samantha," he said softly. His feelings were apparent in the tone of voice and the way he carried his body as he crossed the room toward her, as though she were drawing him to her and he had no control of it.

"Brian," she said gently. The fire lit the soft planes of her face and heightened the shadows under her eyes. She seemed so slender and fragile to him. He couldn't think of a word to say. He wanted just to stand there and let the peacefulness of her flow around him. He saw the tense look about her mouth, and felt the nervous flutter of her whole being, as though she were in great fear of something—something terrible, something that she could not stop.

"It's—it's a beautiful night," he said calmly, but the words screamed out in his mind. "Don't fly away from me, Samantha. I need you. I need you more than I have ever needed anyone before."

Her soft moist lips turned up at the corners, and her eyes smiled at him.

"Yes, it's lovely."

"Sit down, son," Howard said. "Samantha, get Brian something to drink."

Samantha moved away from him, and he was painfully aware that she took the warmth with her. He sat in the chair beside the fire, and Howard sat opposite him. Only half listening to what Howard was saying, he watched her pour him a drink and walk toward him with it. Her eyes were downcast as she handed him the drink, and he deliberately closed his fingers over hers around the glass. Her eyes widened quickly, and Brian was struck dumb with what he saw for one flickering moment. Fear, raw and painful fear.

"Why in God's name should she be afraid of me?" he wondered. Then as swiftly, he understood. She wasn't afraid of him, she was afraid of herself. She was afraid that Brian could reach an emotion, a place she had guarded for so long against intruders. She withdrew her hand quickly as though the touch of his fingers had burned her. Then she moved to a small stool by the fire and sat down.

Brian tried his best to listen to and answer Howard, but his eyes continually wandered back to Samantha, who sat quietly, her hands folded in her lap and her eyes concentrating on them as if they were the utmost importance at the moment.

"Did Devlin go for that last batch of seed, Brian?"

"Yes, sir. He went yesterday. They should be bringing a few bags over for you tomorrow."

"Good. The ground's ready."

"I'll come over with it and help you with the planting."

"That's not necessary," Samantha said, her voice low and trembling. "I'm sure we can get the planting done without help. You have done so much for us already."

"I want to, Samantha," he said quietly. She lifted her eyes and looked at him intently now. They were saying something to him he could not, or would not understand.

"That's wonderful, son," Howard said with a smile. Then he rose from his chair and stretched.

"Well, if you two will excuse me, this tired old body has to get some rest if I'm going to get up early in the mornin' and do all that plantin'."

"Papa!" Samantha looked at him with a look of almost anger on her face. Howard chuckled.

"Don't be distressed, Sam," he replied. "I'm sure Brian plans on leaving in a few minutes."

"Yes, sir," Brian said softly. But his eyes went to Samantha and held hers firmly. "I just want to talk to Samantha for a few minutes. Then I'll be on my way."

Howard nodded, then turned and walked down the short hall to his bedroom. The door closed softly behind him, and there was a deep and poignant silence that followed.

Brian got up slowly from the chair and stood in front of the fireplace with one shoulder leaning against it. He looked down on Samantha who had seemed, without moving, to have curled up within herself. When it came to Samantha, Brian never ceased to be amazed at himself. Brian, with the magic tongue, who was never afraid to seek out the favors of any girl, suddenly found himself without words, without charm and worst of all, with a shaken courage that was completely alien to him.

He watched the red glow of the fire play across her pale skin and the way she seemed to be drawing away from him and he knew. He knew that all her fears had nothing to do with him, that she was fighting a desperate battle within herself. He wanted to hold her, and tell her that, no matter what, he had the strength she needed. He wanted to ease the burden of whatever held her away from him.

"Samantha," he whispered softly.

"Yes?" The hands began to quiver restlessly in her lap. He reached down and gently took both hands in his and drew her slowly from the chair. She stood close beside him, and then he lifted both hands to his lips and kissed them gently. Slowly her eyes raised to his, and he saw they were filled with tears and a pain that was becoming unbearable.

"Don't be gentle with me, Brian, I don't deserve it. Let me be. Go away from me for your own good. I cannot give you what you want, what you need, what you deserve."

"I love you, Samantha."

"No, don't love me," she said with a choked sob.

"Then you tell me," he said firmly, "where is this magic thing with which I can turn love off and on. I love you. There's nothing I can do about it or want to do about it. I want you, and I need you as I've never needed anyone before in my whole life."

He pulled her closer. "Samantha, don't run away from me. Let me help you with whatever it is that hurts you so. There is nothing in this whole world we cannot overcome together."

"Brian, I'm not worth the effort. There is nothing in me to give," she cried out in real anguish. "Don't you think I've tried. I tried to love Daniel, but he knew before he left to fight that I couldn't. He used to look at me with those sad eyes and never condemn me as he should have." She was crying now, deeply and painfully. "And when he came home, so hurt, so in need of me, I still couldn't love him. I nursed him, but I did not love him and he died . . . he died," she whispered, "needing something I could not give. He deserved so much better. He was a good man, a kind and gentle man as you are. I will not do that to you. It is better you leave me now."

"One cannot be guilty of anything by not loving someone. It's not something you have control of just as the way I have no control of how much I love you," he replied tenderly. "And my feelings for you cannot be changed." He took hold of her shoulders and held her a little away from him. "Samantha, look at me."

She lifted her tear-stained eyes to his and saw the truth. But the guilt and the pain had been carried so deeply within her for so long it felt like a part of her being. She had punished herself with it daily.

"You didn't love your husband when you married him?"

She shook her head negatively.

"Can you tell me why you married him, then?"

She searched quietly, far into the depths of her heart, then began to speak slowly and very softly.

"I was so young and foolish, Brian. It was just as the war started. Emotions ran high then since all the men were leaving. Daniel had told me he loved me for a long time. When he came home for the first time after he had fought, he seemed so lost, so frightened that I accepted his proposal. It seemed to make him happy for a while. Then he was . . . well . . . always seeming to expect something from me that I didn't know or understand or at least I had none to give. He never condemned me or said a word against me, and that made everything worse. I felt so helpless. I wanted to make him happy," she whispered in an anguished voice, "but I couldn't. Then Daniel was badly wounded, and they brought him home." Her voice deepened as though she could barely control the grief she felt. "He used to watch me in silence as I nursed him. He would show me his gratitude in every way, yet deep in his eyes I could always see that searching, disappointed look. I—I almost hated him before he died. Hated him!" she said, as though she still could not believe it. "Hated a man who loved me and wanted to give me everything in the world. How could a normal person do such a thing? Why did God allow me to be such a cold, unfeeling person?" she was sobbing heavily, as for a moment, she leaned against him. He put both his arms gently about her and let her cry, her face buried against his chest. He felt that maybe the uncontrolled outlet of some of her grief would help ease the burden she carried.

"Samantha," he said gently against her hair, "if you were a cold, unfeeling person, none of this would have affected you. But you are a gentle, compassionate person, and so you have magnified the guilt in your mind. You're guilty of nothing but honesty. You cannot give love to a person without it coming from your heart. I've told you it is something you cannot turn off and on. I'm sure that he must have understood. If he did not condemn you, it is because he did not blame you for not being able to pretend."

She lifted her head from his chest and wiped away the tears. Then she stepped back from him. Their eyes met across a foot of space that seemed to Brian like miles.

"I—I cannot think of it any longer, Brian, not right now, maybe not for a long time. Please," she said in a voice that was almost inaudible, "please go."

Brian may have been temporarily stopped by Samantha's words, but he was far from finished.

"I'll go tonight. But I want you to understand something, Samantha. I love you, and I'm going to do everything in my power to keep you from sacrificing the rest of your life for an old memory. I'll be here day after day, night after night until I reach you, until I make you understand that you've never really known love and it isn't fair to you, or for that matter, to me, either."

Before Samantha could answer him, he reached out and pulled her into his arms. His hold was firm although she was too surprised to struggle, but his lips were gentle against hers. Then he was gone, and she stood very still and watched the closed door. A strange feeling of deep pain crowded her chest. She felt short of breath and sagged back down on the stool by the fireplace. Then she buried her face in her hands and cried.

Brian rode home slowly. He was angry. Not angry with Samantha, but angry with the husband who let her go on with her guilt. Angry with fate that made him fall in love with the only girl he could not get.

"Why," he wondered, "does life always give you freely the things you don't care for and holds just out of your reach all the things you really want."

Chapter 41

Dixon and Amanda's wedding was the brightest and happiest thing that had happened in the family since the war ended, and it was given all the attention and loving care that was possible. Amanda and her mother had shopped for the ivory satin material and soft pale lace for her wedding gown and veil. They sewed and fitted for long patient hours.

Mother nature cooperated with their happiness by creating a soft warm day with a cool breeze from the river that rustled through the trees and brushed gently against the bright summer gowns of the women.

It was, to the amusement of the others, Dixon who was tense and nervous. They watched his pale face during the ceremony and noticed the trembling hand and the way his eyes clung to Amanda's face. It was a beautiful ceremony, and Amanda made, they all agreed to her embarrassment, the most beautiful of brides. Her gown, cut in the latest fashion, hugged her figure and was drawn back to a full bustle in the back. Sleeves, full from shoulder to elbow, fit tightly about her lower arms.

Brian complimented Amanda on what a beautiful bride she made, then stated mischievously that it was about time that fashions considered the men. "At least," he remarked happily, "we've gotten rid of all those petticoats. Now if we can get rid of those cast iron corsets, a man might stand a chance."

Amid all the laughter and gaiety, Brian took an opportunity to get Adam aside. They stood together in a secluded corner.

"What's going on, Brian?"

"I got word from my informer. They're going to hit two places at once."

"Whose?"

"Grayson's and Beauregard's."

"When?"

"Tomorrow night."

"Well, I'm afraid for once Dixon's not going to be part of this. I'm not going to ruin Amanda's honeymoon."

"Well, then we'd better not say anything. You know how Dixon is. He can smell a rat for miles."

Brian had never been more right, for Dixon, at that moment, was watching them narrow eyed across the room. He followed his instincts well. He knew beyond a shadow of a doubt something was brewing, and he was determined to find out just what it was. He and Amanda had planned a short trip, since she understood, he wanted to be back before anything else might happen.

Making his way to Amanda's side, when she was in a conversation with some of their guests, he put his arm about her waist and was rewarded by her smile and the sway of her body against his.

"I'd like to talk to you alone for a minute, darling," he whispered in her ear. She nodded and excused herself. They walked out into the deep shadows of the veranda. Amanda stopped and turned to him.

"What is it, Dixon? Is something wrong?"

"No," he laughed. "Does something have to be wrong just because I want to have you alone for a minute?"

He put his arm about her and pulled her close to him and laid his cheek against her hair. He could feel her relax against him, and she wrapped her arms about his waist and sighed contentedly. Slowly he kissed the top of her head, then her forehead, each cheek, and finally his lips found hers. The kiss was a gentle touch, and his mouth caressed hers in a leisurely, yet thorough fashion.

"This is what I wanted," he whispered, "to have you to myself for a minute, to kiss you, to remind myself that this is not a dream."

Amanda looked up at him, and her smile glimmered brightly.

"Do you realize, Dixon Gilcrest, that this afternoon you and I, two separate people, became one? I'm so happy to have you as my husband, my darling. I want to do so much for you. I want to make you happy in every way I can. I love you."

"And I you," he replied, as his lips found hers again.

This time, the kiss was deep and searching, and it found the answering passion in hers. Reluctantly, he released her.

"Amanda—"

"Would you please tell me what is on your mind?" she said. "I know something is bothering you, and you might just as well tell me now."

"I think there's going to be a lot of trouble in the next few days over the sharecroppers, and I think Brian and Adam are up to something to keep me out of it and—"

"And, you'd like to postpone our trip for a few days to see just what is going on," she finished.

"Just for a day or two," he replied anxiously. "I'll make it up to you. I'm really sorry, Amanda, but if I went away and there was any serious trouble, I'd feel guilty for not being here to help."

"Oh, my dear, wonderful husband." She smiled and put both her arms about his neck. "Do you really think it matters where we are as long as we're together? I don't really care one way or the other if we take a trip or not as long as I'm with you. We'll stay here, and you do whatever it is you feel you have to do."

He kissed her again and again until she laughed breathlessly and clung to him.

"I love you, God, how I love you!" he murmured against her warm, parted lips.

"Dixon," she said quietly, "don't you think we'd best go back to our guests before they wonder where we are?"

He agreed reluctantly, and they went back in. They stood together and watched their guests.

"Brian's dancing with Samantha Grayson again," Amanda observed. "I think the young man's breaking a lot of hearts tonight."

Dixon nodded in agreement. It was obvious that Samantha received a lot of cold looks from quite a few of the young ladies present. Brian's forte had always been the ability to flit from one girl to the other, in some way keeping them all happy without arousing jealousy. But tonight was a different story. It seemed that everyone knew that Samantha was someone special to Brian. From the moment she and Howard had arrived, Brian had been seeking her out as often as possible to dance with or just to talk to. Whispers had gone from girl to girl, "Who is she? "Where did Brian meet her?" "I heard she's a widow and living with her father-in-law, really!" "A widow, with all these pretty unmarried girls here!" Grudgingly they had to admit that Samantha was beautiful. Her black hair had been coiled about her head like a thick rope, and her blue eyes seemed to sparkle. The dress she wore was plain and simple, pale blue cut with a scoop neck and long fitted sleeves; it accentuated the small waist with the bustle. A thin blue ribbon about the slenderness of her neck with a tiny cameo was all the concession she gave to accessories. Brian smiled down into her blue eyes and relaxed to the sound of the music as they swayed about the floor.

"Brian, this is the fourth time we've danced together,"

Samantha said. "Maybe you shouldn't pay so much attention to me. You're getting some rather nasty looks from a few others."

"Who cares about anyone else, Samantha? As far as I'm concerned, you're the only girl in this room. Did I tell you how absolutely beautiful you are tonight?"

Samantha's smile faded. "Don't, Brian."

"Don't what? Tell you how pretty you are?" he said with a hurt sound in his voice. "Tell you how much I love you, want you?"

Samantha dropped her eyes from his, but he could still see the shine of tears at the corners.

"Still beating yourself, Samantha. Still trying to pay for something you're not responsible for. Just how long do you intend to keep yourself nailed to this cross?"

Samantha's face paled, and he could feel her whole body tremble beneath his hand.

"I'll tell you something, Samantha," he said softly. "You can say anything you want against us. You can fight me with every argument you've got about your guilt. But somewhere, deep inside I know you care as much about me as I do about you. I won't give up. I told you that before. Someday, somehow, you're going to realize all this guilt is wrong. You're going to know the truth, admit the truth of how you feel, and I'll be here . . . waiting."

The music stopped and Samantha, with a small sound almost like a sob, moved away from Brian to stand beside her father-in-law. It was almost like she used him as a shield to protect herself from Brian's truth, for she did, in the hours when she was alone after he'd left the first time, admit to herself that she was drawn to him. But she had determinedly put the thought aside, not wanting Brian or any other to see inside her defenses. If she fooled anyone, it was not Howard. He looked at her with sympathy and pity in his gaze.

363

"Sam, Sam," he said softly.

"Don't, Papa," she said in a weak, broken voice. "If you say another word, I shall not be able to bear it."

"Can't I help you in some way, Sam?"

"Papa . . . I want you to understand. You know I love you, but I must leave. I must go back to my family," her voice faded. "I must get away from here."

"You can't run away from it, Sam. All the misery and pain, you'll take it with you wherever you go."

"I'll take that chance, Papa. Next week I'll make arrangements to leave, and," she looked up at him, her voice became firmer and her features stiff and hard, "I must have your word, you will tell nobody . . . nobody."

"Sam—"

"Nobody, Papa."

He sighed deeply. "All right, Sam, I give you my word. I won't say anything, but it's wrong, Sam, wrong. That boy loves you with the kind of love you should have had at the beginning. The giving kind, not the taking."

She looked at him in alarm. This was the last thing she had ever expected him to say. Anything against his son was alien to him.

"Sam, don't you think I knew how things were between you and Daniel. You certainly aren't to blame just because you couldn't love him the way he loved you. Put the past behind you, Sam. There have been others wounded in the war just like you, but they've picked up what's left of their lives and started over."

"Leave me be, Papa," she said, her voice kind but firm. "I will live my life the way I think best."

Howard knew there was no sense in arguing with her. He only hoped and prayed something would happen to bring her to her senses before it was too late, before she wasted the best years of her life.

Brian and Adam were both wondering why Dixon and Amanda were taking so long to leave. Brian had already told Devlin, Graham and Bram, and they were all waiting as patiently as they could for the couple to leave on their honeymoon before they met to discuss their plans. They watched with puzzled frowns as the guests began to leave, and soon the house was empty of all but family. Of course, it was the outgoing Deline who asked, "Aren't you two ready to leave, yet?"

"Deline!" Jessica said sharply, then smiled. "Will you ever be a lady?"

"Probably not, Mother," she chuckled. "But aren't you all curious. I just asked what you all were thinking," she added innocently.

Brian and Devlin exchanged amused glances. Deline would never change in a lifetime, and neither of them would have wanted her any different. Dixon stood next to the fireplace with his arm about Amanda's waist, and watching their faces closely, he stated calmly, "Amanda and I have changed our plans. We're staying here for now. We'll take our trip later."

He watched with amusement as he got the reaction he expected: complete silence. He laughed aloud at their shock and knew immediately that all four of the men knew exactly why they were staying, and Deline and Steffany were only a heartbeat behind their thoughts.

It was with a great deal of effort that they swallowed their remarks and questions, and Jessica quietly and diplomatically said that it was time they all retired for the night. The hour was late and Dixon and Amanda should be left alone.

Amanda kissed them all good night. Dixon stood leaning against the fireplace and watched them all climb the steps. They were alone, and as Amanda turned to face Dixon across the room, he smiled and extended his hand toward her. And she walked to him. He held her gently against him. They remained without speaking in a contented silence. Her cheek against his chest, she closed her eyes and listened to the slow steady beat of his heart. He kissed the top of her head gently, then rubbed his cheek across the silky smoothness of her hair. She tipped her head up and looked into his eyes. His head bent forward, and he touched her lips softly with his.

"Our room is the second door from the top of the stairs," he said quietly. "I'll stay here and finish my cigar and my drink, then I'll join you."

She nodded, realizing he was giving her time alone to make things as easy for her as he possibly could. For one second, as she watched him, she could see some fleeting fear cross his face. Then like a shadow it was gone, and his eyes smiled again into hers.

She nodded, stood on tiptoe and brushed her lips across his cheek.

"Don't be too long, darling," she whispered. Then she left him and, without looking back, walked up the stairs.

Dixon watched her, his face expressionless. Then he walked to the side table and poured himself a stiff drink. As he lifted it to his lips, he saw his hand was trembling. He was afraid. Not afraid to go to Amanda's side, but afraid the sight of his naked body with the lost arm would repulse her. He realized he was terrified with the thought that Amanda could turn from him. He closed his eyes for a second and felt the nauseous desire to run. With intensity, he willed himself still until he felt himself again in some kind of control. Slowly, he brought the glass to his lips and drank the contents.

Amanda sat in front of the mirror and brushed her hair. She was looking into the mirror but not at her own reflection. Instead, she saw Dixon's eyes, and suddenly it became clear to her, that fleeting look of fear she had seen. She stopped brushing. His arm, she thought. Why, he's actually afraid to show it to me. How could he possibly think I could love him any less? She sat very still. She wanted to get up and run down the stairs and throw herself into his arms and tell him it didn't matter, that nothing mattered, except their love for one another. No matter how much she wanted to, she knew she couldn't. She couldn't hurt him so. No, she must wait, and show him in every way that it didn't matter.

She heard the muffled footsteps coming down the hall and stop in front of her door. He opened the door, stepped inside and closed it behind him, leaning against it and staring at her in profound admiration.

She had stood up slowly and turned toward the door. There were only three candles lit in the room, and Amanda's gold-flecked hazel eyes reflected their brilliant glow. The gown she wore was honey colored, almost the exact color of her hair which she had brushed out and let hang free about her in a thick mass of waves that fell to her waist. The gown had a small border of ivory-colored embroidered flowers about the low-cut neckline; from this, it hung straight to the floor in small pleats. He could see the outline of her body through the sheer material.

"How beautiful she is," he thought. Then he moved slowly from the door and walked to her side. He reached out and gently touched her hair, feeling the soft fine strands of it drift through his fingers. Then he let his fingers slide to the nape of her neck, caressing it gently. Their eyes clung to each other, and very slowly, he pulled her to him until they touched. Holding the back of her head, he brought his lips close to hers until he could feel the soft moistness against his.

"Amanda," he breathed softly. "Do you want me to put out the candles?"

"No," she said in a kind but firm voice. She could feel the trembling of his hand against her head. Now was the moment, she thought desperately. I cannot let him be hurt; I cannot be afraid.

She backed up one step from him, and without her eyes leaving his, she raised her hands and slid them under his jacket, pushing it off his shoulders. Then very slowly she began to unbutton his shirt. He reached up and held her hand against his chest.

"Amanda, it's not the prettiest sight in the world. Let me put out the light. It would be easier for you."

"Easier for me, Dixon, or easier for you?"

Again the grief-filled look flashed across his face, and the hand that held hers shook.

"You are my husband. I love you more than anything, and I love you the way you are. Do you really think, Dixon, that seeing you will change anything? There is nothing that could make any difference to me."

Her hands moved again to the buttons of his shirt, and slowly, she unbuttoned each button, her eyes never leaving his. She felt the hard muscles of his chest tighten as she gently slid her hands across it and slowly pushed the shirt away.

Dixon's arm had been removed just a few inches above his elbow. Skin had been folded over the end of the stump so that it healed smooth and round. But a jagged scar ran up the front of his arm to his shoulder.

She thought of how much pain and suffering he had gone through, and her eyes filled with tears. But she held in check the pity that Dixon didn't need or want. Instead, her eyes lifted to his and he searched her face for any sign of disgust or pity. There was none; only love for him brightened her golden eyes.

With a choked sob, he pulled her tightly against him overwhelmed by the flood of love that flowed like molten lava through him. This was a woman beyond any other that he had ever known before.

"Now," she whispered softly in his ear. "Do you still want the candles out?"

He looked at her and grinned. "And miss seeing what I have found. Not on your life."

She laughed with him. He let his fingers caress her

368

shoulders. Then unfastening the hook at the neckline of her gown, he pushed it from her shoulders and let it fall to a heap at her feet. Her skin felt like warm satin under his hand as he let it drift down over her breasts to her waist. Then sliding his arm about her, he led her toward the large oak double bed. He watched her as she got on the bed. Sitting in the center, she made a lovely picture against the dark blue cover. He seemed bolted to the floor as he stood and watched the candlelight flicker over her body. Then suddenly, as though awakening from a dream, he hastily removed the balance of his clothes, discarding them carelessly. He caught her to him and enjoyed the feel of her body molded against his.

Amanda had always been told that "nice" girls were not supposed to enjoy being with a man. That it was something that had to be endured and only if one wanted to have a child. Consequently, she had always been curious, but had never met a man before that she wanted to touch her.

Now as Dixon's kisses set her mind reeling and caused the brilliant flash of hot desire that flooded through her body, she was glad she had waited for him. She whispered his name against his shoulder as she felt the hardness of his body against hers. If she was a little afraid, it was drowned in the aching desire for him that caused her to lift her body against his and cling to him as he found his way deep within her.

They were both past knowing anything else but each other. Her hands caressed his back, sliding down over his hips, urging him to possess her even more fully.

They lay in each other's arms in silence, too overcome by the magic of their love to talk. Amanda lay with her head against his shoulder and closed her eyes in deep contentment. She was lying so when she heard the gentle chuckle that Dixon gave, and she raised her head to look at him. He was smiling, and her lips twisted in a grin in response to the glitter in her eyes.

"Well?"

"I must remember to give my sister my heartfelt thanks."

"For what?"

"If it hadn't been for Deline, I'd never have gotten up the courage to propose to you." He looked at her, his eyes turning serious. "When I think of what I could have missed, believe me, I'm very grateful."

"Well, you're no more grateful than I. You were so shy of me, and I've loved you for so long. I prayed and prayed for you to notice me."

"Well," he hesitated, "I thought—"

"I know what you thought. That because you had only one arm, I would not be able to love you. What an impossible man you are. And besides," she smiled wickedly, "knowing what you are capable of with one arm, I don't know if I could bear what you could accomplish with two."

All barriers between them were broken as they laughed together, and it wasn't too much longer before Dixon proved his capabilities again to Amanda's deep satisfaction.

Brian lay awake, with his hands folded behind his head in deep and unhappy thought. Dixon, not going away as they had planned, worried Brian. Being newly married, it distressed Brian to think of the possibilities of something happening to him. His thoughts then, as they always did, centered on Samantha. What could he ever do or say to make her believe in love again. To open that door she had so tightly closed against the world. He cursed over and over the dead husband who died letting her believe it was her fault, letting her carry around this guilt that was too much for her. Samantha, he thought with a mental groan, how much I love you. I wish you knew that it's enough for both of us. He drifted off into a dream-filled sleep.

Holly also lay awake. She could hear Adam's breathing as he slept beside her, one arm across her body as though he were afraid she would disappear if he did not hold her.

She thought of the Gilcrest brothers and the sweet and bitter things they had experienced in the past few years. Next to Adam, Brian was the closest to her. The one she could talk to the easiest and the one for whom she carried a special kind of sisterly affection. She knew how Brian felt for Samantha and could not understand the way Samantha seemed so cold to him.

At one time during the reception, she had been watching Samantha's face when she thought no one was looking at her. Brian was dancing with another rather pretty girl, and Holly was surprised at the look on her face. She watched Brian with a sad look. Then Brian had laughed heartily at what the girl was saying to him, and Holly was again amazed at Samantha's reaction. Her look changed from a sad one to one of pain-filled hunger. Holly could almost feel the pain that emanated from Samantha's eyes, but at that moment, Brian looked directly at her and quickly the mask fell back into place, but not soon enough for Holly not to know that she loved Brian also.

But, why, she wondered, why should she deny Brian's love when she wanted it so desperately? She vowed silently that she was going to do her best to become good friends with Samantha. Maybe she could find a way to help her and, in the process, help Brian, too.

The house was quiet as slowly the stars began to flicker out as the first rays of the sun spread over the horizon.

Jessica and Matthew rose early and were sitting in the kitchen. Adam and Holly were the first to join them, and the two men talked quietly while Jessica and Holly began to prepare breakfast. Heavy footsteps descending the stairs heralded the appearance of Brian who stretched

371

and yawned.

"My, you're up early," Holly said with a laughing gleam in her eyes.

"Oh," Brian grinned nonchalantly, "I just wanted to be among the first to welcome the newlyweds to breakfast."

Adam muffled his laughter as his mother turned to him. Then she looked back at Brian.

"Brian Gilcrest!" she said firmly. "You will behave yourself this morning, or I'll take you in hand, young man."

"I—I, Mother, behave myself! Why I'm the soul of discretion."

Jessica eyed him suspiciously and was about to say something else when Dixon and Amanda appeared.

"Come, Amanda," Jessica said, "sit by me, breakfast is almost ready."

Amanda did, and it left Brian and Dixon standing together. Brian opened his mouth to speak when Dixon bent close to his ear and whispered something. Brian's mouth closed, and to Adam's amazement, he kept a respectful conversation during the meal. It was only after that Adam got him alone and asked him just what Brian said to keep him under control.

"Man's in an evil mood," Brian muttered in laughing mock anger. "Said if I opened my mouth and said one wrong thing, he was going to kick my seat so hard, I'd have to eat standing up for a week. Nasty man, isn't he?" he added, as he and Adam walked toward the barn laughing uproariously.

Chapter 42

Adam divided the group in two. This time Matthew and Tyler Jemmison rode with them. One group was to take its place near the Grayson house and the other near the Beauregard's. Adam led the first, which consisted of himself, his father and Devlin. They were to stand guard at the Beauregard's. Dixon led the other, with Graham, Brian and Tyler who took cover in the woods near the Grayson's.

The time set by Stella had been well after midnight. They waited in silence, midnight came and passed. Another hour, then another. Everyone realized something was wrong, for it was obvious the raiders had no intention of attacking that night.

The first gray light of dawn was appearing when Dixon's group was joined by Adam's.

"Something's gone wrong," Adam said quietly. "I hope our informer hasn't been discovered."

"All we can do is go home and wait to see if Brian is contacted again. If he isn't, we'll know for sure. Maybe they just changed their plans for some other reason," Bram replied.

Brian, who had been watching the Grayson home, noticed a small plume of white smoke from the chimney. Someone was up early, either Samantha or her father. No matter, he thought, he wanted to talk to either one of them. He paid no attention to the conversation until Adam said, "Brian, you coming? We're going home."

"You all go on ahead, I'm goin' down to talk to Mr. Grayson for a while."

He nudged his horse ahead and walked slowly down to the house, dismounted and knocked gently on the door. Howard opened it, and when he saw who it was, he cautioned Brian to silence and motioned for him to enter.

"Is Samantha not up, yet?" Brian whispered.

"No, she was awake pretty late last night. She'll be angry with me for lettin' her sleep late, but she needed the rest."

Brian waited quietly while Howard poured him a cup of coffee, then motioned him to a seat.

"What brings you out this early, son?"

"Mr. Grayson, I have to talk to you."

Howard watched the younger man hesitate. He felt a little sorry for Brian.

"What is it you want to say?"

"It's about Samantha, sir. I know it isn't decent to go behind her back, but . . . well, I guess you'd say I'm desperate. I just got the feeling that if I don't do something to stop it, she's going to be gone, and I'll never get the chance to prove to her how I feel, to make her understand."

"And just how do you feel?" Howard asked gently.

Brian sat forward with his elbows on his knees, holding the untasted coffee between his both hands.

"I suspect that you, and everybody else but Samantha knows how I feel," he said bitterly. "Why, why can't I reach her? Why can't I make her understand?" He looked up at Howard. "I want her happy, and I don't think running away from a problem is going to make her so. Even—even if she wouldn't marry me, if I just knew she had peace of mind. If I just knew there could be a beginning somewhere, that would be enough for now."

Brian met Howard's eyes across the table.

"Tell me what really caused all this?" he asked.

Howard contemplated Brian. He had promised not to tell Brian she had plans to leave, but he had not promised not to tell him all about the past. He began slowly, and Brian leaned forward intently listening.

"Samantha," he began, "was probably the prettiest girl in the country. I think my son wanted her from the time they were children. Her parents were much wealthier than we were, but Sam was not a snob. She was happy and sweet. I know that Daniel asked her to marry him more than once, and Sam refused. When the war came along, Daniel joined up. For a while, things were kind of exciting with the girls all marrying their men before they left. But it wasn't that way between Sam and Daniel. He left without being able to convince Sam to marry him. Then things began to turn bad for us. A kind of funny panic swept through. There was some fighting around our place and Sam's father was killed. Her mother . . . well, her mother was never quite the same after his death. Then things began to get hard. Sam was young, and I guess she was kind of afraid, too. When Daniel came home on leave, she consented to marry him. I tried to talk him out of it. I felt it was wrong, because I knew it was fear in Sam, not love. They married. I guess for a while things went along all right. I know Sam tried her best, but every day I could see that look in her eyes. She knew what she'd done was a mistake, but instead of doin' anything about it, I guess she took some kind of guilt on her shoulders. When Daniel came home so badly wounded, Sam nursed him, but it didn't do any good. The thing that's so terrible is that even when my son was dying and knew he was dying, he didn't release Sam. Instead, he built on her guilt." Howard wiped his eyes and said tiredly, "I guess I can understand how he felt, and I guess I can forgive him. He loved her so much, he never knew that he was helping Sam build a wall of guilt so big, nobody could break through it. I've tried." He looked at Brian closely. "I promised Sam I wouldn't say anything about her plans, and this is the first time in my life I've ever broken a promise, but I know if Sam runs now, she'll never quit running all the rest of her life. She's plannin' on leavin', plannin' on goin' back to the rest of her family."

Brian looked up at Howard with a deep frown, drawing his brows together.

"I think maybe you could stop her, Brian."

"How? Don't you think I've tried every argument I can think of? What can I say to her to make her see things as they really are?"

"There are times in life, Brian, when one cannot get through a wall with words, sometimes you just have to batter the walls down." He stood up and looked down on Brian with a half smile on his face. "Now I'm going to do something that Sam will think of as betrayal, but I'm sure in my heart that it's the best for her. I'm goin' to saddle my horse and go visitin' for the day and leave you here to figure out what to do against walls."

Brian smiled in return. "If I fail, sir, she'll probably hate you for the rest of your life."

Howard clapped Brian on the shoulder and gave it a friendly squeeze.

"If this could make the rest of her days happy, son, I'll take the chance."

"Thank you, sir," Brian said quietly. "You know I'll do everything in my power to keep Sam here and make her happy."

Howard chuckled, "Brian, I probably knew that even before you did." Brian watched him with a grin on his face as he took his coat and hat from the peg behind the door and put them on. Then with a half salute and a wink, he opened the door and left.

Brian sat down slowly; a million thoughts swirled about in his head. The main one was that he was not going to leave this house again until Sam belonged to him.

It was over another hour before he heard any signs of movement from Sam's room. He steeled himself and watched the closed door. Sam opened it and stepped out. Her eyes widened in surprise when she saw him sitting there. Then she looked around for Howard.

"He's not here, Sam," Brian said softly, as he rose slowly from the chair.

Samantha had thrown her old cotton robe over her nightgown and slipped into her slippers. Her hair, braided for the night, hung over her shoulder in two thick long braids. It gave her a young defenseless look. Now she put her hand to her chest as though to hold the robe closed and backed up a step.

"Where—where is he, outside? I'll call him for breakfast."

"He isn't outside either, Sam. He's gone for the day."

He could see clearly that she was frightened. He felt terrible, but he would not, could not back up one inch.

The soft sound she made, as she backed up another step was as painful to him as to her.

"Sam, I got to talk to you, and for once, you're really going to listen to me. He told me you were leavin'."

"He promised," she whispered. "He promised."

"How could he keep a promise like that when he knew he was only hurting you?"

"Brian, leave me alone. I'm going away. I'm going home," she said. Her voice tried for firmness but trembled uncontrollably.

"You are home, Sam, and I'm not letting you go."

He took another step in her direction, and she put one hand out toward him, palm outward as though it would hold him away from her. She knew deep in her mind that she must not let him near her. With his charm, his understanding, his strength, he had the power to reach her where no one else could. She was terrified as the carefully built walls began to crack and crumble.

"Don't Brian. I don't want you here," she said. "I don't love you, Brian. Please go away and let me be."

"You're whistling in the dark, my love," he said softly. "You know how deeply you care, just as I do. You're afraid, Sam, afraid if you let me too near, you'll find you've been living a lie all this time. I've been as patient as I can be, Sam, watching you punish yourself every day. I thought that after a while you would see the truth. Well, maybe you did, and now you're too much of a coward to admit it."

"No! No!" she sobbed. Then she whirled about, and before he could move, she slammed her door and locked it. He stood still for just a moment; then, grimly determined, he went to the door. Brian was a muscular young man; with one blow of a well-aimed foot, the lock gave, and the door flew open.

She stood clutching the bedpost and stared at him in open-mouthed terror. He walked to her and stood only a few inches away. Then he reached out and took hold of her shoulders. She put both hands against his chest, but her strength was no match against his, and slowly, he pulled her toward him. He saw clearly the tears on her face and felt the trembling fear in her body, but determinedly he ignored them as his mouth sought and found her moist, warm lips.

Samantha's marriage to Daniel had left her as unknowing of love as a child. She had never felt any passion for him and had only submitted to his lovemaking because she felt it was her duty. She was completely unprepared for the attack upon her senses at Brian's kiss. His arms were wrapped tightly about her like two steel bands from which she had no power to move. She tried to turn her head away from him, but it was useless for he simply held her with one arm and held her head firmly with the other.

Slowly, his lips moved against hers, firmly but gently pushing them apart. Her world reeled out of her desperate grasp, and she felt herself being lost in a wave of warmth that started somewhere in the center of her being and flooded her body.

He released her mouth for a moment and looked at her, then slowly, he began to untie the front of her robe. She fought now like a tigress, but without any effort at all he stripped the robe away from her. "No, Brian! Don't! Please, don't!" she begged. There was no way to get the nightgown off without releasing her, and he had no intention of doing that. Putting his hand at the neckline, he gave one jerk and ripped away the front.

Her body was pale in the early sunlight; she was slender and her breasts were small. He cupped one in his hand, very gently despite the firm way he held her. She writhed in his arms, as she began to feel an emotion she had never felt before. His mouth found hers again and took it hungrily like a starving man at a feast. The balance of the nightgown fell away, and she could feel his hands move over her body. Now, she seemed unable to move. All her bones seemed to her to have turned to liquid fire. She felt him lift her and put her on the bed. She did not want to surrender to this passion, but irreparable damage to the high walls was already done. Softly, she began to cry, but Brian was not going to let tears defeat him, either.

How he got out of his clothes, Samantha did not know; she did not know either that Brian had a great deal of experience along that line. Suddenly, she could feel the warmth of his naked body next to hers, and she moaned aloud at the wild demand of her wayward body. Then suddenly, he was filling her, easing the need of her long, hungry body. Her lips accepted his eagerly now as she felt

379

him move deeply within her touching a spring of white hot desire that had never been reached before. She clung to him now, blind to everything except the answering thrusts of her body. She felt as though something deep within her had burst into a million fiery stars that consumed her and whirled her about in a brilliant storm.

He held her tightly to him and prayed silently that when he looked in her eyes he would see love there and not hate. Slowly, he lifted his head from the softness of her body and looked into her eyes. He had tasted, he thought, a piece of heaven. Now he would see if he were going to be faced with the pits of hell.

"Sam?" he said gently. Her eyes were brilliant with tears and filled with wonder at the beauty she had never known before. His eyes searched hers desperately. Then slowly, he smiled as he saw deep within them an acceptance he had longed for for so very long. "I love you, Sam."

"Are you always so violent with your lovemaking?" she whispered.

"Oh, Sam, that wasn't lovemaking, that was rape." He kissed her throat and drew her body tight against him. "If you give me a little while to catch my breath, I'll show you what lovemaking really is."

"Again, you can do that again?"

He grinned. "With you, if you tell me just once that you love me, I could probably fly."

She laughed lightly, then took his face between her hands. "I love you, you stubborn, stubborn man."

This time, there was a deliberate slowness in the way he aroused her. Things she was unaware could happen became a reality. His lips and hands seemed to move over her body, drawing forth sensations she could never have imagined in her wildest dreams, and when he took her, she cried out her urgent need for him which he filled in a cataclysmic release that left them both weak and clinging silently to one another.

They sat in the small parlor of the house and made plans for their future while they waited for Howard's return. Samantha took a short time to prepare something for supper. It was just before dusk when they heard the sound of Howard's returning. Brian and Samantha exchanged looks of amusement as Howard walked across the porch with loud clomping feet and whistling loudly as he tried to warn them of his approach. He opened the door and stepped inside. There was no need for anyone to tell him anything. With one glance, he took in the broken bedroom door and Samantha's flushed but happy face. He grinned at Samantha who returned his look with a straight face, but laughter in her eyes.

"Traitor," she said softly.

He chuckled. "I guess I don't have to ask what plans you kids have." He looked at Brian, the devil dancing in his eyes. "You are goin' to make an honest woman out of my gal aren't you, sir?"

For a minute, Brian looked at him as though he were seriously considering the idea, until Sam, with a squeal of mock anger, threw her dishcloth in his face. Both men roared with laughter as Brian caught the cloth before it struck. He went to Samantha and put his arm about her, pulling her tight against him.

"The question is, sir," he laughed, "is she goin' to make an honest man outta me? I think I've asked her fourteen times, this makes fifteen, to marry me. She ain't answered me yet." Then he looked down on her, and his eyes lost their laughter and became serious. "How about it, Sam?"

"Yes, Brian. Give me a few days to get ready. I'll marry you."

Brian gave a jubilant whoop and swept her up in his arms. Samantha was going to see this often in her life with Brian. The easy way it was to turn on his good humor and sense for fun.

"And just where are you two goin' to live?" asked Howard.

"I thought, sir, I might move in here. We could build a couple of rooms on the house, and who knows, if we're lucky you might be bouncing grandkids on your lap."

Howard's eyes became moist. He knew it was consideration for him that Brian hadn't planned on taking Samantha to the big house to join his family. He knew Howard would be lonely without her. His voice was choked and gentle as he replied, "That ain't necessary, boy."

Brian smiled at him. "Sure it is. Think I want to cheat my kids out of a doting grandpa. Besides," he added, "I have some repair work to do." He looked pointedly at the door, and they all laughed. He shared supper with them, then told them he was going home to tell his family the news. Samantha walked him to his horse and stood in the yard watching him ride away. Neither of them saw the three mounted men who sat on the hill in the shadows.

Brian was greeted at home with questions. "Where have you been all day?" his father asked. "We've saved supper for you in case you're hungry, son," Jessica added, affectionately. Holly and Adam exchanged knowing glances, but kept silent, and Amanda and Dixon, so much in love with each other, recognized the same emotion in someone else.

"I'm not hungry, Mother. I had supper down at the Graysons. I've something to tell you all."

They looked at him with expectant faces, all except Holly who knew exactly what he was going to say.

"Samantha Grayson and I are getting married in a few days. I'm going to move in with them." His mother hugged him, delighted with the news, and he looked over her shoulder to Holly who smiled in satisfaction at the happy light in his eyes.

382

He stood for some affectionate razing from his brothers, and they sat about talking. He explained why he was going to stay at the Grayson Farm. "Besides, Adam. With the two of us, the farm could produce better and that would be good for Briar Hill, too."

"It's a good idea, Brian." Adam replied, "when are you getting married?"

"As soon as possible," he answered fervently. Adam stood up and held his hand out to his brother. "Congratulations. Samantha's a beautiful girl. I hope you'll be as happy as Holly and I are."

"Thanks, Adam."

"Well, I don't know about the rest of you, but I've a lot to do tomorrow and I'm tired," Adam said. He stood up and stretched. "I'm going to bed." This seemed like an agreeable idea to all of them, and they drifted toward the stairs, except for Brian who was, at that moment, still too excited to go to sleep. He wished the others a good night, then stepped out on the porch to have a smoke and relax a little before bed.

He lit a cigar and walked out into the yard. The stars were bright, and a huge white moon seemed suspended in a sea of black. He breathed in the cool evening air and let himself slowly begin to unwind. He thought of his future with Samantha. He would settle down now, he thought. All the wild ideas were gone from him, and he smiled. A new beginning, a new kind of life. Now he had someone to share it with, someone he loved beyond reason, beyond thought.

Throwing the stub of his cigar away, he turned to go back into the house. At the top of the steps, he turned for one last look in the direction of Samantha's house, and his heart froze. It was a few seconds before his unbelieving eyes accepted what they saw. The bright glow on the horizon could only be fire, and the place could only be the Grayson farm.

383

"Sam," he whispered to himself. "God no, not Sam." He turned and ran into the house shouting at the top of his lungs. Doors flew open, and they were all milling about him.

"Brian, what is it? What is the matter?" Adam asked shaking Brian's arm.

"We've got to get to Sam's fast," Brian cried. "It's on fire. You can see it from the porch!"

"We'll be with you in one minute," Dixon said, as he turned to get the clothes he had just removed.

"I can't wait for you," Brian said. "I've got to find out if Sam is all right. I'm going over now. You follow as fast as you can." He said the last words as he was slamming the door behind him. He ran to the barn, and instead of taking enough time to saddle his horse, he simply put a bridle on it and threw himself up on his bare back. Pushing the horse to his fastest run, he prayed all the way that Samantha was all right. The heavy smell of smoke was stronger and stronger as he neared the house. Riding into the yard, he could see that the house was over half consumed, and the flames were too bad for him to get near. He searched around, then found Howard Grayson about forty feet from the porch. He was alive and Brian knelt by his side. Howard's eyes flickered open, and when they saw Brian, they were filled with agony.

"Sam," Brian choked, "where's Sam?"

Howard could barely speak, and Brian could not understand what he was trying to say.

"Howard," Brian shouted, beside himself with fear. "Goddamn it, where's Sam?"

Howard raised his arm and pointed. Brian turned about to follow where his finger indicated, and a hoarse, agony-filled sound came from him. He rose to his feet and ran to the huge tree that bordered the woods.

Samantha had been stripped and tied to the tree with her arms stretched about it. She hung unconscious against the tree. The bark cut into her soft skin, and little rivulets of blood trickled down her body. Someone had taken a whip and beat her. Crisscross welts ran over her body from the back of her neck to the back of her legs. Most of them had cut deeply, and her back was a mangled mess of torn skin and blood.

He touched her head, and it fell back revealing her face. Whoever had used the whip on her had obviously struck her several times first. Her eyes were swollen shut, bruises ran down her face and blood seeped from the corners of her lips. Nailed to the tree beside her was a piece of paper that read: "Sharecroppers, this is the last warning. Get off Gilcrest property."

A violent burst of rage exploded in his brain. He would find the ones responsible for this, and there would be no revenge but his. No punishment but his.

He worked feverishly at the ropes that bound her, and gently lowered her to the ground. Stripping his shirt from his body, he wrapped her in it, hoping she would stay alive, yet praying she would remain unconscious through the agony of being carried to Briar Hill.

The others arrived, and he could see the pity in their eyes. He told them to take care of Howard. Then he had Adam hold Samantha until he could mount. Adam handed her up gently, and Brian cradled her against him.

He rode toward home, but before he could get there, Samantha began to stir in his arms and moan softly. Her eyes fluttered open, and he could see the look of pure agony cross her face.

"Brian," she sobbed, "oh, Brian."

Tears fell endlessly, as he stopped his horse for a second and gently caressed her hair.

"I'm here, Sam, I'm here. I never should have left you. I'll never leave you again. Oh, Sam," he cried, "I'm sorry."

The pain was too much for Samantha, she lapsed again

385

into unconsciousness for which Brian was grateful. He put aside any other thought but Sam. Nothing else mattered until she was out of danger, he thought. Then and only then could he open his mind toward revenge.

After he had taken her home, he laid her on his bed on her stomach and ordered warm water and clothes. No one interfered or said anything. He gently washed her body and covered her lightly with a sheet. Then he sat and held her hand in silence waiting for the doctor while deep in his own murderous thoughts of death.

Chapter 43

Stella had pulled her dark shawl tighter over her head and made her way back to the cabin she shared with Jessie Colton. The cabin was empty, and she wondered where he was. Since, as she had told Brian, there were no plans until the night after the wedding, she was surprised that Colton wasn't here drinking.

She sat at the table, and folding her arms, she laid her head upon them to wait. Jessie was always angry if she went to bed before he got home. She was half asleep when she heard him open the door. Quickly, she rose to her feet. It was always wise to be ready to move quickly, depending on the mood Jessie was in.

He came in quietly and said nothing to her. She stood still and watched as he hung his coat and hat on the nail behind the door. He turned to face her. His eyes were fathomless, and somehow it alarmed her, for she had always been able to read his face.

"What's the matter, Jessie?"

He took a few more steps toward her, and she suddenly became afraid.

"Jessie, what's wrong? Why are you looking at me like that?"

Now he was almost beside her when he lifted his hand and slapped her hard, knocking her back against the table.

"Jessie, what's wrong? I ain't done nothin'. What you mad at me for?" she cried, as she backed away from him. He stalked her, and she was near terror. Reaching out, he grabbed her by the arm, then methodically, he slapped her again and again until her senses reeled, and she collapsed on the floor. Climbing to her hands and knees, she whimpered softly, "Jessie, why?" she sobbed. Slowly, she stood up and reached out a beseeching hand to him, only to receive another blow and another until she dropped half conscious to the floor. She heard the sound of his feet going to the door. He flung it open and shouted.

"Zekel!"

Zekel stepped inside the door. Vaguely through her tears, she could see him standing over her. His face had a gloating smile.

"Zekel, you always wanted her," Jessie said coldly. "Within the next week, I want her dead. What you do to her in the meantime is of no importance. Just make sure she's dead in a week. You understand me?"

"Jessie!" she screamed. "There's others responsible besides—"

She never finished. This time it was Zekel who silenced her. Licking his lips in anticipation, he bent and lifted her unconscious form and slung her over his shoulder. Then he looked at Jessie.

"I'll make her pay for what she's done to us, Jessie," he said.

"Just make sure she's dead," Jessie said coldly, "and get rid of that kid of hers, too."

"I already done that tonight, Jessie. Just now while you was takin' care of Stella, I got rid of the kid."

Jessie nodded and turned his back on Zekel who smiled and went to the door. He carried Stella to his cabin and laid her on the bed. Slowly and with enjoyment, he tied her hands over her head to the bed posts. Then he began

388

removing her clothes. When she lay naked before him, he sat back and waited for her to regain consciousness.

Slowly, Stella's eyes blinked open. He sat still until her eyes focused on him. He could tell when she realized what had happened to her by the look of fear in her eyes. He chuckled. "Now Stella," he said in a soft velvety voice, "you can scream, yell, do anything you want, and it won't matter. You see, Jessie already told everyone that you squealed on them, that you told Brian Gilcrest all about what we was plannin'. They all know you're goin' to pay for what you done."

"You filthy rat!" she cried. "You told Jessie about me."

"Of course, Stella," he said calmly. "And when he saw you and Gilcrest together tonight, he was so mad he wanted to kill you then, but aren't you lucky I like you, Stella. I talked him into givin' you to me, givin' you an extra week of life."

"I'd rather die now," she said scathingly.

"Oh, no, Stella, not now, and not so easy," he said. "You belong to me for a week." He bent close to her face, his foul breath making her ill and his ugly rat face frightening her. "When I'm through, when I've had all of you every way I want you, then I'll kill you. Not until then." Stella's eyes widened with pure horror as he rose slowly and began to remove his clothes. For the next three days, Zekel kept his word to Stella with a vengeance. He did things to her that she had never imagined could be done, and her cries and pleading, her moans and weeping seemed to exhilarate him. The fourth day, he came in and sat down on the bed beside her and told her they had changed the plans she had given Brian.

"He's sure goin' to be surprised when no one shows up like you told him, won't he?" he laughed.

Stella glared at him in hatred, which seemed to bring him a great deal of enjoyment. He watched her face as he

389

slid his hands roughly over her, pinching her breasts painfully and squeezing until she cried out.

He rose again and stretched, then began to unbutton his shirt. Always, he watched her face intently as he moved. She tried not to show her fear of him, but he had hurt her too often and for too long to be able to hide it. She watched as he reached up and untied her right arm, then he pulled it across her and tied it to the same post her left one was tied to. Then he took her left arm and, pulling it under her, turned her on her stomach and tied it again to the opposite post. She looked back over her shoulder at him frightened, speechless. She watched him climb on his knees on the bed behind her. Then suddenly she screamed again in paralyzing fear as his hands fondled and separated her buttocks.

"No, Zekel, please. Please don't!" she sobbed, but again her screams and cries made it better for him. She moaned and cried and tried to move away from his thrusting organ, but it was impossible. Then the agonizing pain of his entrance was so bad she almost fainted.

"Ahhh," he sighed contentedly. He began to talk to her accentuating every word with another thrust until she thought her body was being torn apart. "Stella," thrust "if you had" thrust "just said yes" thrust "to me when" thrust "I asked you," thrust "maybe" thrust "I wouldn't" thrust "be so hard" thrust "on you." thrust "But" thrust "you got" thrust "to pay."

Now he was panting heavily as he hammered himself against her listening with his malignant enjoyment as she sobbed and cried and begged him to stop.

After he had left her, she cried brokenly into the pillow, her body too exhausted and filled with pain to move. All that remained in her world was the blind fear of his return, and he did return. The next night, he came to her and told her what Jessie had done to Brian Gilcrest's woman. He told her how he had enjoyed tying her to the tree for Jessie and watching him whip her until she was unconscious.

"It gave me an idea, Stella," he said softly. She jerked her head up and looked back over her shoulder again to see the long wicked whip he carried in his hand.

"Zekel," she whispered. "Don't. I'll do anything you want, anything."

"Of course, you will, Stella. You don't have a choice. But you've had lessons comin' to you for a long time." He stood a few steps from the bed just where she could see and know of the coming of each blow. She watched the arm raise and felt the first bite of the whip across her buttocks. She cried out as the second one fell, then the third, fourth, fifth, until her world was a blinding sea of pain.

It was a few minutes after that, she saw through a red haze that he had dropped the whip on the floor. From the corner of her eye, she watched him move toward her, fumble with the ropes, then suddenly she was turned roughly over on her back. She screamed with pain as her back touched the bed, but that was not the worst, for he fell upon her and listened to her moans as he took her violently until blessed darkness swirled over her and she fell into unconsciousness.

It was the final night of her torment that Zekel really broke her. He had taken her and used her as brutally as ever. Then he had lain down beside her and watched her face.

"Tonight's the last night, Stella. You want to know what I'm goin' to do with you. I'm goin' to take you out to that tree where you always met Gilcrest. I'm gonna tie you to it and let you have another taste of the whip. Then he'll be free to find out what's left of you, if there's anything when the night animals get done with you."

Hot weary tears fell from under her closed lids. She

was too broken to even be afraid any longer. It was not enough to satisfy Zekel. He had to have his last little piece of revenge.

"And I want you to know, Stella," he whispered against her face, "I dug a nice deep hole to bury your boy in."

A shrill agonizing wail was torn from the depths of her soul, from a pain so deep she could no longer bear it. It was the deepest pleasure Zekel had enjoyed yet.

He lifted her broken body from the bed, and taking his rope and whip, he carried her out to his horse where he threw her over the saddle and mounted behind her. He made his way slowly to the spot where Stella and Brian had met. He pulled her down from his horse and dragged her limp body to the tree. Throwing her against it, he tied her arms about it as though to embrace it. There was no sound from her. She stared dazedly into the world about her with blank, expressionless eyes.

Zekel stood back from her and uncurled his whip. Tonight he was going to whip her until there was nothing left, then let Brian Gilcrest wonder when he found her. He flung back his arm and snapped the whip against her flesh. Her body jerked spasmodically, but there was no sound. She was beyond that now. In anger he snapped his arm back again and suddenly found himself jerked from his feet and landing solidly on the ground looking up into the murderously cold gray-blue eyes of Brian Gilcrest.

Brian had sat beside Samantha as she had awakened. He heard her moans of pain as consciousness slowly returned. Kneeling beside her bed, he lay his head on the pillow next to her so she could see him without moving. Her eyes were filled with tears of pain but shone with pleasure when she saw he was there.

"Brian," she whispered.

"Shhh, don't talk, darling, try to rest."

He had some medication the doctor had left, and he got

up and mixed a little of the powder in water. Going back to the bed, he gently lifted her head just enough to allow her to drink it. From the trembling of her body, he knew that every movement caused her pain. He knelt down beside her again, and his eyes shone with tears.

"Sam, I'm sorry. I'm so damn sorry," he said gently, his hand lightly touching the softness of her hair. "I should have stayed with you. I should have known something was wrong the other night when they didn't come. I should have had enough sense not to leave you alone."

"I love you, Brian," she said softly. "It's not your fault. There was no way for anyone to know. It's not your fault, Brian."

He did not disagree with her for fear of upsetting her. "How is Papa?"

"He'll be fine. The doctor left him something, so he should be all right in a few days. It's only you that was hurt so badly, Sam."

There was no doubt in Brian's mind that they had caught the informer, and he was scared about what would happen next since he had no way of finding out.

"Brian?"

"Sam, try to let the medication help you sleep."

"I must tell you, or I won't be able to rest."

"What, what do you have to tell me so badly?"

Slowly and painfully, Samantha described Zekel and Jessie and how they had broken into the house minutes after he had left. Howard tried his best to defend her, but it was impossible. She described all that had been done to them, and Brian clenched his teeth in silence.

Slowly, her voice began to die, and she dropped again into an exhausted sleep. Brian stood up and paced the floor, the rage so violent in him it felt like a seething volcano. He had to do something, but he didn't know what. Maybe, just maybe, they were wrong about his

393

informer. If he just took one ride out to their meeting place to check, at least it would give him something to do.

He went downstairs to find Graham, Dixon, Bram, Adam, Devlin and his father along with Tyler Jemmison waiting for him.

"How is she, Brian?" his father asked.

"She's going to get well, Pa. But the scars will be bad, I imagine."

Adam looked at Brian in alarm. His voice was too calm, too easy. Looking around he could see that the others were mirroring his thoughts.

"I'm going for a ride," Brian said quietly.

"I'll go with you," Devlin offered.

"No, no, I want to go alone. Thanks anyway, Devlin. I know Sam probably won't wake up until morning. I'll be back before then."

He turned without another word and left the room. Adam turned to the others.

"He's about to explode. I think it would be wise for a couple of us to follow him," Adam said.

Dixon agreed quickly. "You and I, Adam. If he does explode, I think we would have the best chance to control him."

They left the room immediately and watched Brian leave. Then they ran across the yard, saddled their horses and mounted, moving slowly in the direction they had seen him go. They moved after that by following the receding sounds of his horse, stopping now and then to listen.

As Brian neared the appointed place, he stopped and tied his horse to a tree. Moving forward quickly, he came upon the scene that stopped him cold and brought back, with boiling hatred, what Sam had just suffered. A man had a woman tied to a tree and was about to beat her. Several things registered on Brian's consciousness at the same time: One, that the girl tied to the tree was his informer and was half dead already, and two, but most important, from Sam's description, the man wielding the whip was the same one who had helped in her beating. Then this obviously was one of the raiders, not just any one, but one of the main ones. He walked closer as the man smacked the whip back and struck out at the woman. When he drew the whip back again, Brian was right behind him. He grabbed the other end of the whip handle and jerked the man off his feet.

"You enjoy beating women, don't you?" he asked softly. The gun in his hand pointed at Zekel's head.

"Suppose we find out just how much you enjoy the other end of this little beauty."

He waved the gun in Zekel's face. "Get up on your feet." Zekel obeyed rapidly, then stood trembling in fear and watching Brian closely. Brian backed to where the girl was tied to the tree, but she did not look to him as though she were alive.

"Untie her, and be gentle, my friend, I'd hate to kill you so easy."

Zekel untied Stella and lowered her to the ground.

"Give me the rope," Brian said. Zekel brought the rope to him. Brian loosened one end that had been tied about Stella's wrist. Making a large loop, he hooked it about Zekel's wrist and drew him tightly against the tree, then he brought the other end about the trunk and tied Zekel firmly. Putting his gun away he went to Stella's side and knelt beside her. He was surprised to find that she was still breathing. Very slowly, Stella opened her eyes, and when she saw Brian, she smiled. Her eyes wandered restlessly until they fell on Zekel tied to the tree.

"Kill him," she whispered vehemently. "Kill him so I can die in peace."

She looked up at Brian, then slowly, haltingly, she began to speak. She told Brian who the leader was and where to find him. She also told him where Colton was and that he was partially responsible for what had happened to Samantha. She told him all the things she knew, and as her voice faded away in death, she was satisfied that Colton would pay for what he had done to her poor, helpless son.

Brian stood up from her body and looked at Zekel. His eyes were so filled with blazing hatred that Zekel shook with terror. Brian reached down and picked up the whip. Slowly he waved it back and forth and walked a few paces away from Zekel, who had begun to whimper. He heard Brian tentatively crack the whip a few times in the air. Then there was complete silence. Zekel twisted frantically to see what Brian was doing. He was just standing there watching Zekel.

"I want you to remember something, Zekel," Brian said very softly. Then suddenly the whip cracked against Zekel's back. He yelped with pain.

"Remember the girl at the Grayson farm, Zekel?"

CRACK!

"You put your filthy hands on her, Zekel?" came the soft voice again.

CRACK!

Zekel cried out as the whip cut through his shirt and raised a welt on his skin.

"You hurt her, an innocent girl who'd done nothing to you."

CRACK!

This time, a small line of blood appeared on his shirt, and Zekel knew with finality that Brian meant to beat him to death. Brian was allowing the black fury in him to have complete control. That he fully intended to kill Zekel was beyond doubt. All that he could see in front of his eyes was Samantha's limp, beaten body. The whip cracked again, then again, and he enjoyed the cry of pain that was torn from Zekel's lips at each blow. Each one echoed in his ears—Sam, Sam, Sam.

Zekel fainted from pain and terror, but Brian had no intention of stopping, until a gentle voice at his side spoke calmly and clearly.

"That's enough, Brian."

Brian was panting, and he ignored the voice. He raised the whip to strike again, and a strong hand closed around his wrist. He looked around in surprise, stunned that someone was there. Adam held his wrist tightly, and their eyes met across their arms.

"It's enough, brother," Adam said gently. "This won't help Sam one bit, and it will do you a lot of harm."

Brian licked his dry lips. His mind still would not register the fact that Adam was stopping him. His head jerked around, and he stared again at Zekel.

"I'm going to kill him," he croaked.

"No, Brian. You can't. We love you too much to let you."

"Adam," he sobbed. "You saw what he did to Sam. She's so little, Adam. He hurt her so bad. He deserves to die like the animal he is."

"After what he did to Sam, Brian, there's no way the law can ignore it. He will be punished, but not by you, brother. It would kill you, too."

"No, I can't take that chance, Adam," he cried. "What if they let him get away with it?" Again he tried to jerk the whip free from Adam's grasp, but Adam's grip held like iron. Dixon came up on the other side of Brian and put his hand on his brother's shoulder. Brian turned and looked into Dixon's compassionate eyes. Dixon, who knew pain as no other did and who understood him so well, smiled gently and said quietly, "Give me the whip, Brian."

Brian stood frozen for several minutes. Then suddenly they felt the stiffness go out of his body, and he sagged against Dixon who held him and nodded to Adam who removed the whip from his hand.

"I'll take him home, Adam. Will you see to those other two if I send some help back?"

Adam nodded and watched Dixon lead Brian to his horse and help him mount. When they arrived home, Dixon sent Devlin and Bram back, then took Brian to his room where he collapsed into a sleep of nervous exhaustion. He slept for several hours, and it was dawn when he awoke. Quietly, he changed his clothes and went to Samantha's room. Under the drug, she was still sleeping. He sat beside her and took her hand in his. He knew she would need him when the drug wore off and the pain was there. But somehow, he felt stronger now as if some great load had been lifted from his shoulders. It was a long silent time before he really remembered what happened the night before.

It was several hours before Sam awakened, and Brian held her hand through the worst of the pain. Talking gently to her, caressing her hair and staying by her side. He forced nourishment on her when she didn't want it and bathed and applied the medicine to her back with hands so gentle that Sam herself was surprised.

In a week, she was improved enough that she could get along without the medicine. In another week, she was well enough that Brian could lift her gently out of her bed. From then on, she rapidly regained her strength. With nothing but Samantha on his mind all this time, he realized he had forgotten to tell the others just what Stella had told him about the raider group.

Led by one man, they were determined that some way they would drive the sharecroppers out. Once they did, the big plantations would fail and could be taken easily for back taxes. But it was Brian who knew that in this case that was not the reason. The man behind all this hated Adam, hated Adam with a malignant cancer of hatred that had eaten at him for the past five years.

Brian called the others together.

398

"We have to make plans about what to do to end the raiders forever."

"Brian, how can we do that when we don't know who leads them or where they're centered?" questioned Bram. "With my place in danger like it is and Devlin's and Graham's, we all feel the same way, but what can we do?"

"But you're wrong. I know who leads them and why. I know where they stay and how to get them. We've got to plan one single attack that will clear that Yankee garbage out of our area once and for all."

"How do you know who the leader is?" Graham asked.

"Stella told me the night she died. I've just been confused about everything else, but now it's time to put a stop to all this."

"This Yankee who leads them," Devlin asked. "Who is he?"

"Oh, I didn't say the leader was a Yankee," Brian answered. "I just said he was surrounded by Yankee garbage. He's a Southern boy. The kind that preys on his own kind for profit."

"Who?" Adam said shortly.

"Oh, you know him well, Adam, even better than I do. His name is Jarrod. Raff Jarrod."

Chapter 44

Adam stared blankly at Brian for a few minutes before what he had said registered with him.

"Raff Jarrod!" he said softly. "After all this time, Brian. Does a man really hate that deeply?"

"I think he hated you more than you ever realized, Adam. Zekel has told us that after Devlin took us out of that prison camp and cared for us at his house, Jarrod was going to tell the new commander, he was going to raise such a big uproar that we would have been put back in. It seems your two friends set about stopping him. I don't know how, but in the process, he lost an eye. He wears a black patch over it. No one had any idea that the war would end before the new commander got there. Nevertheless, Jarrod has always blamed you."

"But, God, Brian, enough to track me down?"

"He didn't have to track you down. After I got there, we forgot he was keeping such a close watch on us, listening to us. Remember, Adam? Home, Mother and Father, Dix, Deline and Holly were about all you could talk of. I bet when we left there, he knew as much about you as I do."

"Then where did he get enough money to back up what he planned to do?"

Brian shrugged. "Who knows, Adam. The kind of man Jarrod is, he could have gotten money anywhere."

Adam nodded, and Graham spoke up. "Why don't you two fill the rest of us in on what happened and what's going on, now?"

The idea was seconded quickly by Brian. "It's always a good thing to know who you're fighting and why."

Brian exchanged glances with Adam. Adam grinned bitterly. "You go ahead, explain to them, Brian. It's still pretty hard for me to really grasp this, yet."

Brian began to tell them the story of their stay in the prison camp and how Jarrod's and Adam's paths had crossed.

"So you see," he said as he finished the story, "Jarrod is combining his feelings for Adam with his greed to own Briar Hill. I think that getting back at Adam is something he does not intend to do directly, but he'll carry out his vengeance against any of Adam's family no matter where he finds them."

The other men were grim faced as they realized that there was no way a member of Adam's family could be hurt without touching them all. Bram through Deline, Devlin through Steffany and Dixon and Brian through Amanda and Samantha.

"Well," Brian said quietly, "we know now who and why. I guess our job now is to put together some plan to do something to stop him."

"You know there's only one way, Adam," Devlin agreed. "We've got to stop them for good. We've got to clean out all Jarrod's followers, and," he paused as his eyes held Adam's firmly, "Jarrod has got to die."

"Killing a man deliberately, no matter how necessary, goes against the grain. I know it has to be done," he added hastily, as he saw Brian about to interrupt, "but I don't have to like the idea."

"If you don't, Adam, I do," Brian replied vehemently. "Any man who could do to a woman what he did to Sam deserves anything he gets, and I would be glad to do

401

it personally."

"No, it's me he's after, and it's me he'll have to face. Has anyone come up with an idea?"

"Well, first," Graham said, "I think we'd better see to the safety of the women. If he could be that merciless with Samantha, then Holly and Steffany and Deline would probably suffer worse if he got hold of them."

"Right, now," Devlin suggested, "I bet they're watching every move we make. We gather together to come down on them, and they'll know it hours before we get them. There has to be a way of getting together without them realizing what we're up to."

Tyler Jemmison gave a slight cough, then spoke quietly. "If you boys don't mind, I think I could supply an idea or two you might be able to play with." If any of them had changed since the war, it was Tyler Jemmison. He had discovered how fruitless and empty his life had been before, and he saw that all the things of real value he had taken for granted. Tyler had worked with patience to rebuild what he had almost let slip through his fingers. He had worked diligently and patiently to restore his place in Odella's and his children's lives. His daughters had accepted this gratefully, but Odella was not so easy to reach. The severe blow she had taken when she knew of the birth of Tyler's son to the slave, Portia, had almost undone her. Although she would not admit it, even to herself, part of the bitterness she felt was not because he had taken a mistress, but because she had borne him the son Odella had always longed for.

He had become a quiet, patient man. The one thing he wanted more than anything else in the world was to find his way back to Odella. He tried his best and fought every day the desire to find the son he had lost.

The men were watching him expectantly. "I think we should have a party," he said. They stared at him in silence, unable to follow whatever reasoning he was using. "You know, Matthew," he said, "the old-fashioned kind of bar-b-que where we build a big bonfire and invite a lot of people. At those things, there's a lot of milling around and noise. Do you know it's impossible in all the confusion to tell who's there and who isn't? Why," he added softly, "I'll bet eight or nine could leave and no one would be the wiser."

"You're absolutely right, Tyler." Matthew smiled. "A few could leave a party like that and return, and any spies would never know the difference."

All three of the Gilcrest boys would rather not have had their father go with them, not because they didn't respect his ability, but because they were afraid for him.

"Pa," Adam began, "I really think that the six of us could handle this without a problem."

"Sure, Pa," Brian agreed quickly, much too quickly to suit Matthew. "There's nothing to it, really, if we take them by surprise."

"We can hit them and be back between drinks, Pa," Dixon laughed.

Tyler Jemmison's face was red, not from anger but from suppressed laughter. He remembered quite well Matthew Gilcrest before his sons were born, and even when they were young. He was a hard fighter, a companionable drinker and quite a ladies' man before he met and married Jessica. Now here were his three sons trying politely to tell him that he was too old to get involved in their troubles. Tyler waited expectantly for the explosion which was not long in coming. Matthew's face went from understanding to astonishment to absolute fury in two minutes. It was Adam who realized his mistake first. He took a quick step backward out of reach of his father's hand which had fallen on him several times in his childhood. Adam remembered just how hard and heavy that hand could be and was regretting quickly what he had just said. Dixon, too, snapped his mouth shut on any other words and quickly moved from his father's vicinity. But Brian, being raised as the baby of the family, had never really felt the power of his father's angry strength. He had been well protected by older brothers and sisters. But now, Brian was about to regret each word. His father's hand closed heavily on his shoulder; his face almost purple with anger was pushed close to Brian's, and he shook Brian like one would shake a child. Brian's eyes opened in shocked surprise at, not only his father's strength, but his anger.

"You young whippersnapper!" he shouted. "Are you trying to tell me I'm too old to protect my own home and family?" Each word was punctuated by a firm shake. "Who do you think came out here when this was a wilderness and built this place? Who do you think has protected it all this time while you was growin' up?"

"Pa!" Brian gulped. "I didn't mean nothing. God, Pa, let go. You're gonna break my shoulder."

"I'll kick your seat until I break something else you young scalawag," he said, as he gave Brian another quick shake.

"You're right, Pa," Adam smoothly said. "I apologize for saying anything that gave you the idea we didn't want you along. I don't see how we could pull this off without you now that I've given it some thought," he added diplomatically.

Matthew grunted, a little pacified by Adam's remarks. Then giving Brian's shoulder another shake, just to emphasize what he had said, he dropped his hand. Adam and Dixon smothered with laughter at Brian's alacrity in putting distance between himself and his father.

"We can't plan the bar-b-que too fast, or they might get suspicious. We'll wait a few more days until Samantha's really on her feet. How about we plan it for a week from tonight? That should give you enough time to inform the others. We want as big a crowd as we can get,"

404

Matthew said, "and it's best not to tell any of the other men. The smaller this group is, the more chance we have of success."

"Well, we have to tell our wives," Devlin smiled. "Do you have any idea how hard it is to keep a secret from Steffany? I've never been successful yet, and I doubt if it would work this time."

"I second that," Bram replied. "Deline is not the kind you fool very long, and I got to live with her the rest of my life."

They all laughed. Then Adam became serious again. "We have to tell them. We can't pull this off without their help, anyway. They've got to cover for us and keep this party loud and active if we want to succeed."

"Then it's agreed we plan this party for a week from tonight," Matthew said, casting a questioning look around. His eyes fell on a now silent Brian, and he gave him a long affectionate look. "What's wrong, son?"

"Just knowing that the man who's responsible for hurting Sam is walking around loose is a hard thing to take, Pa."

Matthew watched Brian's face and made a promise to himself. There was no way he was going to let this sensitive young man commit murder. He looked across Brian and found Tyler Jemmison's eyes on him. With a quick, almost imperceptible nod of his head, the two old friends made a silent agreement. If killing had to be done, their children were not going to be responsible.

"Well, I'll go tell Jessica to start planning the party," Matthew said. "I suggest you all inform your wives tonight."

They nodded in agreement, and slowly, the group broke up. Adam and Brian walked together.

"Thanks a lot Adam for getting me in that mess with Pa. I thought he was going to yank my head off my shoulders."

"You never should have suggested that Pa was gettin' too old for this," Adam grinned.

"Me! I was just agreeing with you."

"Yes, Brian," Adam said gently, as he draped his arm over his brother's shoulder. "But I'm quicker on my feet than you are."

They laughed and left the room together. Brian was the only one who did not explain what was going to happen to Samantha. The other women were told immediately. Brian knew Samantha would think that he was on a trail of revenge for her and try to stop him, so he planned on keeping it to himself until it was over. That is what he planned, but the planning was done without taking Samantha's love for him into consideration. He was with her every possible minute he could be, holding inside him the desire to take her into his arms each time he looked at her. Some of the pain still remained, for he could see her wince occasionally if she moved. It hurt him, and the deep burning core of anger grew within him. Besieged by the idea of keeping her away from anymore hurt and his own frustrated anger, Brian was on edge and nervous most of the time, a thing he thought he hid well from Samantha. The need for her sometimes overpowered him, and he would leave her, knowing he could not touch her, yet wanting to crush her in his arms, to kiss away the pain and misery she had gone through, to ease not only her pain, but his own hunger and loneliness.

It was two nights before the party, almost three o'clock in the morning. Brian lay wide awake, more aware of Samantha in the next room than he had ever been since he'd known her.

The soft click of his door latch brought a half smile to his face. Mother, he thought, making her nightly rounds as she had since Brian was a child. He saw her shadowed form silhouetted in the doorway for a second as she entered the dark room from the lighted hallway. He closed his eyes and controlled his breathing as though he were in a deep sleep.

He sensed her passage slowly across the room and felt her standing beside the bed looking at him. Then she sat down on the bed gently and reached out her hand and laid it on his bare chest. It took only one touch for Brian to realize this was not his mother:

"Sam?" he whispered.

"Yes."

"What are you doing here at this hour?"

"I couldn't sleep. Brian, I have to talk with you."

"Couldn't it wait till morning, Sam?" he asked. He was having an extremely difficult time controlling the urge to reach out for her. The celibate life he had been leading for the past month was an unusual thing for Brian, and his body spoke out against it in no uncertain terms at the nearness of Samantha.

"No, I couldn't stand being away from you for another minute. Don't you want me here, Brian?"

He groaned mentally. "Want you here!" he said aloud.

"Shhh, do you want to wake the whole house?"

"Damn it, Sam, you sure are makin' it hard on me. You know how much I love you and want you, just the way you know how impossible it is now until you're better."

He heard a hint of laughter in her voice as she whispered softly, "You idiot. Love is a two-way street. You have to be able to give as well as receive."

The last words were said against his lips as she bent forward and touched her mouth to his. Another tentative touch told him that whatever Samantha had on when she entered the room was gone. He was delighted, happy, miserable and frustrated all at the same time. Delighted she was there, happy that she wanted him as badly as he wanted her, miserable with the knowledge that he was afraid to hurt her and frustrated with the fact that he didn't know at that moment just where to put his hands.

Her hands slid slowly and gently down his body pausing here and there to caress and fondle. Her lips left his, and she kissed his cheeks, throat, then his shoulders as they slowly slid down his body touching with little pricks of flame here and there as they traveled.

It was probably the first time in Brian's life he was the seduced instead of the seducer. He heard her muffled giggle, and he could not control the answering laugh.

"You're deliberately tryin' to kill me. You know you got me in a position where I can't take what I want."

"Why not?" she whispered, as she slowly crossed her leg over his body and sat astride him. "It's my back that's been hurtin', not the rest of me."

His hands reached out and touched the flat softness of her belly, then crept up to her breasts, cupping them in both hands, moving his thumbs in small circles about the nipples until he heard her sigh.

"Oh, Brian," she cried as she bent forward. Her hair fell about him, and he could smell the faint touch of her perfume. Gently, he shifted himself into position until their bodies joined.

"Control, control!" shouted his mind, but his body had long ago ignored its shrieks. He could feel only the need for her. Their lips met and blended as she began to move with slow rhythmic strokes that drove him almost to madness. Finally casting aside all his frustrations, he twined both hands in her long hair and began to move with her. He was conscious now of only her as she bent forward more and began to move more urgently against him. Her lips again found his, and her body moved faster and faster raising him to a frenzy of passion as they reached their peak together and tumbled over into the fiery pit of release.

She lay still against him, and he could feel the rapid

pounding of her heart. Then of all things he felt her shaking with laughter.

"What's so funny?" he said. "I think I've just been raped."

"That's what I was laughing about," she answered. "I always thought one good rape deserved another."

He began to laugh, and she giggled helplessly as she lay against him.

"Brian," she whispered, after a few moments of silence, "now that I have you in my power and you're too weak to fight back, suppose you tell me what's been going on behind my back for the past week?"

"What, the party?" he questioned.

"Don't, Brian. I know when you're trying to keep something from me, and I intend to stay here until I find out what it is."

"Boy! Is that a threat," he chuckled. "I think I'll try and see just how long I can hold out."

"Brian, please be serious for a minute. I can't stand this separation from you, as though you were afraid to talk to me or confide in me. I want our marriage to be something very special, something I've always dreamed of, but that starts with the closeness and ability to talk to each other. There should be no secrets between us."

"You're right, Sam," he said quietly, then holding her face between his hands, he kissed her tenderly. "I'll tell you everything," he said. She laid her head against his chest and listened in silence as he began to explain what they were planning to do.

When he was finished, she was quiet, and he thought for a minute that she was asleep. Then she said very quietly, "Brian, I know that what you all are doing is the only way to get rid of that group of terrorists, but—"

"But what, darling?"

"Brian, I don't want you to kill him, not like that, not like the kind of man he is, and I don't want you to kill a

409

man because of me."

"Sam," he began, "I'd like to say I'm a very noble person and I'm doing all this for just the good of my family and the farmers, for all the trouble those rats have caused us and the threat they'd constantly be if we don't wipe them out. But I'm not noble, Sam. I'm not going to tell you anything but the truth. What they did to you put them beyond any mercy I could feel for them. I have two things that are dearest to me, Sam. My love for you and my family and my pride in what we've rebuilt here which I'm a part of. I guess the most important of those is you. Do you believe I could let something like that happen to you and do nothing, feel nothing? Impossible, Sam. Don't ask it of me. It's impossible."

There was nothing left that Samantha could say. She knew he would do what he felt he had to do. She loved him beyond anything else, loved for the first time in her life, and she would do or say nothing to lose what she had found. She lay on her side and gently pressed her lips against his. "I love you, Brian. Those are the only words I have left to say that mean anything. I love you."

When Brian awoke the next morning, Samantha was gone. He knew she would be, yet he wished she were still there curled against him.

Work progressed as usual for the two days before the party, all of them tense and nervous, yet acting as though nothing unusual was happening.

Jessie Colton sat deep in the shadows of the trees, watching the comings and goings of the family. Others joined him reporting the news of the party they had heard. Jessie was puzzled. This didn't seem normal to him after what they had done to Grayson's place and the old man and the girl. He remembered quite well the girl and promised himself to enjoy her more fully when they raided the Gilcrest place. He was sure the boss was planning that, for why else would he send him to spy on

410

their activities.

He made his way back to their cabin and knocked on the door.

"Come in."

He stepped inside and waited to be spoken to.

"What is it, Colton? What are they up to now?"

"They're plannin' a party."

"They're doin' what?"

"They're plannin' a bar-b-que, and it looks like a big one. From what the men found out, they've invited every farmer for forty miles around. Must be somethin' special to celebrate to invite that many people, but we can't seem to find out what the reason is."

"They're havin' it tonight?"

"Yep. People was beginnin' to come when I came here."

"Well, Jessie, you gather all the boys back here. As soon as I ride out and check things over for myself, I'll be back. Then we'll hit all three places and burn those farmers out once and for all."

Jessie nodded and left the room. Raff Jarrod stood still in deep thought. Something wasn't right. They were up to something, and he felt Jessie was too stupid to see what it was. He would look things over himself. Then either way, they would make the Gilcrests and the others learn to fear them. He was becoming impatient. He wanted Briar Hill, and he wanted Adam Gilcrest dead. And he wanted them both tonight.

He left their camp and rode slowly toward Briar Hill. In the distance, he could see the bright light of the bonfire against the night sky.

Keeping himself well hidden, he watched the celebration beginning at Briar Hill. No matter how he tried, he could see nothing unusual happening, and that worried him. His preservative sense of something amiss had never failed him, and now it clamored shrilly for him to

411

notice . . . what . . . what . . . what!

He dismounted and made his way through the shadows and across the lawn between the trees on the side of the house opposite the fire. Slowly, he made his way, keeping close to the house and deep in the shadows until he stood near the patio door that led out toward the fire. Voices filtered from the room. He listened and grinned in pleasure at what he heard.

"Oh, Deline, I hope all this works out."

"Don't worry, Holly. Adam planned it carefully. There's enough men out there to convince anyone watching that everybody's here. By the time they know what happened, they'll be rounded up and that whole nest of scum will be burnt out."

"I hope you're right. I just have the feeling something is wrong. I'm so worried about Adam and Brian. Deline, they're so filled with anger. I hate to see them like that."

"I know how you feel, Holly, but have faith in Adam. He's not a man to murder in cold blood and neither is Brian, you'll see. They will take care of it some other way."

"I know, Deline. I'm not afraid of that. I'm afraid they'll get careless in their anger and get hurt."

"Stop thinking that way. What they're doing is a thing that has to be done, for our protection and all the others that live here."

"Well I guess you're right, Deline, and I didn't mean to sound like a baby. I believe in Adam, and I'm sure after tonight all our problems will be behind us."

"All except one," Deline laughed.

"One?"

"The one you're carrying. If he's anything like the two of you, he should be something to see."

Raff smiled to himself. What better cards could he have for dealing with Adam Gilcrest than his sister, his wife and his unborn child. Slowly he eased out his gun and moved as close to the door as he could. He saw them standing with their backs to him. Amanda stuck her head in the door from inside the house.

"Are you two coming?"

"We'll be right along, Amanda. You go on out."

Amanda smiled and nodded. Leaving the room, she closed the door behind her. As she closed it, Raff opened the outside door and stepped quietly inside. Deline heard the door click and spun around, her face going white as she saw Raff and the gun in his hand. Holly sucked in her breath at the sight of him. From Adam's description, she would have known Raff Jarrod anywhere.

"Well, well, well," he grinned. "It looks like I've finally got Adam Gilcrest right where I want him."

Chapter 45

Adam eased his horse forward slowly until he stood at the edge of the line of cabins that bordered the narrow street. Four or five of the eight cabins had lights inside; the rest were dark, including the cabin that stood on a small knoll away from the rest, which, Adam presumed correctly, belonged to Raff Jarrod. It surprised him that it was also dark.

"They're probably all gathered together," Brian offered.

"They're not plannin' on us being here."

Adam nodded, but he still watched the solitary cabin as though something was trying to force an idea into his mind.

"Well," he said in a low whisper. "There are eight of us. Brian, you and Devlin take that first cabin with the lights. Bram, you and Pa take the second one. Graham, you and Tyler take the one opposite. Dix, you and I will take the other one. Remember, hit them hard and hit them fast. We only have one chance. If they get together, they outnumber us."

They nodded silent agreement. There was a pause, then Adam shouted, "Now!"

They burst down the line of cabins as though they were shot from cannons. A wild rebel yell from Brian pierced the night air. Men, confused and excited and some a little

414

frightened burst from cabin doors, unprepared for what they believed to be the host of the devil riding down on them. Unarmed and completely off guard, it took less than an hour for the eight of them to have the raiders herded into a large group in the middle of the dirt road.

Looking over his shoulder, it alarmed him that no lights came on in Jarrod's cabin. He pushed forward to the edge of the circle of cabins.

"Jessie Colton," he said sharply. "Step out here."

Jessie stepped out of the circle of men and looked defiantly at Adam.

"Where is Raff Jarrod?"

"I don't know who you're talkin' about."

"Your boss."

"I ain't got no boss, Gilcrest. I don't take orders from no one."

Brian moved slowly forward, his eyes frozen to Jessie's face. The look was one of slow and imminent death, and Jessie recognized it for exactly what it was.

"You're the one who beats innocent defenseless women with whips," he said, his voice deceptively soft. "And you do it all on your own without a boss to blame."

Jessie's face went white, and he cast an imploring look at Adam who gazed back with a cold merciless look. He gulped, but the lump of fear remained in his chest, and he found it suddenly difficult to breathe.

"You go on, Adam, herd this head of cattle away, but leave this one to me."

Adam nodded, and with a quick sign to the others, he jerked his head toward one of the cabins.

"Over that way, gentlemen, we have some talking to do, and when you all get finished baring your souls, I'm sure the law will have no choice except to give you free room and board at the state prison."

They began to move slowly into one of the cabins. Jessie, paralyzed now with terror, turned and looked into

Brian's eyes and saw no quarter there at all.

Brian gave his gun a little jerk in the direction of the horses.

"Find a horse and get mounted, Colton. We're goin' for a ride."

"What—what you goin' to do to me?" Colton asked, his voice cracking with fear.

"Only what you've long deserved, my friend." Brian laughed bitterly. "Long deserved," he added softly. He let his horse move slowly forward until he was almost beside Colton, and lifting his foot, he gave Colton a shove toward the horses. Trembling with fear, Colton mounted and moved ahead of Brian toward the trees.

Just inside the rim of trees, Brian told him to stop.

"Dismount!"

Colton obeyed, eyeing Brian and wondering what he was going to do to him.

Brian threw a piece of rope about three feet long to Colton.

"Make a loop at each end."

Colton obeyed.

"Put one loop around each wrist."

Again Colton followed orders, fear gnawing at his insides. Brian came up to him and grabbed the rope in the center pullin' it taut, effectively tying Colton's hands. Brian dismounted, and jerking Colton after him, he walked to a huge tree. Over the lower limb of the tree, he threw the end of another long rope. Looping this about the rope tied to Colton's wrists, he pulled heavily on the end jerking Colton's arms above his head. He pulled on the rope until Colton's toes barely touched the ground. His arms felt like they were being pulled from the sockets. Then, Brian stepped away from Colton and walked back to his horse. From the corner of his eye, Colton saw him lift something from the saddle horn. Then he moaned in real terror, for Brian turned toward

416

him and began to walk slowly in his direction uncoiling a long black whip.

Adam slowly and methodically lit every cabin on fire. Then he moved to Jarrod's cabin. But he almost knew what to expect there. Jarrod must have seen them coming and gotten away somehow. No matter how he questioned the other prisoners, none of them knew anything about Jarrod. Then for the first time in over an hour, he looked around for Brian and Colton. He was relieved when he saw Brian moving in his direction.

"Where have you been, Brian?"

"Repaying an old debt."

"What did you find out?"

"Nothing, he knew nothing. I hate to say this, Adam, but I think Jarrod has slipped through our fingers."

Adam sighed in disgust. There was nothing more they could do here. Jarrod's affairs in the area had come to an end, but both Brian and Adam knew it was only temporary if they couldn't locate Jarrod.

"I think we've put the fear of God into this group. Let's turn them over to the law with their confessions and go home."

Brian agreed, saying nothing more to Adam regarding the man he had left dangling from the tree half alive from the beating Brian had given him.

They rode home slowly, deep depression settling on them, for they realized, with an angry Jarrod loose, their troubles could be just beginning.

Colton swayed to-and-fro, half conscious, his body a blazing flow of agony. He sobbed, his throat raw and aching. Slow murderous hatred began to blossom in his pain-filled mind and surprisingly not toward Brian, who had beaten him, but toward Jarrod, who had made him do what he had done to bring on Brian's revenge. As Brian had left, he had taken his knife and cut three fourths of the way through the rope that held Colton. He knew in a

417

few hours, the weight of Colton's body would break the ropes. He wanted Colton to have that much time to think about what he had done to cause this, and Colton did think, of Jarrod, of pain and of death.

As they crested the hill, Adam drew his horse to a stop. He stared at Briar Hill, deep frown lines between his eyes.

"Adam?" his father said.

"Something's wrong, Pa," Adam whispered. "The fire is dying down, and I don't see anyone there. I gave them definite instructions there was to be a lot of noise, a lot of people and they were to keep the fire going."

Without another word, Adam urged his horse into a run and rapidly closed the area between him and Briar Hill. The others followed him in silence, all of them afraid of what they would find for they had left their loved ones practically defenseless to perform their unsuccessful maneuver tonight.

Dismounting in front of the steps, he stood and stared about him in amazement and fear, for the grounds were deserted. Taking the steps two at a time, he threw open the front door and looked across the room at the smiling face of Raff Jarrod.

Their hands tied together before them, Deline and Holly stood next to him, his gun pointing directly at Holly's temple.

"So, we finally meet again, Lieutenant Gilcrest."

Adam ignored him for the moment.

"Holly, Deline, are you all right?"

"We're fine, Adam," Deline said defiantly. "Why don't you kill this scum so we can fumigate this house?"

If Jarrod was angered by her words, he showed no sign as the others who followed Adam crowded in behind him.

"Deline!" Bram cried out and started to move forward.

"I wouldn't if I were you, my friend, unless you want to see her dead."

Bram stopped dead in his tracks, and Jarrod chuckled

418

at his look of rage and impotence. It was Devlin who spoke next. "Where are the other women, Jarrod? What have you done with them? If you've hurt Steffany, I'll kill you, one way or the other."

"I think not, my friend," Jarrod replied. "The others are upstairs, locked safely away so they won't cause me any problems. What I came for and what I'm leaving with is Adam Gilcrest, his sister and his wife. I'm afraid I'm being forced to leave town, but not before I kill the man I came to get. Oh," he laughed, "not right away. Not until he suffers a bit, and I believe these are the two ladies who can make him do just that. Now, are all your horses out front?"

Adam nodded, his eyes on Holly's frightened face, trying to give her the encouragement and strength she needed.

"Is there a key to this room?"

"No, it's never been locked."

"What about the room across the hall?"

"There's a key to that, it's hanging above the door. It has hardly ever been used. You see there was no need to lock doors around here until you came."

"Shut up," Jarrod said. "You all move slowly backward and into that room." They did as he said, and he followed slowly pushing Holly and Deline ahead of him. They stepped into the room all except for Adam who was told to lock the door and throw the key away. Adam did exactly as he was told, his eyes never leaving Holly who had relaxed a little and watched him, hope overcoming her fear.

Jarrod urged them outside. He mounted a horse, then told Deline to mount with him. With her on the saddle in front of him and the gun pointed at her head, Adam had no choice but to mount a horse himself.

"Get up on a horse," Jarrod snarled at Holly.

"Goddamn it, Jarrod, she's pregnant. Let me hold her

419

in front of me."

Jarrod eyed him with disgust, then motioned her to go to Adam. She did with a murmured cry of relief as Adam's arms came about her. He lifted her up in front of him and held her close, letting her head rest on his shoulder and the weight of her body against his to ease her in traveling.

Slowly making their way through the woods, Adam was surprised to find them heading back toward the cabins they had just come from. Obviously, Jarrod had left something valuable behind and didn't want to leave without it.

At Briar Hill, Brian, Dixon, Bram and Devlin were putting their shoulders heavily against the door, as soon as they heard Jarrod and the prisoners he took with them leave.

Finally the heavy oak door gave under their combined weight and flew open. The men ran to the upstairs bedroom to release the other women and see if they had been harmed in any way. Reassuring them that they were all right, the women urged them to see if they could follow the trail to find Adam, Holly and Deline.

Bram needed no urging from anyone. He was well ahead of them and had his horse saddled before they reached the barn. His mind could only contain one thought: to find Deline before any harm could come to her.

Within minutes, he was joined by the others. It was Devlin who voiced their main worry.

"Where in the hell could he be taking them?"

"Do you think we should split up, and if anyone finds any sign, they could fire a few shots to signal the rest?" Brian suggested.

"Good idea, Brian," Dixon replied. "You and Devlin head toward Heritage, and me and Bram will go back along the route we came from tonight. Matthew, you and Tyler head toward Cross Oaks. We ought to run across

420

some kind of tracks. Remember, fire two shots in the air if you find anything, all right?"

They nodded in agreement and split rapidly into three groups. Soon the sound of their horses faded into the dark night, and the women were left to wait.

When they reached the cabin, Jarrod dismounted first, pulling Deline down roughly from the horse which brought a sharp, painful cry of protest from her. Adam clenched his teeth. He could do nothing now without endangering both Holly and Deline, but he watched closely for any opportunity that might present itself.

Jarrod motioned Adam to dismount, too, and kept his gun close to Deline's head which caused Adam to be as slow and as cautious as he could be. He dismounted, then gently lifted Holly down to stand beside him.

"Get inside and move slow, Gilcrest. I'd hate to shoot your pretty little sister, but I will if you make one false move."

"Jarrod, it's me you're out to get," Adam said. "Why don't you let them go?"

Jarrod laughed shortly. "No, I don't think so. You might die easy, but I think you'll beg before you die if you see what I plan to do to them."

Adam spoke quietly, his eyes meeting Jarrod's. "I'll beg now, if that pleases you. Let them go Jarrod. Please let them go."

"That sounds good for a beginning, Gilcrest. But," he added in a cold gentle voice, "I'm sure before I'm done, you'll do better, much better."

Adam looked at Holly. She was terrified, but her head was high and her fear kept under control. Deline also was doing her very best to control her fear.

"I'll crawl, if that's what you want, Jarrod. I'll do or say anything you want, only let them go home."

"Stop talking and get inside," Jarrod snapped. He jerked Deline roughly against him and pushed the gun

421

tight against her. Adam took Holly's hand, and they slowly moved into the cabin with Deline and Jarrod following. Jarrod motioned the two women to sit in the straight back chairs that stood beside the fireplace. Then he threw a rope at Adam that had been hanging on a hook behind the door.

"Tie them both up. I think I'll let them watch while I start on you, then we'll let you change places with one of them."

Adam knelt, first by his sister, then by Holly and tied them both as gently as he could. Then he turned to Jarrod. Desperate ideas had been forming in his mind. He realized without doubt that Jarrod's hatred for him was close to insanity. He wondered just how far he could push him to make him break and get careless enough for Adam to jump him.

"You know you aren't going to get away with this, Jarrod. My brothers will follow you to the end of the earth, if necessary. They will never let you rest. They'll track you down and kill you like the crazed animal you are."

"Where I'm going, Gilcrest, I'll have all the protection I'll need."

"From the men who backed you financially in an attempt to get our land? You're really crazy, Jarrod," Adam chuckled. "You failed in getting what they wanted. Do you really think they'll protect you?" Adam threw back his head and laughed. "They'll be only too happy to throw you to the wolves. You poor, stupid jackass. Don't you know what kind of men they are? They can buy your kind for a nickel. You're very expendable, and they'd drop you without blinking an eye."

"Shut up, Gilcrest," he snapped, but Adam could see the faintest shadow of doubt in Jarrod's eyes.

"With Deline's husband and my brothers, you don't stand the chance of a snowball in hell. Let the women go, and I'll go with you wherever you choose. You can do with me whatever you want."

"No!" Holly cried. "Adam, I want to stay with you. I won't leave you!"

"Holly, don't," Adam said gently. "Think of the other life you guard."

Holly's eyes filled with tears, but she remained silent.

Adam turned back to Jarrod.

"What do you say, Jarrod, my life for theirs?"

Jarrod watched Adam. Then he grinned slowly.

"Too easy for you, Gilcrest. You think I'm going to let you off that easy after what happened to me because of you."

"I don't even know what you're talking about. What happened between us in that prison camp was hardly enough to kill me for. The most I ever did was to defend myself from you and your thugs."

Adam was amazed at the maniacal gleam in Jarrod's eye. The positions they were in at the moment put Adam a step or two away from Holly and Deline, but a little behind them. Jarrod stood about three to four paces in front of them. Adam had been doing everything in his power to keep Jarrod's attention on him, while slowly he eased backward hoping Jarrod would follow him, and if he got a chance to jump him, Deline and Holly would not be in the line of fire.

Jarrod stepped one step closer to the women, but his angered gaze was focused on Adam.

"Everything that happened to me there was your fault, Gilcrest. The loss of my eye, done by your two friends, was your fault. Why should you and your brother have had special treatment when the rest of us starved? Maybe they didn't care, but I did. I did!" he shouted, and took another step forward which put him only a few inches from Deline.

Adam, who was watching his face, trying to pick the right second to jump, was as unprepared for what Deline did as Jarrod was.

Putting both feet together she brought her knees up and rammed both her feet into Jarrod. He was a large man, and the blow could not knock him off his feet. But it did cause him to stumble and brought the gun in his hand out of line with Adam who leapt upon him, grasping the gun with both of his hands.

They struggled furiously for the gun, and Adam received several blows to the ribs that almost caused him to lose his hold. He knew if he did, even for a second, that the three of them were as good as dead. They fell together to the floor, and the gun was shaken from Jarrod's hand and flew across the floor to land at Holly's feet. She stared at it helplessly.

Slowly, but surely, Jarrod's size was overcoming Adam's desperate battle. He felt himself weakening. One blow at the side of his head sent him sprawling with brilliant stars exploding in his head. At the same time, Jarrod dove again and came up with the gun, pointing it directly at Adam who had risen to his hands and knees. Adam was looking squarely at death, and he knew it. There was no more time, no reprieve. Jarrod was so angry, he intended to kill them all now. The hammer of the gun clicked back, and Adam inhaled a deep breath for the blow he knew was coming.

But it didn't come. Instead, a soft thud could be heard. Jarrod's eye widened in surprise. Then very slowly, the gun fell from his hand. He sagged slowly to his knees, then fell forward with a solid thud. From the center of his back protruded the handle of a hunting knife. Adam looked at him in shock, then looked up at the open door. None of them had seen the door swing open, nor the man who stood there . . . Jessie Colton.

Jessie stood weaving in the doorway. His eyes focused on Jarrod. Then the sound of hoofbeats could be heard, and before the arrival of help, Jessie slowly faded away.

Adam crawled to Holly's side and untied both girls. Then he pulled Holly into the safety of his arms and rocked her gently back and forth as she cried.

Within a few minutes, Bram and Dixon ran into the room.

"Deline!" Bram said, his voice shaking with fear. Deline ran to him, and threw herself into his open arms.

Dixon went to Adam.

"Are you all right, Adam? God you look like you've been mauled by a grizzly."

"I'm all right," Adam gasped.

"How'd you manage this?" Dixon asked as he waved his hand toward Jarrod.

"I didn't. Jessie Colton did."

"Let's go after him. He can't be far."

"No, whatever debt we owe, we paid back. He saved not only my life, but Holly's and Deline's. We'll let him go. We owe him that much."

Dixon nodded. Adam looked down into Holly's face.

"Shall we go home, love?" he whispered. "I don't think there will be any more trouble at Briar Hill."

"Oh, Adam, I was so afraid he was going to kill you."

"So was I," Adam chuckled. "In fact, I don't remember being so scared in a long time. But it's all over."

He gently lifted her chin and kissed her. Holding her close to him, his lips told her that the strength of their love was as new and as solid as ever.

"Let's go home," he whispered.

Putting her arm about his waist, she leaned her head against his shoulder, and they left the cabin where they buried all their past pain and started a new and rewarding future.

425

Epilogue

Leah Gilcrest sat on the edge of the porch at Briar Hill, dangling her short legs over the edge. She sat patiently waiting for the first sight of her father's horse coming up the drive. Her five year old mind was busy working out a problem her older brother, Brandon, had presented.

Brandon was older than she by three years. He was tall for his age and bore a great resemblance to his father, Adam, except for the clear emerald eyes he inherited from his mother.

Leah herself was a tiny, bubbly child who seemed, or so all her family thought, to have inherited more of her spirit and sense of humor from her uncle Brian than from anyone else. She found laughter in everything. She had her mother's auburn curls, but under her straight auburn brows were two clear gray-blue eyes that found nothing but good in the world.

She thought back over her family in search of the answer to Brandon's question. They had been playing together, and he had asked her suddenly, "Who do you like best, LeLe?"

She looked at him in surprise. She loved everyone so much it was very difficult to pick out one she cared for the most.

"Let me see," she thought. "There's Mama and Papa." She thought of them and knew she loved them in a special

426

way that touched no one else. Mother who hugged and kissed her and cared for her, and Papa who lifted her to his shoulders or held her in front of him on his big horse, who was gentle and kind and always listened to her problems. And then there was Grandpa Matthew and Grandma Jessica who fell into the same category as Grandpa Tyler and Grandma Odella. She loved them dearly. Oh, my, she thought, overwhelmed with the people she had to love. It would be impossible, she felt, to ever pick out one person she cared for the most. Uncle Brian and Aunt Sam? When she was at their house, she loved them most, but then there was Uncle Bram and Aunt Deline who were what she considered "specialest people." Of course, there was a small place reserved in her little heart just for Uncle Dixon and Aunt Amanda and Uncle Devlin and Aunt Steffany.

She was worrying the problem about in her mind when her bright eyes spied the lone figure who rode the black horse up the drive.

"Papa!" she squealed. Jumping to her feet, she flew down the drive. She was not the least bit afraid of the huge black horse. Papa would never let anything happen to her. She could see her father's quick smile as he bent forward and held out his hand. She reached out hers, and effortlessly, he lifted her up beside him.

Adam kissed the top of her head and drew her tightly against him. She liked the feel of his hard strength against her little back and the rumbling sound of laughter deep in his chest. She twisted about a little to look up into his face and was contented when the gray eyes smiled down at her.

"Been a good girl, today, LeLe?"

"I think so, Papa."

He chuckled. "You're always Papa's good girl, aren't you, my love? I don't know what I'd do without you."

"Papa?" she questioned. "Who do you like most?"

427

"Now, what brought on a question like that, little one?"

"I just want to know, Papa, if you love everybody, how you pick out the one you love most?"

Adam contemplated the answer to this question as he rode with her up the drive. At the front of the house, he lifted her down.

"Would I be safe in saying that this question came from your brother?"

Her curls bounced as she nodded affirmatively.

"And he wants to know who you like most?"

Again the nod as her wide serious eyes contemplated him.

Adam knelt down beside her and put both hands on her little face.

"LeLe, I think you know everybody loves you, and I know you love all of us the same. But I think your brother's a little afraid you love someone more than him. So just for this time, why don't you tell him you love him the most. The rest of us will understand."

The door opened and Holly came out accompanied with Brandon. Adam looked at his son with pride. At eight, he was a straight bright-eyed intelligent child.

"C'mon, LeLe," he said. "Mama said we can go down to Uncle Brian's for supper."

Leah ran to his side, and he took her small hand in his. They kissed their parents, then walked together down the road toward Brian and Amanda's. Holly looked up at Adam who was following them with a half-suppressed smile on his face.

"Adam?"

"Look at them, Holly, our future, Briar Hill's future. They're so fine." Again his eyes met hers. "Thank you, Holly, for the greatest gift of my life." He bent and kissed her; then he laughed. "You know, I think I love you the most."

428

"You, what?"

"That's a secret between LeLe and me." He put his arm about her, and they walked inside. Leah and Brandon walked down the road in silence for a while, then Leah stopped. Brandon stopped and looked at her.

"What's the matter, LeLe?" he questioned.

"I just know the answer to your question."

"What question?"

"Who I like best of everybody."

"Well, who?"

Leah slid her little hand in his and smiled up at him.

"I like you best of everyone, Brandon."

Brandon smiled with the bright smile of Adam Gilcrest, and giving her hand a squeeze, they walked down the road together.

And so the roots of the Gilcrest family were pushing forth a new life, a new spirit for the South. The old branches may have been bent or broken, but the roots were solid and firm. The Gilcrest story begins.

GILCREST

Matthew — Jessica

Adam
&
Holly
Jemmison

Brian
&
Samantha
Greyson

Dixon
&
Amanda
Merriweather

Deline
&
Abraham
Forrester

Leah — **Brandon**
Gilcrest — Gilcrest
& &
Alexander — Aubrey
Raymond

Roberta
Gilcrest
&
Guy

Philip — **Dixon** — **Cassandra**
Gilcrest — Gilcrest, Jr. — Gilcrest
& & &
Lorna — Karalee — Brad

Jenny — **Jeremy**
Forrester — Forrester
& &
Brady — Lara

FORRESTERS

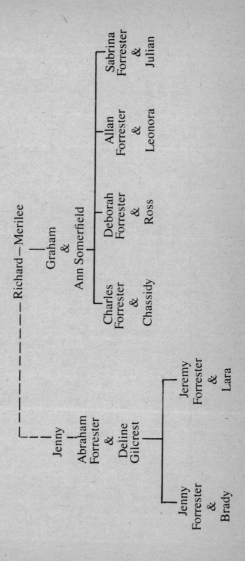

Richard — Merilee

Graham
&
Ann Somerfield

Jenny

Abraham
Forrester
&
Deline
Gilcrest

Charles
Forrester
&
Chassidy

Deborah
Forrester
&
Ross

Allan
Forrester
&
Leonora

Sabrina
Forrester
&
Julian

Jeremy
Forrester
&
Lara

Jenny
Forrester
&
Brady

JEMMISONS

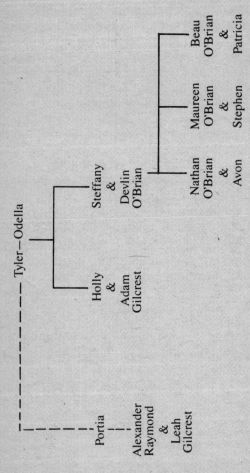